Ao (Awa) Is.

Sanse

u Barrier

awafune

HIGO

Sakata

D E W A

Ōizumi

Daibonji

Mt. Haguro

Mogami River

Kiyogawa River

White Thread Falls

Mt. Gassan

Aizu

Kamewari Mts.

W A

(ŌSHŪ)

Kimbokuzan

Kamo Lagoon

DO IS.

Yahiko

Teradomari

Kanazu

I G O

C

Sakata

Kanazawa Fortress

Kuriyagawa

Kamewari Mts.

D

Kurihara Temple

Hiraizumi

Ancha Pine

Inamu Barrier

Miyagino Plain

Mt. Atsukashi

Shinobu

Date

Matsushima

Chiga Beach

Tsutsuji Hill

Takekuma

MUTSU

Asaka Marsh

TSUKE

Shirakawa Barrier

tsunomiya

no-yashima

TACHI

Kikuta Barrier

D

MUSASHI

Ukishima Plain

SAGAMI

Mishima

Hōjō

Dohi

Cape Manazuru

Edo

Ichikawa

I Z U

Koshigoe

Kamakura

Kurihama

Miura

Kisarazu

KAZUSA

Cape Sunosaki

Kominato

A W A

Yoshitsune

YOSHITSUNE

A FIFTEENTH-CENTURY JAPANESE CHRONICLE

Translated and with an Introduction by
Helen Craig McCullough

Stanford University Press
Stanford, California
1966

UNESCO COLLECTION OF REPRESENTATIVE WORKS
JAPANESE SERIES
This work has been accepted in the Japanese translation series of the
United Nations Educational, Scientific, and Cultural Organization
(UNESCO).

Stanford University Press
Stanford, California
University of Tokyo Press
Tokyo

© 1966 by Helen Craig McCullough

Library of Congress Catalog Card No. 65-19810

PRINTED BY GENERAL PRINTING COMPANY, LTD., YOKOHAMA, JAPAN

Preface

All known texts of *Yoshitsune (Gikeiki)* are substantially the same; there are no important variants. Premodern editions fall into three categories.

1. MANUSCRIPTS

These include texts with the variant titles *Hōgan monogatari* and *Yoshitsune monogatari*, which lack "The Memorial Services for Tsuginobu and Tadanobu" in Chapter Eight but otherwise resemble the common editions closely. *Hōgan monogatari, Yoshitsune monogatari,* and others in this group, such as the Tanaka text, appear to be relatively old and reliable. (*Yoshitsune monogatari* is probably not later than the beginning of the Tokugawa period.) They are frequently more detailed than the common editions.

2. WOODBLOCK EDITIONS (common editions)

There were major woodblock printings in 1633, 1635, 1640, 1645, 1659, 1670, 1673, 1689, 1698, 1708, and 1724. The 1698 edition, which was apparently the most widely circulated, is still to be found in secondhand bookstores in Tokyo. These editions, which are marred by numerous inaccuracies, were the basis of all prewar modern editions.

3. OLD MOVABLE WOODEN PRINT EDITIONS

There are at least four old movable print editions, some of which may date back to 1600, and none of which is later than 1633. They are good texts, closer to the old manuscripts than to the woodblock editions.

In the translation, I have used the *Nihon koten bungaku taikei*'s *Gikeiki* (Tokyo: Iwanami Shoten, 1959), edited by Okami Masao, a carefully collated edition based primarily on a movable print version dating from around the beginning of the seventeenth century. Professor Okami's annotations have been of invaluable assistance. I have also been greatly aided by Takagi Taku's excellent modern Japanese translation (*Koten Nihon bungaku zenshū*, Vol. 17 [Tokyo, 1961]). I should like to thank Donald Shively, Edward Seidensticker, Jeanne Smith, and Patricia Milford for reading the manuscript, and J. G. Bell of Stanford University Press for distinguished miscellaneous labors.

HELEN CRAIG McCULLOUGH

Contents

Japanese Historical Periods

Nara	710–794
Heian	794–1185
Kamakura	1185–1333
Muromachi	1336–1568
Azuchi-Momoyama	1568–1600
Tokugawa (Edo)	1600–1868
Meiji	1868–1912

ABBREVIATIONS

(The following abbreviations are used in the notes. The place of publication of all Japanese sources cited is Tokyo.)

Azuma kagami   *Azuma kagami*, in Kuroita Katsumi, *[Shintei zōho] Kokushi taikei*, 32–33 (Yoshikawa Kōbunkan, 1942).

GSSK   *Gempei seisuiki* (Yūhōdō Shoten, 1912).

Gyokuyō   Fujiwara (Kujō) Kanezane, *Gyokuyō* (3 vols.; Kokusho Kankōkai, 1906–7).

HM   *Heike monogatari*, in Takagi Ichinosuke *et al.*, eds., *Nihon koten bungaku taikei*, 32–33 (Iwanami Shoten, 1959–60).

Kuroita   Kuroita Katsumi, *Yoshitsune-den* (Sōgensha, 1939).

Okami   Okami Masao, ed., *Gikeiki*, in Takagi Ichinosuke *et al.*, eds., *Nihon koten bungaku taikei*, 37 (Iwanami Shoten, 1959).

Shimazu   Shimazu Hisamoto, *Yoshitsune densetsu to bungaku* (Meiji Shoin, 1935).

Introduction

Introduction

By the middle of the twelfth century A.D., the politically corrupt, economically unstable, and militarily impotent court nobles of Japan's ancient regime—the superb aesthetes known to us from *A Tale of Genji*—had entered the twilight of their rule. For more than two centuries these nobles were in gradual retreat before the incursions of provincial warrior families. Taira Kiyomori, the head of one such fighting clan, was from 1160 on the most powerful man in Japan. He had an economic base firmly founded on unrivaled landholdings and maritime trade with China; he had daughters married into the imperial and Fujiwara families, and relatives in major court offices. But in twenty years or so Kiyomori's unwise policies and dictatorial behavior had weakened the Taira, and they were in their turn overthrown by the military house called Minamoto.

The victory of Yoritomo, the Minamoto chieftain, signified more than the appearance of a second military tyrant in Kyoto. Unlike Kiyomori, who had been content to rule within the framework of existing political institutions, Yoritomo established his own independent government, the so-called *bakufu*, at Kamakura in eastern Japan, the ancient seat of Minamoto power. The avowed function of the new government was to control the military vassals of the Minamoto, not to usurp the prerogatives of the emperor and his officials. Nevertheless, since warriors in every section of Japan had hastened to declare allegiance to Yoritomo after the collapse of the Taira in 1185, Kamakura's actual jurisdiction was far more extensive than that of the court. Yoritomo's was, in short, a feudalistic government, transforming the private ties between the Minamoto and their vassals into a political relationship by virtue of which

Yoritomo controlled the nation. This system of dual government was
so closely attuned to social and economic conditions in Japan that
it persisted in one form or another until the latter half of the nineteenth century.

The clash of arms between the Taira (also called the Heike) and
the Minamoto (or Genji) was thus laden with momentous conse-
quences. It was also an intensely dramatic conflict in itself, enduring
for five years, ranging widely over large areas of the nation, and
bringing into confrontation adversaries whose similarities were less
striking than their points of difference. Although both the Taira and
the Minamoto were warrior houses of provincial extraction, the
former, through long residence in the capital, had taken on many of
the attributes of their noble associates. In the legends which soon
sprang up they were depicted, with only modest exaggeration, as
essentially aristocrats in taste and training, better suited to turning
a verse, playing the flute, or inditing a love letter in an elegant hand
than to campaigning in the provinces and withstanding the challenge
of Yoritomo's fierce easterners. The exploits of the Minamoto and
their retainers were retold admiringly again and again to appreciative feudal audiences, but at the same time the gallantry of the
outmatched Taira youths and the pathos of their family's tragic
destruction were keenly felt.

The cultural impact of the war was profound and lasting. The
great land battles in the north and west, the vicissitudes of the ancient capital and its proud imperial family, the climactic clash of
opposing armadas in the treacherous waters of the Inland Sea, and
the deeds of individual warriors quickly assumed central importance
in the national folklore.[1] In particular, tales of the mighty heroes of
the struggle were repeated, discussed, and embellished until they
had shaped an enduring image of the ideal Japanese warrior: a man
of imposing appearance, magnificently appareled in costly armor
and mounted on a stalwart war horse, who so valued family pride
and personal honor that he stood ready to sacrifice his life for his

[1] Even in modern Japan the memory of this old war lingers, finding expression in the
invariable choice of Taira red and Minamoto white as the colors displayed by opposing
teams, in television programs bearing such titles as "Minamoto-Taira Battle of Songs," in
the annual sale of dolls representing famous Gempei warriors, and in countless other aspects of everyday life.

lord, to kill himself to protect his good name, to risk death in order to be the first man to attack an enemy position, and to fight against overwhelming odds to take the head of an adversary of consequence.

Warriors of this sort, Minamoto retainers for the most part, were revered and emulated throughout the long centuries of feudalism. One of them, the subject of this book, remains the greatest romantic hero, and probably the single most famous man, in all of premodern Japanese history.

Minamoto Yoshitsune (1159–1189) was a younger half-brother of Yoritomo, entrusted by him with partial command of the campaign against the Taira. Little is known of his life before 1180, when, as a small, pale youth with crooked teeth and bulging eyes,[2] he arrived at Yoritomo's camp to join the rebellion. In 1184 and 1185, as one of Yoritomo's two field commanders, he crushed the Taira decisively in a series of brilliantly executed engagements, but after the final victory Yoritomo turned against him, hunted him remorselessly, and forced him to commit suicide. Given the paucity of historical records, we shall probably never be able to account satisfactorily for Yoritomo's behavior. The immediately pertinent fact, however, is that a man with Yoshitsune's history could scarcely fail to become a popular hero, especially when it was widely believed that his downfall had been the result of jealous slanders.

The legend of Yoshitsune began to take shape in the thirteenth century, when the first stories of the war came into existence. In *Heike monogatari* ("A Tale of the Heike"), one of the masterpieces of Japanese literature, and in other early works, Yoshitsune is treated almost without exception as a public figure, the fiery young leader whose military genius forced the Taira to their knees. Later, as knowledge of his romantic story became more widespread, fanciful tales concerning his obscure childhood and last fugitive years tended to supplant the more sober accounts. Every child knew how Yoshitsune had learned the art of swordsmanship from supernatural creatures, and how, a frail, effeminate boy, he had effortlessly bested the ferocious warrior-monk Benkei in combat on a bridge in Kyoto; theater-goers of all ages thrilled to *Ataka*, *Funa Benkei*, and other

---

[2] GSSK, II, 605; *kōwakamai Oisagashi* (Shimazu, p. 135). This unflattering description was either ignored or explained away as the Yoshitsune legend developed.

dramas which related the hazards of his flight from Yoritomo's wrath.

Yoshitsune (Gikeiki), the anonymous fifteenth-century work translated in this volume, is the oldest extant collection of stories concerning Yoshitsune's boyhood and fugitive years. Its unknown author, who dismisses the great victories of Ichi-no-tani, Yashima, and Dan-no-ura in a sentence or two, seems clearly to have intended to supplement *Heike monogatari* and other tales of the war by offering an account of the portions of Yoshitsune's life to which such works made little or no reference, using as sources stories which were currently in circulation. The historical value of *Yoshitsune* is so slight that it need not detain us. The interest of the book lies in its relationship to, and influence upon, the Yoshitsune legend as a whole, and to a lesser degree in its importance as a well-known variant form of the war tale *(gunki monogatari)*, an important literary genre of the medieval period.

To appreciate the extent to which *Yoshitsune* contributed to the legend of Yoshitsune, one must review the salient features of the legend itself. That will be the primary function of the pages that follow. First of all, it is necessary to have in mind the factual basis upon which the legend was constructed.[3]

I. THE HISTORICAL FIGURE

Emperor Seiwa (850–880; r. 858–876)
|
Prince Sadazumi (873–916)
|
Tsunemoto (Rokusonnō)[4] (d. 961)
|
Mitsunaka (912–997)
|

[3] The best sources for the historian are *Heike monogatari*; its lengthier and less literary alter ego, *Gempei seisuiki* ("A Chronicle of the Fortunes of the Minamoto and Taira"); *Gyokuyō* ("Leaves of Jade"), the celebrated diary of the court noble Fujiwara Kanezane (1149–1207); and *Azuma kagami* ("The Eastern Mirror"), an official record compiled by the military government *(bakufu)* in Kamakura. We are also indebted to these works and to another, *Heiji monogatari* ("A Tale of Heiji"), for scattered bits of information which, taken as a whole, account for most of our scanty stock of accurate knowledge concerning Yoshitsune's youth and last years.

[4] "Son of the Sixth Imperial Prince," so called because his father was Seiwa's sixth son.

Yorinobu (968–1048)
|
Yoriyoshi (999–1075)
|
Yoshiie (1041–*ca.* 1108)
|
Yoshichika (d. 1108)
|
Tameyoshi (1096–1156)
|
Yoshitomo (1123–1160)
|
Yoshitsune (1159–1189)

A. Antecedents

Minamoto Yoshitsune was a direct descendent of Tsunemoto, a grandson of Emperor Seiwa, who received the Minamoto surname in the year of his death, after an official career which began with the vice-governorship of Musashi Province in the 930's and included numerous other provincial and military appointments. Although Tsunemoto is famous as the founder of the most illustrious branch of the Seiwa Genji,[5] he was himself not a distinguished warrior. His son, Mitsunaka, succeeded in becoming a local chieftain in Settsu Province, with military strength sufficient to recommend him to the attention of the regent house of Fujiwara, which had need of the services of warriors to protect its members and their possessions and to implement its political operations. Mitsunaka was eager to acquire powerful friends at court in order to extend his influence among other provincial landowners, who were willing to offer military allegiance in return for protection of their properties from government tax collectors and rapacious neighbors. He readily assisted the Fujiwara in their ruthless elimination of potential rivals and unwanted incumbents of the imperial throne, making his warriors the "teeth and claws" of the regents, and finding his reward in the increasingly close connection between the Seiwa Genji and the Fujiwara.

Yoshitsune's ancestor, Yorinobu, like Mitsunaka's other sons, served the Fujiwara. By his time, the Minamoto family was so wealthy that it was able to shower its patrons with princely gifts and marry its daughters into the nobility, but its military resources,

[5] The name Genji is the Sino-Japanese equivalent of Minamoto. Similarly, Heike and Heishi are equivalents of Taira.

which centered primarily in the provinces of Settsu, Yamato, and Kawachi, still furnished barely enough men to guard the houses of the nobility and dispose of robber bands. In 1030 Yorinobu was sent to put down the Kantō revolt of Taira Tadatsune; in the process he contrived to make vassals of Tadatsune's entire family and to establish a Genji sphere of influence in eastern Japan. The lucrative governorships with which he was rewarded added to his wealth and power, and consequently to the number of his adherents.

Yorinobu's son, Yoriyoshi, one of the greatest warriors in this great fighting family, won an immense reputation by ending a revolt in northern Japan (the so-called Former Nine Years' War, 1051–62), where a family known as the Abe had ruled vast areas in virtual independence of the central government. Even before this campaign, Yoriyoshi's influence had extended over most of the east, but his position there was immeasurably enhanced by the victory of Minamoto arms in the face of stubborn resistance, adverse and unaccustomed climatic conditions, and acute logistic problems. Many of his difficulties stemmed from the scantiness of the support that he received from the indecisive court nobles in Heian, who were so little alive to political realities, and so contemptuous of the warrior class in general, that they considered it unnecessary to reward a dozen or so deserving chieftains after the final victory. A contemporary chronicle of the campaign[6] dwells at length upon the spiritual bond which united Yoriyoshi, the dispassionately fair feudal lord, to his loyal followers, who were ready to lay down their lives for his sake. It is undoubtedly true that Yoriyoshi's personality and the rigors of the long war fostered the growth of such ties, but the basic relationship was one of mutual self-interest. Unless a lord provided concrete rewards for loyalty on the field of battle, he would sooner or later find himself without vassals. Yoriyoshi therefore reached down into his own pocket to compensate for the court's niggardliness, an act which profoundly impressed the warrior class.

During the lifetime of Yoriyoshi's son, Yoshiie, the Minamoto prestige reached new heights. Even as a boy, Yoshiie showed himself a warrior of remarkable bravery and skill, fighting by his father's side against the Abe. Some twenty years later, while serving as governor of Mutsu Province, he intervened in a family quarrel which

[6] *Mutsu waki* ("A Chronicle of the Pacification of Mutsu").

was disrupting the province (the Later Three Years' War, 1086–87), and after arduous efforts succeeded in restoring peace. When the court refused to recompense his warriors on the ground that the war had been a private affair, he followed his father's example by paying them himself.

Yoshiie, like his father a dependable and generous lord, acquired so many lands by commendation that the court repeatedly forbade farmers to present him with property. The Kantō came completely under his influence, and he was also a figure of consequence in the capital, where, as the nation's foremost warrior, he enjoyed the coveted honor of direct access to the presence of the former sovereign.

The bond between the Genji and the eastern warriors depended to a considerable extent upon Minamoto political influence at court. After the death of Yoshiie, the family's position in the capital deteriorated steadily, and this resulted in a corresponding diminution of its strength in the Kantō. Arrogance, bloody internal strife, and lack of a leader of stature were chiefly responsible for the decline. As governor of Tsushima, Yoshiie's son, Yoshichika, so tried the patience of the court in a series of outrages against public order and private morality that he was ultimately put to death. His executioner was one of ex-Emperor Shirakawa's trusted personal guards, a warrior named Taira Masamori.

The Taira family, soon to become the mortal foes of the Minamoto, had originally been powerful eastern warriors. Many Taira still remained in the Kantō, and, like other warriors in the area, were for the most part Minamoto vassals. This was a situation that had prevailed since the time of Tadatsune's revolt. Those elements of the family to whom the prospect of Minamoto domination was unpalatable had moved west after the revolt, gradually establishing themselves as chieftains in Ōmi, Ise, Chūgoku, Shikoku, and Kyushu. With the rise of Masamori, who seems to have been put forward by Shirakawa for the express purpose of checking the Genji, the western Taira for the first time entered the central arena.

Yoshichika's son, Tameyoshi, the new head of the Genji, was a rough and hotheaded warrior, unable either to keep the peace within his quarrelsome family or to compete with the more polished Masamori in the race for rank and office. He held only minor positions, and was stripped of those after being found guilty of complicity in an intrigue fomented by one of his sons. Thereafter he lived in relative obscurity until the War of Hōgen, when he espoused the losing cause and was put to death.

Meanwhile in the west, Taira Masamori's son and grandson, Tadamori and Kiyomori, were building on the foundation that Masamori had laid. Tadamori's immense financial resources, garnered from provincial governorships and maritime trade with China, were freely expended on the construction of religious edifices and other projects close to the hearts of ex-emperors Shirakawa and Toba, and they rewarded him with desirable offices and other marks of favor. Kiyomori, who along with his inherited wealth and position had great natural abilities, rose even more rapidly in the official hierarchy.

On the eve of the Hōgen War, Kiyomori was the powerful head of a united family, while the divided Genji, though they still retained a certain amount of strength in the east, were negligible as a political force. The most important Minamoto leader was Tameyoshi's son, Yoshitomo, the father of Yoshitsune. Yoshitomo, who was not on friendly terms with his father or brothers, had lived for many years in the east, where he commanded a fairly large following among warriors who still remembered Yoshiie. Shortly before the war he had gone to the capital and had been granted a provincial governorship.

The Hōgen War of 1156 broke out against a background of friction between Emperor Sutoku and his father, ex-Emperor Toba, whose cloister government had usurped most of the functions of the court. The way in which Toba arbitrarily dictated the imperial succession was particularly vexing to Sutoku. In 1139 he forced Sutoku to abdicate in favor of Konoe, the two-year-old child of his own favorite, and in 1155 he further disregarded Sutoku's wishes by selecting another of his sons, Go-Shirakawa, to succeed Konoe. Immediately after Toba's death in 1156, Sutoku joined forces with Fujiwara Yorinaga, a disaffected member of the regent family, and the two summoned warriors for an attempted coup d'état. But the court faction behind Go-Shirakawa enlisted the support of Kiyomori and Yoshitomo and crushed the opposition in a single battle, a night attack suggested by Yoshitomo and fought largely by his eastern warriors.

In spite of its brevity and limited scale, the Hōgen War was a crucial event in Japanese history. The military, erstwhile servants of the nobility, were suddenly revealed as the strongest force in the country, and the only question left undecided was whether the dominant figures in the new era were to belong to the Taira family or to the Minamoto.

Kiyomori and Yoshitomo at once began to compete for rank and office. Notwithstanding the leading role that Yoshitomo had played in the Hōgen victory, he was easily outdistanced by the astute Kiyomori, who prospered spectacularly in alliance with one of the ex-Emperor's most influential officers, Fujiwara Michinori (also known by the religious name Shinzei). Yoshitomo, resentful of Kiyomori's good fortune, and smarting under Shinzei's rejection of a proffered marital alliance, was easily persuaded to join a plot against the two, instigated by another of Go-Shirakawa's favorites, a young man named Fujiwara Nobuyori, who had been frustrated by Shinzei in his attempt to obtain a coveted office. Yoshitomo and Nobuyori acted while Kiyomori was away on a pilgrimage to Kumano. They enjoyed an initial success, during which Shinzei was beheaded, but after some adroit political maneuvering Kiyomori struck back decisively. Nobuyori was seized and executed, and Yoshitomo was killed by a treacherous retainer as he fled east to recruit fresh adherents. That was the Heiji War of 1160.

With Yoshitomo's death, the Minamoto vanished from the scene, leaving Kiyomori to consolidate his position as the most powerful man in Japan.

B. Early Life

Yoshitomo
|
Yoshihira Tomonaga Yoritomo Yoshikado Mareyoshi Noriyori
Zenjō Gien Yoshitsune girl girl

Yoshitsune was one of nine sons.[7] At the time of the Heiji War, he and his two elder full brothers, Imawaka (Zenjō) and Otowaka (Gien), were living in the capital with their mother, Tokiwa, a minor lady-in-waiting whose beauty had caught Yoshitomo's eye. Yoshitsune, then known by the childhood name Ushiwaka, was less than a year old at the time of his father's death in the first month[8] of 1160, and his brothers were seven and five *sai*,[9] respectively.

There is no completely reliable source of information concerning the manner in which Tokiwa met the crisis precipitated by Yoshitomo's revolt, nor indeed concerning any part of Yoshitsune's life from then until his first meeting with Yoritomo in 1180, twenty years later. The account which follows is based primarily upon two war tales, *Heiji monogatari* and *Gempei seisuiki*.[10]

After the war, the Taira searched assiduously for Yoshitomo's sons. Yoritomo, the eldest survivor, who was captured early in 1160, was banished to Izu instead of being executed, thanks to the intercession of Kiyomori's stepmother. Meanwhile Tokiwa, after hiding briefly at Kiyomizu Temple with her three children, had set out with them at night toward Yamato Province, and after severe hardships

[7] The two eldest, Yoshihira and Tomonaga, lost their lives in the disastrous aftermath of the Heiji rising. The third, Yoritomo, whose mother was the daughter of the chief priest at Atsuta Shrine, was destined to become one of the great figures in Japanese history. The fourth, Yoshikado, died young. The fifth, Mareyoshi, who was exiled in Tosa after Heiji, was forced by the Taira to kill himself when Yoritomo revolted in 1180. The sixth, Noriyori, who was the son of a harlot at Ikeda post station in Tōtōmi, joined Yoritomo in 1180, served as one of his two lieutenants in the campaigns against the Heike, and returned to Kamakura after the final victory at Dan-no-ura. In spite of determined efforts to live amicably with his brother, he was exiled and killed in 1193. Of the last three, who were all children of the beautiful Lady Tokiwa, the two eldest became monks. The first, Zenjō, attached himself to Yoritomo's cause in 1180. He lived at Ano in Tōtōmi until the opening years of the thirteenth century, when he was executed on charges of conspiracy. The second, Gien, fought for Yoritomo under the command of his uncle, Yukiie, and was killed in battle at the Sunomata River by the Taira in 1181. The third, Yoshitomo's ninth and last son, was Yoshitsune.

[8] Dates refer to the lunar calendar.

[9] According to the old Japanese system, a man's age *(sai)* was reckoned in terms of the number of calendar years in which he had actually lived, rather than on the basis of his birthdays. Thus, the age of a child born on December 31 of one year would be regarded as one *sai* until January 1 of the following year, when it would become two *sai*. Yoshitsune's age in 1160 was two *sai*, though he was still a young baby.

[10] For the biographical material presented in the remainder of this section, I am heavily indebted to Kuroita Katsumi's detailed study, *Yoshitsune-den* ("A Biography of Yoshitsune" [Sōgensha, 1939]).

had finally found shelter with an uncle at a place called Ryūmon-no-sato. When the Taira arrested her mother, she went with her sons to Rokuhara, the Taira headquarters in the capital, where, it is said, her youth, beauty, and filial piety so impressed Kiyomori that he determined to spare the children, giving as justification the lenient treatment previously accorded their elder brother, Yoritomo. The war tales say that Kiyomori made Tokiwa his concubine but soon tired of her. At any rate, it is known that she and the boys remained in the capital, and that she presently married Ichijō Naganari, a member of the Fujiwara family. Imawaka and Otowaka were made monks, and at the age of seven *sai* Ushiwaka, too, was sent to a temple, Kuramadera, for religious training.

When Ushiwaka, by then renamed Shanaō, was eleven *sai*, the chronicles continue, a chance discovery of the Minamoto genealogy apprised him of his true identity. Thenceforth, his sole desire was to avenge his father. Stubbornly refusing to take the tonsure, he secretly devoted himself to military exercises in the unfrequented wilds near Kurama. Finally, in the third month of 1174, he fled the temple with the assistance of a gold merchant named Kichiji, who took him to Ōshū in the remote northeast. En route, at Kagami post station, he officiated at his own coming-of-age ceremony, assuming the adult name Minamoto Kurō Yoshitsune.

Whatever the details, it is clear that Yoshitsune did in fact balk at becoming a monk, and that he made his way from Kurama to Ōshū, the immense northern territory which had passed into the possession of Fujiwara Kiyohira[11] as a result of the Later Three Years' War, and in which for three generations the Fujiwara family, enjoying the vast wealth and formidable military strength accruing from extensive domains and rich gold mines, had presided over a miniature empire, crowned by the brilliant capital of Hiraizumi.[12] He appears to have

[11] Kiyohira's mother, a member of the Abe family, had been the wife of Watari Tsune-kiyo. After Tsunekiyo's death, she married into the Kiyowara family, taking Kiyohira along as a stepson. In the last phase of the Later Three Years' War, the main contestants were Kiyohira and Minamoto Yoshiie versus Kiyohira's stepbrother, Iehira, and others of Kiyohira's relatives by marriage. Kiyohira and his descendents subsequently took the name Fujiwara. They ruled Ōshū for almost exactly a century, from the end of the Later Three Years' War in 1087 until Yasuhira's defeat by Yoritomo in 1189.

[12] As a cultural center, Hiraizumi rivaled Kyoto itself. The finest craftsmen in Japan were commissioned to construct and adorn its splendid temples, in which gold, silver, and precious stones were employed in imposing profusion. The city's chief ornament was the

remained there for several years, shielded from Taira enemies by Kiyohira's grandson, Hidehira.

In the meantime, Kiyomori's highhanded methods and increasing intransigence were alienating ex-Emperor Go-Shirakawa, the court nobles, the great religious institutions, and the provincial warriors. In the fourth month of 1180, Minamoto Yorimasa, a seventy-six-year-old warrior-poet who had been living quietly in the capital, suddenly joined forces with an imperial prince, Mochihito, in an open revolt. They were quickly suppressed, but Prince Mochihito's summons to arms against the Heike, carried to every important Genji in Japan by Yoshitomo's brother, Yukiie, furnished a long-awaited pretext for action. Yoritomo revolted in the eighth month of the same year, and his cousin Yoshinaka in the ninth.

When news of Yoritomo's uprising reached Ōshū, Yoshitsune rushed off to join him, unmoved by Hidehira's counsels of prudence. As a farewell present, Hidehira sent two of his own warriors after him —the Satō brothers, Tsuginobu and Tadanobu, who were destined to become part of the Yoshitsune legend by sacrificing their lives gloriously for their new master.

C. Military Career

Yoshitsune reached his brother on the twenty-first day of the tenth month of 1180. The reunion occurred at Kisegawa, near the scene of Yoritomo's successful Fuji River brush with the Taira.[13] Cordial relations were established and the two returned together to Kamakura, where both remained for the next three years while Yoritomo consolidated his hold on the Kantō and neighboring provinces. Meanwhile the hard-driving Yoshinaka had forced the Taira to flee from the capital to their western base, taking with them the imperial regalia and the infant emperor, Antoku (seventh month, 1183). By late 1183, there were three nearly equal military powers in Japan:

---

great Chūsonji Temple, founded by Kiyohira, which is said at its height to have contained more than forty religious edifices and three hundred monks' residences. The mummified remains of the three great chieftains, Kiyohira, Motohira, and Hidehira, are preserved in the Chūsonji's magnificent Golden Hall, one of the best surviving examples of the art of the Fujiwara period.

[13] The meeting is recorded in *Azuma kagami* under date of 1180.10.21. From this time until his flight from the capital late in 1185, Yoshitsune's major activities can be traced with some assurance.

Yoritomo, whose strength lay in the east; Yoshinaka, who held the provinces from the Hokurikudō to Ōmi, plus the capital and the person of ex-Emperor Go-Shirakawa; and the Taira, who dominated some twenty provinces in the west. This was the stalemate which Yoshitsune broke.

Yoshitsune's first military campaign, a march against the Taira ordered by Yoritomo in the tenth month of 1181, had ended without incident after the enemy had turned away to avoid a confrontation. He was therefore quite inexperienced when, late in 1183, Yoritomo sent him with his brother Noriyori to oppose Yoshinaka, whose outrageous behavior in the capital had caused Go-Shirakawa to turn to Yoritomo as the lesser of two evils.[14] Aided only by a co-commander of mediocre ability, Yoshitsune faced the immediate challenge of a seasoned, always victorious opponent, while in the background the resurgent Taira waited, ready to strike at the capital.

Yoshinaka's initial reaction to the threat from the east was an attempt to conclude a temporary peace with the Taira; this he succeeded in doing on the ninth day of the first month of 1184. He also considered a strategic withdrawal to his home base in the north, but he abandoned the idea when he received word from a scout that Yoshitsune's command did not exceed 1,000 men.

At this juncture, threatening moves by Minamoto Yukiie in Kawachi prompted Yoshinaka to send part of his small army in that direction. The decision left him with a force of barely 1,000, but he counted on the natural advantages of his position to withstand any assault by Yoritomo.

The two main approaches to the capital were guarded by the deep, swift-flowing Uji and Seta rivers. At Uji the defenses were particularly strong. The bridge had of course been dismantled, the ford was extremely narrow, and the river was strewn with obstacles. It soon became apparent, however, that Yoshitsune's force was much larger than Yoshinaka had been led to believe—55,000, according to the enthusiastic author of *Gempei seisuiki*, but probably actually in the

---

[14] The complex political and military history of these years, which is largely peripheral to our main interest, is of necessity drastically abridged here. Sir George Sansom, *A History of Japan to 1334* (Stanford, Calif.: Stanford University Press, 1958), pp. 264–338, provides a useful summary in English, and there are detailed accounts in standard Japanese histories. See, in particular, Ōmori Kingorō, *Buke jidai no kenkyū* ("*A Study of the Feudal Era*" [Fuzambō, 1927–37]), Vols. I and II.

neighborhood of 3,000 or 4,000. Vying recklessly for the glory of being first across, the veteran eastern warriors struck at Uji as soon as Yoshinaka's main army had been drawn out of the capital by Yukiie (first month, twentieth day) and quickly overwhelmed the numerically inferior defense force. Yoshinaka fell back toward Ōmi, where he was attacked and killed by Noriyori's contingent, now safely across the Seta River.

Yoshitsune's debut as a military commander was marked by the decisiveness, speed, and aggressive spirit that were to characterize all his subsequent campaigns. In view of his many later demonstrations of superb strategic and tactical skill, it is perhaps not going too far to suggest, as Professor Kuroita has done, that he may have deliberately misled Yoshinaka with regard to the size of the attacking force and also may have arranged for Yukiie's convenient demarche.[15]

At Yoritomo's direction, Yoshitsune and Noriyori promptly asked Go-Shirakawa for permission to attack the Heike; the permission was granted on the twenty-sixth of the same month. The Taira, who had earlier moved east from Yashima in Shikoku, were then engaged in establishing a strong position in a narrow strip of land extending for seven miles along the Settsu coast near the modern city of Kobe, well protected by mountains on the north, by the sea on the south, and by the two fortresses of Ikuta-no-mori, to the east, and Ichi-no-tani, to the west. The mountains were precipitous, Taira vessels controlled the seas, and the natural advantages of the terrain at Ikuta-no-mori and Ichi-no-tani had been reinforced by ditches, obstacles, and archers' towers. The size of the defending force has been fairly reliably estimated at around 20,000.[16]

Two Genji armies, headed by Noriyori and Yoshitsune, respectively, set out from the capital on the fourth day of the second month. Noriyori was to attack Ikuta-no-mori on the seventh; Yoshitsune was to make a quick detour through Harima Province in order to strike simultaneously at Ichi-no-tani from the rear. Since only a few days had elapsed since the fighting at Uji and Seta, it seems unlikely that the easterners were able to muster an appreciably larger force than

---

[15] Kuroita, pp. 91, 93.
[16] *Gyokuyō*. *Gempei seisuiki*'s figure is 100,000; *Azuma kagami*'s, "several myriads."

the one that had confronted Yoshinaka, and *Gyokuyō*'s estimate of 2–3,000 is probably not far off.[17]

On the night of the fourth, Yoshitsune inflicted a decisive defeat on a small Taira force in an outlying position. He then turned over his westbound Ichi-no-tani army to a subordinate commander and headed across the mountains north of Ichi-no-tani with a picked force of some thirty men. He reached the ridge overlooking the fortress midway through the night of the sixth. Shortly afterward, Noriyori's Ikuta-no-mori forces launched their attack, and around dawn the Genji rear army assaulted Ichi-no-tani. By seven or eight o'clock the outnumbered eastern warriors had still failed to breach the stubbornly held Taira positions, in spite of gallant and bloody fighting. It was at this juncture that Yoshitsune and his men rode shouting down the unguarded cliff to the rear of Ichi-no-tani, threw the astounded Taira into confusion, and set fires which a strong west wind fanned into a general conflagration. Caught between the flames and the enemy, the Heike abandoned their positions, fled to their ships, and retreated over the seas to Yashima, losing some of their chief warriors in the process.

After this spectacular victory, Yoshitsune returned to the capital to act as Yoritomo's deputy in the Ki'nai area. At the age of twenty-five, he was a popular hero, well liked by the proud court aristocrats and treated with marked distinction by the ex-Emperor himself. Already, however, the seeds of his tragic estrangement from Yoritomo had been planted.

One of Yoritomo's trusted retainers was Kajiwara Kagetoki, an eastern warrior of Taira extraction who had joined him after saving his life in the perilous days of 1180. Kagetoki was a haughty, vindictive, and unscrupulous man, with a slanderous tongue which made him hated and feared in Kamakura, and ultimately led to his destruction after death had robbed him of Yoritomo's protection. He and Yoshitsune seem to have been antagonistic from the start—the one arrogantly insistent on his privileged position as a senior warrior and favorite of Yoritomo, the other youthfully cocksure, blunt, and impetuous. A coolness had developed before Ichi-no-tani, with the result that Kagetoki switched from Yoshitsune's command to Nori-

---

[17] *Gempei seisuiki* says that Noriyori commanded 50,000 men and Yoshitsune 10,000; *Azuma kagami* places the figures at 56,000 and 20,000.

yori's, and soon after the end of the campaign Kagetoki was back in
Kamakura, well primed with tales of Yoshitsune's headstrong behavior. These reports from a valued adviser, plus the obvious signs of
Yoshitsune's military genius and general popularity, doubtless
aroused jealous misgivings in Yoritomo, who was by nature a suspicious man.

At Yoritomo's request, in the sixth month of 1184 the court a-
warded Noriyori a provincial governorship and Junior Fifth Lower
rank; Yoshitsune, to his astonishment, received no recognition,
even though he had repeatedly asked his brother for a recommendation, arguing that his lack of a court title hampered his effectiveness as Yoritomo's representative in Kyoto. The wily Go-
Shirakawa, who was quick to realize the meaning of the slight, took
the occasion to indulge in his favorite tactic of maneuvering one
strong power against another in the hope of controlling them both.
Acting on his own, he awarded Yoshitsune joint appointments in the
imperial police and Left Gate Guards *(kebiishi saemon no shōjō)*[18] two
months after Noriyori's appointment. A few weeks later (third day,
ninth month) he conferred Junior Fifth Lower rank upon him, and
in the tenth month he granted him audience privileges, receiving him
for the first time with great pomp.

Although Yoshitsune reported his appointments to Kamakura
promptly, alleging that he had not been in a position to refuse, Yoritomo in anger relieved him of his commission to attack the Heike
(eighth month of 1184). Yoritomo was determined that his government should control all warriors, particularly in the crucial area of
their relations with the court, and had issued strict orders that court
honors were to come through him alone; he found it intolerable that
his policy should be openly flouted by his own brother. Yoshitsune's
position can only be conjectured. Possibly he was harboring rebellious thoughts, or possibly he underestimated the dark currents in his
brother's nature and allowed himself to be persuaded to accept
rewards to which he felt eminently entitled. At any rate, his behavior
pleased Go-Shirakawa, who, whatever his view of Yoshitsune as a

[18] Yoshitsune thus acquired the sobriquet Hōgan, or Hōgan-dono (sometimes pronounced *hangan*), another name for an official of his status, by which he was commonly
known thereafter. Earlier he had usually been called Onzōshi, a title of respect for a youth
of good family. Both these names eventually came to be associated specifically with him,
and are so identified in modern dictionaries.

person, was bent on driving a wedge between the two brothers in order to increase his own power.

During the ensuing months the campaign against the Taira was entrusted to Noriyori. Since the battle of Ichi-no-tani, the main Taira base had been at Yashima in Shikoku. Yashima, today a peninsular area jutting into the Inland Sea about four kilometers northeast of Takamatsu city, was then a flat island with a steep, mesa-topped mountain in the middle, cut off by a river from Shikoku proper. The Taira had fortified the position and installed Emperor Antoku in a palace on the flat land near a deep inlet, which served as their anchorage. From there they controlled the Inland Sea. Their most able commander, Tomomori, was in charge of a secondary base at Shimonoseki Straits in Kyushu. Instead of striking at Yashima, Noriyori attempted to attack Tomomori, venturing deeper and deeper into hostile territory and encountering mounting logistic problems. By the beginning of 1185 he was so hopelessly bogged down that Yoritomo was obliged to conquer his irritation and reinstate Yoshitsune.

Yoshitsune set off at once to attack Yashima, telling Go-Shirakawa that he would not return without destroying the Taira, even if it meant pursuing them to Korea. According to *Gempei seisuiki*, he left the capital on the tenth day of the first month of 1185. If this is true, he must have spent approximately a month at Watanabe port in Settsu, preparing for the crossing to Shikoku and incidentally clashing again with Kajiwara Kagetoki.[19]

Since the eastern warriors were horsemen with no knowledge of naval warfare, Yoshitsune's strategy was to strike Yashima from the rear, or land side, instead of challenging the Taira on the sea. Relying as usual on the element of surprise, he set out in five vessels with a small advance party of 150 men. The departure took place at two o'clock in the morning on the eighteenth day of the second month, during a gale so violent that the boatmen refused to embark until Yoshitsune's warriors threatened to shoot them down.[20] The three-day trip was accomplished in three or four hours, and around daybreak the party disembarked at Awa-no-katsuura. They made a two-

---

[19] This was the famous "reverse oars" controversy. See p. *32* below.

[20] The bulk of the army, under Kagetoki, was to follow as soon as possible in the remaining 150 boats. *Gempei seisuiki* gives the total size of the army as 100,000, but judging from the fact that five boats were required to transport Yoshitsune's 150 men and their mounts, 2,500 or 3,000 is a more likely figure.

day march in one, burning houses as they went, and arrived at the palace on the morning of the nineteenth. The Taira were caught completely by surprise. The island was shorthanded, since many of the garrison were off fighting in Iyo, and the billowing clouds of smoke and fierce yells of the attackers made it appear that they were being invaded by a mighty army. They fled to their boats, while the Satō brothers and others set fire to the palace and adjacent buildings. Soon, however, the small size of the Genji contingent became apparent, and a fierce battle at the water's edge ensued. Yoshitsune, who in his general's armor was a conspicuous target, would undoubtedly have lost his life had not Satō Tsuginobu stood in front of him to receive a fatal arrow from the bow of Taira Noritsune.

On the twenty-first, after determined resistance, the Taira withdrew from Yashima, pursued by Yoshitsune with eighty men. Local warriors and Kumano monks with naval experience joined the Genji, forcing Munemori and his band of fugitives to abandon Shikoku and flee toward Tomomori's base on Kyushu. On the twenty-second, Kajiwara and his men finally arrived. According to *Heike monogatari*, the newcomers joked good-naturedly about the swiftness of Yoshitsune's victory, which had denied them an opportunity to distinguish themselves in battle. There seem to have been many, however, who felt that Yoshitsune was attempting to monopolize the limelight. This was certainly true in the case of Kajiwara, as his subsequent behavior showed.

The Yashima victory had brought the Minamoto the local support essential for a decisive naval confrontation with their elusive foes. On the twenty-fourth of the third month, after a month of preparation, Yoshitsune set out by sea for the Taira base. Tomomori at once advanced to meet him.[21] The engagement took place at Dan-no-ura in the Shimonoseki Straits, an area of dangerous tidal currents. Both commanders had studied the currents carefully and laid their plans accordingly. The fighting began with an arrow exchange around noon, with the tide favoring the Heike. Yoshitsune fought a basically defensive battle, falling back bit by bit until the tide turned. Then the

[21] Kuroita, who has made an exhaustive study of the battle of Dan-no-ura, estimates the size of the Genji and Heike flotillas at 500 and 800 vessels, respectively, and concludes that the Minamoto contingent consisted of about 3–4,000 men and the Taira of 4–5,000. *Yoshitsune-den*, pp. 159–60.

Minamoto vessels closed with the enemy and soon won a decisive victory. The waters claimed the young Emperor, his grandmother (Kiyomori's widow), and most of the ill-fated clan who had fled the capital three years earlier. Of the imperial regalia, the sacred seal and mirror were recovered but the sword was irretrievably lost. The most important persons taken alive were Antoku's mother, Kenreimon'in; the cowardly commander-in-chief, Munemori; and Munemori's son. With this victory Yoritomo became the undisputed master of Japan.

The following passage from *Heike monogatari* (II, 328–29) indicates the nature of the relations between Yoshitsune and Kajiwara at the time:

[On the day of the battle of Dan-no-ura, there was an incident which brought] Yoshitsune and Kajiwara to the point of blows.

"Let me lead the attack today," Kajiwara proposed.

"I am here, am I not?" Yoshitsune replied.

"For shame! Are you not the commander-in-chief?"

"Not at all. Yoritomo is our commander-in-chief. Like yourself, I am merely his deputy."

"This is not the kind of man to lead warriors," muttered Kagetoki in disappointment.

Yoshitsune overheard him. "You're the biggest fool in Japan!" he shouted, clapping his hand to his sword.

"I owe allegiance to the Lord of Kamakura and nobody else," Kajiwara retorted, gripping his own weapon.

Kajiwara's three sons joined their father, and Yoshitsune's matchless warriors promptly surrounded them, ready to cut them down. But Miura-no-suke took hold of Yoshitsune and Dohi Jirō restrained Kajiwara.

"It will merely help the Heike if we quarrel among ourselves at a time like this," they implored. "Besides, Yoritomo won't like it at all if he hears about it." Yoshitsune regained his composure, and Kajiwara also released his weapon.

From that time on, so people say, Kajiwara lied about Yoshitsune to Yoritomo, and he finally succeeded in causing his death.

D. Yoritomo's Hostility

After Yoshitsune's dazzling victories at Yashima and Dan-no-ura, Yoritomo may well have concluded that his brother was a potential menace. If so, his apprehensions were no doubt heightened by a report from Kajiwara which reached Kamakura on the twenty-first day of the fourth month. Kajiwara accused Yoshitsune of claiming all the credit for a joint victory at Dan-no-ura, alleged that his subsequent behavior had been intolerably arrogant and dictatorial, and asked leave to return to Kamakura.

As chief and assistant chief of the Kamakura organ responsible for the conduct of military operations (the Samuraidokoro, or Warrior Office), Wada Yoshimori and Kagetoki had accompanied Noriyori and Yoshitsune on their western campaigns. Whereas Noriyori had consulted Wada at every step and had also kept in close touch with Yoritomo through letters, Yoshitsune had made decisions quite on his own, brusquely rejecting Kajiwara's advice and even, if the war tales are to be trusted, subjecting the older man to lectures on the conduct proper to a warrior. Regardless of the reliability of anecdotes such as the one quoted above from *Heike monogatari*, there can be no doubt that Yoshitsune and Kagetoki were continually at odds. From this time on, Kagetoki worked unremittingly to alienate Yoshitsune from Yoritomo.

On the twenty-fifth day of the fourth month, Yoshitsune made a triumphant entry into the capital. One of his first acts was to contract an unauthorized marital alliance with a noble family.[22] It was at about this time that Yoritomo privately issued orders to *bakufu* retainers not to obey Yoshitsune, although Yoshitsune was still Kamakura's official representative in the capital.

Learning of Yoritomo's displeasure, Yoshitsune dispatched a retainer to the Kantō with a sworn statement of loyalty. The *Azuma kagami*, in describing the statement's reception, clearly indicates the nature of Yoritomo's chief grievance:

1185.5.7. Kamei Rokurō, an emissary from Yoshitsune, arrived from Kyoto bearing a written oath in which Yoshitsune disclaimed treasonable intentions. It was addressed to Ōe Hiromoto.[23]

[22] He married the daughter of Taira Tokitada, a high-ranking noble captured at Dan-no-ura, who no doubt hoped to use Yoshitsune's popularity as a means of restoring his own fortunes. From Yoritomo's point of view, this was not only a disobedient act but an affront to the daughter of an eastern warrior, Kawagoe Shigeyori, whom Yoshitsune had earlier married at Yoritomo's command.

[23] It was usual to employ an intermediary when communicating with an exalted personage. Hiromoto, the head of the *bakufu*'s supreme judicial organ, the Monchūjo, was a crafty

Instead of acting on his own initiative, Noriyori constantly sends messengers from the west with detailed reports of the situation there. This is most gratifying to Yoritomo. Yoshitsune, on the other hand, does exactly as he sees fit, and only now, after having become aware of Yoritomo's irritation, has he finally sent the present message. Such unpardonable conduct has merely increased His Lordship's anger.

Yoshitsune's next move was to set out in person for the east, taking the prisoners Munemori and his son with him, in order to talk directly to Yoritomo. When he arrived at Sakai post station in Sagami on the fifteenth of the fifth month, he found instructions to wait there for further orders. In the meantime, one of his warriors became involved in a brawl with men in the following of Yoritomo's brother-in-law, Ichijō Yoshiyasu, and this incident increased Yoritomo's annoyance.

From Sakai and the neighboring post station of Koshigoe, Yoshitsune sent repeated declarations of loyalty to Kamakura, but with no effect. Finally, on the twenty-fourth, he addressed the famous Koshigoe letter[24] to Ōe Hiromoto. This moving plea also failed to elicit a response. Instead, he was ordered to return to the capital with his prisoners (who had meanwhile been interviewed by Yoritomo), and on the ninth day of the sixth month he started back, resentful and unforgiven. Four days later, Yoritomo repossessed twenty-four Taira properties which he had previously granted to Yoshitsune.[25]

Only a few short months were to elapse before Yoshitsune became a hunted man. His tragic fate was precipitated by the enmity between

---

scholar-statesman whose counsels carried great weight in Kamakura. He was almost fanatically dedicated to the service of the *bakufu* and dealt ruthlessly with potential threats to its security. He appears to have deliberately fostered ill-feeling between Yoritomo and Yoshitsune as a means of driving the latter into the arms of Go-Shirakawa, the *bakufu*'s chief opponent in the capital, with the ultimate aim of forcing the opposition into the open where it could be crushed. He played a leading role in the rejection of the Koshigoe letter and the dispatch of Tosabō (see below), and was the author of the protector-steward scheme which Kamakura imposed upon the court after Yoshitsune's flight. See Ryō Susumu, *Kamakura jidai* ("The Kamakura Period" [Shunjūsha, 1957]), I, 32.

[24] See the translation, p. *137*.

[25] Yoshitsune's appointment as governor of Iyo two months later, which at first glance seems to represent a softening of Yoritomo's attitude, was the result of a recommendation made much earlier. After Yoshitsune's acceptance, Yoritomo in effect nullified the gift by placing *bakufu* stewards in the province.

Yoritomo and Yukiie, the uncle who had carried Prince Mochihito's
historic summons to the Genji and had subsequently created the
diversion in Kawachi which had proved so costly to Yoshinaka. As a
general, Yukiie had by that time amassed an impressive record of
defeats. He was essentially not a military man, merely a petty schem-
er, one might say a lesser Go-Shirakawa. After falling out with Yoritomo early in the Gempei struggle, he had bestowed the dubious
benefits of his assistance on Yoshinaka, while at the same time working assiduously to intensify the bad feeling between the cousins. Later,
because of a fancied slight, he parted company with Yoshinaka and
intrigued with Go-Shirakawa for Yoshinaka's downfall. Between
Yoshinaka's death and the events about to be related, he appears to
have remained quietly in the capital.

On the fourth day of the eighth month of 1185, Yoritomo ordered
a *bakufu* retainer in Ōmi, Sasaki Sadatsuna, to attack Yukiie, whom
he accused of fomenting rebellion. Given the history of the relations
between Yoritomo and his uncle, and in particular Yukiie's dangerous proximity to the disgruntled Yoshitsune, the order to Sasaki was
a predictable move. Yukiie called upon Yoshitsune for protection,
and Yoshitsune agreed to help him.

Owing to the scantiness of the record, one can do little more than
speculate on the reasons for Yoshitsune's friendly response to Yukiie.
If his overriding concern was to maintain Genji solidarity by avoiding
trouble with Yoritomo, his espousal of the shabby Yukiie's cause was
unwise, to say the least. If his intention was to ally himself with Yukiie
in a military revolt against Yoritomo, the apparent indecision which
characterized his subsequent behavior contrasted remarkably with
his earlier boldness. From the uncertain evidence of the military
romances, one could argue that he was a proud, quick-tempered
youth, who, though brilliant on the battlefield, was a political novice
incapable of grasping the subtleties of minds like Yoritomo's, Go-
Shirakawa's, and Yukiie's, and that his action was partly an impetuous defiance of Yoritomo, partly a chivalrous gesture on his uncle's
behalf.

In actual fact, it is unlikely that Yoshitsune could have taken any
position that would have healed the breach between him and Yoritomo. Yoritomo had apparently made a firm resolve to rid himself of
his popular and gifted brother, and the appearance of Yukiie, it may

be supposed, merely hastened the inevitable. On the second day of the ninth month, Kajiwara Kagesue and others were sent from Kamakura to the capital, with instructions to see Yoshitsune, observe his behavior, and order him to attack Yukiie. When the mission returned, its members reported that Yoshitsune was using a pretended attack of beriberi as an excuse for procrastination.[26]

Yoritomo took Yoshitsune's temporizing reply as confirmation of his suspicions. On the ninth of the tenth month, three days after Kagesue's return, he convened a council of warriors to select his brother's assassin. According to *Gempei seisuiki*, the retainers showed a marked reluctance to volunteer, but at last Shōshun Tosabō, a warlike monk from Shimotsuke, stepped forward and was accepted. Tosabō set out at once for the capital, accompanied by a few dozen followers.

It appears that word of Tosabō's approach may have reached Yoshitsune, and that Yukiie, with the encouragement of courtiers in Go-Shirakawa's entourage, had meanwhile been insistently urging his nephew to revolt. Twice while Tosabō was en route to Kyoto, once on the eleventh and again on the thirteenth, Yoshitsune went to the ex-Emperor's palace and said in effect: "Since Yoritomo is trying to kill his innocent uncle, Yukiie has finally determined to rebel against his authority. I have tried to dissuade him, but he refuses to listen. Far from being rewarded for my own services against the Heike, I too am about to be attacked, and for that reason I have agreed to join Yukiie. Please grant me a warrant to attack Yoritomo." *Azuma kagami* reports that Go-Shirakawa put him off with counsels of moderation.

Tosabō entered the capital on the seventeenth and attacked Yoshitsune's Horikawa mansion on the same night. The premises were almost deserted, but Yoshitsune and Satō Tadanobu held off the

---

[26] According to *Azuma kagami*, the gist of the interview was reported by Kagesue to Yoritomo in these words: "Yoshitsune refused to see us when we called the first time, alleging an indisposition... We called again a day or two later and he received us in an emaciated condition, supporting himself on an arm rest. He had had moxa cautery in several places. When we tested him by mentioning the attack on Yukiie, he said, 'My illness is quite genuine. I consider it my duty to apprehend even a common thief as soon as he commits a crime, to say nothing of someone like Yukiie. However, Yukiie is a Minamoto —a descendent like ourselves of Rokusonnō, and a warrior of outstanding ability. It will do no good to try to take him by sending out subordinates. I shall treat my condition promptly and take suitable steps as soon as I recover.' " [1185.10.6.]

attackers until the commotion attracted Yukiie and others, and with
their assistance the fighting was soon over. The luckless Tosabō fled
to Kurama, where Yoshitsune's old friends, the monks, were instru-
mental in his detection. He was executed on the twenty-sixth.

After repulsing Tosabō, Yoshitsune at once repeated his request for
an order to attack Yoritomo. The ex-Emperor and his advisers
appear to have encouraged the revolt but at the same time to have
shunned actual participation in it, for, resentful though they were of
Yoritomo's interference in court affairs, they dreaded his wrath.
After Tosabō's night assault, however, one of the rumors that swept
the capital was the persistent report that Yoshitsune was preparing to
carry off Go-Shirakawa and the rest of the imperial family to Kyushu.
With this alarming prospect to help tip the scales, the order was
issued on the eighteenth.

On the twenty-second, word of Tosabō's failure and the ex-Emperor's order reached Kamakura. Yoritomo, apparently certain that
Yoshitsune would strike east with his usual speed, immediately
issued orders for a large-scale mobilization of *bakufu* forces to con-
verge upon Ōmi and Mino, and himself left Kamakura for the capital on the twenty-ninth.

Since Yoshitsune had not a single hereditary retainer of his own,
much less an economic base of power, his sole hope lay in suborning
Yoritomo's men. Some of these, moved either by sympathy for Yoshitsune or by fear of his fighting skill, had at first shown signs of uncertainty;[27] but the *bakufu*'s prompt action effectively intimidated
the waverers—the more easily because Yoshitsune himself remained
strangely passive during this critical period—and it was soon clear
that there would be no major defections. Almost at once Yoshitsune
prepared to quit the capital without a struggle. On the second day of
the eleventh month, he obtained letters of appointment for himself
and Yukiie as stewards (*jitō*) of Kyushu and Shikoku, respectively,
with authority over all western warriors, and on the third he quietly
left the city, accompanied by a small personal following of some two
hundred men.[28]

[27] The electrifying news from Kyoto reached Kamakura just as Yoritomo's vassals had
assembled for the grand dedication of a chapel in memory of Yoshitomo. When, after the
conclusion of the ceremonies, the 2,916 principal chieftains in attendance were queried,
only 58 expressed willingness to march toward the capital at once.

[28] "It must be said that Yoshitsune behaved like a gentleman," wrote Kanezane in his

E. The Fugitive Years

Yoshitsune and Yukiie headed for the Settsu coast, fighting off hostile warriors on the way. On the night of the fifth, as they attempted to sail from the port of Daimotsu-no-ura (now a part of Amagasaki city), still harassed by enemies, they encountered a devastating storm, which sank over half their vessels and tossed the battered skeletons of the remainder onto near-by beaches. The few survivors were almost all killed or captured, but, miraculously, the two captains escaped death. They made their way in a small boat to a point on the Izumi coast near the modern city of Sakai, after which they separated, their prospects in ruins, each to hide as best he could from the Lord of Kamakura. Yukiie, who had friends in the Izumi area, managed to remain at large there for about six months before he was captured and executed.

After parting from Yukiie, Yoshitsune spent the night of the sixth at Tennōji Temple in Settsu, attended by his concubine, Shizuka, and two or three retainers. Then he dropped out of sight.

When Yoritomo learned of Yoshitsune's flight and its disastrous sequel, he returned to Kamakura. He made no secret of his anger to the ex-Emperor, who made haste to issue orders for the apprehension of the fugitives, nervously assuring Yoritomo that he had acted under duress (eleventh day, eleventh month). Yoritomo, unimpressed, at once set about strengthening his own position. He banished Yoshitsune's chief friends among the nobility, removed a number of Go-Shirakawa's favorites from office, and installed Fujiwara Kanezane as regent; he forced the court, despite its objections, to authorize the appointment of *bakufu* retainers to supervisory positions[29] in local areas that had not previously been under Kamakura control; and he imposed special levies on hitherto tax-exempt noble and imperial domains, ostensibly to defray the cost of suppressing the rebellion. Thus Yoshitsune's services to his brother did not end at Dan-no-ura.

In spite of intensive investigation, Yoshitsune's whereabouts remained unknown. Rumors placed him in the wilds of the Kii Peninsula, at Nara, on Mount Hiei, and in the capital itself. As month

---

diary, after a description of the agitation of the citizenry, many of whom had gone into hiding on the assumption that Yoshitsune's warriors would follow the usual practice of looting and burning as they departed. [*Gyokuyō*, 1185.11.3.]

[29] Wardens *(shugo)* and stewards *(jitō)*.

succeeded month, Shizuka and the retainers were accounted for, one by one, but Yoshitsune himself eluded the grasp of the infuriated Yoritomo, who suspected with reason that he was being shielded by sympathetic persons among the nobility, clergy, and warrior class. Shrines and temples were ordered to pray for his discovery, and the court and Ki'nai religious institutions were subjected to constant pressure from Kamakura. Additional search orders were issued by the court in the sixth and eleventh months of 1186. At last it became so difficult for Yoshitsune to remain in the capital area that he fled in disguise with his family to Fujiwara Hidehira's Ōshū domain, choosing a time and a route that are not clearly known.[30]

F. The End

News of Yoshitsune's escape, which reached the *bakufu* soon after his arrival in Ōshū, may well have cheered Yoritomo. Not only was Yoshitsune now far removed from such potential allies as the court and the remnants of the Taira, but his flight had furnished an admirable excuse for bringing northern Japan under *bakufu* control. The Ōshū Fujiwara were formidable adversaries, however, particularly with Yoshitsune's military genius to aid them, and for some time Yoritomo prudently refrained from intervening directly. At his instance, the court requested Hidehira to turn over Yoshitsune, but the old chieftain replied evasively. Hidehira had installed Yoshitsune in a fortress residence close to his own home, on a bluff overlooking the confluence of the Koromo and Kitakami rivers, and it was persistently rumored that he had placed his domains on a wartime footing.

Less than one year after Yoshitsune's arrival—on the twenty-ninth day of the tenth month of 1187—Fujiwara Hidehira died. The current gossip, as reported in Fujiwara Kanezane's diary, was that he called his sons to his deathbed, made them swear to serve Yoshitsune faithfully, and commanded them to formulate plans for an attack on Yoritomo. Yoritomo, still cautious, continued to with-

[30] It is likely that he traveled via the Hokurikudō around the second, third, or fourth month of 1187, assuming a *yamabushi* (wandering monk) disguise. The brief account above outlines the most important known facts concerning Yoshitsune's activities during the period between his flight to the west and his arrival in Ōshū. Additional details are supplied, and interesting inferences drawn, in Kuroita, Chapter 11, relevant portions of which are summarized in Appendix A.

hold his hand. With the start of the new year, he informed the court that he was engrossed in the construction of a stupa to be dedicated to his mother, a pious work incompatible with martial activities, and that the year 1188 itself had been pronounced dangerous for him, making avoidance of bloodshed desirable; he asked that the court call upon Hidehira's heir, Yasuhira, to give up Yoshitsune. Kyoto promptly responded with two separate orders to Yasuhira, one from the reigning sovereign and one from the ex-Emperor (twenty-first and twenty-sixth of second month).

On the surface, these demands from the distant court were no more effective than the earlier ones addressed to Hidehira. Actually, however, the situation at Hiraizumi had greatly altered since the death of Hidehira. The new chieftain, Yasuhira, was unsure of himself and his position and at odds with his brothers; he was fearful of the might of Kamakura, but only lukewarm in his allegiance to Yoshitsune, whom he gradually came to regard as a menace to the survival of the Ōshū Fujiwara. Yoshitsune, for his part, was restless in Ōshū. During the seventh and eighth months of 1188, the capital was subjected to a series of raids by robber bands, which, it was said, were inspired by Enryakuji monks in league with the fugitive Minamoto general. Orders for the arrest of a monk called Senkōbō, who had been identified as the ringleader, were issued in Kamakura in the tenth month. When Senkōbō was finally apprehended in the first month of 1189, he was found to be carrying a letter from Yoshitsune announcing his imminent return to the capital area. This news caused great consternation in the city. Moreover, a few days later the *bakufu* discovered a shadowy anti-Kamakura conspiracy at court, in which nobles friendly to Yoshitsune were involved. After Yoritomo received word of this development (twelfth day, second month), he roused himself to action. On the twenty-second of the second month, and again on the twenty-second of the third month, he pressed the court for permission to attack Ōshū. On the twenty-first of the intercalary fourth month, having been invited to select his own date by the ex-Emperor, he indicated that he would start north after the dedication of the stupa in the sixth month.

Several months earlier, as a result of the activities of Yoshitsune's Hiei partisans, a second set of two strongly worded court orders had been forwarded to Yasuhira (tenth and eleventh months, 1188). The shaken Fujiwara chieftain was doubtless also well aware of the massive military effort already underway at Kamakura early in 1189. Correctly assessing the extent of his peril, he appears to have concluded that cowardice, broken promises, and treachery were the purchase price of safety—an unfortunate misreading of Yoritomo's character and policies.[31] On the thirtieth day of the intercalary fourth month of 1189, he sent a force of several hundred mounted warriors against Yoshitsune's Koromogawa castle, overwhelmed the handful of defenders, and forced Yoshitsune to kill himself, his wife, and his three-year-old daughter.

Yasuhira at once sent word to Kamakura. On the thirteenth of the sixth month, after a delay to avoid conflict with the dedication of the stupa on the ninth, a messenger arrived in Koshigoe with Yoshitsune's head, preserved in sweet sake in a black lacquer box. The trophy was viewed by an official inspection party consisting of the two chief officers of the Samuraidokoro, Wada Yoshimori and Kajiwara Kagetoki, and twenty armored horsemen. When it was presented, even Kajiwara turned away, it is said, and Wada and the others could not keep back their tears.[32]

II. THE LEGEND

During or shortly after the lifetime of Kurō Hōgan Yoshitsune,[33] a new expression, *hōgan biiki* (sympathy for Hōgan; by extension, sympathy for the underdog), entered the Japanese language. More than anything else, *hōgan biiki*—sympathy, admiration, respect for a tragic hero—was responsible for the growth of the Yoshitsune legend and the idealization of its protagonist. The temper of the Muromachi period, during which the legend took shape and *hōgan biiki* achieved the status of a proverb, could scarcely have been more propitious: it was a period of strong and uncritical reverence for the past, with a deep interest in preserving the national cultural heritage, and a period also of widespread illiteracy, devotion to the external trappings of religion, and military enthusiasm. However fantastic, the exploits

[31] Yoritomo completely destroyed the Ōshū Fujiwara in a brief campaign which began only a few weeks after Yoshitsune's death.
[32] Kuroita, p. 294.
[33] Kurō means ninth son. For Hōgan, see note 18 above.

of ancient warriors were sympathetically treated in the pages of the characteristic prose and dramatic forms of the day—the war tale,[34] the Nō,[35] the dramatic dance *(kōwakamai)*,[36] and the short story *(otogi zōshi* or *chūsei shōsetsu)*[37]—and if the pedestrian Muromachi prose writers produced little of distinction in the process, they at least, by giving written form to earlier traditions, by elaborating and re-working old tales, and by creating new legends, assembled a rich legacy of source materials for the more fertile imaginations of a later age. The overwhelming majority of these warrior stories came from the stirring era of the Minamoto-Taira war, and the great hero who overshadowed all others was Minamoto Yoshitsune, whose gallant deeds and romantic history appealed irresistibly to the popular imagination.

The major elements in the Yoshitsune legend[38] fall naturally into

[34] For a discussion of war tales, see Section III below. The most important Muromachi war tale is *Taiheiki* (40 chapters; anonymous; probably dates from the sixth or seventh decade of the fourteenth century. Its subject is the civil wars of the first half of the four-teenth century). Of less intrinsic historical and literary value, but significant for their in-fluence on later literature, are *Yoshitsune* and *Soga monogatari*. (*Soga monogatari*: 12 chapters; anonymous; mid-fourteenth century? It deals with the attempt of two brothers in the twelfth century, Soga Jūrō and Soga Gorō, to avenge their father's murder.)

[35] Of approximately 240 Nō now being performed, between 50 and 60 are based on hero legends. Pieces about Yoshitsune *(hōgan mono)* constitute the largest single category of Nō plays; there are over 30 extant, of which 12 are currently performed. (This figure does not include *Futari Shizuka* and *Yoshino Shizuka*, two plays in which Yoshitsune's concubine, Shizuka, is the protagonist.)

[36] Also *kōwakanomai*. A dance form with chanting and musical accompaniment, named for its fifteenth-century originator, Momonoi Kōwakamaru Naoaki. The dance texts, which were also available in book form for the reading public, were devoted almost ex-clusively to martial subjects, as is clear from the categories into which they were divided: stories from *Heiji monogatari*, stories from *Heike monogatari*, stories dealing with Yoshitsune, stories dealing with the Soga brothers, stories from *Taiheiki*, etc. Their literary value equaled that of the short stories *(otogi zōshi)*, which they closely resembled. There are 44 *kōwakamai* in all, of which 14 deal with Yoshitsune. (The addition of borderline cases raises this figure to 19.)

[37] *Otogi zōshi* and *chūsei shōsetsu* are general terms for a large corpus of anonymous short stories written during the late Kamakura, Muromachi, and early Edo periods, apparently by minor court nobles, monks, recluses, and commoners. They were usually illustrated profusely, and seem frequently to have been read aloud to juvenile or illiterate listeners. Though crude and stereotyped in form and vocabulary, they are the repositories of old and new tales on a wide variety of subjects. Of some fifteen or sixteen *otogi zōshi* which belong to the general category of hero tales, eight deal with Yoshitsune.

[38] An exhaustive discussion of literary themes directly or indirectly involving Yoshitsune would occupy at least another volume the size of the present one. For the summary which

two categories. The first, and smaller, consists of half a dozen stories dealing with Yoshitsune's career as a public figure, all of which appear in the relatively reliable *Heike monogatari* and *Gempei seisuiki*, date from around the Kamakura period, and seem to contain a strong historical element. As a group, these stories are of particular interest for the light they cast on Yoshitsune's character. They present him as a military genius, a warrior first and last, with virtues and faults natural to a young man with his background and predilections. He was loyal, affectionate, kind hearted and trusting in his relations with kinsmen, friends, and women, as well as courteous and considerate to subordinates and defeated enemies, fearless in battle, and scrupulously honorable. But he was also impetuous, short tempered, naive, blunt, tactless, arrogant, and willful. Briefly, the most important of these stories are as follows.

A. Legends Dealing with Yoshitsune's Public Career

1. The Descent at Ichi-no-tani *[saka-otoshi]*. (Sources: *Heike monogatari, Gempei seisuiki*.)

The essential features of this legend have been outlined above (see the description of the battle of Ichi-no-tani). The legend in its fully developed form departs from fact primarily in its exaggeration of the difficulties of the terrain. A subsidiary element is the first encounter between Yoshitsune and Washinoo Saburō Yoshihisa, a local youth pressed into service as a guide, who becomes one of Yoshitsune's loyal retainers. The man who recruits Washinoo is the warrior-monk Saitō Musashibō Benkei, who in the legend rivals Yoshitsune himself in importance, although he is barely mentioned in *Azuma kagami* and the war tales of the Kamakura period. This is one of the rare occurrences of Benkei's name in *Heike monogatari* and *Gempei seisuiki*.

2. The Reverse Oar Controversy *[sakaro]*. (Sources: *Heike monogatari, Gempei seisuiki*.)

This famous dispute between Yoshitsune and Kajiwara Kagetoki occurred at a council of war in Settsu before the battle of Yashima,

---

follows, I wish to make clear my great indebtedness to Shimazu Hisamoto, whose encyclopedic *Yoshitsune densetsu to bungaku* ("The Yoshitsune Legend and Literature" [Meiji Shoin, 1935]) has been of invaluable assistance.

when the eastern warriors were considering the problem of naval warfare. The most complete description is given in *Gempei seisuiki* (II, 560–61):

"I think we ought to equip the vessels with reverse oars so we can maneuver freely during the battle," said Kajiwara Kagetoki.

"What is a reverse oar?" asked Yoshitsune.

"An oar in the bow oriented toward the stern. In a land battle a man mounted on a fast horse can advance and retreat whenever he needs to, but it's awkward to move backward in a naval engagement. Let's use bow oars to retreat when the enemy is strong and stern oars to attack when we have the advantage."

"Warriors always retreat if their commander so much as remains in the rear when he orders an attack," Yoshitsune objected. "How can we possibly hope to win if we prepare ahead of time to run away?"

"A good general protects himself until he can destroy his enemy," said Kajiwara. "It's dangerous to be a wild-boar warrior who charges dead ahead without thinking. If you weren't so young you wouldn't talk like that."

Yoshitsune flushed slightly. "I don't know anything about wild boars. I'm only interested in winning. The main thing in fighting is for a man to be ready to die from the day he leaves home. Anyone who wants to take care of himself had better stay away from the battlefield. A warrior's duty is to die engaging an enemy. He's not a man if he runs away to save his life. If you ever become a commander-in-chief, make all the preparations for flight you like—put in a hundred or a thousand reverse oars. I refuse to have the detestable things on my vessels."

The warriors burst out laughing, while Kajiwara reddened with chagrin.

"What do you mean by setting yourself up in opposition to me and comparing me to a wild boar?" Yoshitsune demanded. "Seize him, men!"

Ise Saburō Yoshimori, Kataoka Hachirō, and Musashibō Benkei stepped in front of Yoshitsune, ready to collar Kagetoki.

"People are supposed to say what they think in a council of war," said Kagetoki. "It's up to you to accept good advice and disregard bad ideas. If you were loyal to Yoritomo, you wouldn't humiliate me for suggesting a way to protect ourselves and destroy the Taira. I used to have one master, but now I seem to have two. This is a strange state of affairs!" He fitted an arrow to his bow and faced Yoshitsune.

As Kajiwara's sons moved forward, Yoshitsune confronted them furiously with his naked sword.

Cooler heads prevailed, the account continues, but Kajiwara found his revenge in slandering Yoshitsune to Yoritomo.

This anecdote, one that is generally accepted as a true story, became important to the Yoshitsune legend because it supplied a simple explanation for the estrangement of Yoshitsune from his brother, Yoritomo. As the legend developed, Kajiwara became increasingly villainous, and Yoshitsune's own arrogance was smoothed over.

3. The Dropped Bow *[yumi-nagashi]*. (Sources: *Heike monogatari, Gempei seisuiki*.)

In this incident, which is said to have occurred during the battle of Yashima, Yoshitsune is shown as a high-spirited, audacious, and proud commander:

In some manner or other Yoshitsune's bow was knocked out of his hand. He leaned forward, trying vainly to secure it with his whip, while his warriors shouted, "In heaven's name, let it go!" At last he retrieved it and rode out of the water laughing.

"That was ill advised," said a senior warrior reprovingly. "However expensive the bow may have been, it isn't worth as much as your life."

"Do you think I was worried about losing a bow?" asked Yoshitsune. "If it were like my uncle Tametomo's, which had to be strung by two or three men, I wouldn't mind letting it be captured. I risked my life to get it back because it's such a poor thing. I didn't want the enemy to sneer, 'Look here! This bow was used by the Genji general, Kurō Yoshitsune.'"

His men were deeply impressed. [HM, II, 321–22]

4. The Koshigoe Letter. (Sources: *Heike monogatari, Gempei seisuiki, Gikeiki, [kōwakamai] Koshigoe*.)

The story of the appeal sent by Yoshitsune to Yoritomo from Koshigoe post station, one of the best-documented episodes in the legend, is reported with essential accuracy by the author of *Yoshitsune* (see Chapter Four), who probably drew upon the accounts in *Heike monogatari* and *Azuma kagami*. In the *kōwakamai Koshigoe*, Yoshitsune orders Benkei to write the letter, a modification reflecting the increasing prominence of the role assigned to Benkei in the Muromachi period.

5. The Attack on the Horikawa Mansion. (Sources: *Heike mono-*

*gatari, Gempei seisuiki, Yoshitsune, [kōwakamai] Horikawa yo-uchi,
[Nō] Shōzon.)*

The dramatic night assault of Yoritomo's would-be assassin,
Tosabō, is very succinctly disposed of in *Azuma kagami* and *Gyokuyō;*
virtually the whole of the *Azuma kagami* account (the fuller of the two)
is included in the brief mention earlier in this Introduction.

In *Gempei seisuiki*, Yoshitsune's concubine, the dancer Shizuka,
makes her appearance, efficiently dispatching spies to observe
Tosabō's movements, as in *Yoshitsune* (see Chapter Four). When
Tosabō appears with sixty warriors, there are only seven men in the
mansion, but Yoshitsune calmly arms, mounts, and launches a
furious attack, shouting encouragement to his comrades, and scat-
tering the foe "like leaves in a gale." As Tosabō and his men flee
toward the Kamo River, Yukiie gallops up to complete the rout.
[GSSK, II, 707-8]

The *Heike monogatari* version, though close to *Gempei seisuiki* in most
respects, introduces Benkei's name and omits all mention of Yukiie.
In *Yoshitsune*, in the *kōwakamai Horikawa yo-uchi*, and in the Nō *Shōzon*,
Yukiie is similarly ignored.[39]

As the legend develops, increasing prominence is given to Shizuka
(who in *Horikawa yo-uchi* joins the battle, wielding a halberd), to
Benkei, and to lesser figures who enter the scene, while Yoshitsune
himself becomes little more than a spectator. In *Gempei seisuiki*, Yoshitsune is still the indomitable general, fighting fearlessly against great
odds; in *Yoshitsune*, he is effeminate and hesitant.

To history-conscious Muromachi minds, Yoshitsune's dizzying
plunge from victory and fame to disgrace and ruin must surely have
evoked vivid memories of the fall of the Taira. Though everything
that was known of Yoshitsune's life and personality bespoke the
tough professional man of arms, and though the early legends just
discussed had for the most part already been accepted without substantial modification, the new legends which took shape in the fourteenth, fifteenth, and sixteenth centuries were profoundly influenced
by what we may call the Heike fallen-warrior tradition fostered by
Heike monogatari: the concept of a once-mighty warrior hounded by

[39] Shimazu (p. 373) points out that Yukiie is also eliminated in the Funa Benkei legend
(see below), and suggests that there may have been unwillingness to associate Yoshitsune
with this rather shoddy symbol of defeat.

fate, divested of his military attributes, and transformed into an elegant, ineffectual courtier.

B. Muromachi Legends

The Muromachi legends, the second of the two categories postulated above,[40] themselves fall into two subdivisions, those dealing with Yoshitsune's childhood and those dealing with the period following the final break with Yoritomo. The first, or Ushiwaka group, on the whole present a composite figure, part warrior and part court noble. Ushiwaka is uniformly brave and resolute, and a remarkable swordsman despite his youth and frail appearance; he is also a model young aristocrat, rivaling the beauties of Chinese antiquity in face and figure, who astonishes his teachers with his aptitude for learning, plays the flute with marvelous skill, and effortlessly captures the hearts of susceptible maidens. In the second group, the warlike qualities have virtually disappeared and only the courtier remains. It is as though the authors and transmitters of these tales, relieved of the necessity of preparing the audience for later martial exploits, gratefully stripped their hero of attributes uncongenial to their interpretation of Yoshitsune's character. Chronologically, the two groups are separated by the manly warrior of the older Kamakura legends, an incongruity which must forcibly impress the reader of any work which, like *Yoshitsune,* attempts to bring together all the threads of the legend.

Another general difference between the two Muromachi subdivisions is the strong admixture of fantasy in the Ushiwaka group. Although *Yoshitsune* is by far the largest single early repository of Yoshitsune legends, its author, who usually rejects the supernatural, has included only about half the major Ushiwaka stories. For most of the extravagant flights of imagination, one must turn to a group of some half-dozen *otogi zōshi;* these stories seem on the whole to be somewhat later than *Yoshitsune* in origin, and many of them appear to be little more than variations on or elaborations of the subject matter of *Yoshitsune.* The Ushiwaka legends are also well represented in Nō plays and *kōwakamai,* and two of the best known appear in *Heiji monogatari.*

---

[40] In spite of the tremendous numbers of Yoshitsune pieces produced during the Edo period, little of importance was added to the legend after 1600.

1. Ushiwaka Legends

Taken in approximately the order in which they are presumed to have occurred, the Ushiwaka group can be summarized as follows.

a Tokiwa's Journey to Fushimi. (Sources: *Heiji monogatari, [kōwa-kamai] Fushimi Tokiwa*.)—One of the characteristic features of the Yoshitsune legend is that it includes stories about Yoshitsune's mother, Tokiwa, his retainers, his favorite concubine, Shizuka, and others close to him, stories in which he himself often figures only incidentally, if at all. The legend known as Fushimi Tokiwa, a case in point, was originally little more than a sentimental account of Tokiwa's flight through the snow toward Fushimi, with Ushiwaka clasped to her breast and her two elder sons clinging to her skirts. Tokugawa writers added numerous touches, of which the most important was Munekiyo, a Taira warrior who took pity on her and helped her in her distress.

This episode is unaccountably omitted in *Yoshitsune*, in spite of the author's general reliance upon *Heiji monogatari* as a source for Yoshitsune's boyhood.

b Ushiwaka and the Kurama *Tengu*. (Sources: *Heiji monogatari, Taiheiki*, [Nō] *Kurama tengu, [kōwakamai] Miraiki*.)—There are brief mentions of the Kurama *tengu*[41] legend in two war tales, *Heiji monogatari* (possibly interpolated) and *Taiheiki*, but the chief Muromachi sources are the Nō *Kurama tengu* and the *kōwakamai Miraiki*. Although this legend, too, is omitted from *Yoshitsune*, the author was very likely aware of its existence, since *Taiheiki* is believed to antedate *Yoshitsune*.

In the *Miraiki* version, Ushiwaka steals by night into the mountains

---

[41] The *tengu* (sometimes translated goblin) is conceived of in modern Japan as a supernatural being resembling a *yamabushi*, or wandering monk, with a long nose and a red face, who lives in remote mountain areas, possesses the ability to fly, and is capable of influencing the fortunes of men. The present view represents well over a millenium of evolution, in which Indian and Chinese notions have blended with indigenous religious beliefs and customs. In early times the tendency was to regard all *tengu* as enemies of Buddhism and practitioners of the dark arts—malevolent spirits who delighted in persecuting and abducting human beings, and who appeared to men in the guise of peasants, monks, ascetics, and the like. In later literature, they invariably appear as *yamabushi*. Sōjōbō, the Great Tengu of Sōjō-ga-tani, represents a relatively new category, who use their supernatural powers to assist virtue and punish evil. For a study of the subject, see M. W. de Visser, "The Tengu," *Transactions of the Asiatic Society of Japan*, 36.2 (1908), 25–99.

behind Kurama Temple to practice swordsmanship. He is aided by
the Great Tengu of the area and his followers, who teach him their
secret arts and are so struck by his resolute spirit that they promise
him their protection in the future. They prophesy that he will destroy
the Heike, but they warn him against Yoritomo's wrath and Kajiwara's slanders.

In *Kurama tengu,* the Great Tengu of Sōjō-ga-tani, disguised as a
wandering monk of menacing appearance, encounters and frightens
away a party of flower viewers—a Kurama monk and a group of
temple pages which includes Ushiwaka and some boys of the Taira
family. Ushiwaka, or Shanaō, as he is called in the play, remains
behind alone. The *tengu* announces his true identity and offers to
teach him the principles of warfare. On the following day, the *tengu*
and several of his followers meet Shanaō at a prearranged spot; there
they acquaint him with their secrets and agree to protect him.

The secret "military principles" *(heihō)* transmitted by the *tengu*
were at first interpreted to mean swordsmanship, and the legend
itself can be taken as an attempt to explain Ushiwaka's supernatural
ability and skill with his blade, attributes which figure prominently
in most of the anecdotes of the Ushiwaka group. (Needless to say, the
existence of the *tengu* legend must in turn have fostered the birth of
such stories.) Later, there was a tendency to interpret *heihō* more
broadly, as including strategy and tactics in addition to proficiency
in the use of weapons. The idea of secret instruction in a jealously
guarded art or skill is typically Muromachi.

This legend not only furnished material for many Tokugawa
writers[42] but also inspired later schools of swordsmanship to claim
that their founders had been taught by *tengu.*

c Ushiwaka's Visit to Supernatural Regions. (Source: [*otogi zōshi*]
Tengu no dairi.)—In this story, Ushiwaka learns of the existence of a
tengu palace deep in the mountains, and by offering prayers to
Bishamon succeeds in visiting it. The Great Tengu welcomes him
hospitably and offers to take him to see Yoshitomo, who has been
reborn in the Pure Land as a buddha. Following a tour of the 136
Buddhist hells, the two finally reached the Pure Land. Yoshitomo
urges Ushiwaka to destroy the Heike and then predicts his future.

42 For details, see Shimazu, p. 211 ff.

Back in the *tengu* palace, Ushiwaka and the Great Tengu exchange pupil-teacher vows and Ushiwaka returns to Kurama.

The strong religious element in *Tengu no dairi* is characteristic of Muromachi literature in general. The author begins, typically, with the statement that Ushiwaka himself is a reincarnation of Bishamon; he then, with obvious gusto, describes the various hells; and he closes by recommending cultivation of the Confucian virtues as a means of attaining Buddhist enlightenment. Since Yoshitomo's prophecy is extremely detailed, containing virtually all the elements in the Yoshitsune legend, the story probably dates from the late Muromachi or Azuchi-Momoyama period. (It lacks the legend of Yoshitsune's escape from Takadachi, one of the few Edo additions to the corpus.)

Buddhist stories of adventures in the nether regions originally came into Japan from India via China. They have a long history in the national literature, dating back at least to the Nara period. The birth of this legend was predictable, especially in view of the existence of the similar "island journey" legend (see below).

d Benkei at the Bridge. (Sources: *Yoshitsune, [otogi zōshi] Benkei monogatari, [otogi zōshi] Hashi Benkei,* [Nō] *Hashi Benkei.*)—This is not only one of the best known of the Yoshitsune legends but one of the most significant as well, since it describes the first meeting between Yoshitsune and his celebrated retainer, Saitō Musashibō Benkei.

In the historical record, Benkei is far less important than Ise Saburō and the Satō brothers: indeed, he is little more than a name which appears at infrequent intervals in unimportant contexts. In the legend, however, this monk-warrior dominates the stage almost completely after the flight from Kyoto transforms Yoshitsune into a hesitant and melancholy aristocrat. He is a great bull of a man with bloodshot eyes and a booming voice, a swarthy, menacing figure in his black armor, capable of prodigious feats of strength, fearless in battle, indomitable in his self-imposed role as Yoshitsune's protector. His wit and good humor are irrepressible, his wisdom, resourcefulness, and patience are inexhaustible, and he is as learned and talented as Yoshitsune himself.

The Benkei legend at its height appears in the Nō *Ataka* (see below) and its kabuki adaptation, *Kanjinchō*, the two most famous of all the Yoshitsune pieces, which deal with an episode during Yoshitsune's flight to Ōshū in 1187. Though we shall probably never know exactly how the image of Benkei took shape, or how the Benkei legend became attached to Yoshitsune's biography, it is entirely possible that one or more Hiei monks did in fact accompany Yoshitsune on his journey north (see Appendix A), and it is tempting to speculate that we have here the germ of the Benkei legend as we now know it.

At any rate, the *Ataka* stage of the Benkei legend appears to have preceded the legends dealing with Benkei's early life and his first meeting with Yoshitsune. He emerged full-blown, and it was therefore necessary to fill in the missing portions of his career, and particularly to account for his association with Yoshitsune. Of extant literary works in which this attempt is made, *Yoshitsune* is probably the oldest. Similar accounts of Benkei's miraculous birth and turbulent youth appear in two short stories *(otogi zōshi)*, *Hashi Benkei* and *Benkei monogatari (Benkei no zōshi, Musashibō Benkei monogatari)*.

In its most familiar version, the legend which explains Benkei's association with Yoshitsune runs as follows: Benkei, a lawless warrior-monk who has vowed to rob 1,000 men of their swords, accosts passers-by nightly in the vicinity of Gojō Bridge in Kyoto. As he awaits his one thousandth victim, Ushiwaka approaches, a slight, elegant youth, playing a flute, who wears a woman's cloak over his head and shoulders in the usual manner of temple pages. A duel follows; Benkei is defeated and acknowledges himself Ushiwaka's man.

This precise form does not occur in any of the major Muromachi literary sources, nor do any two agree completely, as the summary below will show.

(1) *Yoshitsune.*—In the *Yoshitsune* version, which is probably the oldest extant, all the main elements are present: Benkei's determination to steal a thousand swords, the flute, the David-and-Goliath fight, and the forging of the lord-retainer bond. Two meetings are described, however, and neither one is at Gojō Bridge.

(2) *Benkei monogatari.*—In this short story, Benkei hits upon the notion of relieving 100 Taira warriors of their swords in order to make a contribution to the court's project of rebuilding the temple on Mount Shosha (see the translation, Chapter Three). He particularly wishes to obtain Ushiwaka's famous gold-mounted blade as his hundredth prize. Benkei and Ushiwaka encounter each other three

times, the third time at Kiyomizu Temple (as in *Yoshitsune*), before the
final test of skill at the bridge.

The author of *Benkei monogatari* has obviously consulted *Yoshitsune*.
The main differences between the two are in the number of swords
involved and the introduction of the bridge.

(3) *Hashi Benkei (otogi zōshi)*.—In *Hashi Benkei*, Ushiwaka, at the
age of fourteen *sai*, resolves to kill 1,000 Taira warriors as a pious act
in memory of his father. He goes from Kurama to Gojō Bridge, where
in the space of three days and nights he dispatches 700 victims. Word
quickly gets around in the city that a murderous ghost is lying in wait
for the unwary at the bridge, and soon the only passers-by are country
people ignorant of his presence. Nevertheless, Ushiwaka manages to
kill 999 people by the end of the seventh day and night. Benkei, who
has been living at Sagano following his departure from Mount Hiei,
hears of Ushiwaka's activities and goes to Gojō. He runs away when
he sees a huge mound of corpses and a river running red with blood,
but presently he collects himself and returns to do battle. After a
furious duel in which he loses his sword, he promises to serve Ushiwaka, escorts the boy back to Kurama, and himself returns to Sagano.

(4) *Hashi Benkei* (Nō).—In this celebrated Nō, Ushiwaka has left
Kurama and is killing passers-by at Gojō Bridge. Benkei determines
to confront him.

BENKEI   The night grows late. Eastward the bells of
              the Three Pagodas toll.
          By the moonlight that gleams through leaves
              of these thick cedar-trees
          I gird my armour on;
          I fasten the black thongs of my coat of mail.
          I adjust its armoured skirts.
          By the middle I grasp firmly
          My great halberd that I have loved so long.
          I lay it across my shoulder; with leisurely step
              stride forward.
          Be he demon or hobgoblin, how shall he stand against me?
          Such trust have I in my own prowess. Oh, how I long
          For a foeman worthy of my hand!

As Benkei approaches the bridge, he catches sight of Ushiwaka,

dressed in a woman's cloak. He is about to pass on when Ushiwaka
challenges him.

> And so they fought, now closing, now breaking.
> What shall Benkei do? For when he thinks that he
>   has conquered,
> With his little sword the boy thrusts the blow
>   aside.
> Again and again Benkei strikes.
> Again and again his blows are parried,
> Till at last even he, mighty Benkei,
> Can do battle no longer.[43]

In a later version of the legend, it is Benkei who vows to kill a
thousand men, no doubt because such indiscriminate slaughter, while
conceivable on the part of an outlaw monk, finally proved incompatible with Yoshitsune's highly idealized character. The somewhat
bizarre notion of offering a thousand murders for the repose of a
loved one's soul is not original with *Hashi Benkei* but occurs in other
Muromachi works as well, some of which link it to an Indian Buddhist legend.[44] Indeed, none of the major elements in the story is new.
The idea of doing something ninety-nine or nine hundred ninety-nine
times without incident, only to come to grief on the one hundredth or
one thousandth attempt, was a well-worn theme, as were the David-
and-Goliath encounter and the sword-stealing monk. One is reminded of the *Yoshitsune* episode in which Yoshitsune kills the Nara monks,
an anecdote very similar in general outline to the Hashi Benkei
legend—sword-stealing monks, flute-playing youth, David-and-
Goliath battle. The flute is an important recurring motif in the Yoshitsune legend as a whole, not so much because of any particular
historical association as because the "Heike" idea of Yoshitsune as an
accomplished courtier-musician appealed strongly to Muromachi
tastes.[45]

[43] Translations from Arthur Waley, *The Nō Plays of Japan* (London: Allen and Unwin,
1956), pp. 117–18, 119.

[44] For details, see Shimazu, p. 306 ff.

[45] In the Nō *Fue no maki*, which is essentially a variant of *Hashi Benkei*, the flute detail is
strongly underlined. Tokiwa learns that Ushiwaka is leaving Kurama at night in order to
cut down passers-by at Gojō Bridge. After reprimanding him, she tells him the history of a
rare flute, brought to Japan by a famous monk, which she has given him. Later, Ushiwaka

Most of the works mentioned place the Hashi Benkei episode during the Kurama period, without explaining Benkei's subsequent long disappearance; the author of *Yoshitsune*, who was attempting to fit all the parts of the legend together, was obliged to come to grips with the problem. He was faced with a similar difficulty in the case of the Oni-ichi episode (see below), which seems to be of common origin either with the Kurama *tengu* legend (Kurama period) or with the island-visiting legend (first Ōshū period), and is correspondingly vague as to date. Having decided to assign the Oni-ichi episode to the Ōshū period, the author had to risk straining the reader's credulity by bringing Yoshitsune back to the capital; but this chronology at any rate gave him the opportunity to introduce Benkei in a fairly plausible manner. We are apparently intended to believe that Benkei accompanied Yoshitsune when he returned to Ōshū and remained with him constantly thereafter.[46]

e Yoshitsune Vanquishes the Brigands. (Sources: *Yoshitsune, Soga monogatari, [kōwakamai] Eboshi-ori,* [Nō] *Kumasaka,* [Nō] *Eboshi-ori.*)— This is the first of two major legends dealing with Ushiwaka's journey to Ōshū. It appears in its fullest form in the dance *Eboshi-ori,* which may be summarized as follows.

As Ushiwaka is traveling east in company with the gold merchant Kichiji, he stops for the night at Kagami post station in Ōmi and there decides to conduct his own coming-of-age ceremony *(gembuku).* He orders a man's cap from a near-by shop and pays for it with a sword. The hat seller's wife, who is a sister of one of Yoshitomo's old retainers, recognizes the sword as a Minamoto heirloom and returns it. That night Ushiwaka assumes the name Kurō Yoshitsune.

The journey continues, with Kichiji calling Yoshitsune by a servant's name and forcing him to act as his sword-bearer. When the party arrive at Aohaka post station[47] in Mino, they are entertained at the mistress's establishment (see Chapter One, note 10). Kichiji continues to treat Yoshitsune as a menial. He orders him to serve

---

encounters Benkei at the bridge as he waits there for the last time. There is an almost identical dance *(kōwakamai)* of the same name.

[46] *Benkei monogatari*, which is based upon *Yoshitsune*, specifically states that the two returned to Ōshū together.

[47] Where Yoshitomo killed his wounded son, Tomonaga, at the latter's request.

wine and reprimands him severely when he spills it. Yoshitsune attracts the mistress's attention by his remarkable skill as a flautist. She comments on his resemblance to Yoshitomo's two eldest sons, and tells him that she has borne Yoshitomo a daughter. That night the spirits of Yoshitomo and the two dead sons warn Yoshitsune that a large band of cutthroats, led by the notorious Kumasaka Chōhan, are preparing to steal Kichiji's goods. When the robbers appear, Yoshitsune kills a number of them and chases the rest away. His encounter with their chief, Chōhan, comes when he is already exhausted, but he kills him by using the secrets taught him by the Kurama *tengu*.

The Nō *Eboshi-ori* is similar in content, but the locale is Akasaka in Mino rather than Aohaka. The Nō *Kumasaka*, in which Chōhan's spirit tells a traveling monk how he has been killed by Yoshitsune, is essentially a reworking of the last part of *Eboshi-ori*.[48]

In *Soga monogatari*, where the incident figures as one of the digressions characteristic of that work, the scene is Tarui post station in Mino.

In *Yoshitsune* there is no suggestion of Ushiwaka's being treated as a menial. The recognition by the mistress and the encounter with the brigands both occur at Kagami, and the coming-of-age ceremony, in which the episode of the hat seller[49] is omitted, comes later, at Atsuta in Owari. The main point of difference between *Yoshitsune* and the other accounts is that Kumasaka Chōhan is replaced by two robber chieftains, Yuri Tarō and the Fujisawa Novice (who wears armor and weapons corresponding exactly to those ascribed to Chōhan in the Nō and dance). The reason for the dichotomy is obscure.

Of particular interest are (1) Yoshitsune's relationship to the merchant Kichiji, (2) the sociological implications of the incident, (3) the typical idealized treatment of Yoshitsune's valor and military prowess, and (4) the recurrence of the flute motif.

Heiji monogatari, Heike monogatari, and *Gempei seisuiki* all agree that a gold merchant took Yoshitsune to Ōshū; the first two identify the man by name as Kichiji. This tradition, whether based on fact or not,

---

[48] *Eboshi-ori* and *Kumasaka* are translated by Arthur Waley in *The Nō Plays of Japan*, pp. 92–114.

[49] Shimazu traces this story in the Nō and dance to an anecdote in *Gempei seisuiki*, in which a sympathetic hat seller presents Yoritomo with a cap, identical in design to the one in question here, after an early setback in his campaign against the Taira. Shimazu, p. 275.

was clearly well established by the Kamakura period. In describing Kichiji's ungenerous treatment of Yoshitsune, the dance *Eboshi-ori* was also drawing on an existing legend. *Gempei seisuiki* (II, 575) quotes a Taira warrior at the battle of Yashima as sneering, "When the capital got too hot for Yoshitsune, he went off to Ōshū as a gold merchant's lackey, with a straw raincoat and hat on his back"; Yoshitsune himself may have been referring to something of the sort when he wrote in the Koshigoe letter of "serving commoners." The author of *Yoshitsune* seems to have rejected this particular legend, no doubt because he wished to avoid showing his hero in such ignoble circumstances.

Since Heian times Japan had been overrun with robber bands, usually led by impoverished or embittered warriors. Diaries and other contemporary records refer again and again to their depredations in the capital, where the mansions of the wealthy were looted (sometimes, it was suspected, with the connivance of delinquent members of the nobility), and where even the imperial palace itself was not safe. One of the principal functions of Yoshitsune's tenth-century forebears had been to protect the property of the great Fujiwara regents from this sort of outrage. An anonymous social critic of the fourteenth century might have been referring to any period from Heian to Muromachi when he noted: "Today's fashions in the capital—night attacks, armed robbery, and forged edicts."[50] Conditions in the provinces were undoubtedly worse. The most notorious robber chieftains achieved national reputations, and stories of highwaymen and thieves became so numerous that—to cite a single example—the well-known prose anthology *Konjaku monogatari* ("Tales Ancient and Modern"; late Heian period) devoted an entire section to them.

It is not surprising that this social phenomenon should have found a place in the Yoshitsune legend. The encounter with Kumasaka's band is merely the most conspicuous of a number of similar incidents: the sword stealing by Benkei and the Nara monks, Yoshitsune's first meeting with Ise Saburō, and the introduction of the outlaw Tankai (or Tōkai) in the Oni-ichi story. Such bullies and desperadoes were natural adversaries for the brave, supernaturally endowed young

[50] From the *Nijō River-Beach Lampoon*, a satirical poem posted in the dry bed of the Kamo River in 1335. Shimazu, p. 281.

Minamoto hero, and all his successive encounters with them follow
the same basic David-and-Goliath pattern.

Apropos of the flute, it may be noted that in the dance *Eboshi-ori*,
not only does this instrument in Yoshitsune's expert hands lead to his
recognition by the station mistress, but the entire history of a famous
flute is included for the enjoyment of music-loving readers (cf. *Fue no
maki.*)

There are minor variations in the legend in addition to the ones
previously noted. For example, the size of the robber band varies, and
Kichiji is sometimes accompanied by one or more brothers. The differences in locale are not striking, since all the places involved are
relatively close together. In later versions, Kumasaka is almost invariably the chieftain; Fujisawa and Yuri tend to disappear. Numerous subsidiary legends grew up around Kumasaka, who gradually
became one of the two or three most famous robbers in Japanese
history, but we need concern ourselves only with the one called
Tokiwa at Yamanaka.

(1) Tokiwa at Yamanaka. (Sources: *[kōwakamai] Yamanaka
Tokiwa, [otogi zōshi] Yamanaka Tokiwa zōshi, [otogi zōshi] Tengu no
dairi.*)—This legend relates how Tokiwa, having learned of Yoshitsune's departure from the capital, sets out in search of him and is
attacked and killed by Chōhan's band at Yamanaka post station in
Mino. Yoshitsune unknowingly avenges her murder when, later on,
the brigands attempt to rob Kichiji.

There is, of course, no historical basis for the legend. According to
Azuma kagami, Tokiwa was living peacefully in the capital when
Yoshitsune and Yukiie left in 1185.

(2) Sekihara Yoichi. (Sources: *[kōwakamai] Kurama-ide*, [Nō]
Sekihara Yoichi.)—Although it belongs earlier, we may here briefly
note a less influential legend which, like the meeting with Kumasaka,
shows the gallant young Ushiwaka en route to Ōshū, calling upon
techniques learned from the Kurama *tengu* in order to overcome a
numerically superior foe. It does not appear to have been in existence
at the time *Yoshitsune* was set down. The sources are a dance, *Kurama-
ide* (or *Azuma kudari*), and a Nō, *Sekihara Yoichi*.

The first part of *Kurama-ide* parallels the description in *Yoshitsune*
of Ushiwaka's initial meeting with Kichiji and the latter's stories
about Ōshū. As in *Yoshitsune*, the merchant and Ushiwaka agree on a

rendezvous at Awataguchi, but Kichiji fails to appear. Ushiwaka sets out alone on the road to Yamashina. At Matsusaka he encounters Sekihara Yoichi, a Heike warrior from Mino who is on his way to the capital with nine men. Yoichi's horse splashes muddy water on Ushiwaka's clothing, and when Ushiwaka protests the men answer him contemptuously. Yoichi taunts Ushiwaka with being an unworthy adversary and tries to cut him down, but Ushiwaka slashes the neck of Yoichi's horse and topples him into the mud puddle. Ushiwaka then enjoys a hearty laugh, which so mortifies Yoichi that he forsakes his horse and men and goes into retirement near Yamashina Temple.

The Nō *Sekihara Yoichi*, which appears to be somewhat later, corresponds to the second half of *Kurama-ide*. In this version Yoichi's seventy followers are all either killed or chased off. Yoichi himself then enters the battle, but he too is speedily disposed of by Ushiwaka, who rides off toward Ōshū on Yoichi's horse.

f Lady Jōruri. (Source: *[otogi zōshi/jōruri] Jūnidan zōshi*.)—The highly imaginative story of Lady Jōruri, probably the best known of the legends concerning Ushiwaka's journey to Ōshū, seems to have been set down from oral tradition around the middle of the Muromachi period or even somewhat later. It is recorded in a short story *(otogi zōshi)* usually referred to as *Jūnidan zōshi* (also *Jōruri jūnidan zōshi*, *Jōruri-hime monogatari*, *Jōruri gozen jūnidan zōshi*, *Jōruri monogatari*), the name, it is thought, being derived from the twelve sections into which it is customarily divided.[51] The gist of the tale is as follows.

Section 1. Yoshitsune, a youth of fifteen *sai*, is on his way to Ōshū with Kichiji. They stop for the night with the mistress of Yahagi post station in Mikawa. The mistress, it is explained, was once the most famous courtesan on the Tōkaidō and was for many years the consort of the late Minamoto Kanetaka, a court noble posted to Mikawa as a provincial official. Grieved by their childlessness, the couple prayed to Yakushi Buddha, who appeared to them as an aged monk and told them that their difficulty was due to the karma of a previous existence, in which the mistress was a snake and her husband a hawk. Yakushi Buddha responded compassionately to their entreaties, and the mistress gave birth to a jewel-like daughter, whom they named

[51] There are variant texts with eight, fifteen, and sixteen sections.

Jōruri.[52] Jōruri is now a lovely and cultivated maiden of fourteen *sai*.

Section 2. Yoshitsune chances upon the elegant building in which Jōruri lives and is dumbstruck by the profusion of flowering plants in her garden.

Section 3. Peeping through the hedge, Yoshitsune catches a glimpse of the exquisitely attired maiden as she sits composing verses and playing music in company with two hundred forty beautiful attendants.

Section 4. As Jōruri and twelve of her ladies play an air, Yoshitsune begins to accompany them with his flute. When Jōruri is told that he is traveling with Kichiji, she suspects at once that he is a Genji in disguise.

Section 5. A lady-in-waiting, sent to inspect Yoshitsune more closely, reports that he must certainly be a Minamoto. She describes his handsome costume in detail.

Section 6. Jōruri sends a second lady to test Yoshitsune by reciting a verse. He caps it instantly.

Section 7. Late that night, one of the ladies-in-waiting guides Yoshitsune to Jōruri's private chamber. He extinguishes twelve of the thirty lights and declares his love.

Section 8. Jōruri resists Yoshitsune's advances, explaining that she must remain pure in body because she is in the midst of reciting a thousand sutras on behalf of her father, who has died in the preceding year. Yoshitsune counters with Buddhist arguments.

Section 9. Jōruri's scruples are overcome.

Section 10. The next morning, the suspicious mistress appears at Jōruri's residence. Yoshitsune makes himself invisible by means of magic arts learned from the Kurama *tengu*. He leaps across a series of moats and sets out again along the Tōkaidō, bearing Kichiji's sword. After passing a succession of famous spots, he arrives at Fukiage in Suruga.

Section 11. At Fukiage, Yoshitsune falls critically ill of a mysterious disease. Kichiji abandons him among the pines on the beach. One of the local people attempts to steal Yoshitsune's sword, which is instantly transformed into a snake one hundred twenty feet long.

---

[52] A *ruri* is a precious stone, green in color and indestructible; *jō* means pure. In Buddhist usage, *jōruri* is a metaphor for purity. It is also an abbreviation for *jōruri sekai* (Pure World), Yakushi's paradise.

Meanwhile the god Hachiman in monk's guise informs Jōruri that her lover is dying. Because she has incurred her mother's wrath by her liaison with a seeming servant, Jōruri has been banished to a tiny hut with a single maid. The two make their way on foot to Fukiage, where, with Hachiman's help, Jōruri raises the lifeless form of Yoshitsune from the sand. While she prays, sixteen wandering monks appear and restore Yoshitsune to life with their incantations.

Section 12. Aided by Yakushi Buddha, who assumes the form of an ancient nun, Jōruri spends the next twenty days nursing Yoshitsune back to health. After his recovery, he reveals his identity to her for the first time. The two lovers recite poems of farewell and exchange a copy of a Buddhist scripture and a gold hair ornament as keepsakes. Then Yoshitsune summons a number of his *tengu* friends to transport Jōruri and the maid back to Yahagi, while he continues on his way to Hiraizumi.

Although the origins of the tale are unclear, there are indications of kinship with other Yoshitsune pieces. In the dance *Eboshi-ori,* Yoshitsune's flute playing brings him to the attention of the Aohaka mistress, just as it does to Jōruri's; Kichiji's attitude is similar to his attitude here; and the description of Yoshitsune's dress at the time of the battle with Kumasaka resembles the lady-in-waiting's report in Section 5. In the island-visiting tale (see below), there is a similar love story, even greater emphasis on the role of the flute, and a similar use of religious elements.[53]

As the *Jūnidan zōshi* legend developed, there was a tendency to consign the unfortunate Lady Jōruri to a tragic fate, doubtless under the influence of the island-visiting and Oni-ichi tales. Her end is unclear in *Jūnidan zōshi,* but Chikamatsu and other Edo writers show her either dying of a broken heart or casting herself into a river. In a more cheerful variant, she appears to Yoshitsune as her true self, Yakushi Buddha, when he visits her grave.

In its alternative form as a ballad recited by blind minstrels, *Jūnidan zōshi* enjoyed a tremendous vogue during the late Muromachi period. The attraction of Yoshitsune's name, along with the liberal

[53] In *Jūnidan zōshi,* Jōruri is said to be a child born as a result of divine intervention, and there is a strong suggestion that Yoshitsune may be an incarnation of Kannon or some other bodhisattva. In the island-visiting myth, Yoshitsune and the lady are specifically identified as manifestations of Bishamon and Montoku (Yoshitsune) and Enoshima Benzaiten (the lady).

use of florid descriptive passages,[54] was reinforced by other elements calculated to please Muromachi audiences, notably the frequent mention of music, literature, and religion. To make the ballad even more appealing, the entertainers employed a novel method of chanting which was gradually being adopted by certain reciters of war tales, Nō choruses, and the like.[55] So phenomenal was *Jūnidan zōshi*'s success that *jōruri* achieved currency as a generic term for ballads recited in the new manner; and when puppets and the shamisen were added in late Muromachi, the result was a new dramatic form, the *jōruri*, which Chikamatsu Monzaemon (1653–1724) raised to the level of serious literature.

  g Yoshitsune's Voyage Among the Islands. (Source: *[otogi zōshi] Onzōshi shima-watari*.)—This is one of two closely related legends vaguely ascribed to the period of Yoshitsune's first sojourn in Ōshū, and it is by far the most mythical component of the tradition. It is not included in *Yoshitsune*, though it was probably known to the author. It consists of two parts; (1) a fantastic odyssey, in which, as Shimazu remarks, the hero might as well be Momotarō[56] as Yoshitsune, and (2) a quest for a secret military treatise, with a subsidiary love story. The *locus classicus* is a short story, *Onzōshi shima-watari*.

  On Hidehira's advice, Yoshitsune decides to go to Ezo (which is equated with Chishima in the text) in order to learn the contents of the "Law of Dainichi Buddha", a secret military treatise in the possession of a demon king named Kanehira. Setting sail from Tosa in Shikoku, he passes a series of islands—Cat Island, Dog Island, Pine Island, Bamboo Island, Helmet Island, Bow Island, and so on—and on the seventy-fifth day reaches a place where the inhabitants are one hundred feet tall and have equine heads and trunks and human legs. These giants carry drums, which they beat to attract help when they fall down. Yoshitsune next visits an island of naked people, for whom he provides clothing by magically summoning a fleet of cargo boats.

---

  [54] For example, in Section 2 (Jōruri's garden), Section 3 (the 240 fair attendants; Jōruri's bewitching appearance), and Section 10 (Yoshitsune's journey *[michiyuki]* past famous places on the Tōkaidō).
  [55] There is insufficient evidence to substantiate the view, sometimes expressed, that the new style originated with *Jūnidan zōshi*.
  [56] The child-hero of a favorite nursery tale, who journeys to an island of devils in order to put an end to their wicked deeds.

Then he stops at an island of women, who propose to kill him in order to make his spirit their guardian god. He dissuades them by playing his famous flute, Taitōmaru, and departs in an atmosphere of cordiality, promising to find husbands for them. After another month, he chances upon an island of tiny men two inches high, who enjoy a life expectancy of eight hundred years and are visited six times a day by a heavenly host from Amida's paradise. He lingers to observe one of the visitations and then resumes his travels. Three months later he puts in to a hostile shore where barbarians prepare to shoot him down. The flute again comes to his rescue, and presently he finds himself in Kikenjō, the capital of Ezo. The huge iron gates of the king's palace are guarded by horse- and ox-headed demons one hundred feet tall. At first the guards threaten to devour him, but after listening to his captivating performance on the flute they decide to escort him to the king.

The demon king Kanehira is one hundred sixty feet tall, with eight hands and feet, thirty horns, a voice audible for two hundred fifty miles, and eyes as dazzling as the morning sun. After he has been put in a friendly humor by the flute, he asks Yoshitsune the purpose of his visit, and affably quizzes the youth when he begs to be accepted as a disciple. Since Yoshitsune not only has mastered the arts of the Kurama *tengu* but is also a manifestation of Bishamon and Montoku, he passes the examination easily. The king teaches him a number of secrets, but retires without a word about the crucial "Law of Dainichi Buddha."

Later there is a great banquet in the palace, at which Yoshitsune plays the flute for the king (who appears in the form of a Kyoto noble) and his beautiful young daughter, Asahi. Yoshitsune and Asahi fall in love.

At the first opportunity, Yoshitsune and Asahi exchange lovers' vows. Yoshitsune prevails upon Asahi to purloin the "Law of Dainichi Buddha." To their horror, however, the precious document becomes blank paper after Yoshitsune has copied it. Asahi urges him to flee and shows him how to evade pursuit. Meanwhile the sky has turned black as night, a sign to the king of what has happened. Kanehira chases Yoshitsune's boat with a thousand demons mounted on water-treading horses, but Yoshitsune uses Asahi's magical arts to block the way with mountains of salt. Then Yoshitsune conjures up a mighty wind which blows him to Tosa in seventy-five days.

After Yoshitsune has returned to Ōshū, Asahi appears beside his pillow to tell him that her father has torn her to bits. Yoshitsune sorrowfully commissions Buddhist rites on her behalf. She was a manifestation of Enoshima Benzaiten, born in order to give him the treatise.

Through the efficacy of the "Law of Dainichi Buddha," the Minamoto became the rulers of Japan.

There is no known prototype for the island-journey portion of this tale, although stories resembling some of the individual incidents are extant. The credulous and ignorant people of Muromachi times, who had no notion of Ezo except that it was an unimaginably remote and barbarous place, were probably not at all disturbed by Yoshitsune's peculiar decision to set sail from Tosa in Shikoku, rather than directly from northern Japan.[57] The stock ingredients of popular Muromachi literature are present in abundance in this wild adventure: Buddhist beliefs, evidence of the irresistible power of music, romance of a rather stilted and perfunctory nature, and jealously guarded professional secrets.

For our purposes, the most interesting aspect of the tale is its striking resemblance to the Oni-ichi episode (see below), in which Yoshitsune is again represented as gaining access to a secret military treatise through the good offices of its owner's daughter, who pays with her life for betraying her father. Internal evidence seems to suggest that the island-voyage tale is the older of the two, but in any case there can be no question of coincidence. There is nothing to indicate a factual basis for this secret-treatise motif; it no doubt merely represents a persistent desire to account for Yoshitsune's success as a military strategist, just as the Kurama *tengu* legend explains his remarkable swordsmanship.

(1) Oni-ichi Hōgen. (Sources: *Yoshitsune*, [Nō] *Tankai*, [otogi zōshi] *Oni-ichi hōgen*, [otogi zōshi] *Minazuru*.)—If the Oni-ichi story is later

[57] Some modern scholars have tried to explain this by saying that Tosa is a mistake for Tosa (written with different characters), a port in modern Aomori Prefecture, and that the mention of Shikoku is a later interpolation, but one is inclined to agree with Shimazu (p. 244) that the story merely reveals the vagueness of contemporary notions of geography.

than its counterpart, it perhaps reflects an attempt to remove the adventure from the realm of fantasy to a more credible setting. It is included by the author of *Yoshitsune*, who boggles at the island voyage.

The legend appears in its fullest form in a long short story, *Oni-ichi hōgen* (5 chapters; probably mid-Muromachi or later; also known as *Hōgan miyako banashi*), which takes the incident described in Chapter Two of *Yoshitsune* as a point of departure. In this story, Yoshitsune returns to the capital from Ōshū in order to be introduced to Oni-ichi, a teacher of military skills who boasts 6,000 disciples among the nobility and Buddhist clergy. Yoshitsune's sponsor, a Minamoto retainer named Kamada, persuades the avaricious Oni-ichi to interview the youth by describing his gold-mounted sword, but Oni-ichi is so intimidated by Yoshitsune's appearance that he turns him away.

By stubbornly remaining on the premises day after day, Yoshitsune makes friends with some of the ladies of the household. One night he hears music emanating from the chamber of Oni-ichi's unmarried daughter, who is the most beautiful girl in the capital. He takes up his flute, joins the concert with his usual proficiency, and secures an invitation to enter. He and the lady exchange vows.

Presently Oni-ichi goes off on a pilgrimage to Kumano. With the daughter's assistance, Yoshitsune gains access to the master's secret treatises and copies out important sections. Upon his return, Oni-ichi at once perceives that the volumes have been disturbed. He flies into a jealous rage and determines to do away with Yoshitsune. Feigning affability, he asks Yoshitsune to kill his son-in-law, a formidable outlaw known as Tōkai (Tankai, his brother-in-law, in *Yoshitsune*), with whom he pretends to be at odds. Then he summons Tōkai and orders him to waylay Yoshitsune and murder him. Yoshitsune fortunately learns of the plot through Oni-ichi's daughter; he kills Tōkai, takes his head to Oni-ichi, and departs, his aim accomplished. The daughter dies of grief, whereupon her distracted father burns his books and ascends to heaven. Yoshitsune uses the knowledge he has acquired to destroy the Heike.

2. The Final Period

The most notable characteristic of the legends of the final period, as contrasted with those of the Ushiwaka and public periods, is the passive role assigned to Yoshitsune. In *Funa Benkei*, Benkei is the pro-

tagonist; in the Yoshino episodes, Shizuka and Tadanobu play the
main parts; and throughout the journey to Ōshū, Benkei is again the
leader in fact, as well as in name. The transformation in Yoshitsune's
character is doubtless to be explained as a reflection of the Muromachi taste for a rather effeminate type of hero—the same taste
responsible for the adulation of handsome temple pages *(chigo)* and
the idealization of the fleeing Taira as elegant and bewildered aristocrats.[58] In any case, one important consequence was the opportunity
thus presented for the development of a Benkei legend within the
Yoshitsune legend. Although the Nō *Ataka* is the classic example of
Benkei in his role of loyal retainer and protector, his character is most
fully realized in *Yoshitsune,* where he emerges life size: a great, bold,
brawling monk, ingenious, irrepressible, and irreverent, who is nevertheless sensitive, patient, subtle, learned, and accomplished. Yoshitsune himself is so highly idealized that he is dull by comparison.
(Only in the public-career legends, omitted in *Yoshitsune,* is there any
suggestion of individuality.)

Most of the legends in this group are developed in detail in *Yoshitsune.*

a Benkei in the Boat. (Sources: *Yoshitsune,* [Nō] *Funa Benkei,*
[kōwakamai] Shikoku-ochi, [kōwakamai] Oisagashi.)—In this story, the
first major episode in the last period and one of the most famous in
the entire legend, Benkei has already emerged as the central figure.
Its essential elements are these: Yoshitsune sails for western Japan
from Daimotsu-no-ura in Settsu Province. The angry spirits of Taira
warriors slain at Dan-no-ura suddenly appear, riding on a dark cloud,
but are vanquished by Benkei's Buddhist prayers.

This pattern, which is still incomplete in *Yoshitsune,*[59] appears

[58] The importance which the Japanese have traditionally attached to civilized deport-
ment, scholarly and literary pursuits, and mastery of polite accomplishments can be attributed partly to the influence of Confucianism, which was imported from the Asiatic
continent at a very early date, and partly to the generally peaceful conditions which prevailed during the Nara and Heian periods. The great Taira-Minamoto conflict, together
with other military convulsions which ushered in the feudal structure of society and accompanied its development, fostered the acceptance of a more virile type of hero in Kamakura
times, and to a lesser extent through the remainder of the premodern period, but the appeal of old values persisted, enhanced by nostalgia for past glory in the case of the Kyoto
nobility, who were still the cultural arbiters.

[59] See Chapter Four. The spirits do not actually appear, and Benkei disperses the
menacing clouds not by praying but by shooting arrows.

in three Muromachi dance dramas: the *kōwakamai Shikoku-ochi*, the *kōwakamai Oisagashi* and the Nō *Funa Benkei*.

(1) *Shikoku-ochi*—Yoshitsune has set out from the capital to go to Kōno in Iyo. Benkei's prayers save him from Heike spirits at Daimotsu-no-ura. Benkei also beats off an attack by a local warrior, Ashiya Saburō Mitsushige. (A variant form of the battle appears in *Yoshitsune*, where Ashiya is replaced by three chieftains, Teshima Kanja, Komizo Tarō, and Kōzuke Hangan. The battle is also the subject of a Nō, *Ashiya Benkei*. According to *Azuma kagami*, the skirmishes between Yoshitsune's party and local partisans of Kamakura occurred earlier, between the capital and the port.)

(2) *Oisagashi*—*Oisagashi* is a sequel to the dance *Togashi* (see below). After Benkei reads the subscription list at Togashi's house, he rejoins Yoshitsune and the rest of the party. At Naoe in Echigo, their baggage is searched by suspicious warriors, but they are finally able to put out to sea, heading for Ōshū. Taira spirits threaten the vessel but are driven away by Benkei.

(3) *Funa Benkei*—In this favorite of the Nō repertoire, Shizuka joins Yoshitsune at Daimotsu-no-ura, but Benkei insists that she return to the capital. She does so after a farewell dance, and Yoshitsune sets out for Shikoku. A storm arises, carrying with it the angry spirits of the Taira commander, Tomomori, and his slain kinsmen.

> TOMOMORI   Behold me!
>   I am the ghost of Taira-no-Tomomori,
>   Scion of the Emperor Kammu,
>   In the ninth generation.
>   Hail, Yoshitsune!
>   I have come
>   Guided by your oarsmen's voices,
> CHORUS   As your boat cleaves
>   The waters of Daimotsu Bay,
>   As your boat cleaves
>   The waters of Daimotsu Bay.
> TOMOMORI   I, Tomomori,
>   Will drag down Yoshitsune
>   Under the waves beneath which I sank.
>   Grasping his halbert,
>   He whirls it round him like a flail,

> Churning up the waves
> And belching forth noisome vapours.
> Dizzy-eyed and mind distraught,
> None knows where they are.[60]

As Tomomori attempts to pull Yoshitsune down into the sea, he is driven off by Benkei's prayers.

The first half of *Funa Benkei* seems to be the product of the author's imagination; the second half is based on *Yoshitsune*.

One can trace the origin of this legend back through successive stages to *Azuma kagami*, which merely states that Yoshitsune and his men encountered a storm. *Gempei seisuiki* hints that unquiet spirits of Taira dead may have caused the bad weather, *Yoshitsune* conceals Taira spirits within dark clouds, *Shikoku-ochi* produces spirits in plain view, and *Funa Benkei* identifies Tomomori by name.

b The Yoshino legend.—Although reliable sources indicate that Yoshitsune went not only to Yoshino but also to Tōnomine, Totsu-gawa, and Nara after the shipwreck, the legend concentrates upon Yoshino, and particularly upon the adventures of Shizuka and Tada-nobu, which are elaborated with tireless ingenuity by Tokugawa writers. Both Tadanobu and Shizuka appear in Nō plays,[61] but by far the most complete Muromachi treatment is to be found in *Yoshi-tsune*, to which the reader is referred.

c Shizuka at Kamakura. (Sources: *Yoshitsune*, [Nō] *Tsurugaoka*, [Nō] *Futari Shizuka, [kōwakamai] Shizuka*.)—All Muromachi descriptions of Shizuka's dance in Yoritomo's presence agree substantially with the *Yoshitsune* version (see Chapter Six), which itself closely resembles *Azuma kagami*, the main difference being that in *Azuma kagami* the dance precedes the birth of the child. This story, which presents Shizuka as beautiful, talented, brave, and passionately loyal to Yoshitsune, is the most important legend in which she figures, and the one chiefly responsible for her fame.

In a subsidiary and apparently somewhat later development,

---

[60] Translation from Nippon Gakujutsu Shinkōkai, *Japanese Noh Drama* (Tokyo, 1955), p. 181.

[61] For example, Tadanobu is the subject of *Tadanobu*, which describes the manner in which he covers Yoshitsune's retreat, and Shizuka is the principal character in *Futari Shizuka*. In *Yoshino Shizuka*, Tadanobu and Shizuka work together to aid Yoshitsune's escape.

Kajiwara proposes to rip open Shizuka's belly in order to kill the child. Iso-no-zenji goes to Masako, who intervenes on Shizuka's behalf. After the child is born, it is thrown into the sea at Yui-ga-hama.

 d Yoshitsune's Journey to Ōshū.

 (1) Ataka. (Sources: *Yoshitsune*, [Nō] *Ataka*, *[kōwakamai]* *Togashi*, *[kōwakamai]* *Oisagashi*.)—*Yoshitsune* contains what is probably the earliest, and is without doubt the most detailed, account of the experiences of Yoshitsune's party during its flight to Ōshū. The episodes all follow a common pattern, in which Benkei's nerve and resourcefulness save the others from immediate or potential peril. As the false monks flee through Kaga Province, Benkei coolly visits the home of Togashi, the principal local warrior, to collect contributions for the reconstruction of Tōdaiji Temple, destroyed by Taira warriors a few years earlier. The next morning, when the fugitives are questioned by a ferryman, Benkei beats Yoshitsune in order to allay suspicion,[62] and soon afterward he outwits a hostile warrior who searches their baggage.

In the dance *Togashi*, which appears to be an elaboration of the first of these three episodes, Benkei lends verisimilitude to his pose by reading from a subscription list.[63] Another dance, *Oisagashi*, combines the master-beating and baggage search.

In general, when the same subject is treated by *Yoshitsune*, one or more dances *(kōwakamai)*, and a Nō, the contents of the dance tend to represent an intermediate stage between *Yoshitsune* and the Nō. This appears to be the case here. The Nō *Ataka* resembles *Togashi* and *Oisagashi* so closely, not only in content but also in phraseology, that it must certainly have been influenced by them if they were in existence when it was written. There is also evidence to indicate that the author of *Ataka* was acquainted with *Yoshitsune*.

Ataka, a Nō ascribed to Kanze Nobumitsu (Kojirō; 1437–1516), is the only Muromachi source in which the Ataka legend appears fully developed. The process of sharpening and dramatizing the material in *Yoshitsune*, which had begun with the two dances, reached its cul-

---

 [62] This episode is almost certainly borrowed from a similar legend concerning a fleeing Chinese emperor. Shimazu, p. 456.

 [63] An innovation possibly suggested by a *Gempei seisuiki* anecdote concerning a disturbance created by Mongaku, a monk with a personality similar to Benkei's, when he read a subscription list at the ex-emperor's palace. Shimazu, p. 445.

mination in this work, which, with its virtually identical kabuki adaptation, *Kanjinchō* ("The Subscription List"), is easily the best of the Yoshitsune works as literature.[64]

As *Ataka* begins, Togashi enters with a sword-bearer. After identifying himself, he tells his man to halt all passing monks. Next Yoshitsune and his party appear in another part of the stage.

BENKEI AND RETAINERS	Dressed in the travelling robes of monks,
	Dressed in the travelling robes of monks,
	Sweeping the dew, our sleeves are drenched.
BAGGAGE-CARRIER	Torn by dwarf bamboos
	My clothes to me are useless.
BENKEI AND RETAINERS	Crushed is our hope to guard our lord
	Like the shining shield of Kōmon.
	We leave Miyako
	Along the Koshi Road
	For days and nights we travel on;
	How far our journey stretches
	If but in thought we trace its way!
BENKEI	There are among the Hōgan's men
RETAINERS	Ise-no-Saburō, Suruga-no-Jirō,
	Kataoka, Mashio, Hitachibō,
BENKEI	Benkei in leader's guise—
BENKEI AND RETAINERS	Lord and vassals, twelve in all,
	In unwonted traveller's guise,
	This day set forth together.
	Brushing the dew and frost
	With our stoles of silk brocade,
	Knowing not our journey's end,
	In spring through Koshi
	Mantled white with snow, we speed...
BENKEI	Travelling in haste, we have come to the
	port of Ataka. Here shall we rest awhile.[65]

[64] *Ataka* has been translated by Sir George Sansom in *Transactions of the Asiatic Society of Japan*, 38.3 (1911), 149–65, and by Nippon Gakujutsu Shinkōkai in *Japanese Noh Drama*, III (Tokyo, 1960), 153–71. Kanjinchō, written by the third Namiki Gohei, was first performed in 1840. For a detailed synopsis, see A. C. Scott, *The Kabuki Theatre of Japan* (London: Allen and Unwin, 1956), pp. 244–49. Unless otherwise indicated, the translations below are from the text published in Sanari Kentarō, *Yōkyoku taikan* (Meiji Shoin, 1953), I, 77–104.

[65] Translation from *Japanese Noh Drama*, III, 155–57.

[Having heard that a barrier has been erected at Ataka, Benkei sends the baggage-carrier ahead to reconnoiter.]

BAGGAGE-CARRIER   This is a momentous mission. I shall make haste to inspect the barrier... What a sight! An archers' tower, a barricade of standing shields, bramble obstacles. Not even a bird could get through. And what are those two or three blackened objects under the tree over there? Alas! They resemble the heads of wandering monks...

[To make Yoshitsune as inconspicuous as possible, Benkei arranges for him to change clothes with the baggage-carrier.]

BENKEI	Now, my lord, we can resume our journey.
	The red safflower
	No garden growth can hide,
RETAINERS	But never will they cast an eye
	Upon a serving man.
	From their master they remove
	The stole of silk brocade
	And help him on with hempen clothes.
BENKEI	The pannier that the carrier bears
HŌGAN	Yoshitsune on his shoulders takes
RETAINERS	And on it binds the rain-gear
	And the shoulder-chest.
HŌGAN	He hides his face
	Within the deep sedge-hat.
RETAINERS	And clinging to his staff,
HŌGAN	The carrier, weak and weary,
CHORUS	Guides his tottering steps.
	How piteous his plight![66]

[As Yoshitsune and his men approach the barrier, they are challenged by Togashi, who threatens them with death. Benkei and the others calmly begin a Buddhist chant.]

RETAINERS	...A wandering monk is a living Buddha.
BENKEI	Should you venture to strike us down,
RETAINERS	Who can say what the divine Fudō may think?
BENKEI	Nor will you escape the punishment of the
	gods of Kumano...
CHORUS	...They rub their rosaries noisily.

[Togashi is impressed, but perseveres.]

TOGASHI	...Since you claim to be collecting subscriptions for

---

[66] Translation from *Japanese Noh Drama*, III, 160.

Tōdaiji Temple in Nara, you must certainly possess a subscription list. I should like to hear you read from it.

BENKEI   What's that? You want me to read from the subscription list?

TOGASHI   Precisely.

BENKEI   With pleasure. *(Aside.)* Of course I have no such thing. I shall take a scroll from my pannier and pass it off as the list.

[Walking to the front of the stage, he begins a sonorous recital of the history of Tōdaiji Temple, full of recondite Buddhist allusions. As he chants, he cleverly thwarts Togashi's repeated efforts to catch a glimpse of the text.]

TOGASHI   The guardians of the barrier are terrified.

CHORUS   Fearfully they let them pass,
          Fearfully they let them pass.

TOGASHI   Go on quickly.

BENKEI   We shall do so.

[As the party file by, Togashi and his sword-bearer recognize Yoshitsune and stop him.]

BENKEI   Isn't that amazing? So he looks like Yoshitsune, does he? That's something this rascal of a porter can remember for the rest of his life. *(Furiously.)* I had planned to go on to Noto today, since it's still early, but you must needs lag behind with your little load and attract suspicion. It's been one thing after another with you lately. Here, how do you like this! *(He snatches the staff from Yoshitsune's hand and beats him mercilessly.)*

[Yoshitsune's retainers face Togashi and his man threateningly, and the two parties alternately advance and retreat in a series of confrontations.]

TOGASHI   I was mistaken a moment ago. Go on quickly.

[Once the party is beyond the barrier, there is an emotional scene as Benkei tearfully begs his master's forgiveness and Yoshitsune laments his fate. Suddenly Togashi's sword-bearer appears, saying that Togashi wishes to apologize by offering them wine. Togashi enters as Benkei warns the retainers not to relax their vigilance. All drink, and Benkei dances in simulated intoxication, signing with his eyes for the others to depart unobtrusively. When they are safely away, he makes a dramatic exit, while the chorus chants.]

CHORUS   Feeling as men who have trod on the tiger's
              tail
          Or escaped the serpent's jaws,
          Down toward the land of Mutsu
          They make their way.

The immense popularity of this short piece, full of suspense and drama, has immortalized Benkei and made the Ataka legend the best known of all the stories dealing with Yoshitsune's life. Both *Ataka* and *Kanjinchō* are still favorites of their respective repertoires.

(2) The Baggage Search. (Sources: *Yoshitsune*, *[kōwakamai]* *Oisagashi*.)—The baggage search mentioned above, in which Benkei again demonstrates his quick wit, is a less well known story, preserved in *Yoshitsune* and in a dance, *Oisagashi*.

(3) The Meeting with the Mother of the Satō Brothers. (Sources: *[kōwakamai]* *Yashima*, [Nō] *Settai*.)[67]—This is another minor episode on the journey to Ōshū. Yoshitsune and his men, now nearing their destination, stop at the home of the Satō brothers' widowed mother, where they reveal their identity and relate the story of Tsuginobu's gallant death.

The story has no known historical basis (according to *Azuma kagami*, the father of the brothers was still alive at the time). It may be an elaboration of the meeting described in Chapter Eight of *Yoshitsune*.

e The Fates of Yoshitsune and Benkei.—The most famous Muromachi legend in this last group, the one dealing with the manner of Benkei's death, is fully presented in Chapter Eight of *Yoshitsune*. It also appears in a major dance, *Takadachi*.

The chief Edo additions to the Yoshitsune legend have to do with Yoshitsune's end. In one story, known as Noguchi Hōgan (Hōgan at Noguchi), the chief *tengu* of Kurama rescues Yoshitsune when he is on the point of suicide and flies with him to Noguchi in Harima Province, where he becomes a monk to pray for the souls of his dead retainers. It was also alleged during the Tokugawa period that Yasuhira had sent the head of another man to Kamakura in order to protect Yoshitsune, that Yoshitsune had escaped to Manchuria, where he was known as Genghis Khan, or where, alternatively, he became the ancestor of the Ch'ing dynasty, etc. The best known of these theories, to which some people in Hokkaidō are said to subscribe even today, is that Yoshitsune escaped with his men to Hokkaidō, subdued the island, and became its benevolent ruler.

[67] *Settai* is translated in Nippon Gakujutsu Shinkōkai, *Japanese Noh Drama*, II (Tokyo, 1959), 109–22.

III. "YOSHITSUNE"

Yoshitsune is thought by modern scholars to have been written during the first half of the Muromachi period, or between about 1336 and 1450. (This could also be interpreted to mean between 1333 and 1450 [1453], or between 1392 and 1480 [1482], depending upon which of several possible boundaries for the Muromachi period are accepted.) Its close resemblance to other Muromachi literature, such as *Soga monogatari*, the short stories *(otogi zōshi)* and the dance texts *(kōwakamai)*, in vocabulary, style, and intellectual orientation leaves little doubt that all belong to the same general period. The ascription is further supported by mention in Chapter Six of the Tenryūji, a temple founded in 1340, and by *Yoshitsune*'s apparent reliance on *Taiheiki*, a work which describes events occurring as late as 1367. The mid-Muromachi cut-off date depends largely on the probability that *Yoshitsune* was available to the authors of certain Nō and dance texts written in the second half of the fifteenth century.

To the reader who has reached this point, little need be said concerning the content of *Yoshitsune*. It is clearly the single most important source for the Yoshitsune legend as a whole, a fact which, more than any other, recommends it to our attention. One may say of it what Shimazu wrote of Yoshitsune works in general:

> For the most part, the interest and importance of a study of Yoshitsune pieces reside not in the individual works considered as literature, but in the legends upon which those works have drawn; not in the accuracy with which the historical Yoshitsune's character and actions have been described, but in how popular sympathy has idealized him in legend and literature. [p. 84.]

In addition to its value as a collection of legends, *Yoshitsune* is of interest to the student of literary history because of its key position in the corpus of Yoshitsune works. *Heike monogatari*, *Gempei seisuiki*, and *Yoshitsune* are the three chief sources for the hundreds of literary works, most of them written in the Tokugawa period, that have been based on episodes in Yoshitsune's life. As we have seen, numerous Muromachi dances, Nō plays, and short stories are identical with portions of *Yoshitsune*. Relative ages are seldom clear, but in many cases it seems likely that *Yoshitsune* is the older. A considerable number of the dances were later adapted as puppet plays, and many other Yoshitsune puppet plays were also written for the Edo theater (Chikamatsu alone produced ten). *Kanjinchō* was merely the most popular of some seventy Yoshitsune kabuki plays (mostly adapted from puppet plays) which were written in the Tokugawa and Meiji periods; and Yoshitsune pieces not only claimed a substantial place in most of the major Edo fiction genres but also persisted in the Meiji era as children's stories and historical novels. Of all these literary works, at least 110 have drawn on *Yoshitsune,* either directly or indirectly.[68]

Yoshitsune is usually classified as a war tale *(gunki monogatari).* The war tales, as their name implies, are prose works which take warriors and battles as their main subject matter. They are not basically products of the imagination, but, rather, dramatized accounts of historical events and persons. Whether dealing with a single military engagement or with an extended series of campaigns, they typically include digressions of many kinds—elegant anecdotes of court life, romantic interludes, instructive tales from Chinese and Japanese history, Confucian moralizing, and invariably stories about buddhas, bodhisattvas, monks, temples, and Buddhist doctrines and rites. Most of the best ones were recited to illiterate medieval audiences by itinerant entertainers, a circumstance which helps to explain their loosely knit structure and varied content. *Heike monogatari,* the best from a literary standpoint, is written in a graceful, vigorous style, with many rhythmic poetic passages; and *Taiheiki,* though somewhat self-conscious in its efforts to match the standard of *Heike,* has a certain lofty dignity. In general, however, the war tales depend for their appeal not upon subtle literary effects but upon straightforward and lively accounts of historical events of interest to a warrior society. With the single exception of *Taiheiki,* all the great thirteenth- and fourteenth-century war tales deal with the twelfth-century disturbances which culminated in the destruction of the mighty house of Taira.

Even today, something remains of the poignance of that long-ago clash between two great warrior families: the Heike, fatally weakened by participation in the life of the capital nobility, and the Minamoto, tough provincials to whom bravery, loyalty, and honor were the

---

[68] Fujimura Saku, *Nihon bungaku daijiten* (Tokyo, 1950–52), II, 171.

supreme values, but who nevertheless were moved to pity by the
plight of their adversaries.

> Now the clan of Taira, building wall to wall,
> Spread over the earth like the leafy branches of
>   a great tree:
> Yet their prosperity lasted but for a day;
> It was like the flower of the convolvulus.
> There was none to tell them
> That glory flashes like sparks from flint-stone,
> And after,—darkness.
> Oh wretched, the life of men!

These lines are from *Atsumori*, a Nō which describes the pathetic
death of a young Taira noble at Ichi-no-tani. In the play, Kumagai,
the eastern warrior who has killed Atsumori, appears as a Buddhist
monk, explaining:

I am Kumagai no Naozane, a man of the country of Musashi. I have
left my home and call myself the priest Rensei; this I have done because
of my grief at the death of Atsumori, who fell in battle by my hand. Hence
it comes that I am dressed in priestly guise.

And now I am going down to Ichi-no-Tani to pray for the salvation
of Atsumori's soul.

Presently he encounters Atsumori's spirit, and the two exchange
melancholy reminiscences.

> ATSUMORI   ...But on the night of the sixth day of
>   the second month
>   My father Tsunemori gathered us together.
>   "To-morrow," he said, "we shall fight
>   our last fight.
>   To-night is all that is left us."
>   We sang songs together, and danced.
> PRIEST   Yes, I remember; we in our siege-camp
>   Heard the sound of music
>   Echoing from your tents that night;
>   There was the music of a flute...

ATSUMORI   The bamboo-flute! I wore it when
I died.[69]

The valor and military prowess of some of the fugitives, the bewilderment or cowardice of others, the spectacular exploits and internal quarrels of the Genji, led by their brilliant young commander,
Yoshitsune, the magic names of Ichi-no-tani, Yashima, and Dan-no-
ura, the inscrutable Lord of Kamakura in the background, the
intrigues in the Kantō and at the capital—all these furnished ample
material for the most tireless of medieval reciters.

The author of *Yoshitsune*, familiar, as were his contemporaries, with
the whole Minamoto-Taira corpus, and likewise acquainted with the
legends that had grown up around Yoshitsune's name during the two
and a half centuries[70] since the great hero's death in 1189, produced
a work which resembled other war tales in its choice of period, its cast
of characters, and its emphasis upon military lore, martial skills, and
fighting. It differed from its predecessors, however, by concentrating
upon the life of a single man, by admitting a far larger element of
fiction than the others, and by omitting the digressions characteristic
of the genre. Furthermore, it was written in a style which could hardly be considered elevated, even by the unexacting standards of the
war tales. As a result, *Yoshitsune* is but grudgingly permitted to join
the company of other war tales, where it is regarded as not only different but inferior; and from time to time one hears that it is not a
war tale at all, but merely a superior short story *(otogi zōshi)*.

The manner in which *Yoshitsune* is labeled is of less concern to us
than its intrinsic literary qualities. These the reader will be able to
judge for himself. It has seemed to me that the work deserves kinder
treatment than it ordinarily receives. The narrative flows along
smoothly, with effective use of humor and dialogue, and some of the
characterizations (notably Benkei and Shizuka) surpass anything in
Taiheiki, if not in *Heike monogatari* itself. The abrupt and unexplained
transformation of Yoshitsune from a gallant youth and indomitable
general into an ineffectual court noble, which is probably the most
obvious artistic flaw from a modern point of view, was not disconcert-

[69] Translations from Waley, pp. 70, 64, 71–72.
[70] In ascribing the work to the fifteenth century, I follow Shimazu, who argues cogently
(p. 641 ff.) for a date somewhere between 1400 and 1450.

ing to Muromachi audiences, to whom such a figure was in the highest degree sympathetic. Given the intent to present Yoshitsune as a private person, with the consequent abridgment of the section dealing with his public life, *Yoshitsune* is also well constructed, fast paced, and dramatic. As a Muromachi product, it could scarcely be entirely free of Confucian and Buddhist influence, but the relative absence of wordy and didactic digressions contrasts refreshingly with other war tales, particularly with *Soga monogatari,* a work with which it is often bracketed. *Yoshitsune* is popular fare, admittedly, but good of its kind, perhaps the best of the Muromachi period.

Yoshitsune

Chapter One

In the old days in Japan there were heroes like Tamura, Toshihito, Masakado, Sumitomo, Hōshō, and Raikō—and in China Fan K'uai and Chang Liang—but all we know about them is what people tell us.[1] Certainly we have never laid eyes on any of them ourselves. If it is a question of actually seeing a warrior perform amazing feats, then to my mind our country has never had anyone to compare with Kurō Yoshitsune, the youngest son of Yoshitomo, the Chief of the Imperial Stables of the Left from Shimotsuke.

Yoshitsune's father, Yoshitomo, suffered a defeat in the capital on the twenty-seventh day of the twelfth month of the first year of Heiji [1159], in alliance with Fujiwara Nobuyori, the Commander of the Gate Guards. After most of his hereditary retainers had been killed or wounded, he fled toward the east with a band of twenty men, including his grown sons, while his younger children remained in the capital. The oldest son was Kamakura Akugenda Yoshihira; the second was sixteen-year-old Tomonaga, a fifth-rank secretary in the Empress's household, and the third was twelve-year-old Yoritomo, the Assistant Chief of the Military Guards of the Right.

Yoshitomo sent Yoshihira toward Echizen with instructions to search for friends in the north, but Yoshihira, it appears, was unable to find help. At any rate, he was hiding at Ishiyama Temple in Ōmi when the Heike learned of his presence and sent Senoo and Namba to fetch him back to the capital. He was beheaded at the Rokujō River Beach.

---

[1] For identification of persons and places mentioned in the text, see Appendix B.

Yoshihira's younger brother, Tomonaga, died at Aohaka, a post station in Mino Province, of a wound in the left knee inflicted by a mountain brigand's arrow.

There were a number of other sons in various places, including one whose mother was a daughter of the chief priest at Atsuta in Owari Province. At first, as a consequence of having grown up at Kaba in Tōtōmi, that boy was called Kaba Onzōshi, but he later became known simply as the Governor of Mikawa. Three other children, Imawaka, aged seven, Otowaka, aged five, and Ushiwaka, not yet a year old, were the offspring of Tokiwa, a minor lady-in-waiting in the service of ex-Empress Teishi. Kiyomori gave orders to seize and execute all of them.

TOKIWA'S FLIGHT FROM THE CAPITAL

At dawn on the seventeenth day of the first month in the first year of Eiryaku [1160], Tokiwa set out from the capital with her three sons. The times were still sadly troubled, and after she had sought shelter in vain at the home of a relative who lived at Kishi-no-oka in Uda District, Yamato, she was obliged to go into hiding at a place in Yamato called Taitōji. There she presently learned that Taira warriors from Rokuhara had seized her mother, Sekiya, at her home in Yamamomo-machi and were questioning her pitilessly.

Tokiwa's distress was extreme. If she attempted to save her mother's life, her three sons were certain to be put to the sword; if she protected her sons, it must be at the cost of her aged mother. May one sacrifice a parent for the sake of a child? Over and over she told herself that those who treat their parents lovingly are regarded with favor by the earth spirits, and at last she concluded that it would probably be best for the children in the end if she returned.

Weeping bitterly, she began the journey to the capital with her three sons. The Taira officials, who had been told of her departure, directed Akushichibyōe Kagekiyo and Kemmotsu Tarō Yorikata to escort her to Rokuhara.

Meanwhile Kiyomori had been thinking, "Torture by flames or torture by water..." but at the sight of Tokiwa his fury vanished, for not a woman in Japan was her equal in appearance. The ex-Empress, a shrewd judge of feminine charm, had once summoned a thousand of the fairest maidens in the capital. She had selected a hundred from the thousand, ten from the hundred, and one from the ten, and To-kiwa had been that one.

"If she can be persuaded to listen to me, I won't worry about the future enmity of her children," Kiyomori thought. "I will let them live." After instructing Yorikata and Kagekiyo to take her to Shichijō Shushaka, where Yorikata kept watch over her, he began showering her with letters. At first she refused even to touch them, but at length, for the sake of her sons, she capitulated. That was how she managed to keep the three boys alive until they reached maturity.

Imawaka, who was sent to study at Kannonji Temple in the spring of his eighth year, entered holy orders at eighteen and was called the Honorable Monk. Later, after he went to live near the foot of Mount Fuji in the province of Suruga, he became known as the Honorable Militant Monk.

The son at Hachijō,[2] though also a monk, was of a violent temper, always on the alert to murder a Taira whenever there was a festival at Kamo, Kasuga, Inari, or Gion. Later, when Shingū Jūrō Yoshimori of Kii rebelled, that son was killed at the Sunomata River on the Tōkaidō Road.

Ushiwaka remained with his mother until he was four years old; at about that time his precociousness came to the attention of Kiyomori, who fell into the habit of remarking that it was a dangerous business to rear the son of an enemy in one's own house, and so the boy was sent east of the capital to Yamashina, a place in which successive generations of Genji had lived after retiring from active life. He remained there until he was seven.

HOW USHIWAKA WENT TO KURAMA

As her sons matured, Tokiwa became more and more concerned about their future. She was reluctant to make them military retainers of another family, and since their lack of experience barred them from careers at court, the only possible course seemed to be that of training them as monks to pray for Yoshitomo's enlightenment. She sent a messenger to Yoshitomo's old prayer-monk,[3] the Deacon of Tōkōbō, who was the abbot at Kurama.

---

[2] Otowaka. He entered the service of a monk-son of Emperor Go-Shirakawa, Prince Hachijō En'e, where he was known as Kyō-no-kimi Enshin.

[3] *Inori no shi*, a monk entrusted by a layman with the recitation of prayers on his behalf.

"I am sure you have heard of me, and also of Ushiwaka, Yoshi-tomo's youngest son," she wrote. "I am but a woman, and it frightens me to keep Ushiwaka here when the Taira are so powerful. It is best for him to go to Kurama. He is rather boisterous; please teach him to be gentle. Show him how to read as well as you can, and have him learn the holy writ, even if it is only a single character."

"I shall be delighted to see one of Yoshitomo's sons," Tōkōbō replied, and he sent a man to Yamashina to fetch Ushiwaka.

After Ushiwaka had climbed the mountain to Kurama early in the second month of his seventh year, he spent every day with his teacher, reciting sutras and poring over Chinese classics. When the sun sank in the west, he read on with the teacher until the image lamps flickered out. Day and night he studied, working at his books until four or five o'clock in the morning; Tōkōbō was quite certain that not even Mount Hiei or Miidera could boast such a page.[4] His devotion to learning, his irreproachable character, and his great beauty also charmed the Deacon of Ryōchibō and the Canon of Kakunichibō. "If he continues in this fashion until he is twenty, he will make a good successor for Tōkōbō himself—someone Tamon can be proud of," they said.

When Ushiwaka's mother heard all this, she sent a letter to Tōkōbō. "He is doing well enough in his studies now, but I am afraid that it may make him rude and lazy if you let him visit home too often," she wrote. "If you will tell me when he wants to see me, I shall come to him at the temple."

"A page cannot go home whenever he feels like it anyway," commented Tōkōbō. Ushiwaka was thus permitted to leave the temple only once in two or three years.

What devil could have gained the ear of such a brilliant scholar? In the autumn of his fifteenth year, Ushiwaka's feelings toward his books underwent a startling change, all because a family retainer urged him to rebel against the Taira.

---

[4] *Chigo*, a name applied to a boy from a noble or warrior family who was sent to study at a Buddhist monastery. Some *chigo* eventually became monks, while others returned to their homes. As early as the Heian period some became involved in homosexual relations with the monks, and in the Kamakura and Muromachi periods, when homosexuality was an accepted custom in monastic and warrior society, girlishly beautiful, elegantly dressed *chigo* were much sought after. A *chigo* was easily recognized by his distinctive hair style, his use of cosmetics, and his rich apparel, which was sometimes indistinguishable from that of a woman.

SHŌMON

Near the Shijō-Muromachi intersection there lived a Genji retainer of long standing, a shaven-headed monk from a warrior family, whose father had been Kamada Jirō Masakiyo, the son of Yoshitomo's wet nurse. During the Heiji war, a maternal kinsman had saved the life of Masakiyo's son by hiding him from the Osada bailiff (the future monk was then a boy of eleven), and the same relative had named the boy Kamada Saburō Masachika at his capping ceremony when he was nineteen.

At the age of twenty-one Masachika took stock of his situation. "The Minamoto have fallen on hard times since Tameyoshi and Yoshitomo died in Hōgen and Heiji. They don't act like warriors at all. And since my own father was killed by Kiyomori too, the best thing I can do is to wander through the provinces as a monk, praying for our lord's enlightenment and my father's happiness."

He directed his steps to Kyushu, where for a time he studied at the Dazaifu Anrakuji, a temple situated in Mikasa District in the province of Chikuzen. When homesickness drew him back to the capital, he devoted himself to pious observances at a temple in Shijō. He was known as Shōmon, which was his name in religion, and also as the Holy Man of Shijō.

Whenever Shōmon's devotions permitted him the leisure to observe worldly things, he was shocked by the flourishing fortunes of the Heike. "Why should a Taira rise to the office of chancellor, or the most insignificant of the Heike connections lord it over other people at court?" he thought. "Nothing was left of the Genji after the Hōgen and Heiji battles—the men were killed and the young boys were packed off to such out-of-the-way places that they've never been heard of again. If only a brave, lucky Minamoto would lead a rebellion! I would go anywhere as his messenger if it would help destroy the Taira."

When he was not busy with religious works, he counted over the provincial Genji on his fingers. There were at least a dozen,[a5] but they were so far away that there was no hope of communicating with them.

"Lord Yoshitomo's youngest son, Ushiwaka, is at Kurama near the capital," he reflected. "Why shouldn't I go to see him? If he is a

[5] Superscript letters indicate abridgments. For the complete text, see Appendix C.

courageous youth, he might give me a letter for Yoritomo in Izu. If only the provinces would revolt!"

Although the summer retreat was then in progress at the Shijō temple, Shōmon started at once for Kurama, heedless of his neglected devotions. Soon he was standing outside the abbot's veranda.

"The Holy Man of Shijō is here," reported the monks.

"Have him come in," said the abbot. He gave Shōmon accommodation in his own quarters, not for a moment suspecting that he had come with the wicked intention of stirring up a rebellion.

One night when there were no offices to perform and everyone was fast asleep, Shōmon went to Ushiwaka's lodgings.

"Why are you wasting time?" he whispered in Ushiwaka's ear. "Hasn't anyone told you that you're a son of Yoshitomo, the Chief of the Imperial Stables of the Left, and a tenth-generation descendent of Emperor Seiwa? My own father was Kamada Jirobyōe, the son of Yoshitomo's wet nurse. Doesn't it matter to you that your relatives are hiding miserably in the provinces?"

"The Heike run everything nowadays. This may be a trap," thought Ushiwaka. He responded distantly, but the monk soon dispelled his suspicions with intimate family reminiscences. Although Shōmon himself was a stranger, Ushiwaka had often heard of him.

"We cannot stay together, but let us meet wherever we can."

With these words Ushiwaka sent Shōmon home.

USHIWAKA'S VISITS TO KIBUNE

After his encounter with Shōmon, Ushiwaka thought of nothing but rebellion day and night. He forgot his studies as completely as though they had never existed. "The leader of a revolt must be a real warrior," he thought. "It would be a good thing if I learned how to fight."

His present quarters, in which people were constantly coming and going, were clearly unsuitable for military exercises. Far back on Kurama Mountain there was a ravine called Sōjō-ga-tani, where someone had long ago dedicated a shrine to a wonder-working spirit known as the Divinity of Kibune, and where famous and learned monks had practiced devotions. It had been a place of marvels, echoing to the sound of Buddhist bells and the boom of the priests' holy drums, but the miraculous powers of the buddhas and gods had become weakened in the degenerate climate of a later day.[6] The abandoned buildings were now the abode of goblins, and weird apparitions shrieked in the ravine after the western sun had set, frightening away all those who might otherwise have selected Sōjō-ga-tani as the site of a pious retreat.

After Ushiwaka heard about Sōjō-ga-tani, he made a pretense of working at his studies as usual during the daytime, but at night, without a word even to his sworn brothers among the monks, he began going regularly alone to Kibune Shrine, wearing a corselet called Shikitae (a gift from the abbot) and a sword with gold fittings. "Hear me, great and all-merciful god! Hear me, Great Bodhisattva Hachiman," he would pray with joined palms. "Preserve the Genji! If my wish is granted, I shall build you a magnificent shrine endowed with twenty-five hundred acres of fields." This vow pronounced, he would stand erect with his face toward the southwest. He would pretend that the surrounding bushes and shrubs were various members of the Taira family and would slash away with all his might at a towering tree which he dubbed Kiyomori; then he would draw objects resembling *gitchō* balls[7] from his blouse, suspend them from branches, and call one of them Shigemori's head and another Kiyomori's. At daybreak he would return to his quarters and lie down with a cover over his head without anyone's being the wiser.

In time, however, a monk named Izumi, who was acting as Ushiwaka's servant, became puzzled by his master's behavior and began watching him closely. One night he followed Ushiwaka and observed his goings-on from the shelter of a clump of bushes; then he hastened back to inform Tōkōbō.

"Tell everybody we are going to shave Ushiwaka's head," Tōkōbō instructed Ryōchibō in great perturbation.

"We ought to consider each boy's case separately," protested Ryōchibō. "It would be a shame to force such a pretty lad to take his vows this year. Can't we wait until next spring?"

"Everyone finds it hard to say good-bye to the world, no matter

[6] Buddhist doctrine divided the propagation of the faith into three successive eras, one of true Buddhism, one of formalized religion, and one of religious decline. In late Heian times it was generally believed that the era of decline had begun.
[7] Wooden balls shaped like tops and hit by a special kind of mallet *(gitchō)* in a game played during the New Year season.

who he is," the abbot replied. "Both for my sake and for the boy's,
I will not condone this kind of misconduct. Cut off his hair!"

When they approached Ushiwaka, he seized the hilt of his sword.

"Anybody who comes near me to shave my head will be run
through, regardless," he warned. It was not going to be an easy task
to make him a monk.

"I don't wonder that he refuses to study in such a noisy place,"
said Kakunichibō. "Let him learn quietly in my secluded quarters."

Perhaps the compassionate Tōkōbō pitied Ushiwaka. "All right,"
he agreed, and he put the boy in Kakunichi's charge.

It was then that Ushiwaka changed his name to Shanaō. He
abandoned his visits to Kibune and went daily to the Main Hall,
where he prayed before the image of Tamon for the success of his
revolt.

KICHIJI'S TALES OF ŌSHŪ

So the year drew to a close and Shanaō became sixteen. One day
toward the end of the first month or the beginning of the second,
while he was performing devotions before Tamon, it chanced that
another worshiper was also paying his respects to the deity. He was a
rich gold merchant from Sanjō, Kichiji Nobutaka by name, who was
in the habit of making an annual journey to Ōshū.

"What a handsome lad," thought the merchant when he saw
Shanaō. "I wonder who he is. If he belongs to one of the great
families, he should have a retinue of servants among the monks, and
yet he always seems to be alone. Can it be true that one of Yoshitomo's sons is living here? Hidehira has often said to me, 'One of
Yoshitomo's sons is at Kurama Temple. Kiyomori boasts that he
rules the sixty-six provinces of Japan, but if you could bring me a
single one of the young Genji, I would gladly establish a capital for
him in Iwai District, make my two sons governors of the Two Provinces, and act as the steward and devoted servant of the Minamoto for
the rest of my life.' If I could persuade the boy to go with me, there
might be a nice profit in it."

Approaching Shanaō deferentially, Kichiji said, "To which of the
capital families do you belong? I'm a city man myself, a gold merchant who travels to Ōshū every year. Do you know anyone there?"

"My home is in a remote place," Shanaō replied evasively. But he was thinking, "This must be Kichiji, the famous gold merchant. He would be just the man to ask about Ōshū."

"How large a province is Michinoku?" he inquired.

"It covers an immense area. There are fifty-four districts between the Hitachi-Michinoku boundary at Kikuta Barrier and the Dewa-Ōshū boundary at Inamu Barrier," Kichiji replied.

"How many of the men would be useful to the Genji in a struggle with the Taira?"

Kichiji, who was well acquainted with the history of the area, began to explain. "A general named Oka Tayū controlled the Two Provinces long ago. His only son, Abe Yoritoki, had six sons of his own: Kuriyagawa Jirō Sadatō, the eldest, Torinomi Saburō Munetō, the second, Ietō, Moritō, Shigetō, and Sakai Kanja Ryōzō, the sixth and last. Ryōzō was a remarkable man. He could make fog and mist whenever he wanted to, or stay under water all day long to outwit an enemy. The brothers were taller than Chinese. Sadatō was nine feet five inches tall, Munetō eight feet five inches, and every one of the others at least eight feet. Sakai Kanja's height was ten feet three inches.

"Until Yoritoki's day, the Abe feared the court's majesty enough to journey to the capital every year as the Emperor wished, but after his death they showed no respect for imperial commands. On one occasion they agreed to go to the capital if the court would pay half the cost of the journey there and back through the seven Hokurikudō provinces. When a meeting was held to consider their message, the principal courtiers said, 'Those men have defied an imperial edict. A Taira or Minamoto general will have to be sent to punish them.' By order of the court, Minamoto Yoriyoshi set out for Michinoku with 110,000 mounted warriors, led by Takahashi Ōkura-no-tayū Mitsutō, a Suruga chief.

"When Sadatō learned that Mitsutō had reached Imō in Shimotsuke, he left Kuriyagawa Fortress, prepared a stronghold in Adachi District with the mountains of Azukashie behind him, and galloped to Yukigata Plain to wait for the Genji. The general, Mitsutō, passed Shirakawa Barrier with 500 riders, and at once attacked Sadatō at Yukigata.

"Sadatō fell back toward Asaka Marsh as a result of that day's fighting. He entrenched himself near Azukashie in Date District,

while the Genji occupied positions at Hayashiro on the bank of the
Surukami River in Shinobu Village. The fighting continued day and
night for seven years until all the 100,000 Genji warriors were either
killed or wounded. Then Yoriyoshi went back to the capital in despair
and admitted to the Emperor that the Abe had been too much for him.

" 'If you can't overpower them, send a deputy to do it for you,'
commanded His Majesty.

"Yoriyoshi went home to Rokujō Horikawa and sent his thirteen-
year-old son to the palace.

" 'What is your name?' asked the Emperor.

" 'I was born at the hour of the dragon on the day of the dragon in
the year of the dragon, so people call me Ganda,'⁸ said the boy.

"Since there was no precedent for making a commander of someone without a court title, they ordered a capping ceremony for
Ganda. In rites performed at Hachiman Shrine with Gotōnai Noriakira as sponsor, he took the name Hachiman Tarō Yoshiie. The
suit of armor presented to him by His Majesty was called 'Ganda's
Swaddling Clothes.'

"Yoshiie set out for Ōshū with Chichibu Jūrō Shigekuni as the
leader of his vanguard. He attacked Azukashie Fortress, but the Genji
lost again. Then in great alarm Yoshiie dispatched a swift courier to
the capital.

"When the nobles heard the courier's report, it occurred to them
that the era designation might be at fault. They changed the name of
the year to the first year of Kōhei [1058]—Peace and Tranquility—
and Azukashie Fortress fell on the twenty-first day of the fourth
month. From positions at Shikarazaru the Abe fought past Inamu
Barrier to strongholds in Mogami District, but the Genji attacked
again, forcing them to cross Okachi Pass to Kanazawa Fortress in
Sembuku. There was another year or two of fighting, and then Kanazawa Fortress fell before a desperate attack by Kamakura Gongorō
Kagemasa, Miura Heidayū Tametsugi, and Takahashi Mitsutō. The
Abe retired to Shirokiyama and occupied Koromogawa Fortress, but
Tametsugi and Kagemasa attacked again.

⁸ *Yoshitsune monogatari* has, "...I am called Kuwatatsu [Accumulated Dragons?]."
Although it is quite possible that Yoshiie was born in 1040 (a dragon year, according to
the traditional chronology), rather than in 1041, the date given in standard references,
Ganda seems clearly to be a variant of Genda [Eldest Minamoto Son], which according to
Heiji monogatari was Yoshiie's childhood name. Okami, p. 50, n. 1.

"On the twenty-first day of the sixth month of the third year of Kōhei [1060], Sadatō, mortally wounded, lay down for the last time on the Iwate moorland, dressed in a yellow robe. His younger brother Munetō was taken prisoner, and Sakai Kanja was captured and executed by Gotōnai Noriakira. Yoshiie himself galloped back to the capital to be received in audience by the Emperor. His name will never be forgotten.

"One of Yoshiie's men was left behind to guard the conquered area—a certain Fujiwara Kiyohira, known as the Mitsū Lesser Captain, who was an eleventh-generation descendent of Tankaikō. Since he lived in Watari District, he was called Watari Kiyohira. The Two Provinces fell completely under his domination, and he controlled 500,000 warriors in fourteen circuits. Hidehira still has 180,000 retainers. If there were a war between the Minamoto and the Taira, I am sure he would help the Genji."

SHANAŌ'S DEPARTURE FROM KURAMA

"That is just what I have always heard about Hidehira. He must be a great man," thought Shanaō as he listened to the merchant's story. "Now I know that I must go to Ōshū. If Hidehira would agree to help me, I could leave 100,000 of his 180,000 warriors in Ōshū and march to the Kantō at the head of the other 80,000. Yoshitomo's old provinces in the Kantō favor the Genji. By mustering another 120,000 men thereabouts, I would have a total of 200,000—half of them for Yoritomo in Izu and half for Lord Kiso. Then I could cross over to Echigo, call up the warriors of Ukawa, Sabashi, Kanazu, and Oku-yama, recruit others in Etchū, Noto, Kaga, and Echizen, and ride across the Arachi Mountains to western Ōmi with 100,000 men. After meeting the 200,000 Kantō warriors at Ōtsu, I would invade the capital by way of Ōsaka Barrier, present 100,000 men to the throne, and offer to protect the palace. If I still couldn't overthrow the Heike, death in the capital wouldn't be a bad price for eternal fame." He was a warlike sixteen-year-old indeed!

"I might as well let this fellow know who I am," Shanaō thought. Aloud he said to Kichiji: "Let me tell you a secret. I am a son of Yoshitomo, the Chief of the Stables of the Left, and I want to send a letter to Hidehira. When can you bring me an answer?"

Kichiji slipped down from his seat and touched his cap to the

ground. "Hidehira has told me about you. Why don't you go yourself instead of sending a letter? I shall be responsible for your comfort
on the way," he urged.

"Who knows when the answer might arrive? It would be wiser to
do as he suggests," thought Shanaō. "When do you intend to leave?"
he asked.

"Since tomorrow will be an auspicious day, I plan to hold the departure ceremony then," replied Kichiji.

"Very well, I shall wait for you before the Jūzenji Shrine at Awataguchi."

With a word of acquiescence Kichiji left the temple.

Shanaō returned to the abbot's lodgings to prepare in secret for his
journey. But though he struggled to maintain his composure, sobs
rose in his throat as he realized that he would never again see his
beloved teacher, the constant companion by whose side he had
greeted all the dewy mornings and starlit nights since his seventh
spring. Only by firmly reminding himself of the need for courage was
he able to hold firmly to his plan for leaving.

The departure was at dawn on the second day of the second month
of the fourth year of Shōan [1174]. For traveling, Shanaō chose a
blouse and knickers[9] of Chinese silk over a pair of wide-bottomed
white drawers, and a set of four undergarments, two of them made of
a plain white fabric, another of Chinese damask, and the last of a
filmy pale yellow cloth of hemp and silk woven in Harima. The
corselet Shikitae was concealed beneath his clothing. At his waist
hung two weapons, a short sword with a hilt and scabbard of dark
blue brocade, and a long blade decorated with gold. He applied a
thin layer of powder to his face, penciled two delicate brows on his
forehead, rolled his hair high, and sorrowfully prepared to quit the
empty chamber.

"I hope the abbot will still think of me once in a while even after
someone else has taken my place," he thought.

He took out a bamboo flute and played for an hour; then, in tears,
he departed from Kurama, telling himself that the music would have
to suffice for a farewell present.

That night at Shōmon's Shijō lodgings, Shanaō revealed his plan
to the monk.

 ⁹ The usual dress of the military.

"Whatever happens, I shall be at your side," promised Shōmon. But Shanaō stopped him. "You will have to stay in the capital so that I can know what the Heike are about," he said.

So Shanaō left. Shōmon accompanied him as far as Awataguchi, and waited with him for Kichiji to arrive at the Jūzenji Shrine.

Kichiji was there long before dawn, preceded by a score of treasure-laden beasts. He was dressed for the journey in thickly furred riding trousers and a blouse and knickers with a random design of herbs and blossoms. His mount was a dark chestnut horse with a horn-trimmed saddle. For the boy's use he had brought a pair of spotted deerskin trousers and a cream-colored horse saddled with a gold-trimmed lacquer saddle.

"You have not forgotten your promise?" Shanaō called.

Kichiji leaped jubilantly from his horse, led the extra mount forward, and helped Shanaō up, scarcely able to believe his good fortune.

Shanaō beckoned to him. "If you see a party of horsemen galloping after us, please hurry on without paying any attention to them. When the monks miss me, they will look for me in the capital and along the Tōkaidō Road. If they overtake us and call me back before we reach Surihari Mountain, I won't be able to refuse to go with them. Even if they don't, the capital is full of my enemies. We shall still be in danger until we cross the Ashigara Mountains, but I'm sure we can find post horses in the Kantō provinces, since they are friendly to the Genji. Once we are past Shirakawa Barrier, we shall be inside Hidehira's territory. Then let the rain fall and the wind howl! It won't bother us."

"This is terrible!" thought Kichiji. "He doesn't even have a reliable horse or a decent retainer, and yet he talks about finding beasts in provinces belonging to his enemies." Nevertheless he urged the horses on as Shanaō had directed, past Matsusaka, the Shinomiya River Beach, Ōsaka Barrier, Ōtsu Shore, and the Chinese bridge at Seta, until they reached Kagami post station, where the mistress,[10] an acquaintance of long standing, brought out a number of her girls and entertained the travelers in various ways.

---

[10] The woman in charge of the station prostitutes.

Chapter Two

HOW ROBBERS ENTERED KICHIJI'S LODGINGS AT KAGAMI STATION

Since Kagami was close to the capital, Kichiji reluctantly seated Shanaō far back among the courtesans, where he hoped he might pass unobserved. But when the party was well under way the mistress caught hold of the merchant's sleeve. "You travel this road every year or two, but you've never brought along such a fine-looking youth before. Is he a relative or just a stranger?" she asked.

"Neither one," replied Kichiji.

Tears began streaming down her cheeks. "Of course I've seen many sad things in my lifetime," she said, "but just now something in the past has come back to me as if it were yesterday. That young gentleman looks and acts exactly like Lord Tomonaga, the second son of the Chief of the Stables of the Left. Have you coaxed him into coming along with you? Ever since Hōgen and Heiji, the Minamoto sons have been shut away in one place or another. If any of them has an idea of restoring the family fortunes when he grows up, just bring him to me. As the old sayings go, 'Walls have ears and stones mouths,' and 'There is no hiding a safflower, even though it be planted within a garden wall.' "[1]

"No, no, it's nothing of the sort," Kichiji protested. "As a matter of fact, he is a particular friend of mine."

"Have it as you please," retorted the mistress, rising from her seat. She drew the youth by the sleeve to a place of honor, served him wine, and took him off to her own quarters when it grew late. Kichiji, who had drunk a great deal, also retired.

That night an unforeseen thing occurred at Kagami post station.

[1] She means that it is dangerous for a Minamoto to try to hide in the capital area.

It happened to be a year of famine, and Yuri Tarō, a notorious robber chief from Dewa Province, and the Fujisawa Novice,[2] a powerful warrior from Kubiki District in Echigo, had come to an understanding and crossed over together into Shinano, where they had joined forces with Tarō, a son of San Gon-no-kami. With the addition of other well-known brigands, such as Gama Yoichi in Tōtōmi, Okitsu Jūrō in Suruga, and Toyooka Gempachi in Kōzuke, the size of the band had swollen to a total of twenty-five leaders and seventy followers.

"Conditions are miserable on the Tōkaidō," these men said, "but the mountain hamlets are pretty well off. We can count on their rich peasants to supply our boys with decent wine while we're on our way to the capital, and we can start home again through the northern provinces when the autumn winds begin to blow." So they headed toward the capital, pillaging every post station and mountain dwelling in their path.

On this particular night the brigands had taken lodgings next door to the mistress's house at the Kagami station.

"Kichiji, the famous gold merchant from the capital, is stopping tonight at the mistress's establishment on his way to Ōshū with a mixed consignment of trade goods. What shall we do about it?" Yuri Tarō asked Fujisawa.

" 'Hoist a sail when the wind is fair; wield an oar when the current is right,' " replied Fujisawa. "We'll break in, seize the peddler's goods to keep our boys in wine, and be off."

Half a dozen brawny ruffians at once buckled on their corselets and lighted oil-soaked torches, which when held aloft made the surroundings as bright as day. The two leaders were at the head of the band. Yuri wore a green corselet and a green Chinese blouse and knickers, a folded cap tied under his chin, and a sword three and a half feet long. Fujisawa was dressed in a dark blue blouse and knickers, black armor, and a helmet. He was armed with a long halberd and a lacquer-trimmed sword in a scabbard covered with bearskin.

The night was half spent when the robbers stormed into the mistress's house. Quickly they moved through the deserted outer apart-

---

[2] *Nyūdō*, someone who shaves his head, takes Buddhist vows, and assumes monk's attire without formally joining a religious community. In theory such men retired from active life in order to devote their time to pious works.

ments to the inner rooms, slashing at sliding panels with their naked
blades, and swooped down like demon kings upon the astonished
Kichiji. Never dreaming that they wanted only his treasures, Kichiji
leaped from his covers and rushed away. "They've come from Rokuhara to punish me for escorting a Minamoto to Ōshū," he thought.

Shanaō, awakened, saw Kichiji's flight. "It's never safe to rely on
a fellow with no breeding," he said to himself. "Not even the worst
excuse for a warrior would be such a coward. Never mind! I've been
ready to die for my father's sake ever since I left the capital. It might
as well happen at Kagami." He fastened on his corselet over a pair
of flared drawers, took up his sword, and draped a narrowsleeved
robe of figured Chinese brocade over his head. Then he slipped
hastily through a sliding panel into the main room and hid behind
a pair of folded screens to await the arrival of the robbers.

The robbers soon approached, waving their torches and shouting,
"Keep your eyes on Kichiji." Suddenly they were startled by the
sight of a beautiful face behind the screens. In appearance Shanaō
was still the matchless page whose fame had spread from Kurama to
Nara and Mount Hiei. With his dazzlingly white skin, blackened
teeth, thinly penciled brows, and covered head, he seemed no less
fair than Matsura Sayohime, the maiden who waved her scarf on the
moor year after year. His painted, sleep-smudged eyebrows were as
graceful as the wings of a nightingale in flight. In the reign of Emperor Hsüan Tsung, he would certainly have been called Yang Kuei-
fei; in the day of Han Wu Ti, people would have confused him with
Lady Li. The robbers pushed him against the screens and passed on,
taking him for a courtesan.

"I would rather die than have other men despise me," thought
Shanaō. "It would be intolerable if people said later, 'Yoshitomo's
son Ushiwaka didn't dare risk his life against the robbers he met at
Kagami while he was on his way to Ōshū to start a revolt, but now
he's trying to challenge the august Chancellor of State!'[3] How can I
run away?" Out he flew at the intruders and scattered them with his
sword.

"What a bold wench this girl is!" said Yuri Tarō, turning back to
meet Shanaō. He took a step and swung with all his might, meaning
to dispose of him with a single blow. He was a tall man, however, and

[3] Taira Kiyomori.

the blade of his long sword stuck in the ceiling. As he struggled to extricate it, Shanaō struck off his left arm, sleeve and all, with his short sword. With a second blow Shanaō took his head.

"So you've killed him! Face me then!" bellowed the Fujisawa Novice, lunging forward with a flourish of his mighty halberd. Shanaō matched him blow for blow. Fujisawa grasped the halberd at the very end of the handle and deftly shot it ahead, but the adroit Shanaō's superb blade cut it cleanly in two, and before Fujisawa could draw his sword his helmet and face were split wide open.

"See that! He must think me a miserable coward," thought Kichiji as he watched from his hiding place. He hurried into the sleeping alcove, where he fastened on his corselet and untied his hair so that it hung loose. Then he ran with drawn sword into the main courtyard to join Shanaō, waving a torch dropped by one of the robbers. The two laid about them so vigorously that the six robbers still left quickly fell victim to Shanaō's blade. Two of them managed to escape toward the north, nursing wounds, and another also took to his heels, but the three others all were killed.

The next day five heads were hung up on the east wall of the station, with a sign which read: "Behold the proof of the story you will hear! What wayfarer cut down Yuri Tarō of Dewa, the Fujisawa Novice of Echigo, and three others? He was someone linked by karma ties to Kichiji, the gold merchant from Sanjō. This, his first exploit, was performed at the age of sixteen. If you desire further information concerning him, inquire of Tōkōbō at Kurama. Fourth day, second month, fourth year of Shōan." Later, people said to one another incredulously, "One of the Genji must have started on a journey."

Shanaō left Kagami that day, solicitously attended by Kichiji. He passed Ono-no-suribari, Bamba, and Samegai, and at nightfall stopped at Aohaka post station in Mino, where the mistress had once enjoyed Yoshitomo's warm regard. After asking for the grave of his elder brother, he spent the night on the spot intoning the *Lotus Sutra*. The next morning he built a stupa, made an offering of a Sanskrit character written in his own hand, and then continued on his journey. That day, the third of his travels, he reached Atsuta Shrine in Owari, having glimpsed Koyasu Woods in the distance, crossed the

Kuze River, and witnessed the spectacle of the Sunomata River at dawn.

At Atsuta the former chief priest was Yoshitomo's father-in-law and the present chief priest was his brother-in-law. Yoritomo's mother was also living in the vicinity, at a place called Atsuta-no-soto-hama. Because of these family connections, Shanaō instructed Kichiji to make his presence known. The priest at once sent men to escort him to the shrine, where he treated him with the greatest cordiality. Shanaō had planned to set out again on the following day, but his hosts remonstrated with him in every imaginable way, and with one thing and another he remained at Atsuta until the third day after his arrival.

"I don't want to go to Ōshū as a page," Shanaō said to Kichiji. "I should like to arrive with a man's cap on my head— borrowed, if necessary. Will you see what can be done about it?"

The chief priest obtained a cap, put up Shanaō's hair, and placed the cap on his head. Then Shanaō said, "If I go to Ōshū as I am, I'll have to say 'Shanaō' when Hidehira asks my name. There will be nothing to show that I have become a man. Unless my name has already been changed, Hidehira is sure to propose a capping ceremony for me, but it will cause gossip if my ceremony is sponsored by someone whose family have been hereditary retainers of the Minamoto.[4] I want the ceremony to take place here, in the presence of the gods and the mother of Yoritomo."

He purified himself and went before the august divinities, accompanied by the priest and Kichiji. "Akugenda was the first of Yoshitomo's sons, Tomonaga the second, Yoritomo the third, Kaba the fourth, Zenji the fifth, Kyō-no-kimi the sixth, and Akuzenji the seventh,"[5] he said to his companions. "I myself ought to be called Hachirō, the eighth, but I don't want to seem to be trading on the name of my uncle, Chinzei Hachirō, who acquired such a reputation in the Hōgen War. I have no objection to being last, so let me be

---

[4] The sponsor at a capping ceremony was usually someone whose social standing was superior to the youth's.

[5] Comparison with the list in the Introduction reveals numerous inaccuracies here, the most striking of which is that Zenji and Akuzenji are both sobriquets of Yoshitsune's full brother, the monk Zenjō.

known as Sama Kurō.[6] Since my grandfather's name was Tameyoshi, my father's Yoshitomo, and my oldest brother's Yoshihira, let
my true name be Yoshitsune."

So he who the day before had been Shanaō set out from Atsuta
Shrine as Sama Kurō Yoshitsune. He passed along Narumi Beach at
ebb tide, crossed Yatsuhashi Bridge in Mikawa, and beheld Hamana
Bridge in Tōtōmi, but these and other famous places admired by
Narihira and the Yamakage Middle Captain failed to arouse his
admiration. "I would enjoy seeing them if I had no worries, but there
are other things for me to think about now," he thought as he journeyed on. Soon after crossing Utsu Mountain, he arrived at Ukishima Plain in Suruga.

THE MEETING WITH THE MONK OF ANO

From Ukishima Plain Yoshitsune sent a messenger to the Monk of
Ano, who welcomed him with the warmest delight and gazed on him
with tears in his eyes as they talked of the past.

"It is very odd, is it not?" said the monk. "You were only two
years old when we parted, and all this time I have had no idea what
had become of you. Now here you are—a grown man starting out on
a great adventure! It is wonderful to see you. I wish I could go with
you and face the future at your side, but I have already begun to
study the holy doctrines of Śākyamuni, entered a teacher's retreat,
and dyed my three robes black. It would not be right for me to put
on armor and carry weapons. Besides, there is no one else to pray for
our father's happiness and our family's prosperity. Just the same, it is
very upsetting to have to say good-bye before we have been together
even a month. Yoritomo lives at Hōjō in Izu, but his guards are so
strict that I don't ordinarily venture to write to him—I try to be
satisfied with knowing that he isn't far away. You probably won't be
able to see him, so you had better leave a letter with me. I shall make
sure that he gets it." This Yoshitsune did.

That day Yoshitsune progressed as far as the capital of Izu Province, where during the night he prayed fervently: "Hear me, Great
God of Mito, Sōtō Gongen, and Kichijō Komagata! Let me become
the leader of three thousand horsemen. If I don't, may I never go

[6] Sama, which means Stables of the Left, is an allusion to Yoshitomo's official title;
Kurō means ninth son.

westward from these mountains." He was a warlike sixteen-year-old indeed!

At length Yoshitsune reached Takano in Shimotsuke, journeying by way of Ashigara post station and Horikane Well on Musashi Moor, and marking the spot which Narihira's notice has linked forever to his name.[7] That night he was preoccupied with memories of the capital, which had receded farther into the distance with each passing day, while the east had drawn ever closer. By questioning the mistress of the station, he learned that he was in the province of Shimotsuke.

"Is this public land or a private domain?" he asked.

"Shimokōbe Domain."

"Who is the lord?"

"Misasagi Hyōe, the heir of Misasagi-no-suke, who was the maternal great-uncle of the Lesser Counselor Shinzei."

HOW YOSHITSUNE BURNED MISASAGI'S HOUSE

Yoshitsune was reminded of an incident which had occurred at Kurama when, as a boy of nine, he had lain with his head in Tōkōbō's lap.

"What remarkable eyes the child has! Whose son is he?" Misasagi had asked.

"His father was Yoshitomo, the Chief of the Stables of the Left."

"He'll make trouble for the Heike some day. They might as well turn lions and tigers loose on the moors as to let boys like him live. He'll rebel as soon as he grows up. Remember my words, child, and call on me if you ever need warriors. I live in Shimōsa Province at a place called Shimokōbe Domain."

As Yoshitsune recalled the conversation, he suddenly resolved to ask Misasagi for help instead of traveling the long road to Ōshū.

"Wait for me at Muro-no-yashima in Shimotsuke," he told Kichiji. "I shall overtake you after paying a visit." He set out to see Misasagi, while Kichiji reluctantly journeyed on toward Ōshū.

---

[7] Since Yoshitsune appears to have been following the Sumida River, this probably refers to the place beside the river where the homesick Narihira, having been told that a bird on the water was called *miyako dori* [capital bird], is said to have recited, "If Capital Bird be truly your name, let me speak to you—how fares the person of whom I am thinking?" See Appendix B, Ariwara Narihira.

When Yoshitsune had arrived at Misasagi's house, a prosperous establishment with a number of saddled horses tethered beside the gate, he peered inside and saw about fifty men of various ages on duty in the guard station.[8] He beckoned to one of them.

"I should like to see your master."

"Where have you come from?"

"From the capital. I met him there."

The man conveyed this intelligence to Misasagi, who inquired, "What sort of person is the visitor?"

"He's not at all ordinary-looking."

"Very well, ask him to step in."

When Yoshitsune had been conducted inside, Misasagi asked his name.

"Have you forgotten our meeting when I was a child? When I was staying with Tōkōbō at Kurama, you invited me to call on you in case of need, so here I am," said Yoshitsune.

With two grown sons in the service of Taira Shigemori at the capital, Misasagi was by no means disposed to entertain a request which, he thought in dismay, would certainly lead to their deaths. After a moment's anxious deliberation he said, "I am honored that you should have remembered me, but permit me to remind you that you and your brothers, whose lives were forfeited in the Heiji Rebellion, were magnanimously spared by Kiyomori because of his regard for your mother. Although it is true that the old don't always die before the young, I don't think you ought to rebel until Kiyomori is dead."

Much as this reply infuriated Yoshitsune, he could not protest. So the day ended; but late that night he vengefully burned Misasagi's house to the ground and vanished like a ghost. Fearing that a watch might be set for him at Yokota Plain and Muro-no-yashima in Shimotsuke, and at Shirakawa Barrier, he gave free rein to his horse beside the Sumida River, and in a single day the swift beast carried him to Itahana in Kōzuke, a two-day journey.

HOW ISE SABURŌ BECAME YOSHITSUNE'S RETAINER
The day had drawn to a close. Other than a cluster of humble

---

[8] *Tōsaburai (tōsamurai).* Usually located near a gate in a warrior's dwelling compound. It served as a reception office and guard headquarters.

cottages, none of which appeared suitable for a night's lodging, there was no dwelling close at hand, but farther in the distance Yoshitsune perceived a thatch-roofed house with a bamboo fence and cypress doors, such as a man of sensibility might fancy. The flock of fowl beside an artificial pond also seemed to suggest refined tastes. Yoshitsune walked through the courtyard to the edge of the veranda, calling out to make his presence known. When a servant girl of twelve or thirteen appeared to ask his business, he sent her back inside.

"Is there an older person here? If so, have him come out to hear me," he said.

Shortly after the child had gone in, an attractive girl of eighteen or nineteen spoke to him from behind a sliding door. "What do you want?" she asked.

"I have come from the capital to see someone at a place called Tako in this province, but I am a stranger here and it is getting dark. Will you let me spend the night at your house?"

"It would not be any trouble at all, but our master, who is not here just now, is sure to come back later tonight, and he is such an unfriendly man that there is no telling what he might say. For your own sake, I advise you to go somewhere else," she replied.

"If things get awkward, I'll find shelter on the open moor," he promised. As she hesitated, he urged again, "Please let me spend the night here. You who 'recognize color and scent' must surely know what kind of person I am."[9] So saying, he slipped into the guard station.

The puzzled girl withdrew into the house to seek advice from her mistress.

"Even people who merely sip water from the same stream are linked by ties from another life," the lady said. "What is there to worry about? He can't be comfortable in the guard station. Put him in the small room."

Then they offered Yoshitsune fruit, nuts, and wine, all of which he refused.

---

[9] An allusion to a poem by Ki no Tomomori in the first imperial anthology, *Kokinshū* (*ca.* 905): "To whom, if not to you, shall I show these plum blossoms, whose worth can be measured only by one who understands color and scent?" (The author is asking the recipient to recognize his merits and act as his patron.) Yoshitsune means that he is an unusual person, and will be appreciated as such by the lady because she is a woman of discrimination.

"Our master has a shocking temper," the girl warned. "You must not let him know you're here. Put out the lamp and close the doors before you go to sleep, and set off at once when the cock crows."

Yoshitsune promised to do as he was asked. "What makes them so afraid of him?" he wondered. "I have just finished burning down a house belonging to Misasagi, who is a lot tougher than this fellow. I'll use my sword on him if he objects to the hospitality of his women-folk."

Yoshitsune lay waiting as though asleep, with a naked blade below his knees and a sleeve shielding his face. The doors which he had been told to close were wide open, and the wick was raised as high as it would go. As the night waned, his impatience mounted. At last, around one o'clock, the master returned. Yoshitsune watched him fling open the cypress-wood door and pass to the interior of the house. He was a man of about twenty-four or twenty-five, dressed in a green corselet and a pale yellow blouse and knickers woven in a pattern of fallen rush leaves. He wore a sword at his belt and carried an enormous straight-headed spear in his hand. Behind him strode five or six hulking, battle-weary retainers, armed with war axes carved in heart-shaped designs, long-handled cutlasses, halberds, long thick staffs, and metal-reinforced cudgels.

"They look like the Four Heavenly Kings. No wonder the women are nervous," thought Yoshitsune. "That man probably fights like a fiend."

When the master saw that the small room was occupied, he stood glaring at Yoshitsune from the entry stone, sword in hand.

"Come here," commanded Yoshitsune.

Without replying, the man slammed the door violently. He hurried into his wife's chamber.

"He'll begin to abuse her now," thought Yoshitsune, pressing his ear to the wall.

"I say, wife!" roared the master. "Wake up!"

After a moment's silence, a faint voice murmured, "What is the matter?"

"Who is sleeping in the small room?"

"I don't know," she admitted.

"What do you mean by letting a stranger into the house during my absence?" he demanded angrily.

"Now the trouble is starting," thought Yoshitsune.

"It's true that he is a stranger," said the lady. "We didn't know what you would think about our taking him in while you were away, so we refused him at first, even though he pleaded that it had grown dark and he had a long way to go. Then he shamed us by adding, 'You who recognize color and scent must know what I am,' so we let him stay. What possible harm can there be in sheltering him for a single night?"

"My dear, I had always regarded you as a typical obtuse easterner, 'plain as the owls of Shiga Capital.'[10] You showed commendable delicacy by recognizing his allusion and offering him shelter," her husband replied. "I'll take a chance on letting him stay."

"The gods intervened just in time," thought Yoshitsune. "Still, he'd better mind his tongue if he wants to stay out of trouble."

"Our guest must be an unusual chap," the master went on. "I suspect that he's been in some scrape within the last day or two, or the week at any rate. When a man has to hide, it's never easy for him. I'll take him some wine."

He prepared fruit and nuts, ordered the maid to carry in some wine bottles, and went with his wife to the small room, but Yoshitsune refused both food and drink.

"Drink up; there's no need for caution. Although we're plain folk, you'll be well guarded as long as I live. Hey! Where is everybody?" shouted the master.

The men who had reminded Yoshitsune of the Four Heavenly Kings appeared.

"We have a guest who seems to be on his guard. Don't sleep tonight; watch his room for him," ordered the master.

"We understand!" They took up their posts with a great droning of humming bulbs[11] and twanging of bowstrings. The master meanwhile raised the wooden shutters of the reception room, brought out a pair of lampstands, laid his corselet by his side, strung his bow, untied and loosened a bundle of arrows, and placed his sword and dagger under

[10] The text is elliptical and probably corrupt here, and the meaning of the simile is obscure. The capital was located at Ōtsu, in Shiga District, Ōmi, during the reign of Emperor Tenchi (r. 668–71).

[11] *Hikime.* Also called turnip-heads *(kaburaya)*, from their shape. Perforated wooden arrowheads to which metal prongs were attached. They made an eery droning noise in flight. The master's retainers were apparently trying a few shots.

his knees. All night long he sat there awake, roaring, "Who's there? Cut him down!" every time a dog barked in the neighborhood or two branches rubbed together in the wind.

"That fellow is a first-rate fighting man," thought Yoshitsune.

In the morning Yoshitsune prepared to continue on his way, but the master pressed him to remain, and in the end he lingered for two or three days.

"What do they call you in the capital?" his host inquired. "Since I don't know anyone else there, I'll visit you if I ever have the chance. Please stay another day or two." On another occasion he said, "I'll escort you to Usui Pass if you travel by the Tōsendō road, or to Ashigara if you follow the Tōkaidō."

There was, of course, no prospect of Yoshitsune's being in the capital, so it was idle for the master to plan to visit him there.

"This is a trustworthy fellow; it's perfectly safe to tell him who I am," thought Yoshitsune.

"I'm on my way to Ōshū," he said. "I am Ushiwaka, the youngest son of Yoshitomo of Shimotsuke, who died in the Heiji War. For a while I was at school at Kurama, but now I have come of age and taken the name Sama Kurō Yoshitsune, and I am going to Ōshū to ask Hidehira for help. Henceforth you share my secret."

Too overcome to listen further, the master abruptly placed himself in front of Yoshitsune, caught hold of his sleeve, and began to speak of the past and the future, weeping bitterly.

"How could I have known that you were my family's hereditary lord? Do you wonder who I am? My father, Ise Kanrai Yoshitsura, lived at Futami in Ise Province, where he served as a priest at the Grand Shrine. Once, on his way home from a pious visit to Kiyomizu Temple, he failed to dismount before the retinue of the Holy Man of Kujō, and for that crime he was exiled to Narishima in Kōzuke. After some time had passed, he married in order to forget his old home, but he died unpardoned, leaving his wife seven months pregnant. When I was born, my mother wanted to abandon me because she thought I would not have lost my father if I had not been cursed with an evil karma. But one of her brothers made himself responsible for me, and when I reached the age of thirteen the same uncle told me that it was time for my capping ceremony.

" 'Who was my father?' I asked then.

"At first my mother was too upset to answer, but she finally sobbed, 'I think your father came from Futami Coast in Ise. He was an exile named Ise Kanrai Yoshitsura, a man who was held in the very highest esteem by the Chief of the Stables of the Left until a horrible accident brought him to this province. You were conceived here, and he died during my seventh month.'

"My father was called Ise Kanrai, and I am known as Ise Saburō. His personal name was Yoshitsura; mine is Yoshimori. During these years of Taira rule, every last one of the surviving Genji has been driven into hiding. I knew that members of the family were scattered here and there, but I had no way of telling them that I was loyal. This has worried me a great deal. Of course I understand that the bond between lord and vassal lasts for three lives, but I am certain that the Great Bodhisattva Hachiman himself is responsible for our meeting."

The master's relationship with Yoshitsune may have been somewhat tenuous, but from that time forward he served him faithfully. He was none other than the famous Ise Saburō Yoshimori who accompanied Yoshitsune to Ōshū, stuck with him like a shadow after the beginning of the Gempei War in the fourth year of Jishō [1180], and followed him to Ōshū again after he had incurred the displeasure of the Lord of Kamakura.

Yoshimori went into the house and spoke to his wife. "Our mysterious guest is my hereditary lord; I shall have to go with him to Ōshū. Wait for me until next spring. If I am not back by then, feel free to remarry, but please do not forget me," he said.

His wife burst into tears. "I am lonely for you even when you're away on a short trip. If we're going to part while our love is still fresh, it is not likely that I shall ever forget you," she cried. But her laments were in vain; his mind firmly made up, the strong-willed master set out with Yoshitsune.

After journeying within sight of Muro-no-yashima in Shimotsuke, paying his respects to the god of Utsunomiya, and crossing Yukigata Plain, Yoshitsune came to the Adachi moorland, where, it is said, the Middle Captain Sanekata once strung and twanged a locally made bow of untreated spindle wood, reciting with the weapon on his shoulder, "Parting from mere acquaintances is easy, but how regrettable it is to be separated from a dear one!" From there his road

led past such other famous sights as the iris of Asaka Marsh, Asaka
Mountain, "seen in reflection,"[12] and Shinobu Village. Just at dawn,
as he was traversing Atsukashi Mountain in Date District, he heard a
wayfarer ahead.

"It would be amusing to overtake him and ask about this mountain," he thought. "No doubt it is one of the well-known places here-
about."

The second traveler proved to be none other than Kichiji himself,
who, though he had a nine-day headstart, had been spending time in
one place and another, as merchants will. Nothing could have ex-
ceeded the joy with which he beheld Yoshitsune, and Yoshitsune for
his part was well pleased by the reunion.

"How did things go with Misasagi?" asked Kichiji.

"He was untrustworthy, so I burned his house down and came
along here," said Yoshitsune.

"Who is your companion?" continued Kichiji, shrinking at the
thought of such violence.

"He comes from Ashigara in Kōzuke," Yoshitsune replied.

"Since you don't need retainers yet, you'd better forget about them
until you get to Ōshū. This man's deserted wife must be in a pitiful
state of distress. Let him come to you at the proper time." With these
words Kichiji sent Ise Saburō back to Kōzuke to begin the long vigil
which lasted until the fourth year of Jishō [1180].

From then on Yoshitsune traveled constantly. One by one he
passed the Takekuma pines, Abukuma, and other places of renown—
Miyagino Plain, Tsutsuji Hill, Chiga Beach (where he worshiped the
gods), the Atari pine, Magaki Island, Matsushima (once the home of
the holy Kembutsu), Murasaki Shrine (where he pronounced a vow
before the august deity), and the pine of Aneha. Kichiji found shelter
for him in the quarters of the abbot at Kurihara, and himself continued to Hiraizumi.

YOSHITSUNE'S FIRST INTERVIEW WITH HIDEHIRA

Kichiji lost no time in telling Hidehira of Yoshitsune's arrival.
Although the lord chanced to be confined to his bed with a cold, he
summoned his first and second sons, Motoyoshi Kanja Yasuhira and

---

[12] The allusion is to a verse in *Man'yōshū:* "Little did I suppose your heart to be shallow
as the spring whose clear waters reflect Mount Asaka."

Izumi Kanja Motohira. "This explains it! Not long ago I dreamed
that a yellow dove[13] flew into the house, so I have been expecting
word of some kind from the Genji. I'm delighted to hear that Yoshitomo's son is here." Then he asked his sons to help him up, and,
supported on their shoulders, he put on his cap, blouse, and knickers.
"Even though Yoshitsune is young, he is sure to be versed in the polite
accomplishments and schooled in the Five Virtues,"[14] he went on.
"I suppose the place has been neglected during my illness. See that
the garden is trimmed, and leave at once to welcome him, both of
you. Don't be ostentatious about it."

Yasuhira and Motohira hurried off obediently to Kurihara Temple
with 350 mounted men, and Yoshitsune proceeded to Hidehira's
house, escorted by 50 Kurihara monks.

"I am deeply honored that you have made the long journey here,"
said Hidehira. "Heretofore I have never been able to act freely, even
though I control the Two Provinces, but I shall not need to hesitate
any longer." To Yasuhira he added, "Select 360 of my chieftains to
provide a daily guard for our lord. You and your brother may keep
100,000 of my 180,000 retainers; the rest are for His Lordship. So
much for that. Now, how could His Lordship have reached us if
Kichiji had not been with him? We must see that Kichiji is properly
repaid."

Hidehira's eldest son, Yasuhira, presented Kichiji with a hundred
finely tanned hides, a hundred eagle feathers, three rare horses, and
a silver-mounted saddle. The second son, Motohira, produced gifts
of equal value, and the other kinsmen and retainers, not wanting to
be outdone, also pressed offerings upon the merchant.

"You couldn't possibly need any more deerskins or eagles' tail
feathers. Here is something I think you will like." Hidehira, who had
been looking on, brought out a Chinese lacquer box inlaid with shell;
the lid was completely filled with gold dust. Kichiji felt certain that
nothing short of the miraculous power of Tamon could have preserved him from the perils of the journey as Yoshitsune's companion

---

[13] Another *Gikeiki* text has "two white doves." The dove was regarded as Hachiman's
messenger. Since white was the Genji color, a white dove from Hachiman, the Genji
tutelary god, might be expected to symbolize the family.

[14] The five Confucian virtues: kindness, uprightness, propriety, wisdom, and trust-
worthiness.

and, in addition, rewarded him with such rich profits. He returned to the city immediately, thinking, "I have all the capital I need without any bargaining at all."

So the year ended and Yoshitsune became seventeen. More days and months passed, but still Hidehira made no sign. Although Yoshitsune also remained silent, he began to say to himself, "If I were in the capital, at least I could go on with my studies and keep track of the Heike. Since I can't do anything here, I might as well return. But I shall have to leave without telling Hidehira." When he finally departed, it was as if he were going on a brief outing. He rested for a time at Ise Saburō's home, and then he traveled over the Tōsendō to discuss the rebellion with Kiso Kanja; from Kiso's domains he proceeded to the capital, there to observe the state of affairs from the dwelling of an acquaintance in the countryside at Yamashina.

YOSHITSUNE'S VISIT TO ONI-ICHI HŌGEN

Now there was a certain book of sixteen chapters,[15] a work prized by emperors and jealously preserved by great ministers, which made military geniuses of all who mastered its contents, Chinese and Japanese alike. After studying its pages, Lü Shang of China mounted to heaven from the top of an eight-foot wall; Chang Liang, who gave it the name "One-Chapter Book," flew through the air on a bamboo stalk three feet long; and Fan K'uai, clad in armor, made his hair rise straight through the top of his helmet when he wrathfully confronted an enemy with bow and arrow in his hands. In Japan, it enabled Sakanoue Tamuramaro to capture Akuji Takamaro, and Fujiwara Toshihito to subdue the general called Akagashira Shirō. After long neglect, it claimed the attention of Sōma Kojirō Masakado, a rash Shimotsuke warrior who became a traitor to the state. Since

---

[15] The inconsistencies in this paragraph reflect the author's lack of accurate information concerning the secret Chinese military treatises which were jealously guarded by Muromachi owners. "Book of sixteen chapters" refers to *Liu-t'ao*, a late forgery attributed to Lü Shang, which actually contains sixty sections. "Chang Liang's one-chapter book," which appears to be a Japanese invention of around the eleventh century (there is no such Chinese work), is here confused with *Liu-t'ao*, probably because *Liu-t'ao* and *San-lüeh*, the treatise said to have been given to Chang Liang by the Ancient of Huang-Shih (or, alternatively, to have been written by Chang Liang on the basis of information supplied by the Ancient), were traditionally bracketed together as supreme authorities on military matters. The anecdotes about Lü Shang, Chang Liang, and Fan K'uai are not to be found in Chinese sources.

few defy the mandate of heaven with impunity, Tawara Tōda Hidesato, another Shimotsuke chieftain, went east with an imperial commission to subjugate Masakado, and the rebellious forces were destroyed in four years' time. Nevertheless, when Masakado was in his
hour of extremity, he fixed eight arrows to a single bow, released
them simultaneously, and struck down eight enemies, all because he
had studied this text.

The book was later stored among the treasures of successive emperors, unread and useless, but around the time of which I speak, it
was given to Oni-ichi Hōgen, a talented and versatile yin-yang
master[16] who lived at Ichijō Horikawa, as a reward for offering
prayers on behalf of the nation. Yoshitsune learned that it was locked
away in a secret repository at this master's house, and he left Yamashina to pay him a visit.

Although Hōgen lived in the capital, his house was guarded like a
fortress by a moat, eight watchtowers, a bridge which was drawn up
between four and six o'clock every afternoon, and a gate which remained locked until eleven or twelve each morning. Hōgen himself
was a haughty and arrogant man.

As Yoshitsune entered, he noticed a youth of seventeen or eighteen
standing on the veranda of the guard quarters. He beckoned with his
fan.

"What do you want?" the boy asked.

"Do you belong to this house?"

"Yes."

"Is Hōgen at home?"

"Yes."

"Then will you please tell him that an unknown young man wants
to speak to him?"

"Hōgen is exceedingly proud," said the boy. "Even when a
dignitary calls, he sends out one of his sons instead of greeting the
guest himself. He certainly won't grant an interview to anyone like
you."

"You're an odd chap. Do you always answer questions without
consulting your master? Give him my message and then report back."

"As you wish, but it won't do any good."

---

[16] A professional diviner. The text indicates that Oni-ichi was also a Buddhist monk,
bearing the common honorary title Hōgen [Eye of Buddhism].

The youth went inside and knelt before his master. "A queer thing has happened," he reported. "I saw a boy of seventeen or eighteen standing at the gate. He wanted to know if you were at home, and when I said yes, he asked to see you."

"I didn't think anyone in the capital held me so cheaply. Find out whether he's someone's messenger or whether he speaks for himself, and then send him away," replied Hōgen.

"He doesn't look like a retainer, even though he is wearing a blouse and knickers. He's more likely to be a temple page, judging from his black teeth[17] and penciled eyebrows and his gold trimmed sword and expensive corselet. I wonder if he may not be a Genji chieftain, since everyone is predicting that the Minamoto will revolt any day now. Perhaps he has heard so much about you that he wants to make you one of his captains. If you see him, be careful to avoid the word 'recluse,' or you may feel the back of his sword," advised the youth.

"If he is as unusual as all that, I had better meet him," said Hōgen. He strode heavily along the corridor, dressed in a blouse and knickers of raw silk, a scarlet corselet, straw sandals, and a small cap, with a huge halberd clenched in his fist. "Is the person who wishes to speak to me a warrior or someone of lesser status?" he inquired, staring intently at Yoshitsune.

"I am the one," said Yoshitsune. He mounted to the corridor and sat down calmly opposite his disconcerted host, who had expected him to remain on the ground below.

"You're the person who asked to speak to me?" said Hōgen.

"Yes."

"What is your business? Do you want a bow or some arrows?"

"I wouldn't be likely to come on an errand like that. Is it true that the court has given you a Chinese military treatise called *Liu-t'ao*, which Masakado once studied? It's not right for *Liu-t'ao* to be kept locked up. At any rate, even though you own it, what good is it if you can't read it? Please don't take it amiss if I ask to see it. I will read it in a single day and explain it to you when I give it back."

Hōgen flew into a rage. "Who is responsible for sending this fellow through my gate? He's the worst rascal in the entire city!" he bellowed.

17 See Chapter Five, note 6.

"Detestable wretch!" thought Yoshitsune. "It's not enough for him to refuse—he has to call me names too. Why do I wear a sword? I'll use it on him." But on further reflection he determined to spare him. "Since he and I could be called teacher and disciple, even though we haven't read a single word together, the gods might be angry if I harmed him. Besides, I can find out where he keeps *Liu-t'ao* if I let him live," he said to himself. Hōgen was fortunate indeed!

Yoshitsune loitered quietly about the premises during the days that followed. He showed no signs of being hungry, though no one saw him eat, and he appeared each day in a dazzling new costume, to the bewilderment of Hōgen's people, who little knew that he visited the Holy Man of Shijō every night. Gradually he became acquainted with one of the members of the household, a humble but kindhearted woman called Kōju, who was never too busy to help him. One day while he was talking with her, he asked what Hōgen had been saying about him recently.

"Nothing at all," she replied.

"He must say something."

"He's told us to ignore your comings and goings, and not to mention you to anyone else."

"He distrusts me; that's clear enough. By the way, how many children has he?"

"Two sons and three daughters."

"Are the sons at home?"

"They are captains in a band of rock fighters[18] at a place called Haya."

"Where are the three daughters?"

"They're living in various places, well married."

"Who are their husbands?"

"The oldest is married to the Taira Consultant, Lord Nobunari, and another is the wife of the Torikai Middle Captain."

"It's a mistake for a person of Hōgen's class to take nobles as sons-in-law. They would never avenge him if his highhanded and foolhardy behavior exposed him to an insult. Tell him he would be better

[18] *Inji.* The term *inji* originally meant fighting with rocks, which was considered to be one kind of military skill. It was applied to mock rock-throwing battles, staged during the fifth month on the shores of the Kamo River or a similar place (a common custom from the late Heian period on), and, later, to the unemployed ruffians who participated in such engagements.

off as the father-in-law of someone like me who would protect his honor."

"He would cut off the head of any one who said such a thing, man or woman."

"You and I would not have met like this if we had not known each other in a previous existence, and there is no reason to hide my name from you, though it is a secret. I am Gen Kurō, the son of the Chief of the Stables of the Left, and I mean to get hold of the military treatise called *Liu-t'ao*, whether Hōgen likes it or not. Tell me where it is."

"How should I know? I've heard that it's Hōgen's most cherished possession."

"Then what's to be done?"

"If you'll write a letter," she offered, "I'll do my best to coax an answer from Hōgen's youngest and favorite daughter—the one who's still unmarried. No woman can resist the temptation to read a message from a suitor."

Yoshitsune composed the letter, thinking that Kōju had shown a rare sensibility, however inferior her position; and by means of various persuasions the good woman obtained an answer from her mistress. After that Yoshitsune hid himself in the lady's apartments instead of going to Hōgen's personal quarters.

"What a relief!" exclaimed Hōgen. "He's disappeared, just as I was wishing he would go where I would never see or hear of him again."

Meanwhile Yoshitsune said to the daughter, "I don't like having to behave furtively. We can't go on like this forever. Please tell Hōgen." She burst into frightened tears and clung to his sleeve. "I want to see *Liu-t'ao*," he went on. "If you won't tell your father about us, can't you at least show me the book?"

"Father would kill me if he found out," she thought. Nevertheless she went with Kōju to Hōgen's secret treasury, removed the single scroll in its metal-bound Chinese box, and took it to Yoshitsune, who unwrapped and examined it with the greatest delight. By copying throughout the day and reviewing throughout the night, he committed every character to memory between the beginning of the seventh month and the tenth day of the eleventh month. After that he began to move about freely, and soon attracted Hōgen's notice.

"It's bad enough for the fellow to be here at all. Why must he hang around my daughter's quarters?" Hōgen complained.

"People say that the person visiting Her Ladyship is a son of the Chief of the Stables of the Left," someone suggested.

"What would the Taira do if I let my daughter marry a Genji— someone supposedly living in retirement?" thought Hōgen. "Although he might be my son in this life, he would be my enemy in the next. Nothing would please me better than to cut off his head." Filicide was a violation of the Five Prohibitions,[19] he reflected. "But he isn't related to me by birth. Why shouldn't I earn a reward by killing him and taking his head to the Taira?"

As a man of religion, he could not defile himself by taking a life. Casting about for a stouthearted deputy, he decided to approach Tankai, a famous warrior from Kitashirakawa who chanced to be both his brother-in-law and his disciple. He summoned Tankai by messenger, ushered him into a private room, and entertained him cordially.

"I asked you to come because I cannot continue to show hospitality to a young lord who has been hanging around my house since last spring—a son of Yoshitomo of Shimotsuke. You're the only one who can get rid of him for me. If you will be at Gojō Tenjin Shrine tonight, I shall see that he goes there. Your reward for his head will be *Liu-t'ao,* the military treatise you have wanted for the last five or six years," he said.

"Agreed," said Tankai. "I'll go; you can count on it. How shall I know him?"

"He is still a boy—about seventeen or eighteen, I should say. He wears a fine corselet and a magnificent gold-fitted sword. Be on your guard," said Hōgen.

"It makes no difference to me if some fellow carries a sword that's too good for him. I won't need to strike a single blow in earnest," boasted Tankai as he left.

In the past, Hōgen had not even permitted Yoshitsune's name to be mentioned in his hearing, but now, vastly pleased with himself, he sent a man to summon him. Yoshitsune replied by the same messen-

---

[19] The five Buddhist sins are patricide, matricide, shedding the blood of a buddha, killing a person who has attained enlightenment, and preventing monks from living together amicably. Filicide is not one of them.

ger that he would come at once. "I haven't anything to gain by going, but I don't want to look like a coward," he thought.

Hōgen put on a monk's scarf over a silk robe, placed a copy of the *Lotus Sutra* on a desk in his reception room, and in high spirits began to intone solemnly from the first scroll, "Hail to the Lotus of the Wonderful Law!" As he was thus engaged, Yoshitsune entered unannounced. Hōgen called him close, drew up his knee informally, and sat face to face with him.

"I have known since last spring that you were here, but I took you for a vagrant," Hōgen said. "I am astounded to learn that you are the son of His Excellency the Chief of the Stables of the Left. I can't picture you very well as the son-in-law of a mere monk, but if you succeed in the capital I place myself completely in your hands. By the way, may I ask you to dispose of a fellow at Kitashirakawa called Tankai, who's nursing a senseless grudge against me? I happen to know that he'll be at Gojō Tenjin Shrine tonight. I should be infinitely obliged if you would go there, put him to the sword, and bring me his head."

Yoshitsune concealed his surprise. "Gladly," he assented. "It sounds like a big job, but I will be happy to do it for you. He won't give me much trouble, even though he's probably a good rock fighter. I'll visit Tenjin first and cut off his head on my way out, just like the wind stirring up a little dust."

Hōgen permitted himself a secret smile. "However elaborate your precautions, they won't do you any good against a forewarned adversary," he thought.

"I'll be back soon," promised Yoshitsune.

Although Yoshitsune had intended to go direct to Tenjin, he found himself entering the apartments of Hōgen's daughter, to whom he had grown deeply attached.

"I'm on my way to Tenjin," he told her.

"Why?"

"Hōgen wants me to kill Tankai for him."

She began to sob bitterly. "This is terrible! My father is trying to kill you. I can't tell you more without being a bad daughter, but if I don't say anything I shall be making lies of all my pledges to you and losing you forever. After all, the marriage bond lasts for two lives, but a parent and his child never see each other again. I couldn't live

without you for an instant. I'll have to tell you even if my father dies
for it... Get away from here, no matter where you have to go.
Yesterday around noon my father called Tankai in, gave him wine to
drink, and talked very strangely. 'He's a stout youth,' Father said.
'It won't take a single blow in earnest,' Tankai answered. Of course
they meant you! You may suspect my honesty, but 'A loyal minister
does not serve two lords, nor a faithful wife wed twice.' ''[20] She wept
quietly, with her sleeve pressed to her face.

"It might have been awkward if I hadn't been warned," said
Yoshitsune, "but the scoundrel will have a hard time killing me now.
Good-bye."

It was late on the night of the twenty-seventh of the twelfth month
when Yoshitsune took his leave. He was dressed in two narrow-sleeved
white undergarments, a robe decorated with an indigo-rubbed
design, a pair of flaring drawers made of fine raw silk, a corselet, and
a blouse and knickers of Chinese silk. His sword hung at his side. The
distracted lady prostrated herself in the doorway with a cloak over
her head, despairing of ever seeing him again.

Within a short time he was kneeling at the shrine. "Hail, all-
merciful heavenly gods!" he prayed. "In this holy place, they say,
people are granted divine favors, good fortune, and the fulfillment of
all their wishes. Heavenly gods of this shrine, deliver Tankai into my
hands!"

He walked in a southerly direction about fifty yards to a large tree,
in whose dense shade five or six men could be concealed.

"This is a good spot," he decided. "I shall wait here to kill him."

While he was biding his time there, sword in hand, Tankai came
into sight followed by several ruffians. The famous outlaw captain
had taken pains to look his most dashing: he wore a black blouse and
knickers surmounted by a corselet dyed in a meandering pattern of
white, pale blue, and scarlet, and he carried a gold-trimmed sword,
a great naked halberd, and a foot-long dagger encased in a scabbard
the color of persimmon, ornamented with a tiny white design. The
stubbly growth on his unshaven monk's pate was covered by a small
black Buddhist cap.

Bending forward for a better look, Yoshitsune found a tempting
target in Tankai's unprotected neck. He began to plan his attack,

[20] A tag from *Shih chi*.

while the unsuspecting Tankai walked directly toward him, praying, "All-merciful heavenly gods, let me kill the man Hōgen told me about."

"Little does the great fighter know that death is staring him in the face," Yoshitsune exulted. "Now is the time to cut him down! But wait—since he is praying to the same gods I'm depending on, perhaps I ought to hold off awhile. My prayer is finished, but he's still on his way to the shrine. The gods might be angry if I shed a man's blood in these sacred precincts before he had finished his devotions. I'll wait until he's leaving." As he awaited his enemy's return, the time seemed longer than the thousand generations since the pine sprouts of Settsu first took root.[21]

Meanwhile Tankai had failed to find Yoshitsune at Tenjin. "Has a young man of good family been here?" he inquired casually of a monk at the shrine.[22]

"Someone like that came and went some time ago," replied the monk.

"If I had got here earlier I wouldn't have missed him," said Tankai peevishly. "He must be back at Hōgen's house. I'll drag him out and kill him." He left the shrine with his seven followers, who marched along behind chorusing, "Yes, that's the best plan."

"At last!" thought Yoshitsune in his ambush. But when Tankai was barely ten yards away one of his men, a monk named Zenji, spoke up.

"Yoshitomo's son Yoshitsune is very friendly with Hōgen's daughter. When a woman is in love with a man she lets him dominate her completely. If she has heard of our plans and told him, he may be waiting under a tree just like that one. Keep your eye on it."

"Don't get excited," admonished Tankai. "All right then, let's call out. If he has any backbone he won't hide; if he's a coward he won't dare to face us."

"I'll wait until they challenge me," thought Yoshitsune.

Tankai uttered a derisive shout. "Has a Genji outcast come here from Imadegawa?"

[21] Sumiyoshi in Settsu is famous for its magnificent old pines. There is a pun here on *matsu*, which means both "pine tree" and "wait."

[22] Because of a prevailing tendency to fuse Shinto and Buddhist beliefs, Buddhist monks were frequently attached to Shinto shrines.

Yoshitsune flew at them with a roar, waving his sword. "Am I wrong in taking you for Tankai? I am Yoshitsune."

Forgetting all their bold plans, the rock fighters scattered in every direction. Tankai himself retreated about twenty-five yards before he straightened his halberd and rallied his men. "Live or die, a warrior's greatest shame is cowardice!" he cried.

Yoshitsune rushed toward Tankai, wielding his short sword with the speed of lightning. The outmatched Tankai fought back desperately with his halberd, but Yoshitsune seized upon a momentary opening to slash it in two at the handle. Then, as Tankai threw the weapon at him, he darted in and struck at Tankai's head with the tip of his sword. The head dropped to the ground, and thus Tankai perished at the age of thirty-eight.

As the wine-loving *shōjō* is tied up beside a cask,[23] so the wicked Tankai died of an evil alliance. When Tankai's five henchmen saw what had happened, they took to their heels at once. "If a mighty warrior like Tankai has suffered such a fate, how can we possibly do any better?" they said.

"I won't spare one of you," cried Yoshitsune. "Didn't you swear to share Tankai's lot when you started out? Come back and fight, you cowards!" The sound of his voice only served to make them run faster, but he managed to corner and kill two. The others escaped.

After gathering up the three heads, Yoshitsune recited buddha-invocations[24] under a cedar tree at the shrine, meanwhile trying to decide what to do with his trophies. "Hōgen made a great point of asking to see Tankai's head," he recalled. "I'll surprise him."

When Yoshitsune reached Hōgen's house with the three heads impaled on his sword, he found the gate locked and the bridge withdrawn. Knowing that there was small chance of gaining admittance by shouting his name, he leaped the ten-foot moat and scaled the eight-foot wall as lightly as a bird skimming the treetops. Inside, all the watchmen were asleep. He ascended to a corridor from where he could see Hōgen, poring over the middle of the second scroll of the

---

[23] Apparently a proverb which has not survived. The *shōjō*, defined in modern dictionaries as a chimpanzee or orangutan, was in ancient Chinese literature a sea-dwelling animal with a human face and a weakness for strong drink.

[24] *Nembutsu.* Pronouncing the name of Amida Buddha in order to attain rebirth in the Pure Land (Amida's Paradise). Here Yoshitsune is reciting on behalf of the slain men.

Lotus Sutra with the aid of a dim light. Hōgen was in fact gazing at the ceiling, pondering the ephemeral nature of human existence. "Yoshitsune, who was so eager to read *Liu-t'ao*, is about to be killed by Tankai without having seen a single word of it. Hail, Amida Buddha!"

Only the thought of Hōgen's daughter prevented Yoshitsune from striking him with the back of his sword.

Yoshitsune, as a warrior, did not wish to be guilty of eavesdropping. Suppressing an impulse to enter the house, he returned to the gate with the heads. "Is anyone inside?" he called from the cover of a mandarin orange tree.

"Who is it?" came the reply.

"Yoshitsune. Open up here."

"Something must have gone wrong," the voice said. "We were expecting Tankai. Shall we let him in?"

They were bustling about, running to open the gate and lower the bridge, when Yoshitsune suddenly appeared on top of the wall, clutching the three heads. As they shrank back in horror, he strode into the house and tossed the heads onto Hōgen's lap. "The job was almost too much for me, but since you were so anxious to see Tankai's head, here it is," he said.

Hōgen was far from pleased, but he felt obliged to thank him. "It was very good of you," he murmured, his sour face contradicting his words. "Delighted," he said again, and at once retired to an inner room.

Though Yoshitsune would have liked to linger for the remainder of the night, he took leave of the lady to go to Yamashina. The sorrow of parting brought tears to his eyes, while she for her part lay prostrate where he had left her, sobbing piteously.

Try as she might, Hōgen's daughter could not forget Yoshitsune. When she slept, he visited her dreams; when she was awake, memories of him crowded into her mind. Her all-consuming love finally became insupportable, and late in the winter she fell ill—crushed under the burden of her passion, one must suppose, although people said that she was possessed by a spirit. Despite prayers and medication of every description, she died of a broken heart in her sixteenth year.

Thus Hōgen suffered one blow upon another. His beloved daughter was lost, his trusted disciple was killed, and he was on bad terms with Yoshitsune, who would very likely become a general some day. Indeed, there were countless things to cause him grief, but, as the saying goes, "Regret never precedes indiscretion." People ought to treat one another kindly in this world.

Chapter Three

THE SHOCKING BEHAVIOR OF THE KUMANO ABBOT

Among Yoshitsune's retainers there was an incomparable warrior known as Saitō Musashibō Benkei, the son and heir of the Kumano Abbot Benshō, who was a descendent of the Middle Regent Tōryū, of the august line of Amatsukoyane. Benkei's birth came about in this manner.

It happened that there was a person called the Great Counselor of Second Rank, whose many sons had all predeceased him. Late in life, this Great Counselor became the father of a daughter so beautiful that one high noble after another begged to be allowed to wed her. At first the father rebuffed them all impartially, but the Minister of State Moronaga presented his case with such exquisite tact that the Counselor finally agreed to accept him as a son-in-law. "This is a year in which I must be very cautious. I must not let my daughter become the bride of a man living to the east. You shall have her in the spring of next year," he promised.

On a certain occasion during the summer of that year, while the fifteen-year-old maiden was keeping a nightlong vigil at Gojō Tenjin Shrine to offer a petition of some sort, a sudden gust of wind from the southeast seemed to envelop her body, and from that instant her wits were disordered.

"Heal this illness," prayed the Great Counselor and Moronaga, who were both devout worshipers of the gods of Kumano. "If our request is granted, the lady will journey to Kumano next spring, and she will also offer prayers of thanksgiving at each of the Kumano Ōji shrines."

The maiden promptly recovered. The following spring, she set out to fulfill the vow, duly visiting the Three Shrines with an escort of one hundred pilgrims provided by her father and Moronaga. Late one evening, as she was praying in the sanctuary of the Main Shrine, the abbot chanced to enter. A slight rustling sound made her glance toward the inner sanctum.

"The abbot has come in," someone explained.

Although the abbot was a virtuous ascetic, one glimpse of the maiden in the dim lamplight was enough to make him stop reciting the repentance rites and hurry back to his quarters. Calling the monks together, he asked, "Who was that?"

"The daughter of the Great Counselor of Second Rank and wife of the Minister of the Right," one of them answered.

"As far as I know, the Counselor's daughter is only betrothed to the Minister. They are not married yet," said the abbot. "Here is your chance, you monks who are always saying, 'If only we could have an emergency at Kumano, then everyone would see how much the abbot trusts us and how loyally we support him!' Go out dressed in your armor, drive away the pilgrims at a strategic place, and capture the girl. She shall be my cherished page."

"That would be a violation of Buddhist and secular law," they protested.

"Don't be such cowards! The Counselor and Moronaga will complain to the ex-Emperor, and we shall undoubtedly be attacked by a Ki'nai force under Moronaga's leadership, but no enemy must set foot on the soil of the New Shrine or Kumano!"[1] retorted the abbot.

In the past, the abbot had been unable even with his most earnest pleas to restrain his impetuous monks. Now he was himself urging them on! They snatched up weapons and armor, rushed down the hill to await the pilgrims, and then attacked with shrieks and cries. The warriors, usually so jealous of their honor, took to their heels in panic.

The monks carried the maiden to the monastery in her litter, and the abbot installed her in the temple office. "All kinds of people come to pray near my own quarters. It would be unfortunate if pilgrims from the capital saw her," he said. The two remained in seclusion together day and night, while the monks zealously mounted guard against possible attackers.

[1] Here Kumano means the Kumano Main Shrine. See Appendix B, Kumano.

Meanwhile the maiden's attendants, unable to retaliate by themselves, galloped back to inform the Minister of the Right, who went to the ex-Emperor's palace in a great rage to ask for justice. The ex-Emperor at once named Moronaga and the Great Counselor as the joint commanders of 7,000 local warriors from Izumi, Kawachi, Iga, and Ise. "Expel the abbot and appoint a layman in his place," he commanded.

The 7,000 advanced toward Kumano and launched an attack, but the embattled monks fought back so stoutly that the court warriors quickly grew discouraged. From a camp at Kiribe-no-ōji they dispatched a courier to the city.

"We cannot press the monks too hard," said the court nobles who met to consider the matter. "It would be a sad thing for the nation if this quarrel resulted in the destruction of Kumano. The Minister of the Right would feel better if we gave him Hei Saishō Nobunari's beautiful daughter, who was summoned to the palace by an earlier council of nobles, and the Kumano abbot would be a perfectly good son-in-law for the Great Counselor of Second Rank—after all, he is a remote descendent of Amatsukoyane and the Middle Chancellor Tōryū. There would be no reason for the Counselor to complain."

When a courier was sent to Kiribe no-ōji to announce the findings of the courtiers, the Minister of the Right said, "Nobody can challenge the decree of a council of nobles." Abandoning the quarrel, he prepared to return to the capital in company with the Great Counselor, who said, "It is useless for me to keep on by myself."

It was in this manner that peace returned to the capital and Kumano. Afterward the warrior-monks boasted disdainfully, "Why should we obey imperial commands?"

So the lady remained at Kumano, until to his boundless delight the sixty-one-year-old abbot begot a child. "If it is a boy, I shall make him a monk and let him be the abbot," he said.

Days and months of waiting followed. Not only did the child fail to appear at the expiration of the normal period, but it remained in the womb until the eighteenth month.

BENKEI'S BIRTH

The abbot, who had been greatly disturbed by the late arrival of his son, sent someone to the lying-in place to examine him.

"He is as big as most children of two or three. His hair covers his shoulders, and he has enormous teeth—molars, incisors, and all," reported the messenger.

"He must be a devil. He will be an enemy of Buddhism if we keep him. Tie him up and drown him, or crucify him deep in the mountains," directed the abbot.

"No matter what he may be, I have always been told that the bond between a parent and his child lasts for more than one life. How could anyone be so heartless as to kill his own baby?" lamented the mother.

Just then the abbot was visited by his younger sister, the wife of a man called Yamanoi-no-sammi. "What is so queer about the child?" she asked.

"The human gestation period is never less than nine months or more than ten, but this monster stayed in the womb for eighteen. He will be the destruction of his parents if he is spared. We cannot afford to be sentimental," replied the abbot.

"Parents don't need to fear a child just because his gestation period was long," said the baby's aunt. "Huang-shih of China stayed in the womb for eighty years and had snow-white hair when he was born. He was an odd, stunted, dark-faced man who lived for two hundred eighty years, but all the same he is worshiped as the divine messenger of the Great Bodhisattva Hachiman. Give me the boy to take back to the capital. If he turns out well I shall make a proper man of him for Sammi; if he proves troublesome he can be a monk."

This proposal impressed the abbot as reasonable, and he therefore agreed to relinquish the child to his sister. She went to the lying-in place, bathed the baby for the first time, christened him Oniwaka, and on the day following the fiftieth-day ceremony[2] took him with her to the capital, where she reared him carefully with the assistance of a nurse.

At the age of five, Oniwaka resembled an ordinary lad of twelve or thirteen. In his sixth year he suffered an attack of smallpox. His aunt, contemplating his scarred, swarthy complexion and unkempt, shoulder-length hair, said to herself, "With that kind of face and hair, he'll never look like anything. I had better make him a monk." She took

---

[2] *Ika [no iwai]*, a ritual inaugurated during the Heian period. The baby boy was fed a special kind of cake by his father or grandfather on the fiftieth day after his birth.

him to a learned and venerable prelate in the Western Compound of Mount Hiei, known as the Bishop of Sakuramoto. "I should like you to educate this boy, whom I have thought of as a possible adopted son for Lord Sammi. He is so ugly that it embarrasses me to bring him, but his mind is quick enough. Won't you teach him to read, even if it's only a single chapter of one sutra? Please correct any faults you may notice in him, and in general treat him exactly as you think best," she said.

As the days and months passed in diligent study at Sakuramoto, Oniwaka showed himself to be an exceptional scholar. "No matter how ugly someone's face may be, it's what he knows that counts," the monks assured him.

There would have been no trouble if Oniwaka had devoted himself seriously to intellectual pursuits, but he was a strong, powerfully built youth, who liked nothing better than to persuade a group of pages and young monks to play wrestling games with him behind a deserted building or in a remote area of the mountain. Once the monks learned of these activities, they complained unceasingly to the bishop. "If Oniwaka wants to waste time, it's his own affair, but he has no business corrupting other people's disciples," they said.

Oniwaka, regarding such critics as his enemies, would burst violently into their quarters to smash the shutters and doors. There seemed no way of moderating his excesses, since no one cared to offend the son of the Kumano abbot, the foster son of Lord Yamanoi, the grandson of the Great Counselor of Second Rank, and the disciple of the chief scholar of the entire temple. As a result, he was continually embroiled in quarrels of his own making. A man going from one place to another would detour to avoid his fists, or step aside hurriedly if he chanced to encounter him. Oniwaka would permit the wayfarer to proceed unchallenged, but on meeting him again would collar him and ask, "Why did you turn away on the path the other day? Do you bear me a grudge, fellow?" Then as his unfortunate victim's knees quaked with fear, he would twist his arm painfully, or punch him brutally in the chest.

"Bishop's page or no, he has created a problem that affects us all," the monks said, meeting in council. Three hundred of them went off to wait upon the retired Emperor.

"Get rid of the rascal as fast as you can," His Majesty commanded.

The monks returned to Mount Hiei in high spirits, but soon a council of nobles was convened, in the course of which an old diary was shown to contain the words, "An eccentric person will make his appearance on Mount Hiei sixty-one years from now, and there will be official prayers because of him. If he is disciplined by an ex-Emperor's decree, the nation's fifty-four great imperial-vow temples[3] will vanish in a day." That year being the sixty-first, it was decided to let Oniwaka stay.

"So Oniwaka is more important than 3,000 monks! This is preposterous! Let us take out the sacred car of Sannō," said the monks. The court was able to quiet them only by presenting lands to the shrine.

In spite of the monks' efforts to keep all this from coming to Oniwaka's knowledge, someone must have been thoughtless enough to tell him. In his resentment he behaved even more outrageously than before, until the bishop despaired utterly of controlling him. "If he is here, all right; if he is not, that's all right too," he shrugged.

BENKEI'S DEPARTURE FROM ENRYAKUJI TEMPLE

When Oniwaka learned that the bishop had turned against him, he left Enryakuji Temple. "What's the use of staying at Mount Hiei if even my teacher dislikes me?" he said to himself. "I'll disappear somewhere. As things are now, wherever I go people will say, 'That's Oniwaka from Enryakuji Temple.' There's nothing wrong with my education. I'll make my way in the world as a monk." Seizing his razor and cassock, he ran to the bathroom of a man called Mimasaka-no-jibukyō, where he washed his hair in a tub and wielded the razor until the reflection of his head in the water was as round as a ball.

"I can't stop with this. I'll have to have a proper monk's name," he then determined.

Long ago Enryakuji Temple had harbored a wild monk known as Saitō Musashibō, who, it was said, had sat erect and achieved rebirth on his deathbed at the age of sixty-one, after a career of violence extending back to his twenty-first year. Hoping to become a great warrior by adopting the same name, Oniwaka resolved that he would be known in the future as Saitō Musashibō. For his true name

[3]Temples erected to fulfil vows sworn by emperors or empresses.

he settled on Benkei, a combination of elements from the names of his father, the abbot Benshō, and his teacher, Kankei.

So yesterday's Oniwaka became today's Musashibō Benkei. For awhile he took it upon himself to practice austerities in a deserted building at Ohara-no-bessho, a place frequented occasionally by Hiei monks; but since his appearance and manner had always been unattractive, even during his days as a page, no one offered him sustenance, much less came to call on him, and very shortly he wandered off in disgust, with the notion of traveling from province to province as a pilgrim.*b* Late in the first month of his travels he found himself in Awa.

THE FIRE AT MOUNT SHOSHA

From Awa, Benkei crossed to Harima to visit Mount Shosha and pay his respects to the portrait of the holy Shōgū. As he was just about to travel on, he decided to remain for the summer retreat, an annual occurrence which drew throngs of devout ascetics from every province. Ordinary monks assembled in the head teacher's quarters on the mountain, while wandering ascetics withdrew to an area of their own to practice austerities. According to regulations, the teacher's quarters could be entered only after preliminary instruction at the Kokūzō Hall; Benkei, however, forced his way to the threshold and stood glaring belligerently.

"I don't believe you were here yesterday or the day before. Where is your home temple?" asked the teacher.

"Mount Hiei," said Benkei.

"What part of the mountain?"

"Sakuramoto."

"Are you one of the bishop's disciples?"

"Yes."

"What was your lay name?"

"I am the son of the Kumano abbot, a descendent of the Middle Chancellor Tōryū, of the line of Amatsukoyane," Benkei replied haughtily.

In spite of this inauspicious beginning, Benkei performed his rites so faithfully during the retreat that the monks were astonished. "He is very friendly and good natured—not at all as he seemed at first," they said.

Benkei had intended to resume his pious rounds in early autumn after the end of the retreat, but he lingered on for a time, reluctant to leave. Late in the seventh month, he finally said to himself, "I can't stay here forever," and went to say good-bye to the teacher. It chanced that some pages and monks were holding a lively party. "I'd better not go in now," he said, turning away. "I'll take a nap."

As he slept, stretched out beside a new sliding panel, one of the Shosha monks, a quarrelsome fellow called Shinanobō Kaien, passed by. "I have never seen such an unpleasant wandering monk as that one. If I do something to embarrass him, perhaps he will leave," Kaien thought. Rubbing ink on his stone, he wrote two rows of characters on Benkei's face. One said, "Rain clogs," the other, "Rain clogs for Shosha monks." Then he added a verse:

> Benkei's turned into a pair of low clogs.
> Even if you put your feet on him,
> You don't get any higher.[4]

That done, Kaien called together twenty or so junior monks and persuaded them to beat on the wooden wall and laugh uproariously.

Benkei awoke, thinking, "I should have chosen a quieter place." Straightening his sleeves, he got up to join the noisy group. Immediately on seeing him, they burst into laughter and began exchanging significant glances. At first Benkei grinned amiably. "They seem to find something very amusing," he thought. "I don't know what it is, but they'll be offended if I don't laugh."

The continued odd behavior of his companions began to arouse his suspicion, however. "What's the joke?" he demanded crossly, drawing up one knee and clenching his fists.

"He's very angry. This could mean trouble for the temple," whispered the chief teacher. "It's nothing at all," he assured Benkei. "It has nothing to do with you. They were laughing at something else. It's nothing at all."

Benkei left the room and walked some one hundred yards to the quarters of a monk called the Deacon of Tajima, a place where wandering monks often assembled. There also, to his bewilderment,

---

[4] The last line also means "He won't get up."

everyone began to smile. At last, catching a glimpse of himself in a pool of water, he discovered the writing on his face.

"What the devil!" he exclaimed. "I must get away. I can't stay here after being made a fool of. Still," he reflected, "it would be terrible if I were the one to stain Mount Hiei's reputation. Before I leave, I must wipe out my disgrace by telling these people what I think of them and beating up anybody who tries to stop me." So saying, he set off on a tour of the monks' living quarters, stopping to abuse each monk in a scandalous manner.

"The monks of Shosha are being humiliated," the teacher said. "We must hold a meeting about this. If any of our brothers is at fault, we had better turn him over to Benkei before something dreadful happens."

A conference was duly convened in the Lecture Hall, but Benkei declined to attend, persisting in his refusal even after the teacher had sent a venerable monk expressly to fetch him. When the summons was repeated, he climbed a hill to the east to reconnoiter. Behind the hall, there appeared a monk of about twenty-two, wearing blue and white armor under his robes.

"What is this all about?" Benkei wondered. "They told me there would be a friendly discussion today, but I don't like that fellow's looks. I have heard that when a temple monk does something wrong they simply tell him to repent, but if the wrongdoer is a wandering ascetic they demote him. I shall be powerless if I go out in these clothes and let them surround me. I must prepare myself." Ignoring a shouted challenge, he hastened to break into a forbidden storeroom in the teacher's compound; he dragged out a Chinese chest and found inside a dark blue blouse and knickers and a black corselet. He put these on, tied a soft cap on his head, which had not been shaved for ninety days, and took up a staff of peeled yew, octagonal in shape except for a foot-long rounded section at the base, which was so heavy that he was obliged to drag it behind him. He slipped his feet into a pair of high clogs and hurried off to show himself in front of one of the temple buildings.

"Who is that?" the monks asked one another.[5]

"He must be an outlaw monk."

[5] They fail to recognize Benkei at first.

"Look at the way he's dressed! Shall we call out to him or leave him alone?"

"Whatever we do, he looks dangerous."

"Let's pretend not to notice him."

"I can't understand it," said Benkei, perplexed. "I expected them to ask my business, but instead they all seem to be avoiding my eye. Who knows what people may be saying about me at the meeting while I'm outside? I'd better listen." He hurried over to the Lecture Hall, where some three hundred senior monks and pages were crowded together inside the building, while the lesser orders thronged the corridors. The entire temple community of a thousand persons had come rushing pellmell to the convocation.

Benkei strode noisily forward without a word of apology, trampling on the shoulders and knees of the monks, who submitted to this without a word. "He may start a fight if we object," they thought. At the foot of the stairs, where there was a tremendous array of footgear, he decided against removing his clogs. "It will be safer to wear them," he told himself. Up he went, clattering loudly.

"Saying something will only make things worse," the monks whispered. "After all, we're no match for him." Gradually they shrank back toward the side gate.

At the sight of Benkei, still in the clogs, stalking back and forth along the threshold, the teacher was indignant. "What a disgraceful exhibition! This temple was founded by the holy Shōgū. How dare you walk fully shod beside its respected monks and young pages?"

Benkei stepped back. "You are quite right," he said. "You monks think it's shocking to wear clogs on a veranda—then why did you trample on the face of a wandering ascetic?" This was so reasonable a question that the monks found themselves unable to reply.

Had matters been allowed to rest there, the teacher would no doubt have been able to persuade Benkei to leave. As luck would have it, however, Kaien broke in with a sneer: "This wandering monk has an interesting face, hasn't he?"

Benkei drew himself up. "Some of the monks at your temple are much too arrogant, and I dare say you would prefer them to be less rude to wandering ascetics. I'll punish this fellow for you."

The monks began to exclaim excitedly. "Something terrible is going to happen!"

"This fool hasn't got the sense to pick on somebody he can beat," Benkei went on. "What do you say? Is he too much for me? Will he break my skull? The miserable wretch scribbled on my face!" He stood ready, club in hand.

At this, five or six of Kaien's friends spoke up from within the hall. "We're tired of looking at that lout! Let's throw him off the veranda and kick his head in." They tied back their sleeves and charged at Benkei with loud whoops. Benkei, springing into action, raised the club, and with one sideways thrust swept them all from the veranda.

Kaien had jumped into the fray and was looking around frantically for a club of his own. He snatched up a burning oak brand at the far end of the hall, knocking the brazier aside, and lunged at Benkei. "Do you really want to fight, young man?" he cried.

Benkei took a step back and then brought down his club with a furious thrust. Kaien dodged, and parried skillfully. Benkei lowered his head, took a leap forward, and pulled Kaien's head toward him with his left arm. Gripping Kaien's thigh with his right arm, he raised him aloft and ran out to the main courtyard of the Lecture Hall.

"Forgive him, honorable ascetic," shrieked the monks. "He always fights when he drinks."

"What do you mean?" cried Benkei. "I thought you monks were supposed to control the ascetics when they got drunk, and that they were supposed to do the same for you. I won't kill him."

With a great shout he spun around and hurled Kaien to the roof of the Lecture Hall, eleven feet above the ground. Kaien rolled toward the edge and dropped heavily to the paving stones. Benkei at once commenced stamping on him as though determined to smash his bones to the marrow. Kaien's left forearm was shattered and two ribs on his right side were injured, but no sound passed his lips. Words, it was clear, were useless.

Meanwhile, the smouldering brand, which Kaien had still clutched in his flight through the air, had lodged on the roof of the Lecture Hall and was fanned by a wind from the valley. Quickly it became a spreading blaze, which completely consumed the nine-pillar Lecture Hall, the seven-pillar veranda, the Tahō stupa, the Manjusri Hall, and the five-story pagoda. The Founder's Hall itself and fifty-three other buildings of all descriptions were burned to ashes.

"I suppose I am a real enemy of Buddhism now," thought Benkei as he watched. "Well, as long as I have committed such a crime as this, there's no point in sparing the monks' quarters." He ran down to Nishisakamoto, where he lighted a torch and began setting fire to the thickly clustered cells one by one. Since all the buildings projected out over the valley from perches on the mountainside, every last one was devoured by the flames as they mounted toward the peak. Nothing was left but the foundation stones.

At around ten o'clock on the morning of the twenty-first day, Benkei left Shosha for the capital. All day and all night he walked, and on the morning of the twenty-second he arrived in the city, which was just then being swept by torrential rains and violent winds. All the inhabitants were indoors, but Benkei nonetheless proceeded to dress himself carefully in red trousers and a formal blouse and knickers.

Benkei had come to the capital for a purpose. Late that night when everything was still, he climbed a wall at the ex-Emperor's palace, cupped his palms to light a fire, and shouted at the top of his lungs. Then he ran off toward the east. In a short time he retraced his steps, leaped to the top of a gate, and screamed in a paralyzing voice, "Horrifying news! A shocking thing! Yesterday morning there was a quarrel between a monk and an ascetic at Shosha, the monastery founded by the holy Shōgū himself. All the fifty-four buildings and three hundred monks' cells have been burned to ashes!" Then he vanished like a phantom.

The ex-Emperor, who had heard all this, at once dispatched a courier to make inquiries concerning the cause of the fire at Shosha. "If the monastery actually has been burned, expel the teacher and the others," he commanded.[6]

The courier discovered that not a building remained at the temple. Knowing that he must report without delay, he rode swiftly back to the capital to relate his story at the ex-Emperor's palace.

"Who were the guilty men?" asked the ex-Emperor.

"The ascetic was Musashibō and the monk was Kaien," answered the courier.

"If Musashibō is the same as Oniwaka from the Mountain Gate,

---

[6] The head of a temple and his associates were responsible for the temple to the court, which could dismiss them at will.

measures were taken to quell his spirit before all this happened," the nobles said. "On the other hand, there is no doubt about Kaien's guilt. He has shown that he is an enemy of Buddhism and of the state. Seize him for interrogation."

A commission was bestowed upon Koyano Tarō, a warrior from Settsu, who rode off with a hundred men to take Kaien into custody. Back at the ex-Emperor's palace, the monk was questioned in the imperial presence.

"Were you alone or did you have fellow plotters?" they asked him.

"If they mean to press me as closely as all that, I probably won't leave here alive. I may as well take along some of my enemies," thought Kaien. He made a confession which named eleven monks as his confederates.

On the road back to Shosha, Koyano Tarō encountered the accused men themselves, who had of their own accord started for the capital when they heard rumors of Kaien's accusations. Ignoring this sign of good faith, His Majesty ordered them detained, since they had, after all, been named in a criminal's confession.

Kaien was soon sentenced to death, denied even the permission to enter a plea in his own behalf. Just before the execution he protested, "I am not the only guilty one. If you let the others go free, I will return as an angry spirit." The eleven were no doubt headed for execution in any event, but when the nobles were informed of Kaien's threat they said, "If that's the case, cut off their heads," and this was promptly done.

Benkei, who was still in the capital, was exuberant. "Very gratifying indeed! This is the first time I have ever got rid of an enemy with no effort at all. When I do something wrong, the court merely prays about it." After that his behavior was worse than ever.

HOW BENKEI STOLE SWORDS IN THE CAPITAL

"A man reckons his wealth in terms of a thousand," thought Benkei. "Hidehira of Ōshū owns 1,000 fine horses, Kikuchi of Tsukushi 1,000 suits of armor, and Tayū of Matsura 1,000 quivers and 1,000 bows. Since I haven't the money to buy anything, why should I not collect swords by roaming the capital after dark and relieving other fellows of their weapons?" Night after night he followed this plan, until people began saying, "A goblin monk ten feet tall is stalking the capital streets these days, stealing swords." The year drew to a close, and by the end of the fifth month or the start of the sixth month in the following year, Benkei had accumulated a vast quantity of weapons in the loft of a certain Buddhist hall at Higuchi Karasumaru. On the seventeenth day of the sixth month, he found that he possessed exactly 999 swords. That afternoon he made a pious journey to Gojō Tenjin Shrine. "Grant that I may take a prize blade tonight," he prayed as dusk fell.

When the hour had grown late, he walked south from the shrine to loiter near the wall of a private dwelling, hoping that one of Tenjin's worshipers might be wearing a likely weapon. Toward dawn, just as he had started off along Horikawa Avenue, he heard the distant plaintive notes of a flute. "That must be someone on his way to Tenjin for an early morning visit. I wonder whether it's a monk or a layman. If his sword is any good, I shall help myself to it," he thought. Leaning forward as the music drew nearer, he saw a young man, wearing a white blouse, white knickers, and a silver-plated corselet. At his waist hung a magnificent sword decorated with gold.

"What a superb weapon! I must have it," Benkei said to himself eagerly. He was shortly to learn that the stranger was an adversary to beware of, but how was he to know it then?

Yoshitsune, advancing watchfully, saw a menacing armed monk beneath a *muku* tree.[7]

"That fellow has a strange appearance. He must be the one who has been stealing swords in the capital," he thought. He walked on steadily in Benkei's direction.

"I've taken swords away from plenty of seasoned warriors. If I walk up to that boy and tell him to hand his over, my face and voice alone will throw him into such a panic that he'll agree. If he refuses, I'll knock him down and grab it," thought Benkei. He stepped out and accosted Yoshitsune. "Waiting here quietly for enemies, I find it singular that a fine fellow like you should come along dressed in armor. I can't let you pass without a word. Hand me your sword if you want to go on."

"I've heard that some ass has been around here lately," Yoshitsune answered. "I'm afraid I can't give you my sword as easily as all that. You'll have to come after it if you want it."

[7] *Aphananthe aspera.*

"That's all right with me." Benkei drew his sword and lunged at Yoshitsune.

Unsheathing his own weapon, Yoshitsune ran toward his adversary's position near the wall. Benkei sprang back with a tremendous blow in Yoshitsune's direction. "Not even a god dares oppose me!" he shouted.

"The rascal isn't a bad fighter at all," said Yoshitsune, darting under Benkei's left arm like a streak of lightning. Benkei had put such a thrust into his sword that the tip became embedded in the wall. As he sought to release it, Yoshitsune kicked him in the chest with his left foot, lashing out so vigorously that the weapon flew from Benkei's hands. Yoshitsune snatched it up and sprang with a shout to the top of the nine-foot wall, while Benkei stood motionless, half-believing in his astonishment and pain that he had met a devil.

"In the future, don't try any more of your lawless tricks," admonished Yoshitsune. "I've been hearing about you for a long time. I ought to keep your sword, but I don't want you to think I need it. Here!" Holding Benkei's sword against the top of the wall, he bent it out of shape with his foot and threw it down.

With a bitter glance at Yoshitsune, Benkei straightened the weapon. He began to move away, muttering, "You're a better fighter than I imagined. You seem to favor this neighborhood... I may not have done so well tonight, but next time I won't be so careless."

"He certainly has the look of a Hiei monk," thought Yoshitsune. "Ah, Hiei monk! You're not what you seem to be!"[8] he mocked.

Benkei was silent, but he resolved to kill him. As Yoshitsune jumped toward the ground, he lunged forward, brandishing his sword; but Yoshitsune leaped blithely back onto the wall while he was still three feet in the air.

When people heard about King Mu of China, who ascended to heaven from the summit of an eight-foot wall after reading *Liu-t'ao*, they always used to say, "That's the kind of miracle that could only have happened in antiquity," but even in our own degenerate times the same book taught Kurō Yoshitsune to jump back from mid-air to the top of a nine-foot wall. That night Benkei went home frustrated.

[8] He means that Benkei does not live up to his fierce appearance.

HOW BENKEI BECAME YOSHITSUNE'S SWORN RETAINER

On the eighteenth of the sixth month, people from all around came flocking to Kiyomizu Kannon to worship. "That fellow I met last night is bound to turn up at Kiyomizu. I'll just have a look," Benkei said to himself. He loitered in the vicinity of the main gate, but Yoshitsune was nowhere to be seen.

It grew late, and Benkei was about to leave in disgust when he heard the strains of a flute floating up from Kiyomizu Hill.

"What an elegant air! It can't be anybody else," he thought. He remained where he was in front of the gate, praying, "This temple was dedicated by Sakanoue Tamuramaro to Kannon, the En-lightened One, who has vowed to remain in the world of men, defer-ring omniscience, until he has answered all the petitions of humanity in his thirty-three guises. He has also sworn to bring good fortune to everyone who enters the temple precincts. I don't ask for good luck. Simply allow me to take that sword."

Meanwhile Yoshitsune was beginning to feel inexplicably ill at ease. He glanced warily toward the top of the hill and saw that last night's monk was awaiting him, dressed in a corselet and armed with both a sword and a halberd. "The scoundrel! Here he is again to-night!" He continued to advance toward the gate.

"Well, if it isn't the gentleman I met at Tenjin last night!" said Benkei.

"It is," said Yoshitsune.

"Will you give me your sword or won't you?"

"You may ask as much as you like, but I'm not going to hand it over. If you want it, you'll have to come after it."

"Still boasting!" Benkei exclaimed. Waving his halberd, he charged down the hill, but Yoshitsune, with discouraging adroitness, parried the long blade. "I can't compete with him," Benkei was forced to admit to himself.

"Much as I should like to go on with this for the rest of the night," said Yoshitsune, "I have made a vow to Kannon." And he resumed his progress toward the temple. Benkei was left thinking, "I feel like a man who has lost something he was holding in his hand."

Yoshitsune was reflecting, "He is a brave man. If he's still there at dawn, I'll knock down his sword and halberd, wound him a bit, and capture him. It's no fun doing things all alone. I'll make him my retainer."

The unsuspecting Benkei followed along behind, still intent on the sword. As he entered the Kannon Hall, which was filled with the murmur of worshipers' voices, he heard someone beside the inner lattice reverently reciting the opening lines of the first chapter of the *Lotus Sutra*. "That's the voice of the fellow who called me a scoundrel. I'll just have a look," he thought. He laid his halberd on the threshold and, unarmed save for his sword, pushed rudely through the crowd inside, saying "I'm a temple official; make way, please." When he reached a position behind the chanting Yoshitsune, he planted himself with his legs wide apart. People who saw him in the light from the altar lamps said, "What a grim-looking monk! He's a giant!"

"How did he know I was here?" Yoshitsune wondered. To Benkei's surprise, he was now dressed as a woman, with a cloak over his head. Confused but determined, Benkei rapped him smartly in the side with his sheath. "Whether you're a page or a lady, I'm a worshiper too. Move over," he demanded. When Yoshitsune failed to reply, Benkei gave him a powerful shove, thinking, "This is no ordinary person. It must be my man."

"You pest!" exclaimed Yoshitsune. "A beggar like you can pray under a tree or a thatched roof; you'll be heard right enough. What do you mean by creating a disturbance where important people are worshiping? Get out!"

"That's an unfriendly thing to say to someone you've known since last night. Make room." While the spectators watched in shocked disapproval, Benkei jumped nimbly across two mats to Yoshitsune's side, snatched up the sutra, and flipped it open. "What a handsome sutra! Is it yours or somebody else's?" As Yoshitsune remained silent, he began to recite, saying, "Come, read it with me."

Benkei had been one of the most famous sutra readers in the Western Compound, and Yoshitsune had been well trained as a page at Kurama. As they read the first half of the second scroll in alternation, with Benkei taking the lead and Yoshitsune following, the noisy crowd of pilgrims grew still, and the devotees stopped ringing their bells. An indescribable aura of sanctity pervaded the quiet night.

After a time Yoshitsune arose, saying, "I must speak to an acquaintance. We shall meet again."

"If I can't hold onto a man while he's right in front of me, am I likely to see him again? Let's go together," said Benkei, pulling him by the hand. When they reached the south door, he continued, "I am in earnest about wanting your sword. Will you give it to me?"

"I can't do that; it's an heirloom," Yoshitsune replied.

"All right, then, let me win it from you in a fair match."

"Very well. We shall fight for it."

The two drew their swords and began to fence briskly.

"What's the meaning of this?" complained the spectators. "Imagine fighting in a cramped space like this—to say nothing of picking on a boy! Put away your sword, monk." Benkei ignored them.

When Yoshitsune threw off his outer cloak, revealing the blouse, knickers, and corselet beneath, the awed spectators knew that he was no ordinary person. Such was the excitement among the visiting ladies, nuns, and children that some of them fell off the veranda, while the men rushed to close the doors to the hall so as to keep the combatants outside.

Presently Yoshitsune and Benkei made their way down to the dance platform, without a break in their fighting. The spectators, who had at first been afraid to venture close, now began to walk around them in fascination, like people performing a circumambulation ritual.[9]

"Who will win, the page or the monk?" someone asked.

"The page can't lose. The monk's out of his class; he's tired already," replied someone else.

"It looks as if I were done for," thought Benkei, disheartened by this judgment, but he fought doggedly on. Suddenly, Yoshitsune seized a chance opening to run forward and thrust the point of his weapon into Benkei's left side below his arm. Then, as Benkei faltered, he struck him again and again with the back of his sword until he lay stretched out with his head toward the east.

"What do you say? Are you willing to follow me?" Yoshitsune demanded, planting a foot on the monk's prostrate body.

"This must be my karma from a previous existence. I will serve you," Benkei promised.

Yoshitsune put on Benkei's corselet over his own, took up both swords, and before daybreak had come, marched him to Yamashina,

[9] A Buddhist ceremony in which chanting monks circle a sacred image or hall.

where he remained with him until the wound had healed. Then the two went to the capital to observe the activities of the Heike.

Once Benkei had become Yoshitsune's retainer, he followed him as faithfully as a shadow, performing innumerable gallant deeds during his master's three-year campaign against the Heike. He was that very Musashibō Benkei who remained with Yoshitsune to the end and fell beside him in the last battle at Koromogawa in Ōshū.

Meanwhile a rumor spread in the capital that Kurō Yoshitsune was conspiring against the Heike with a ruffian named Musashibō. Someone sent word to Rokuhara that Yoshitsune was lodging with the holy man of Shijō, and a great company of Taira warriors descended upon Shijō. They seized the holy man, but Yoshitsune, who was also there, contrived in some way to escape.

"I had better return to Ōshū before I am caught," Yoshitsune decided. Setting out on the Tōsendō, he called upon Kiso Yoshinaka. "I can't stay in the capital any longer, so I'm on my way to Ōshū. I am counting on you to do your best here. Rally the warriors of the eastern and northern provinces. If I can join you with men from Ōshū, it won't be long before we get what we want. You're close to Izu—keep in touch with Yoritomo," he said. Kiso provided him with an escort to Ise Saburō's home in Kōzuke, and from there he and Saburō continued to Hiraizumi.

YORITOMO'S REBELLION

Minamoto Yoritomo rebelled against the Taira with a night assault upon Izumi Hangan Kanetaka on the seventeenth day of the eighth month of the fourth year of Jishō [1180]. He lost a battle at the Kobayagawa River in Sagami on the nineteenth, and hid at Sugiyama in Dohi until he was attacked by Ōba Saburō and Matano Gorō. At dawn on the twenty-sixth, he embarked over the waves toward Miura from Cape Manazuru in Izu. A violent gale prevented his landing at Miura, and late on the twenty-eighth he was obliged to land at Cape Sunosaki in Awa, where he began an all-night vigil at Takinoguchi Shrine. As he prayed, it seemed to him that the door of the shrine was pushed open by a finely shaped hand, revealing this verse: "I am the very god who dwells at Iwashimizu. Arrest the decline of the Minamoto; raise their fame higher than the clouds." When he awoke from his dream, he bowed to the god three times, chanting, "You who are the very god of Iwashimizu: let me arrest the decline of the Minamoto and raise their fame higher than the clouds."

The next day Yoritomo left Sunosaki.[e] When he arrived at Ryō-shima, one of his retainers, a man named Katōji, remarked, "It's a sorry state of affairs, isn't it? Since the deaths of Tameyoshi and Yoshitomo in Hōgen and Heiji, all the Genji have been living as quietly as though they were not warriors at all. The only one who tried to revolt failed because he was allied with an unlucky prince. It is a discouraging thing to think about."

"You're too pessimistic," said Yoritomo reprovingly. "The Great Bodhisattva Hachiman will never forsake us." Those were words to inspire confidence!

While the Genji were still at Ryōshima, two members of the Miura family[d] came to join them in small boats from Kurihama, leading 300 men. Five hundred other allies arrived on horseback, captained by two prominent Awa warriors.[e] Then the revitalized Genji, 800 strong, whipped their mounts over the Awa-Kazusa border at Tsukushiumi, surged across the beach at Sanuki-no-edahama in Kazusa, passed Ise Cape, and arrived at Shinobe and Ikaishiri. At the Suekawa River, more than 1,000 men galloped to Yoritomo's side.[f]

Chiba Hirotsune had not yet declared his allegiance. "Yoritomo has been rallying all the warriors in Awa and Kazusa. I can't understand why he hasn't sent me any word. Unless I hear from him today, I'm going to ask Chiba Tsunetane and the Kasai family to go with me to Kisōto Beach and put him down," he confided to his men. At that very moment Adachi Morinaga appeared, wearing a dark blue blouse and knickers and a black leather corselet, and carrying a lacquered bow, bound in rattan, with arrows trimmed with black eagle feathers.

"I wish to see Lord Hirotsune," he said.

When Hirotsune was informed of the arrival of Yoritomo's emissary, he was so delighted that he went out at once to meet him. "Yoritomo is probably asking for some of my relatives and retainers," he thought as he opened the letter. To his surprise, he read: "Why have you not reported to me?"

"That is the message of a real leader," said Hirotsune approvingly. "I can't sit still and do nothing." He sent the letter on to Chiba

Tsunetane, and after the Kasai, Toyota, and Uranokami had hastened to his house, he and Tsunetane quickly joined the Genji at Kaihatsu Beach, leading a band of 3,000 warriors.

Yoritomo arrived at Yakata in Kazusa with 40,000 men. Although many years had passed since the eclipse of the Minamoto, the warriors of the Eight Provinces flocked loyally to his standard,[g] and on the eleventh day of the ninth month of the fourth year of Jishō [1180], he reached Ichikawa (in Matsudo Domain on the Musashi-Shimotsuke border) with a force which was said to number 89,000 men. There he confronted one of the most famous rivers of the east,[10] whose headwaters rose far away in the province of Kōzuke at Fujiwara in Tone Domain, and whose lower reaches had been called the Sumida River by Ariwara Narihira—a stream which might have been mistaken for the sea itself, so obscured were its banks by the heavy sea tides and rain-swollen waters. The army was delayed there five days.

On the opposite bank, meanwhile, Edo Tarō had established positions above and below Sumida Crossing; he had built observation towers and tethered horses to the tower pillars and now awaited the Genji.

"Take that fellow's head," Yoritomo ordered.

When news of this order reached Edo Tarō, he dismantled the towers in great haste, made a raft out of some of the pillars, and crossed over to Ichikawa. Through Kasai Hyōe, he requested an audience, but Yoritomo refused to receive him.

When Tarō again asked for an audience, Yoritomo merely said, "His intentions are unfriendly. Watch him, Ise Katōji." Edo Tarō paled when these words were repeated to him.

Fortunately for Tarō, Chiba Tsunetane had recognized him as an old neighbor. "I can't stand by without a word," he said to himself. "I must speak up for him." Kneeling before Yoritomo, he begged mercy for Tarō.

"It is said that Edo Tarō is one of the richest men in the Eight Provinces," Yoritomo replied. "Since my army has been delayed by the river for several days now, have him build a floating bridge so that we can cross to Ōji and Itabashi in Musashi."

"Even if it costs me my head, I don't see how I can get them across," said Edo Tarō.

[10] The Tone River.

Chapter Four

THE MEETING BETWEEN YORITOMO AND YOSHITSUNE

At Ukishima Plain Yoshitsune made camp to rest awhile, choosing a spot about three hundred fifty yards from Yoritomo's headquarters. When Yoritomo became aware of his arrival, he assigned Hori Yatarō to call upon him with a large party of the chieftain's personal retainers.

"I see nearly sixty fresh warriors with white banners and badges over there,"[1] he said. "They're strangers to me. Any Genji from Shinano should be at home with Kiso, and those from Kai should be in the second line. Who is their leader? Find out his exact name."

Yatarō left his escort in the rear and advanced alone. "The Lord of Kamakura has commanded me to find out who has come here wearing a white badge," he called out.

A warrior on a stout black horse rode forward. He was a fair-skinned, aristocratic-looking man of twenty-four or twenty-five, dressed in a red brocade blouse and knickers under lilac-colored armor embellished with metal ornaments. On his head he wore a silver-studded helmet with five flaps surmounted by a crest in the shape of a hoe. The feathers of his arrows were black in the center, and his bow was of lacquer wrapped with rattan.

"The Lord of Kamakura knows me," he declared. "I was called Ushiwaka as a child, and for the past few years I have been living in Ōshū. I came as soon as I learned of his rebellion. Please let me see him."

When Hori Yatarō understood that the horseman was Yoritomo's

---

[1] The Minamoto traditionally carried white banners. Badges attached to helmets or sleeves distinguished friends from enemies.

brother, he leaped from his saddle and presented his compliments through Satō Saburō Tsuginobu, who was the son of Yoshitsune's wet nurse. He retired respectfully on foot for the first hundred yards, with a subordinate leading his mount.

The usually imperturbable Yoritomo made no attempt to conceal his pleasure at Yatarō's report. "Have him come here. I will see him," he replied. Yatarō hurried to tell Yoshitsune, who presented himself eagerly, accompanied by Satō Tsuginobu, Satō Tadanobu, and Ise Saburō.

Within the great curtains at Yoritomo's camp, which formed an enclosure twelve miles in circumference, the chieftains, great and small, of the Eight Provinces were seated in rows on fur rugs. At Yoritomo's place a padded straw mat had been provided, but the chieftain sat on a rug. When Yoshitsune handed his helmet to an attendant and knelt beside the curtain, bow in hand, Yoritomo moved to the mat. "Sit on my rug, sit there," he said. After many protests, Yoshitsune did as he was bid. Tears rose in Yoritomo's eyes as he gazed at his brother, and Yoshitsune also wept, although he knew nothing of what was in Yoritomo's mind.

Presently Yoritomo composed himself. "I have never once heard your name spoken since our father died. The last time I saw you, you were still an infant, and after the Nun of the Pond succeeded in having me exiled to Izu my guardians, Itō Sukechika and Hōjō Tokimasa, kept me from writing to you, even though I knew you were in Ōshū. I am overjoyed that you have hurried here like a faithful brother.

"Look around you at these warriors. They came to join me from the Eight Provinces and other places as soon as I rebelled, but I am unable to talk frankly with any of them. They are all outsiders—former Taira followers at that—men who watch me constantly for a sign of weakness. The thought of it keeps me awake at night. Of course I have thought again and again of attacking the Heike, but I am only one man. If I went, what would happen to the eastern provinces? I haven't had a trustworthy brother to send as a deputy, and someone from another family might have gone over to the enemy. I couldn't be happier now if our father had come back from the grave.

"When our ancestor Yoshiie attacked Munō Castle during the Later Three Years' War, he lost his army and fell back to the shore of the Kuriyagawa River. He prepared offerings, faced the capital, and prayed, 'Hail, Great Bodhisattva Hachiman! Let your regard remain unaltered; let my life be preserved and my mission accomplished.' Then as though by Hachiman's divine intervention, Yoshiie's brother in the capital, the Secretary of the Punishments Ministry, suddenly slipped away from the imperial palace where he was on duty and left the city with 200 men, saying that he was needed in Ōshū. Gathering recruits on the way, he galloped to the Kuriyagawa River to join Lord Yoshiie with a force of 3,000, and eventually Yoshiie subjugated Ōshū. Even Yoshiie's delight on that occasion couldn't have been greater than my pleasure at this meeting. From today on, the two of us must be as inseparable as a fish and water until we wipe out our ancestors' disgrace and comfort the spirits of the dead. If you will consent, it will please me more than I can say."

As Yoritomo spoke, his tears began to flow anew. Yoshitsune also wept silently, while the assembled lords of all ranks pressed their sleeves to their eyes in sympathy.

"It is true that we haven't met since I was a baby," Yoshitsune replied. "After your exile I lived at Yamashina for awhile, and then in my seventh year I went to Kurama, where I studied in the usual way until the age of sixteen. Later I moved to the capital. Someone warned me that the Heike were planning to kill me, so I went to Ōshū to ask Hidehira for protection. I came as soon as I heard of your revolt. Now that I have seen you, it is as though I had met our dead father. I have already dedicated my life to him, so please use me just as you like. I couldn't possibly object to anything you wanted." His voice broke.

Thus it was that Yoritomo came to send Yoshitsune to the capital as his commander-in-chief.

HOW YOSHITSUNE MARCHED AGAINST THE HEIKE

In the third year of Juei [1184], Yoshitsune went to the capital and drove out the Heike. By fighting valiantly at Ichi-no-tani, Yashima, and Dan-no-ura, he crushed the enemy completely. He returned to the city with his prisoners (the enemy commander, who was the former Interior Minister Munemori, the commander's son, and thirty others), to be received in audience by the former emperor and the ruling sovereign, who had already named him a police lieutenant of fifth rank in the first year of Genryaku [1184]. From there he set out toward Kamakura with Taira Munemori and his son, and presently arrived at Koshigoe.

"What do you make of Yoshitsune's arrival at Koshigoe with Munemori and his son?" Kajiwara Kagetoki[2] asked Yoritomo. "I think he is waiting for a chance to betray you. When Shō Saburō Takaie gave up Taira Shigehira to Noriyori after capturing him during the battle of Ichi-no-tani, Yoshitsune flew into a terrible rage. 'This is intolerable! Noriyori didn't win the battle—why didn't you send me the prisoner?' he shouted. He would have ordered his men to kill Takaie if I hadn't pacified him by arranging for Shigehira to be delivered to Dohi Jirō Sanehira. On the same occasion he said, 'After the Heike are destroyed, I expect to control all the area west of Ōsaka Barrier. Though the proverb says there aren't two suns in the sky or two sovereigns on earth,[3] Japan is going to have two shoguns from now on.'

"He is such a magnificent warrior that he ignored the wind and waves and skimmed over the gunwales of ships like a bird, even though he knew nothing at all about naval warfare. At Ichi-no-tani the Heike had a fortress in a thousand, defended by 100,000 men against our 65,000. When a big army besieges a weak fortress, the opposing sides are usually fairly well matched. The Ichi-no-tani garrison was huge and its men were at home on the ground, while we were outnumbered strangers. Nobody thought we had a chance until Yoshitsune beat them by leading a handful of warriors across Hiedori Pass, through mountains that were almost too wild for birds and beasts. No ordinary man could have done such a thing! In the battle of Yashima, he forced a passage with five vessels through raging winds and towering waves, swooped boldly down on the fortress at the head of fifty men, and drove away thousands of Taira warriors. From start to finish, when the decisive battle was fought at Dan-no-ura, he seemed to have no weakness whatever. Warriors from all over the country agreed that there had never been another general like him in China or Japan.

"Because he intends to rebel, he is thoughtful of everyone—he takes an interest in the personal problems of the humblest warriors. All the

---

[2] Yoshitsune's old enemy. See the Introduction.
[3] From *Li-chi*. Okami, p. 143, n. 17.

men admire and respect him. 'There's a master for you! I would give
my life for him without thinking twice,' they say. It would be foolhardy to let him into Kamakura. Your good fortune is karma from a
previous existence, so it will probably last to the end of your life; but
what about your sons? And can we be quite certain even in your own
case?"

"There is no reason to suspect Kajiwara of duplicity," said Yoritomo. "Nevertheless, a fair ruler hears both sides. Since Yoshitsune is
in Koshigoe now, he and Kajiwara will confront each other here
tomorrow."

"There should be no danger for Yoshitsune, who has certainly done
nothing wrong," said the chieftains among themselves. "Still, who
knows what may happen? Kajiwara's lies show that he hasn't forgotten the reverse oars—to say nothing of his rivalry with Yoshitsune at
the battle of Dan-no-ura, when the two almost came to blows."[4]

Kajiwara, in the meantime, had retired to his home at Amanō. He
submitted a solemn written affirmation of his statements to Yoritomo,
who declared himself entirely satisfied. The prisoners were brought
in alone from Koshigoe, while Yoshitsune, forbidden to enter Kamakura, was left to indulge in useless regrets. "Though it is true that my
main desire was to clear our family name and cheer the spirits of the
dead, I did my best to please Yoritomo too. I had hoped to get a reward, but now it looks as though my loyal service will count for nothing at all. Thanks to Kajiwara's lies, I won't even be granted an
interview. I was too lenient with him in the west," he reflected bitterly. "Instead of killing him as he deserved, I let him live to repay me
with enmity."

At Kamakura, Yoritomo summoned Kawagoe Tarō Shigeyori.
"My brother is secretly planning to start a war by trading on the ex-
Emperor's friendship. Go to Koshigoe and kill him before warriors
from the west join him," he commanded.

"I need hardly say that I will always obey you, but, as you know,
my daughter's marriage to Yoshitsune puts me in an awkward position," Kawagoe replied. "Please ask someone else." And he left the
room.

Yoritomo could not regard this attitude as unreasonable, and
therefore, instead of pressing Kawagoe, he summoned Hatakeyama.

---

[4] See the Introduction, p. *21*.

"Kawagoe has begged off because of his relationship to Yoshitsune, but we can't sit still while Yoshitsune gets ready to start a war. I want you to go, especially since the precedents are auspicious. As a reward, I shall give you Izu and Suruga provinces."

"Of course I will do whatever you ask," answered the forthright Hatakeyama, "but I should like to remind you of the Great Bodhisattva Hachiman's vow, in which he promises to protect our land and our people first of all.[5] How can an outsider compare with your own flesh and blood? Kajiwara is nothing but a temporarily useful tool— Yoshitsune is a brother who has given you years of loyal devotion. Even if you believe there is some truth in Kajiwara's accusations, give Yoshitsune a grant of land—Kyushu, perhaps—and present him with Izu and Suruga, which you have just offered me, to show your good will when you meet. It would be a magnanimous gesture to make him warden of Kyoto, too, and let him guard your rear." With this blunt advice he withdrew.

Yoritomo allowed the matter to drop—perhaps because he agreed with Hatakeyama or perhaps for some other reason, who can say?

After news of these events reached Yoshitsune in Koshigoe, he drew up and dispatched one oath of fealty after another. When they had all been rejected, he sent a letter to Kamakura.

THE LETTER FROM KOSHIGOE

This was Yoshitsune's letter.

To His Excellency the Governor of Inaba:

I, Minamoto Yoshitsune, venture to address you.

Having overthrown the enemies of the court and erased the infamy of military defeat as His Lordship's deputy and the bearer of an imperial commission, I had supposed that my deeds would be commended; yet, to my distress, pernicious slanders have caused accomplishments of uncommon merit to be ignored. Though innocent, I am blamed; though deserving, and guilty of no error, I have incurred His Lordship's displeasure. What can I do but weep bitter tears! Since I have not been permitted to refute false accusations, or even to enter Kamakura, I have been obliged to remain idle for days, with no means of expressing my feelings. I have been denied the privilege of seeing His Lordship for so

[5] He means that Yoritomo should feel a special concern for his relatives, just as Hachiman does for his own people, the Japanese. Okami, p. 146, n. 2.

long that the blood bond between us seems to have vanished. Is this the karma of a previous existence? Am I being punished for evil acts committed in my last life? Alas! Unless the august spirit of my late father chances to be reborn, who will plead my cause or pity my condition?

At the risk of appearing querulous, I must say to you that never since birth have I enjoyed a moment's peace of mind—never, from the time of my journey in my mother's arms to Uda District in Yamato, an infant orphaned by my father's death. Though able to preserve my useless life, I could not safely frequent the capital but was obliged to skulk in out-of-the-way places, dwell in distant lands, and serve commoners. When at last, through sudden good fortune, I was sent to the capital to crush the Taira clan, I first punished Kiso Yoshinaka and then set about the destruction of the Heike. I whipped my mount over precipitous cliffs, heedless of life in the face of the enemy; I braved the perils of wind and wave on the boundless sea, ready to sink to the bottom as food for monsters of the deep. Battle dress was my pillow; arms were my profession—yet, as in the past, my sole desire was to comfort the unhappy spirits of the dead. As regards my appointment as a lieutenant of fifth rank, was that not a remarkable honor for a member of our family? Yet how deep is my present misery; how acute my suffering! Despairing of obtaining a hearing through any means short of divine assistance, I have repeatedly submitted oaths of loyalty inscribed on the backs of talismans from temples and shrines, to which I have sworn by the gods of all the great and small shrines in Japan, and by the spirits of the underworld, but no pardon has been granted.

This is the land of the gods. Since the gods consider my petitions unworthy, my sole remaining recourse is to implore you to do me the kindness of bringing this message to His Lordship's attention at a suitable time in order to persuade him of my innocence. Once his forgiveness is secured, my heirs and I will rejoice in the "superabundant happiness of accumulated goodness,"[6] and I will end my life in peace.

Finding it impossible to write as I feel, I have confined myself to bare essentials.

Humbly and respectfully submitted,

MINAMOTO YOSHITSUNE.

Fifth day, sixth month, second year of Genryaku [1185].

When the letter was read aloud, it drew tears from Yoritomo himself, to say nothing of all the others who heard it, down to the very ladies-in-waiting. The question of Yoshitsune's loyalty was laid

---

[6] From *I-ching*. Okami, p. 149, n. 14.

aside, and Yoritomo inclined to the view that his brother, who enjoyed the favor of the ex-Emperor, would after all be the best possible warden of Kyoto. As for Yoshitsune, he deferred entirely to Yoritomo's judgement. But as autumn drew to a close and winter set in, the vengeful Kajiwara worked so unceasingly to blacken Yoshitsune's character that Yoritomo at length began to believe his stories.

HOW TOSABŌ WENT TO THE CAPITAL TO ATTACK YOSHITSUNE

"Summon Tosabō from Nikaidō," said Yoritomo. He awaited Tosabō's arrival in a small private room.

"Tosabō is here," Kajiwara announced.

"Show him in."

As the guest bowed respectfully, Yoritomo commanded Kajiwara's son Genda to serve him wine, and he entertained him with exceptional courtesy. Then he began: "I have spoken of this matter to Wada and Hatakeyama, but neither of them has given me any help. Yoshitsune has been taking advantage of the ex-Emperor's friendship to plan a revolt in the capital. When I asked Koshigoe Tarō to kill him he refused, giving their relationship as an excuse. You are the only one I can trust. Besides, you know your way around in the capital. If you will go there and kill Yoshitsune, I will give you the provinces of Awa and Kazusa."

"Very well... but it's distressing to be commanded to destroy a member of His Lordship's own family," replied Tosabō.

Yoritomo's expression altered instantly. "Am I to believe that you and Yoshitsune have reached an understanding?" he demanded coldly.

Tosabō assumed a posture of abject humility. "After all," he reflected, "a man must obey his master, even if he is ordered to kill his father. When there is contention in high places, ordinary warriors must be prepared to die." Aloud, he said, "Of course I will obey. I hesitated only for the sake of form, because he is your brother."

"I was right—you are the only man who can stand up to him." Then Yoritomo called for Genda. To the bowing Genda he said, "What has become of that thing?"

From a cupboard Genda withdrew a spear with a foot-long blade, decorated on the hilt with a design of shells. The handle and scabbard were adorned with alternating bands of silver and rattan.

"Lay it in Tosa's lap," ordered Yoritomo. "I have prized this spear ever since Senjuin of Yamato made it for me," he continued to Tosabō. "A long-handled weapon is the best kind for killing my enemies. When this was used in the attack on Izumi Hangan Kanetaka, it decapitated him easily. Take it with you to the capital and bring back Yoshitsune's head on the point." Having uttered these heartless words, he summoned Kajiwara. "See that men from Awa and Kazusa accompany Tosa," he commanded.

Tosa did not in the least relish the prospect of hand-to-hand combat in a full-scale battle. A sudden attack in the night was more to his liking.

"This is not the sort of job for a big party. I can use my own men," he demurred.

"How many do you have?"

"About a hundred."

"That should be enough."

As Tosa drained his wine cup he reflected, "If I took along a great many warriors I would have to divide the reward with all of them. Awa and Kazusa are full of dry fields—there isn't enough good rice land for so many."

Presently Tosa returned with his gifts to Nikaidō. There he called together his kinsmen and retainers. "Yoritomo has granted me a reward. I am going to the capital right away so I can claim my lands. Make your preparations," he said.

"Is this for ordinary services or for something special?" they asked.

"He has ordered me to kill Yoshitsune."

"Yes, Tosa would get Awa and Kazusa if he lived! He'll never return," said the more discerning among his men. The optimistic told one another, "If our lord prospers, we'll share his good luck."

Instead of traveling in the usual way, the clever Tosa ordered his men to provide themselves with white pilgrims' tunics. Laymen and monks alike attached strips of paper to their headgear[7] and to the manes and tails of their mounts, which Tosa proposed to pass off as horses destined for presentation to the gods. The warriors' armor, packed in Chinese chests, was wrapped in coarse straw matting, tied with sacred rope, and labeled "First Fruits for Kumano."

Setting out with ninety-three men on a day auspicious for Yori-

---

[7] Indicating that the wearers had purified themselves.

tomo and inauspicious for Yoshitsune, Tosa spent the first night at Sakawa post station. Since the Kajiwara family seat chanced to be located at the First Shrine[8] of the province, Kagetoki sent his heir, Genda, to present Tosa with two horses, a light brown and a light grey, and two silver-trimmed saddles. The beasts were festooned with paper strips as though intended for the gods.

By traveling early and late, Tosa reached the environs of the capital in nine days. Though the sun was still high when he arrived, he remained on the river beach at Shinomiya until nightfall. Then he divided his party into three[9] groups and rode casually into the city with fifty-six men, followed after a brief interval by the others. He struck out along the Gion Highway, crossed the river beach, and headed south on Higashi-no-tōin Avenue.

As luck would have it, one of Yoshitsune's retainers, a Shinano chieftain named Eda Genzō, was courting a lady at Sanjō Kyōgoku. This Eda encountered Tosa's party at Gojō Higashi-no-tōin while he was on his way from the Horikawa mansion to her home. He paused in the shadow of a building. "There go some pilgrims bound for Kumano. I wonder where they're from," he thought. He watched as the vanguard passed and the rear riders came into view. "That's Tosa from Nikaidō! Why would he be traveling to Kumano just now with all those warriors?" he wondered. Recalling the ill feeling between Yoritomo and Yoshitsune, he thought of stepping forward to question Tosa, but it seemed unlikely that he would receive truthful replies. He resolved to extract the information from Tosa's porters in an innocent manner.

Soon the porters came hustling along. When they saw Eda loitering there, one of them inquired, "How do we get to the intersection of Rokujō-no-bōmon and Abura-no-kōji?" After giving directions, Eda followed close on their heels. "Who is your master and where does he live?" he asked. "He is Lord Tosa from Nikaidō in Sagami," they replied.

Presently another porter came up from behind. "People say the

---

[8] Samukawa Shrine, situated on Mount Miya, north of Ichinomiya Village, Kōza District, Sagami. In principle, the First Shrine of a province was the one officially designated as of primary importance, although in practice there were sometimes two or more competing First Shrines recognized during different reigns.

[9] Probably a copyist's error for two.

capital is the sight of a lifetime. Why did we wait on the road for nightfall instead of entering the city while it was still light? Besides we're carrying heavy loads, and the road is pitch black," he grumbled.

"Don't be so impatient," said another voice. "You'll see the sights if we spend the night here."

"Tonight will be your last taste of peace," retorted the first. "The capital will be in an uproar tomorrow because of that affair. Heaven only knows what will happen to us."

Genzō spoke up as he walked along behind them. "I'm from Sagami myself, but I've been living in the capital with my master. It's nice to meet people from home."

"If you're a Sagami man, I'll tell you something," a voice answered unsuspectingly. "Lord Tosa is in the city on orders from Yoritomo to kill his brother, Yoshitsune. Don't mention this to anybody."

Abandoning all thought of visiting the lady, Eda rushed back to report at Horikawa.

"I'm not surprised," said Yoshitsune coolly. "I want Tosa brought here immediately. Give him this message: 'When Yoshitsune sends a man to the Kantō, his first duty is to report to Yoritomo on the state of affairs in Kyoto. Anyone who arrives in the capital from Kamakura is expected to visit Yoshitsune before he does anything else. Your failure to report is discourteous. Come at once.' "

Eda obediently went to Tosa's quarters on Abura-no-kōji Street, where he found the monk's men busily washing the legs of their unsaddled horses. Fifty or sixty warriors seemed to be engaged in a conference, while Tosabō himself lounged on an arm rest.

When Tosa had listened to Eda's message, he explained, "I'm making a pilgrimage to Kumano for Yoritomo. I had planned to call upon Yoshitsune before doing anything else, but having caught a slight cold on the way, I thought it best to rest tonight and go in the morning. I was about to send my son to tell His Lordship when you arrived. Will you be good enough to convey my apologies to him?"

Although Yoshitsune seldom permitted himself to speak harshly to a warrior, his face paled ominously when Eda returned with Tosa's message. "Only a coward would have let Tosa make excuses at a time like this. You're unfit for military service, you blundering idiot! Get out of here and don't let me see you again!" he shouted. Eda's first inclination was to go home, but he stayed to show that he was not afraid.

Meanwhile Benkei, who had left in the middle of a party at the mansion, came back to assure himself that Yoshitsune did not lack attendants.

"I'm glad to see you," said Yoshitsune. He described Eda's encounter with the porters. "I sent Genzō to fetch Tosa, but the stupid fool accepted an excuse, and after I reprimanded him he went off somewhere. I want you to bring Tosa here."

Benkei bowed and rose to his feet. "Right away! You ought to have asked me in the first place."

"Would it be a good idea to take some warriors with you?" wondered Yoshitsune.

"They would just alert him," Benkei replied. After putting on an ordinary blouse and knickers, a suit of black armor, a helmet with five flaps in back, and a four-foot sword, he mounted Yoshitsune's favorite horse, Ōguro, and went to Tosa's quarters with a single attendant. He rode through the inner courtyard to the side of the house, leaped onto the veranda from Ōguro's back, and flung up a blind, disclosing Tosa and seventy or eighty of his retainers seated in rows discussing plans for their raid.

Without a word of greeting, Benkei strode through the crowd of warriors to a seat next to Tosa at the head of the room. He settled himself rudely with his armor skirts touching Tosa's garments, surveyed the hall, and turned to glare at Tosa. "Deputy or not, it is your duty to go at once to the Horikawa mansion with news of the Kantō. What is the meaning of this delay?" As Tosa began to make excuses, he cut him short, pulling him up by the hand. "My lord has been drinking; don't get me in trouble with him. Come along," he said.

The warriors changed color, ready to fight at a word from their master, but the shaken Tosa gave them no cue. "I'll come at once," he agreed. "Just one minute, while I order someone to saddle a horse."

"I have one right here. Why saddle a beast that's already been used once today? Hurry up and get on." Although Tosa was renowned for his size, Benkei dragged him to the edge of the veranda.

At the sight of his master, Benkei's attendant led Ōguro over. Benkei heaved Tosa into the saddle, jumped on behind, and seized the reins, which he was of no mind to entrust to his companion.

Whipping the horse and urging him on with the stirrups, he galloped
off toward Rokujō Horikawa.

After Benkei had reported, Yoshitsune went to the south veranda.
He called Tosa near to question him.

"I am on my way to Kumano for Yoritomo," Tosa replied. "I had
planned to call here early tomorrow morning, since I'm suffering
from a cold tonight, but now that Your Lordship has sent a second
messenger, I have come in fear and trembling."

"I have been informed that you are here to attack me. Can you
deny it?"

"Such a thought has never crossed my mind. Someone has been
lying about me. I swear by the gods of Kumano that I think of you
and Yoritomo both as my lords."

"Isn't it a pity that men injured in the western fighting should have
to go as pilgrims to Kumano while their wounds are still unhealed?"

"Nobody like that is with me. I've just brought along a few lads to
protect me against brigands in the Kumano mountains. Perhaps
somebody was talking about them."

"Will you keep on with your denials if I tell you that your own
servants are predicting a major battle in Kyoto tomorrow?"

"It is hard to refute such lies. With your permission, I shall prepare
an oath of loyalty."

"By all means—as you know, the gods turn their backs on the un-
righteous." Yoshitsune ordered Tosa to write on the reverse sides of
seven Kumano talismans. "Let three be deposited at Hachiman
Shrine, one at Kumano, and three inside Tosa's body," he said,
setting fire to the last three. He watched Tosa swallow the ashes, and
then let him go.

"Sooner or later the gods and buddhas will punish me. I had better
not sit still tonight," thought Tosa after he had taken his leave. He
set his men to work the moment he reached his lodgings, with the
words, "Our only chance is to attack tonight."

Meanwhile at Yoshitsune's mansion Benkei and the other warriors
were warning their master: "It's all right to accept a loyalty oath in
some trifling matter, but promises aren't enough in a case like this. Be
on your guard tonight."

"Oh, I don't think there's anything to worry about," Yoshitsune
replied, unconcerned.

"Just the same, we must not be careless," they insisted.

"If anything happens, leave it to me. You can all go home," he said.

Yoshitsune had drunk steadily at the party that night, and he soon fell into a deep slumber; but it chanced that he was keeping a courtesan at the time, an uncommonly clever girl called Shizuka, who was so alarmed by his imprudence that she sent a servant girl to spy on Tosa. The girl saw men tying their helmet strings and exercising their horses as though on the point of starting on an excursion. She ventured cautiously forward to peek inside the building, and in so doing attracted the notice of one of Tosa's lackeys.

"There's something odd about that woman," he said.

"You're right. Seize her," replied a second.

They took hold of her and began to question her, alternately cajoling and threatening, until at last, unable to resist further, she confessed the truth.

"It's a mistake to treat such people leniently," they said, and chopped off her head.

Tosa's one hundred warriors approached Rokujō Horikawa around two o'clock in the morning on the seventeenth day of the tenth month, accompanied by fifty Shirakawa rock fighters[10] whom they had enlisted as guides. Yoshitsune's retainers had all quit the mansion, confident that nothing would happen so late at night—Benkei and Kataoka to retire to their homes in Rokujō, Satō Shirō and Ise Saburō to visit women in Muromachi, and Nenoo and Washinoo to go to Horikawa. Except for a servant called Kisanda, not a man remained. Yoshitsune himself lay fast asleep, still stupefied with wine from the previous evening. Though the enemy rode toward the mansion shouting warlike yells, no sound disturbed the silence inside.

Shizuka was the first to hear the hostile cries. After tugging at Yoshitsune and shaking him in vain, she threw open the lid of a chest and flung a suit of general's armor on top of him.

Yoshitsune woke with a start. "What is it?"

"Enemies outside!"

"Nothing beats a woman! It's Tosa, of course. What's the matter, isn't anyone there? Cut him down!"

"There isn't a warrior on the place. They all went home after you excused them last night."

[10] See Chapter Two, note 18.

"Oh yes, I remember now. Isn't there a man of any description around?"

After an excited search, the ladies of the household reported that the servant Kisanda was the only male to be found.

"Have Kisanda come here," Yoshitsune ordered.

Kisanda bowed low at the stepping stone beside the south veranda.

"Come closer," said Yoshitsune. Kisanda, who was not ordinarily permitted such liberties, could not bring himself to obey.

"Suit your conduct to the occasion, fellow," urged Yoshitsune. Kisanda advanced as far as the shutters.

"I have caught a trifling cold, which has made me stupid, but I'm going to arm myself and ride out. Hold them off until I come."

"Yes, Your Lordship." Kisanda ran forward and hastily pulled on a blouse and knickers decorated with a large wheel-and-line crest. Then he put on a corselet braided in a reversed water-plantain pattern,[11] seized a halberd, and leaped down from the veranda.

"Isn't there an extra bow in the reception hall?" he asked.

"Go and look."

Kisanda ran panting into the hall. There he found an unlacquered bow with a thickly bound grip and a number of untreated bamboo arrows with swan feathers, standing fourteen fists above the head. He strung the bow triumphantly against a pillar and hastened to the main courtyard, twanging the string until it rang like a gong.

Although Kisanda was a servant of the lowest order, he was quite as strong as Sumitomo or Masakado. As an archer he surpassed Yang Yu himself. With no trouble whatever he fixed one of the fourteen-fist arrows to the four-man bow,[12] pleased to find that the weapon suited him perfectly. He unbolted the gate, set it ajar, and dropped to one knee at the sight of enemy helmet studs gleaming temptingly in the bright starlight. One after another the arrows sped swiftly from his bow, felling five or six of Tosa's vanguard and killing two men on the spot. Tosa retreated cautiously.

"For shame, Tosa! Is that how you deputize for the Lord of Kamakura?" shouted Kisanda.

Tosa rode up behind the shelter of the gate. "Who has been named

---

[11] A corselet with thongs sewn in a trefoil design resembling the inverted leaf of a water-plantain.

[12] A bow so heavy that four men were required to string it.

Yoshitsune's commander for tonight? Identify yourself! Only a coward makes a sneak attack! I am Tosabō Shōshun, well known as a member of the Suzuki League and deputy of the Lord of Kamakura."

Kisanda remained silent, afraid of being scorned by the enemy because of his low rank.[13]

Meanwhile Yoshitsune had placed a gold-mounted saddle on his horse, Ōguro, and dressed himself in a red brocade blouse and knickers, scarlet armor, and a helmet with silver studs and a crest in the shape of a hoe. His weapons were a gold-fitted sword, war arrows trimmed with black and white eagle feathers, and a rattan-wrapped bow. He led up the horse, mounted, galloped into the main courtyard, and, from the kickball grounds,[14] called out Kisanda's name. Then Kisanda shouted to the enemy, "Though I am the lowliest of menials, my bravery has placed me in the vanguard of tonight's battle. Kisanda is my name, twenty-three my age! If anyone fancies himself a warrior, let him advance to meet me!"

Tosa burst angrily through the half-open gate, taking aim as he approached. He sent off a thirteen-fist arrow which buried itself to the feathers in the protective covering on Kisanda's left arm. Kisanda plucked the missile out and swiftly threw his bow aside. Then he opened both halves of the gate, planted his feet on the threshold, and grasped his great halberd squarely in the middle. The shouting enemy dashed forward bridle to bridle. Stepping back a pace, Kisanda struck out on all sides, bringing down the horses with blows to their heads, chests, and forelegs, and stabbing the riders as they pitched from their saddles. Countless of the foe fell in this manner before their overwhelming numbers forced Kisanda to run back to cling to Yoshitsune's bridle.

Yoshitsune saw that Kisanda's body was dripping with blood from the breastplate down. "You're wounded!" he exclaimed.

"Yes."

"Give up the fight if it's serious."

"A warrior dies on the field of battle."

"Good boy! You and I alone are a match for them."

---

[13] It was a point of honor with a warrior to choose an opponent of the highest social status possible.

[14] Kickball was a pastime of the nobility. From four to eight men kept a small leather ball in play with their feet, the object being to prevent it from touching the ground.

Nevertheless Yoshitsune remained motionless, and Tosa for his part hesitated to penetrate further. It appeared that neither side was eager to resume the battle.

Lying in bed at his Rokujō lodgings, Benkei said to himself, "I can't seem to get to sleep tonight. I suppose having Tosa in the city makes me worry about His Lordship. I'll just take a look at the mansion and then come back." He dressed himself in an ancient but strong suit of long-skirted armor, took up a sword and a staff, and clattered off on a pair of high clogs to Yoshitsune's house, where he gained admittance through a side entrance, supposing the main gate to be barred. As he passed behind the stables he heard horses' hooves thundering through the main courtyard, shaking the ground like an earthquake.

"Curse the luck! They've already attacked!" A glance inside the stables showed that Ōguro was not there. "His Lordship must have gone out to fight." Climbing onto the eastern middle gate, Benkei perceived Yoshitsune, a solitary figure on horseback with only Kisanda by his side.

"This is a great relief, but it's annoying all the same," he grumbled. "He's had a fine scare because he wouldn't listen to me." He began to stride noisily westward along the veranda.

Catching a startled glimpse of a brawny, armor-clad monk, Yoshitsune thought, "Tosa must have got in from the back." He rode forward with an arrow in his bow. "Who are you, monk? Identify yourself or be shot," he called out.

Benkei made no answer, trusting to his thick armor to stop the arrow. Yoshitsune abruptly returned the arrow to the quiver, unwilling to risk a mistake, and placed his hand on the hilt of his sword. He drew the weapon swiftly from its scabbard. "Who are you? Name yourself or be cut down," he demanded, advancing toward Benkei.

"As a swordsman His Lordship is the equal of Fan K'uai and Chang Liang," thought Benkei. He proclaimed aloud, "Let those who are far away listen to what is said of me! You who are close, behold me now with your own eyes! I am Saitō Musashibō Benkei, the eldest son of the Kumano abbot Benshō, who traces his ancestry to Amatsukoyane. I serve Yoshitsune, and I am a man in a thousand!"

"Very amusing," said Yoshitsune. "You should save your jokes for more suitable occasions."

"Very well—only you told me to identify myself, so I did," Benkei replied, not in the least abashed.

"Tosa has attacked me."

"It's a pity that you wouldn't listen to other people or take sensible precautions. You've let those fellows ride right up to your own gate."

"I've made up my mind to capture Tosa alive. Watch me."

"Stay where you are. I'll find him, grab him, and bring him here."

"I've seen a good many men, but none to equal you. Kisanda is a match for anyone too, even though he has never fought before. You'll be my captain—let Kisanda be your fighting force."

Kisanda climbed into the tower. "Night attackers have invaded Yoshitsune's mansion! Can't any of his retainers hear me? Are no citizens of the capital within earshot? Anyone who fails to appear tonight will be treated as an accomplice of the rebels tomorrow," he bellowed.

These shouts, which were audible far and wide, caused a great commotion in the capital and Shirakawa. Yoshitsune's warriors and other men rushed up from every direction. They surrounded the enemy and attacked mercilessly. Kataoka Hachirō plunged into the thick of Tosa's force and reported to Yoshitsune with two heads and three prisoners; Ise Saburō took two prisoners and three heads; Kamei Rokurō and Bizen Hcishirō killed two men each; and all the others took prisoners and trophies to their hearts' content.

The only warrior to suffer from the fortunes of war was Eda Genzō, who on hearing of the battle at Horikawa had immediately returned from Kyōgoku, where he had gone after incurring Yoshitsune's anger earlier that night. Eda began by taking two enemy heads. He entrusted them to Benkei to be presented to Yoshitsune on the following day and was returning to fight again when one of Tosa's arrows buried half its length in his neck. Raising his own bow, he tried frantically to release an arrow, but weakness overcame his arm. He stumbled toward the house, leaning on his sword, and attempted unsuccessfully to mount the veranda. "Is anyone there?" he called.

One of Yoshitsune's ladies in waiting emerged. "What is it?"

"Tell His Lordship that Eda Genzō is fatally wounded."

Yoshitsune, who had overheard, hastily kindled and raised a torch. An enormous black-feathered arrow hung from Eda's neck.

"What has happened? Look here, men!" he shouted.

"I know that I have displeased you," Eda gasped, "but this is going to be my end. Will you forgive me so that I may die content?"

"You know that I would never have cast you off for good. I spoke in the heat of the moment," Yoshitsune said in tears. Genzō bowed his head.

"Genzō, it is hard luck for a warrior to die from the wound of a single arrow," said Washinoo Shichirō, who was close by. "Have you any message to send home?" As Genzō failed to respond, Washinoo continued, "Your head is pillowed on His Lordship's knees."

"To die on His Lordship's lap is all I could possibly want," said Genzō. "When my mother left the capital for Shinano last spring, I promised faithfully to take leave and visit her in the winter. It would be a sin to grieve her by allowing some menial to confront her suddenly with my lifeless bones. I should be grateful if His Lordship would write to her during his stay in the capital."

"Don't worry. I will write often," Yoshitsune assured him.

Genzō wept gratefully. Washinoo urged him to recite Buddha invocations, since the end was near, and presently he died on his master's knees, intoning the sacred name in a clear voice. He was twenty-five years old.

After a time Yoshitsune summoned Benkei and Kisanda.

"How is the battle going?" he asked.

"Only twenty or thirty of Tosa's men are left."

"Eda's death is hard to bear. Don't kill any of Tosa's confederates. Capture all of them and bring them to me."

"It's simple enough to shoot down enemies, but taking them alive is a different matter. However..." Kisanda rushed away, halberd in hand.

"That fellow won't get ahead of me!" shouted Benkei, racing off with his battle-ax.

Kisanda ran past a deutzia hedge and turned west alongside the veranda of the water pavilion.[15] A warrior astride a bay horse was leaning on his bow while his mount rested.

"Who are you?" Kisanda demanded.

---

[15] *Izumidono.* In the mansions of the nobility, a small airy structure situated at the end of a corridor which extended southward from the eastern wing of the main building to an artificial lake in the garden.

The warrior urged his horse toward him. "I am Tosa Tarō, nineteen years old and son and heir to Tosa."

"I am Kisanda." As Kisanda sprang forward, Tarō nervously wheeled his horse to flee. Kisanda set out in pursuit. Tarō's horse, which had already galloped long and hard earlier in the day, had been driven relentlessly in the nightlong battle. It reared on its hind legs and refused to budge, stubbornly enduring its master's lashes, until Kisanda dealt it a sledgehammer blow which penetrated both hocks and made it rear over on top of Tarō. Then Kisanda held Tarō down, loosened his armor sash, and delivered him bound and uninjured to Yoshitsune, who ordered a servant to tie him to one of the pillars in the stables.

Benkei was running here and there, annoyed at having been bested by Kisanda, when he spied a warrior at the south gate, dressed in armor dyed in bands of white, pale blue, and indigo. "Who are you?" he demanded.

"Tosa's cousin, Ihō Gorō Morinao."

"I am Benkei." He lunged forward. Morinao fled in a panic, whipping his horse.

"You coward! Don't think you're going to get away," shouted Benkei. Stepping back, he brought down his ax on the horse's rump, striking with such force that it penetrated beyond the ornamental carving on the ax-head. Then he withdrew the weapon with a grunt, pounced on Morinao as the beast crashed to the ground, bound him with his own sash, and turned him over to be tied alongside Tosa Tarō.

For a time Tosabō fought recklessly at the head of his seventeen remaining warriors, as though life had lost its meaning for him, with most of his men either dead or missing and Tarō and Gorō captured. But at length he appeared to realize that the struggle was useless. Pursued by Yoshitsune's foot soldiers, he fled with his retainers all the way to the Rokujō River Beach, where ten of the seventeen promptly vanished from sight. He retreated up the Kamo River toward Kurama with the others.

Since the Kurama abbot was Yoshitsune's former teacher and the monks were his old comrades, the entire monastery turned out to search for the fugitives. "Whatever happens afterward, let us help Yoshitsune now," they said.

Back at the mansion Yoshitsune reproved his men. "You're a sorry lot! It would be maddening to have a rascal like Tosa slip through our fingers. We can't let him escape." After that all the retainers went off to take part in the hunt, leaving the Horikawa mansion to be guarded by the Kyoto warriors.

Tosa was soon obliged to flee from Kurama to Sōjō-ga-tani. At Kibune Shrine, with the pursuers hot on his trail, he removed his armor and presented it to the gods, and then hid himself in a great hollow tree.

When Benkei and Kataoka realized that Tosa had disappeared, they began to search frantically, afraid to face Yoshitsune's anger.

"I think I saw something move in the hollow tree behind Lord Washinoo," cried Kisanda, who had climbed onto a fallen log just opposite Tosa's hiding place. Washinoo ran toward the tree, brandishing his sword.

Tosa burst out in despair and plunged straight down the hillside. Benkei, arms outspread, gave chase. "Where do you think you're going, you scoundrel?" he bellowed exultantly. The swift Tosa was leading Benkei by a hundred feet when Kataoka called from a ravine far below, "I'm waiting for him. Send him down." Tosa thereupon began to angle upward on the steep face of the mountain, but Satō Tadanobu got above him with a huge two-pronged arrow in his bow, aimed down the hill, and pulled back slightly on the string. Tosa might have been expected to kill himself at that point, but instead he meekly permitted Benkei to capture him.

When the warriors had returned from Kurama, escorted by fifty of Tōkōbō's monks, Yoshitsune ordered the prisoner to be taken to the main courtyard.

"Well, Shōshun, a loyalty oath is supposed to mean something. Why did you write it? I'll let you off if you want to go home. What do you say?" he asked from the veranda.

Tosa touched his head to the ground. "The *shōjō* treasures his blood, the *sai* his horn, and the Japanese warrior his honor.[16] How could I return and face other fighting men? All I ask is that you cut off my head without wasting any time."

[16] Probably a saying current in the Muromachi period. The *shōjō* and *sai*, sea-dwelling semimythical animals in Chinese literature, are sometimes identified with the orangutan or chimpanzee and the rhinoceros. Apparently there were stories in medieval Japan about *shōjō* hunted for their blood (for medicinal use?) and *sai* for their horns. Okami, p. 169, n. 1.

"If you hadn't been a stouthearted fellow Yoritomo wouldn't have relied on you. Should we kill such a valuable prisoner or keep him alive? Let Benkei decide."

"When a man as strong as Tosa is shut up in a prison, he's apt to break out. Rather than risk such a thing, we had better kill him," said Benkei. With Kisanda walking behind to hold Tosa's bonds, he took the monk to the Rokujō River Beach and ordered Suruga Jirō to behead him. Tosa perished at the age of forty-three, Tosa Tarō at nineteen, and Ihō Gorō at thirty-three.

In time, the men who had escaped made their way back to Kamakura. "Tosa blundered. Yoshitsune cut off his head," they told Yoritomo.

"I won't tolerate the seizure and execution of a man who was acting as my representative!" Yoritomo exclaimed. Among themselves his warriors said, "Why shouldn't Tosa have been executed? Wasn't he personally leading an attack on Yoshitsune?"

YOSHITSUNE'S FLIGHT FROM THE CAPITAL

By Yoritomo's order, Hōjō Shirō Tokimasa set out in the direction of the capital as commander of a war party. Hatakeyama at first refused to have anything to do with an attack on Yoshitsune, but upon receiving a second direct command he rode toward Atsuta Shrine in Owari at the head of the Seven Leagues of Musashi.[17] It was also reported that Yamada Shirō Tomomasa would leave the Kantō with a rear guard of a thousand men.

On the first day of the eleventh month [of 1185], Yoshitsune sent a message to the ex-Emperor by the Lord of Third Rank. "When I risked my life to subdue the enemies of the court, I did so in order to avenge my ancestors, of course, but I also thought of myself as serving His Majesty, so it is only right that I should receive special favors from the throne. I had hoped to have all the lands west of Ōsaka Barrier, but now that Yoritomo wants to execute me as a traitor I shall be content with Shikoku and Kyushu. I should like to go there now," he said.

Since this request required a careful reply, the nobles met in council. "What Yoshitsune says is reasonable enough, but Yoritomo will be furious if we issue the edict," they said. "On the other hand,

[17] See Appendix C, note 1.

Yoshitsune may create a frightful disturbance if we refuse, just as Kiso did when he was in the capital. As long as Yoritomo is already marching against him, the best thing we can do is to give him what he wants, and at the same time order the local Genji to attack him at Daimotsu." This decision was presented unanimously, and the Emperor granted the request.

As Yoshitsune was making preparations to leave for the west, a large number of warriors from that part chanced to be in the capital; among them was a certain Ogata Saburō Koreyoshi. Yoshitsune said to him, "I am going to Kyushu, which has been granted to me by the throne. Can I rely on you to help me?"

"Since Kikuchi Jirō is in the city now, you will probably be calling him in. If you slay him, I am at your disposal," replied Ogata.

Yoshitsune summoned Benkei and Ise Saburō. "Who is the better man, Kikuchi or Ogata?" he asked.

"That would be difficult to say. Kikuchi is more trustworthy, but Ogata commands more men," they answered.

Then Yoshitsune called in Kikuchi. "I am counting on your support, Kikuchi," he said.

"I would be very happy to obey your commands if I hadn't let my son go to the Kantō. A parent and his child cannot follow rival leaders," replied Kikuchi Jirō.

When he heard this, Yoshitsune determined to destroy Kikuchi. He set up a siege of his house under a force led by Benkei and Ise Saburō. Kikuchi, his last arrow gone, set fire to the building and killed himself. Ogata Saburō then joined Yoshitsune.

Yoshitsune left the capital with his uncle, the Governor of Bizen, on the third day of the eleventh month. Since he had made a point of telling his men that they must look their best when he entered his own provinces for the first time, they were all dressed in the most elegant manner imaginable. Among the party was the famous *shirabyōshi* dancer[18] Shizuka, the daughter of Iso-no-zenji, who at Yoshitsune's request had attired herself as a man in a hunting costume. Yoshitsune wore a red brocade blouse and knickers, leggings, and arm shields, and sat on a silver-mounted saddle astride a spirited

---

[18] A female entertainer specializing in the performance of *shirabyōshi*, a type of singing and dancing which was extremely popular around the end of the Heian period. The performer dressed as a man in a white tunic and long trousers.

black horse with a flowing mane and tail. His escort consisted of two groups of fifty warriors each, the first party attired in black armor and mounted on black horses with silver-trimmed saddles, and the second wearing light green armor and riding bay horses. These were followed by a host of other riders, streaming along behind in bands of one or two hundred. The entire procession included more than 15,000 men.

With 500 men, a store of valuables, and twenty-five horses, Yoshitsune set sail for Shikoku on board a great ship, the Tsuki Maru, which was famous throughout western Japan.

> Sad is the lot of those
> Who ride the waves in ships,
> Their tear-drenched sleeves
> Damper than the garb of Ise fisherfolk[19]
> As they watch the seaweed-gatherers' boats
> Float drearily at their moorings among the inlet reeds,
> Or hear the island plover's plaintive call
> From desolate shores the oarsmen skirt.
> "Were those an enemy's battle shouts?"—those distant cries
> Of seagulls veiled in mist?
> Borne by the winds and tides,
> They bow on the left to Sumiyoshi's gods,
> On the right to the Western Shrine,
> And glimpsing afar the Ashiya coast
> With the woods of Ikuta,
> Row on past Wada Cape
> Toward the Strait of Awaji.

As they plied the oars with Eshima Shore on their right, Yoshitsune perceived the indistinct outline of a great mountain looming through the winter rain. "Where is that mountain and what is its name?" he asked. His men advanced one theory and another. Benkei, who had been napping with his head against the side of the ship, jumped up to the helm deck. "You have taken it for a distant peak, but it's not far away at all. That is Mount Shosha in Harima," he said.

---

[19] A stock literary expression, used, as here, to convey the notion that a despondent lover's or traveler's sleeve was always wet with tears, unlike the fishermen's garments, which occasionally had an opportunity to dry. Okami, p. 173, n. 24.

"Shosha or not, I am looking at the black cloud to the west of it which has just risen near the peak. A gale will be blowing by nightfall. If it reaches us, we shall have to save ourselves by beaching the vessel on the first island or shore we can find," said Yoshitsune.

"That doesn't look like a wind cloud," said Benkei. "Have you forgotten your words during the campaign against the Heike, after you sent the bodies of all those young Taira nobles to the bottom of the sea and buried their bones beneath the moss? I can hear you now: 'Since Hachiman protects the Genji, we are always safe.' All the same, the cloud is dangerous for you. If it hits the boat, it will be the end of you and me both."

"Nonsense!"

"You have regretted not listening to my advice in the past," Benkei retorted. "Watch me." He put on a soft cap, laid aside his sword and halberd, took up a number of unlacquered arrows with swan feathers and a plain bow, and climbed agilely onto the prow of the boat. There he began to speak in a challenging voice, as if he were addressing a human audience.

"There has never been anything to compare with the battles of Hōgen and Heiji in all the forty-four reigns since the first human emperor—to say nothing of the seven reigns of heavenly gods and the five reigns of earthly gods during the age of the gods. In both of those wars Minamoto Tametomo won praise from everybody by shooting fifteen-fist arrows from a five-man bow. Many years have passed since then, but now there is another great archer among the Genji retainers.

"I am going to shoot at that cloud. If it is only a plaything of the winds, my arrows won't hurt it; but if it is the spirits of Taira dead, it will be powerless to resist me—that is the law of heaven. If these arrows are of no avail, what is the use of worshiping gods and buddhas? Though I am but a retainer of the Genji, I have a proper name of my own. I am Saitō Musashibō Benkei, the son of the Kumano abbot Benshō, who traces his ancestry to Amatsukoyane!" One after another the swift arrows sped from his bow. It was impossible to trace their course over the sea, which was dazzlingly bright in the sunlight of the winter afternoon, but all of a sudden the cloud was gone—it must indeed have been the spirits of the dead.

"That was most frightening," the warriors muttered among themselves. "What might have become of us if Benkei had not been here?"

When the chanting oarsmen had reached a spot from which the eastern part of Mizushima in Awaji Province was faintly visible, the party saw a second black cloud enveloping the northern slopes of the same mountain.

"What about that one?" asked Yoshitsune.

"I am sure that is a wind cloud," replied Benkei. Immediately a savage gale struck the ship. Since it was early in the eleventh month, hail mingled with the driving rain, wholly obscuring the shore to the east and west. Winds howled around the foot of the hills, and violent gusts from Mount Muko in Settsu blew with increasing fury as darkness gathered.

"The wind is appalling. Lower the sail," Yoshitsune told the boatmen. They attempted to do so, but the pulley, wet with rain, stuck fast.

"We ran into typhoons scores of times during the western campaign," Benkei said to Kataoka. "Lower the tow ropes. We'll roll up the matting[20] and fasten it to them." This was of no help whatever, so they tied vines around a number of rocks which had been taken aboard for ballast at Kawashiri; but when they threw them overboard the wind pulled the ropes to the surface, rocks and all. The horses neighed wildly, terrified by the pounding waves, and the wretched passengers, who only that morning had considered themselves perfectly safe, lay vomiting in the hold.

"Rip the sail so the wind can go through," Yoshitsune commanded. His men hacked away with long-handled cutlasses,[21] giving the wind free passage, but foaming crests continued to surge against the prow like a thousand thrusting spears.

Like souls in purgatory, they plunged through the darkness that hung over the empty seas, searching in vain for a beacon or fisherman's fire. Even the stars of the Great Bear had vanished from the clouded heavens.

Had Yoshitsune been alone the matter would have been quite different, but being of a warmhearted nature he had been on intimate terms with some twenty-four ladies during his sojourn in the capital, and of these he had brought along a number of elegant beauties who

[20] Matting was used as an awning to protect passengers from the elements.
[21] *Naigama.* Used in battle for slashing the legs of men and horses.

were his special favorites, including the daughters of the Taira Great
Counselor, the Koga Minister of State, the Karahashi Great Counselor, and the Torikai Middle Counselor. The feminine party aboard
the ship numbered eleven in all, including Shizuka and four other
shirabyōshi dancers. Though each had lived separately in Kyoto, these
ladies were now huddled together. "Any fate in the city would have
been better than this!" they wailed.

"What is the time?" Yoshitsune inquired at last, rising unsteadily
to his feet.

"Around one in the morning," someone replied.

"If only dawn would come! If we could see the clouds, we might be
able to do something . . . Warrior or servant, is there no one here who
can climb the mast to cut the pulley rope?"

"When a man's luck deserts him, his disposition changes," Benkei
muttered.

"I am not asking you to climb it," Yoshitsune said. "A mountain
chap like you could never do it. Hitachibō is used to small boats on
the lake[22] in Ōmi, but he doesn't know anything about ships. Ise
Saburō is from Kōzuke and Tadanobu's from Ōshū . . . But Kataoka
was raised on the wild coast of Kashima and Namekata in Hitachi.
When Shida Saburō Senjō was living on Ukishima Island, Kataoka
used to visit him and boast that if trouble broke out between the
Taira and the Minamoto he could sail a boat as frail as a reed anywhere at all, even to China. Kataoka, climb up."

Kataoka promptly withdrew. Taking off his tunic, blouse, and
knickers, he twisted breechcloths around his middle. Then he loosened and pushed back his top hair, tied a headband over his cap, and
tucked a sharp, long-handled cutlass into his waist. He elbowed his
way through the crowd, mounted the crosspiece, and made as if to
grip the mast. It was so enormous, however, that not even a giant
could have encircled it. It soared to a height of forty or fifty feet, and
its snow- and rain-drenched surface had been transformed by the
piercing blasts from Mount Muko into a silvery sheet of ice.

Yoshitsune, seeing that Kataoka was for the moment at a loss,
cried encouragingly, "Good work, Kataoka!"

"Here goes!" roared Kataoka. He began to climb, sliding down
and reascending again and again. When he had finally gained a point

----

22 Lake Biwa.

about twenty feet above the deck, he heard a weird rumble, like an earthquake, reverberating in the bowels of the ship. A wall of wind and rain was approaching from the shore.

"Do you hear that, sailors?" Kataoka shouted. "Wind from the rear! Watch the waves! Change course!" At once a great wind whistled through the sail and sent the vessel tossing wildly over the waves. Two mysterious reports as loud as thunderclaps drew shrieks of despair from the panic-stricken passengers.

At that instant the top of the mast fell into the sea from a break twenty feet below the pulley. As the lightened ship began to run more buoyantly, Kataoka descended to the deck to cut away the tangle of ropes. For the remainder of the night, they rolled and pitched, still at the mercy of the sea, while the wind tore at the broken mast.

Toward dawn, just when the storm had almost subsided, a new wind sprang up.

"I wonder where this one is coming from," said Benkei.

"Yesterday's storm has returned," replied a sailor of about fifty.

"I say, fellow," objected Kataoka. "Look before you talk. Yesterday the wind came from the north. If it's the same one returning, it ought to be blowing from the south or southeast. This must come from Settsu Province."

"You men don't know anything about it; the sailors are the experts," interposed Yoshitsune. "Just see to it that we have a sail to catch the breeze." They erected an emergency mast and sail, and the ship ran swiftly ahead.

Shortly before daybreak the sailors brought the vessel to an unfamiliar shore.

"Is the tide in or out?" asked Yoshitsune.

"Out."

"All right, we'll wait for it to return."

As they lay with waves slapping against the hull, a great bell began to toll from the direction of the land.

"If we can hear a bell, the shore must be very close. Somebody had better take a boat and see what he can find out," said Yoshitsune. The warriors swallowed nervously, wondering who would be chosen.

"There's no harm in using a good man more than once," Yoshitsune continued. "Kataoka, go and have a look."

Kataoka obediently put on a corselet of reverse plantain[23] and fastened a sword to his waist. Being an excellent sailor, he had no difficulty guiding his small boat to the beach. There he found a cluster of thatched huts used by fishermen for salt curing. He rejected his impulse to question the people there, feeling certain that they would not speak freely to a stranger, and passed on. About one hundred yards inland, he came to a great torii which guarded the deserted precincts of an ancient shrine. When he had approached and made his obeisances, he became aware that an old man, near eighty, was lingering near by.

"What is the name of this place, and what province am I in?" Kataoka inquired.

"This is not a well-known spot, but it is odd that you should have to ask the name of the province... We've been in a sad turmoil here during the past two or three days. People say that Yoshitsune, who left yesterday for Shikoku, will be forced by the storm to land on our coast, and Teshima Kurando, Kōzuke Hangan, and Komizo Tarō, three of the leading warriors in the province, have been ordered to intercept him. They're waiting on the land with 500 mounts saddled, bridled, and ready for instant action, and on the beach with thirty cedarwood boats filled with war shields. If you are connected in any way with Yoshitsune, you had better get away as fast as you can."

Feigning innocence, Kataoka said, "My home is in Awaji. I started out to go fishing two days ago, but I was caught in the typhoon, and now I've landed here. Tell me the truth."

The old man recited an ancient verse, "Watching the flickering fireflies at Ashi-no-sato, I recall the lights of bygone fishing fires,"[24] and with those words was gone. When Yoshitsune and his men learned later that the shrine was dedicated to the god of Sumiyoshi, they understood that a divine being had taken pity on them.

When Kataoka had returned with his report, Yoshitsune said, "All right, we shall put out to sea." But the receding tide had stranded the vessel, so there was nothing to do but spend the night where they were.

---

[23] See Note 11 above.

[24] He is telling Kataoka that the vessel has been blown back to Ashiya (Ashi-no-sato) on Osaka Bay near Daimotsu, which was its point of embarkation. The "ancient" verse appears in *Shinkokinshū*, a poetic anthology compiled in 1206.

THE FIGHTING AT SUMIYOSHI AND DAIMOTSU

Meanwhile there was a great to-do at Daimotsu-no-ura. As the saying goes, "Heaven, which lacks a mouth, must speak through human agents."

"No vessel was there last night; it is queer that that one has suddenly arrived in the dark with its matting spread. Let us go and look at it," said the 500 warriors. They set out in the thirty boats, which were small, shallow-bottomed craft, freely maneuverable even at low tide. Their skilled sailors quickly surrounded the great ship. The warriors shouted menacingly, "Don't let any of them get away."

"Don't be alarmed by these enemies," counseled Yoshitsune. "Once they know I am here, they won't be eager to come any closer. If they start a fight, let the ordinary warriors go, but capture the leaders with grappling hooks."

"A fine plan," said Benkei. "Still, fighting on board ship is a touchy affair. Let me be the one to start the battle."

"The proper functions of a monk are to mourn the dead and guide the living. Why should you take the lead? Stand back and let me shoot an arrow," said Kataoka.

"Are you the only warrior among His Lordship's retainers?" Benkei demanded.

Satō Tadanobu bowed low before Yoshitsune. "The enemy will be on top of us while those two are still arguing about precedence. Please command me to release the first arrow."

"Spoken like a man! I had hoped you would volunteer," said Yoshitsune.

Satō put on a dotted silk blouse and knickers, a suit of green armor, and a helmet with three flaps. He armed himself with a handsome silver-mounted sword, a bamboo bow wrapped with rattan at the joints, and a quiver containing twenty-four arrows with hawk feathers, which he slung high on his back[25] with two large humming bulbs uppermost. Then he strode to the bow of the ship to confront the enemy.

Led by Teshima Kanja and Kōzuke Hangan, the attackers had approached to within bowshot in their small boats lined with shields. "Ahoy there! We know you are Yoshitsune's ship," they called. "We

---

[25] The quiver was customarily worn low on the hip to facilitate withdrawal of arrows. Satō's reason for wearing it high was to cut a dashing figure.

are Teshima Kanja and Kōzuke Hangan, emissaries of the Lord of Kamakura. We shall be disgraced if we allow you fugitives to land."

"I am Shirobyōe Tadanobu." Satō sprang erect.

"A deputy is the same as his principal," cried Teshima Kanja. He fixed a great turnip-shaped arrow to his bow, pulled back hard, and sent the humming missile square into the side of the ship.

"Anyone who begins a fight ought to be able to hit the one he aims at," taunted Tadanobu. "You're hardly the warrior to make light of a Genji retainer like me. Let me show you what I can do." To his three-man bow he affixed a humming-bulb arrow thirteen hands and three finger-breadths long. He pulled the string back as far as it would go and released it. The arrow flew toward Teshima with an ominous moan. Its forked prongs struck him below the visor of his helmet, went all the way through his neckbone, and came to rest in his top neckplate. The bowl of the helmet, the head in it, fell into the sea with a splash.

Kōzuke Hangan stepped into Teshima's place. "I'll put a stop to your big talk," he cried. Instead of a humming bulb, he dispatched an arrow from the middle of his quiver; it grazed the left side of Satō's helmet just as he was preparing to shoot again, forcing Satō's humming bulb to drop into the sea.

"The warriors in this province can't seem to hit an enemy," jeered Satō. "Shall I show you how it's done?" He fitted a spearhead arrow into place, pulled back slightly on the bowstring while the mortified Hangan inserted a second arrow, and then pulled back hard and sent the arrow off as Hangan was raising his own bow. The spearhead entered Hangan's body on the lower left side and emerged on the right, protruding a full five inches. Quite unceremoniously, Hangan toppled into the sea.

Satō thereupon returned to Yoshitsune, stringing another arrow on the way. Since there was no doubt about the quality of his performance, his name was entered at the head of the achievement register.[26] Meanwhile the retainers of Teshima Kanja and Kōzuke Hangan withdrew far beyond arrow range, much shaken by the deaths of their lords.

"Tell me, Tadanobu, what was your strategy?" inquired Kataoka.

"I only tried to shoot as well as I could," Satō replied.

[26] Kept as a reference for use in allotting rewards.

"Stand aside, please. I shall venture an arrow myself." Satō withdrew.

After changing to a white blouse and knickers, yellow-figured white armor, and a folded cap, which he tied on his head in place of a helmet, Kataoka tucked a bow of untreated wood under his arm and placed an arrow box on a crossplank. He took off the lid of the box. The arrows inside were made of natural bamboo smoothed at the tops of the joints. Their feathers were secured by spindlewood bark, and the shafts were reinforced with casings of yew and black oak four inches in circumference and six inches long, fitted with six-inch tips made of horn.

"If I shoot one of those at a captain, people may say I was too weak to penetrate his armor," said Kataoka to the others. "The upper edges of Shikoku cedarwood craft are thin, however, and the waterline on those crowded boats must be five inches higher than normal. A fast arrow at close range will split one like a chisel. Once a boat is swamped and its occupants are in the water, we can kill them all. If other vessels try to rescue them, shoot at random as fast as you can. Don't stop to worry about whether you're aiming at important warriors or ordinary soldiers."

"Very good," they agreed.

Crouching with one knee on the plank, Kataoka released a swift volley of arrows. Fourteen or fifteen of his yew wood-splitters drove home in the enemy ships, and three of them quickly filled to the brim with water. When all three had sunk before the eyes of the onlookers, with the frightened passengers pushing and shoving, the remaining enemy ships rowed to Daimotsu-no-ura and the men returned disconsolately to their homes, bearing Teshima Kanja's lifeless body.

Benkei, meanwhile, complained to Hitachibō: "This is a fine state of affairs! You and I had no chance to fight a real battle. The way we've wasted today reminds me of someone who goes to a mountain for treasure without laying his hands on anything valuable."

As if in reply, Komizo Tarō, who had got wind of the fighting and ridden into Daimotsu-no-ura with a hundred men, was now headed toward Yoshitsune's ship with his eager parties in five of the boats that had been drawn up on the beach. Benkei and Hitachibō put on black armor and commandeered a small boat, which Hitachibō engaged to maneuver, since he was a skilled oarsman. Leaving behind his bow and arrows, Benkei armed himself with a four-foot sword decorated with a crane design, and a shorter sword named Rock Cleaver. He tossed in a long-handled cutlass, a grappling hook, and a battle ax decorated with heart-shaped figures, and jumped agilely into the bow, clutching his favorite weapon, a twelve-foot club of yew wood with an iron base reinforced with bands of rattan and iron.

"This will be easy. If you'll just row our boat in among the others, I'll pull one of them toward us with the hook, board it, and use the club on their helmets, elbows, knees, and hips. Their leader's head will be a sorry sight after I split open his helmet. The rest of you stay here and watch." Benkei shoved off like a descending god of pestilence as Yoshitsune and the others stared after him.

"Who are those two men heading toward us all alone?" asked Komizo Tarō.

"One is Benkei and the other is Hitachibō," someone answered.

"We're no match for them," Komizo exclaimed, and he turned about in the direction of Daimotsu.

"Cowards! I see Komizo Tarō! Come back and fight," Benkei roared. But Komizo continued his retreat.

Urged on by Benkei, Hitachibō rowed furiously with his foot on the gunwale. When they had drawn abreast of the enemy, Benkei engaged one of the five hostile craft with the grappling hook. He sprang aboard and proceeded to clear a path from stem to stern, knocking down and crushing men with his dreadful club. Not one who was struck survived, and those who managed to elude the club were so terrified that they jumped to their deaths in the sea.

"Stop him, Kataoka," commanded Yoshitsune. "He is committing shocking sins."

"Orders from His Lordship: don't commit such sins!" Kataoka shouted to Benkei.

"I am not a very holy monk; don't bother me with orders. Follow me, Hitachi, after them!" roared Benkei, raining blows in every direction. After two of the enemy boats had been sunk, the other three succeeded in escaping in the direction of Daimotsu-no-ura.

The fighting on that occasion thus ended in victory for Yoshitsune. Sixteen of the warriors on the ship were wounded, and eight were killed. The dead were buried at sea off Daimotsu to prevent the enemy from taking their heads.

The remainder of the day was spent on board. At nightfall the
ladies were put ashore. Though their sorrow was heart-rending, it
was impossible for them to stay on. All but one were sent back—the
daughter of the Taira Great Counselor of Second Rank with Suruga
Jirō, the daughter of the Koga Minister of State with Kisanda, and
the rest with kinsmen or other connections. With Shizuka, his particular favorite, Yoshitsune journeyed from Daimotsu to Watanabe,
and on the following day he reached the home of Nagamori, the chief
priest of Sumiyoshi. After spending the night there, he went to a
place in Uda District, Kishi-no-oka by name. There he remained
with a relative of his mother's until he learned that Hōjō Shirō Tokimasa had crossed the provinces of Iga and Ise on his way to Uda.
He then set out again, to avoid involving others in his difficulties.
As dawn was breaking on the fourteenth day of the twelfth month of
the first year of Bunji [1185], he abandoned his horse in the foothills
and sought sanctuary in the Yoshino Mountains, where the famous
cherry trees blossom in the spring.

Chapter Five

HOW YOSHITSUNE ENTERED THE YOSHINO MOUNTAINS

Though spring had already visited the capital, the valley streams at wintry Yoshino were still locked in year-end cold. Entering the inhospitable mountains with Shizuka, from whom he had refused to part, Yoshitsune toiled painfully across chasms and mountain passes to Sugi-no-dan.

"Looking after His Lordship properly on this journey is anything but easy," complained Benkei to Kataoka. "I didn't fancy having a dozen women on board while we were bound for Shikoku, but bringing one into these wilds is even worse. If the foothill villagers hear about us while she is with us, we'll be captured by common fellows. I don't intend to disgrace myself by letting them shoot me down. What do you say, Kataoka? Shall we run off and save our skins?"

"I can't bring myself to do that," Kataoka answered. "Let's pay no attention to her."

Yoshitsune, overhearing this conversation, recognized with a heavy heart that he must either part with his men for Shizuka's sake or relinquish her to retain their loyalty. Choking with tears, he summoned Benkei. "Although I knew you were against it, I was sentimental enough to bring Shizuka here against my better judgment. Now I think it is best to send her back to the city. What do you say?" he asked.

"A splendid idea! I would have suggested it myself if I had dared. As long as you feel that way, send her off right away before it gets dark."

"What on earth am I doing?" thought Yoshitsune. He wanted to say that he had changed his mind, but it was impossible to disregard the feelings of his warriors. He could only repeat, "I wish Shizuka to go to the capital."

Two warriors and three yeomen at once volunteered to serve as her escorts.

"You have made me a gift more precious than life. Be kind to her during the journey. After you have seen her safely to the city, you will be free to go wherever you like," Yoshitsune said.

Next Yoshitsune called Shizuka to his side. "Don't think that I'm sending you back to the capital because I have tired of you. If I had not loved you tenderly, I would never have kept you with me so long, or brought you on this cruel journey in spite of other people's disapproval. This mountain, the Peak of Enlightenment made sacred by En no Gyōja, is forbidden to the impure,[1] so it is quite possible that I have made the gods angry by letting you share the fate which has led me here. I want you to hide with Iso-no-zenji at home until spring. If things are not better for me by next year, I shall become a monk. If you still care for me then, let us enter religion at the same time, read the sutras and pronounce the name of Amida together, and be united both in the present world and in the life to come."

Long before he had finished, Shizuka was weeping bitterly, her face hidden in her sleeve. "Before you tired of me I was allowed to accompany you over the waves toward Shikoku. Now that you have forgotten our vows, all I can do is resign myself to a life of sorrow. Perhaps I oughtn't to say anything, but I haven't been my usual self since last summer, and there's no more doubt that I'm going to have a child. Since everybody knows about our relations, my condition is sure to be reported at Rokuhara and Kamakura. Who knows what terrible thing will happen to me if I'm captured and sent off to those barbarians in the Kantō? I implore you to kill me here," she begged. "Both for your sake and for mine, it is better for me to die than to linger on in misery."

"However unreasonable it may seem, please go back to the capital."

---

[1] That is, to all women and to men who had recently drunk strong liquor, eaten meat, or indulged in sexual relations. Many old works refer to the prohibition against women at Mount Kimpu (the "Peak of Enlightenment") and specifically at the Zaōdō (Kimpusenji) on the mountain. I have found no satisfactory explanation for the author's reference a few pages below to visits to the Zaōdō by Shizuka and other ordinary people of both sexes.

At these words Shizuka buried her face in Yoshitsune's lap, moaning softly, while the watching warriors pressed their sleeves to their eyes.

Presently Yoshitsune handed her a small looking glass, of the sort used by men when dressing their hair. "I have used this every morning and evening. Whenever you look at it, think that you are seeing me," he said. The weeping Shizuka pressed it to her breast as if she were receiving a memento from the dead. A poem came to her mind: "Though I gaze at it, I shall feel no pleasure—this clear glass which no longer reflects the features of my beloved," she recited haltingly. Yoshitsune gave her a pillow, beseeching her to keep it constantly by her side. "In vain do I seek to hasten on my journey—I who have been accustomed to travel with serenity,"[2] he said in reply to her verse. Then he pressed treasures of all kinds on her, including a particularly valuable drum with a sandalwood frame, a sheepskin cover, and multicolored cords. "I prize this instrument highly," he said. "During the reign of ex-Emperor Shirakawa a prelate from Hōjūji Temple brought back two rare treasures from China, a lute called Meigyoku and this drum, Hatsune. Meigyoku was kept in the imperial palace until it burned in ex-Emperor Sutoku's residence during the Hōgen War. Hatsune was given to Taira Masamori, the Governor of Sanuki, who took great care of it. Tadamori inherited it after Masamori's death... I'm not sure who owned it after Kiyomori,[3] but at the battle of Yashima it was dropped into the sea, either accidentally or by design. Ise Saburō recovered it with a grappling hook and I sent it to Yoritomo, who later returned it to the ex-Emperor. It was given to me while I was in the capital after the defeat of the Heike. I had meant to keep it always, but I want you to take it, now that the end has come." Shizuka accepted it tearfully.

Since further delay would merely have increased the sorrow of parting, the two groups prepared to go their separate ways. But when Yoshitsune summoned his resolution, Shizuka could not bear to leave, and when Shizuka steeled herself to go, Yoshitsune's courage failed. Neither could set out in earnest, and every departure was succeeded by a return. At length, however, Yoshitsune drew away on his journey toward the peaks, while Shizuka descended toward the valley,

---

[2] The point of the poem is in a pun on Shizuka's name, which can be translated Serenity.

[3] We are to understand that Tadamori handed it on to his son, Kiyomori.

gazing after his figure as long as it was visible. When they could no longer see each other, they shouted back and forth until the hills rang.

Consoling her as best they could, Shizuka's five escorts descended with her to Sanshi Pass. Then the two warriors called the yeomen aside. "What do you think? Whether Yoshitsune is devoted to her or not, he is a hunted man. How can we hope to escape from such a dangerous area if we leave the mountains with a fugitive? The foot-hills are close enough so that she can easily find her way out if we leave her. Let us escape from here and save ourselves," they proposed.

What could be expected of the lower orders when such words were uttered by warriors—men who presumably understood the meaning of honor and compassion! "The decision is entirely up to you," said the yeomen.

"Rest here awhile," the men told Shizuka, spreading a fur rug under an ancient tree. "A close connection of ours is the abbot of a temple dedicated to Eleven-Headed Kannon at the foot of the mountain. We shall go down to tell him about you, and if he agrees we shall take you to him for the time being. From the temple we can follow the mountains to the capital."

"Do whatever seems best," Shizuka replied.

SHIZUKA IS DESERTED IN THE MOUNTAINS

Shizuka's escorts disappeared at once, carrying Yoshitsune's gifts with them. As the day gradually drew to a close, Shizuka began to await their return with increasing anxiety, until at length, in tears, she left the tree, unable to control her alarm. The only sound was that of the wind sighing in the withered foliage of the cedars; the moonlight shone fitfully through the trees. She wandered, as if in a daze, to the summit of a lofty peak, where she called out as loudly as she could. An answering cry echoed from the valley. "Can someone be calling me?" she thought. She descended, sobbing piteously, to an untracked expanse of deep snow. For a time she fancied that a plaintive voice in the valley was mingling with the gale, but it was only the faint murmur of a snow-covered stream. Still in tears, she returned to the peak, from where she could discern no human footprints except her own.

So in this manner Shizuka descended valleys and climbed peaks. Her shoes were claimed by the drifts and her hat by the wind. Blood from her bruised feet reddened the snow of the Yoshino Mountains, freezing water dripped from her tear-drenched sleeves, and ice formed on the hem of her skirts, weighting her body so that she could scarcely move. All night long she stumbled over mountain paths.

The parting with Yoshitsune had taken place around noon on the sixteenth day of the month. What distress Shizuka must have felt, following wild trails alone until dusk on the seventeenth! At last she chanced upon a path trampled in the snow. This she followed as best she could, in the hope that either Yoshitsune or her faithless escorts might be near at hand, until it came to a road of sizable dimensions. After hesitating for a time, uncertain as to where the road might lead, she struck out along it toward the west. (It was in fact, as she later discovered, the Uda Road.)

A faint light presently became visible deep in a distant valley, giving promise of a settlement of some sort. "Since there are no charcoal burners in the hills at this time of year, it cannot be a kiln fire. If this were an autumn evening," she thought, "I would call it a marsh firefly."

As she drew nearer, she found that the light emanated from a lantern in front of Zaō Gongen. The main gate of the temple compound was thronged with pilgrims. Shizuka entered the compound and paused beside one of the halls. "What is this place?" she inquired of a bystander.

"The Sacred Peak of Yoshino," he replied.

Shizuka realized with joy that, of all possible days, this was none other than the seventeenth, the date of the Mount Kimpu festival. Mingling with the pilgrims, she reverently approached the image; there were countless numbers of people of all degrees in the inner sanctum and outer hall. Then, exhausted, she lay down under her robe while the monks performed their rituals, but at the end of the services she arose and recited the sacred name with the others.

Some of the talented pilgrims performed various dances for the entertainment of the company. Shizuka particularly enjoyed the *sarugaku*[4] dancers from Ōmi and the *shirabyōshi*[5] from Ise. When the *shirabyōshi* had retired after their performance, she uttered a silent prayer to the god. "If I could do as I chose, I too would demonstrate

---

[4] An early form of the Nō. The Ōmi performers were among the best known of several troupes in the capital area.

[5] See Chapter Four, note 18.

my piety by dancing. I beg of you to see me safely to the capital, and to reunite me with my beloved lord. If my petition is granted, I will make a pilgrimage here with my mother, Zenji." When the other pilgrims had withdrawn, she advanced toward the image to pray.

"That lady is extraordinarily beautiful," said a young monk, approaching the altar. "Who do you suppose she is? She must be talented. Let us urge her to perform."

An old monk dressed in a robe of white silk was standing near by, holding a rosary made of crystal and semiprecious stones. "Will you not perform before the sacred image to give pleasure to the god? Anything at all will do," he said to Shizuka.

"I don't know how to do anything," she replied. "I simply come here each month from my home in the neighborhood to pray. I am in no way an artist." ·

"Zaō Gongen has no peer as a worker of miracles. Or if you prefer, your performance might be regarded as a token of repentance for transgressions. This deity takes it very much amiss when a talented person refuses to perform before him, but he is well pleased with anyone who performs to the best of his ability, however inept he may be. These are not my sentiments, but the divine words of the god himself," said the monk.

"Whatever shall I do?" Shizuka thought. "I am a well-known dancer. Since the gods desire truth, it is not safe to refuse like this. But I don't have to dance—there can't be any harm in singing a trifling song. After all, no one here knows me."

Of the many songs in Shizuka's repertoire, none displayed her unique artistry as well as the *shirabyōshi* called "Parting." The beauty of the melody and the exquisiteness of her phrasing were so far beyond imagination or description that all the listeners wept until their sleeves were drenched. The final words of the song were: "Even when a woman has tired of a man, she remembers him fondly after his death. How shall I ever forget the person from whom I was torn asunder while our love was young? The loss of a parent or child is hard to bear, but nothing is so bitter as the separation of husband and wife." Overcome with grief, Shizuka pulled her cloak over her head and sank to her knees.

"It's not often that one hears such a superb voice and flawless technique," the listeners said to one another. "She seems to be deeply in love with her husband. What kind of man can he be to inspire such devotion?"

"It is quite understandable that you should find her singing agreeable," said a monk called Jibu Hōgen. "She is the renowned Shizuka."

"How do you know?"

"In the capital, there was one year a drought that lasted a hundred days. Though the ex-Emperor himself offered prayers and a hundred *shirabyōshi* were commissioned to perform, not a drop of rain fell until Shizuka danced. Then there was a great downpour which lasted for three days and earned her a special imperial commendation. I was there and saw her."

"She must know where Yoshitsune is," said some of the young monks. "Let us stop her and question her." They erected a barricade in front of the clerks' cloister and waited for the pilgrims to leave the temple. When Shizuka appeared, walking inconspicuously among a group of other worshipers, they forced her to halt. "We know you are Shizuka. Where is Yoshitsune?" they demanded.

"I don't know," she replied.

"Don't show her special consideration because she is a woman," shouted the young monks rudely. "Make her talk."

Although Shizuka was determined to conceal Yoshitsune's whereabouts, in the end she tearfully confessed the truth, since she was only a weak and terrified woman. But the monks were touched by her gentleness. They took her into the clerks' cloister, did what they could for her comfort that night, and the next day sent her off toward Shirakawa on horseback, accompanied by an escort. It cannot be said that they were devoid of feeling.

YOSHITSUNE'S FLIGHT FROM YOSHINO

Early in the morning the monks assembled in the courtyard of the Lecture Hall. "Yoshitsune is at Chūindani. Let us capture him and turn him over to Yoritomo," several of them proposed.

"Don't be foolish," reproved the older monks. "Yoshitsune is neither our enemy nor the court's; he has merely disagreed with Yoritomo. It is not fitting that those who wear black ecclesiastical robes should put on helmets and armor, take up bows and arrows, and destroy life."

"That is true," replied the young men, "but don't forget what happened in the Jishō era [1177–81]. Miidera and the rest joined Prince Mochihito's revolt, while Mount Hiei took the other side. Though the Miidera monks did their best for the prince, he fled toward Nara before the arrival of his friends from the temples there, and was killed by a stray arrow in front of the torii at Mount Kōmyō. The Nara monks didn't actually reach him, but Kiyomori destroyed their temples anyway as a punishment for agreeing to help him. Let us not forget what happened to them. If word reaches the Kantō that Yoshitsune is in these mountains, eastern warriors will march against us, and this Zaō Hall, founded for all eternity by Emperor Kimmei, will be burned to ashes in an instant. What could be more disastrous!"

"Very well," the old monks said. "We won't argue any more."

At dawn on the following day, which was the twentieth, the monks rang the great assembly bell.

Yoshitsune was by this time at Chūindani, where massive drifts of snow blanketed the hills and muffled the small valley streams. Since horses could not penetrate to such a place and porters were not to be had, the party had journeyed on foot, doing without even a soldier's simple fare.

In the gray light of dawn, as the exhausted warriors lay sleeping, Yoshitsune heard the booming of a temple gong somewhere below on the mountainside. Disquieted, he awoke his men.

"Why do you suppose they are ringing again after the early morning bell? There is no holier ground in Japan than Yoshino Zaō Gongen, the temple founded by Emperor Kimmei near the foot of these mountains, and many other gods are also worshiped near its compound.^j The monks are so inordinately proud that they consider themselves above taking orders either from the court or from the military authorities. I am sure they are putting on their armor now and meeting to display their loyalty to the Kantō, even though the court has not told them to," he said.

"We must decide at once what to do if they attack," said Bizen Heishirō. "Shall we make off, go back and die fighting, or commit suicide? We can't show indecisiveness when the moment arrives."

"You may think me a coward, but I see no reason for committing suicide while we still have a chance, or for resisting the monks and letting them kill us. The important thing is for His Lordship to reach safety, no matter how many times he has to try," said Ise Saburō.

"Very well put," said Hitachibō. "Everyone agrees; you are entirely correct."

"Don't be absurd," objected Benkei. "If we are going to take to our heels every time we hear a temple bell ringing, we shall never find a mountain where we can feel safe. Stay here while I go down to see whether anything is happening at the temple."

"That sounds like a good idea," said Yoshitsune, "but won't the people at Yoshino and Totsugawa remember you from your days on Mount Hiei?"

"It is true that I spent a long time at Sakuramoto, but nobody here knows me," replied Benkei. Retiring quickly from Yoshitsune's presence, he changed to a dark blue blouse and knickers, a suit of black armor, and a soft folded cap. He tied a headband over his hair, which, in most un-monkish fashion, he had allowed to grow to a length of three inches. Then he armed himself with a crescent-bladed halberd and a four-foot lacquered sword with a rakishly tilted scabbard and set out in the direction of Zaō Gongen, kicking the snow with his bearskin boots as if he were sauntering among fallen cherry blossoms.

Presently Benkei reached a vantage point from which to survey the temple, east of the Miroku Hall and above the Dainichi Hall. The entire compound was astir, the main body of monks milling around excitedly at the South Gate, the senior monks in the Lecture Hall, and the excited lesser orders outside the gate ready to set out. As he watched, several hundred black-toothed young monks[6] attached protective sleeves to their corselets, tied on helmets, slung quivers low on their backs, seized bows and halberds, and began to climb without waiting for their elders.

Benkei hastened back to Chūindani. "Things are in a terrible state at the temple. Enemies are already within arrow range," he reported.

"Are they eastern warriors or Yoshino monks?" asked Yoshitsune.

"Monks from the temple."

"That makes it awkward. They know their way about and are sure to have their strongest men in the lead. We must not let them drive us into a corner. If we had a guide, we might be able to escape."

"Very few men know the lay of this mountain," Benkei answered. "The famous mountains across the sea are Mount Yü-wang, Incense

---

[6] Artificially blackened teeth were considered a mark of good breeding.

Mountain, and Mount Sung-kao. The mountain called Single Vehicle is Katsuragi, and the one called Enlightenment is this one, where the holy En no Gyōja purified himself.

"Once a Buddhist novice who had spent many years at this shrine was disturbed by some water birds who were making a great commotion. When he looked toward the stream, he saw the living figure of the divine Fudō, who was the particular object of his devotions. Since that day the mountain has been too sacred for ordinary people to enter. I myself have seen very little of it, but I have heard that it is almost impassible in every direction except the one the monks are coming from. On the west there is a chasm so awful that bird cries are swallowed in its depths, and on the north there is a cliff called Dragon's Return, with a mountain torrent at its base. Our best plan is to retreat toward the east side, which borders on Uda in Yamato Province."

HOW TADANOBU REMAINED AT YOSHINO

Yoshitsune's men began to prepare for flight, each as he thought best. But along with the sixteen men there was another warrior of great renown, Shirobyōe Fujiwara Tadanobu, who was a descendent of the Minister of State Kamatari and Tankaikō, a grandson of Satō Noritaka, and the second son of Shinobu Satō Shōji. Of all that band, Tadanobu alone advanced into Yoshitsune's presence, knelt in the snow, and spoke.

"As things are going now, we are no more than sheep headed for the slaughter. A way must be found for you to retreat in safety. Let me delay the monks with arrows while you escape."

Yoshitsune thanked him warmly, but he refused his offer. "After your brother Tsuginobu was killed in my place by Lord Noto during the battle of Yashima, your presence made me feel that Tsuginobu was still alive. This year will soon end. If we both survive until the beginning of the next, come with me to Ōshū—see Hidehira and your family at Shinobu Village," he said.

"It is very kind of you to suggest it. When I left Michinoku in the autumn of the third year of Jishō [1179], Hidehira said to me: 'From today on, make a name for yourself by dedicating your life to your lord. If I hear that you have been killed by an arrow, I shall commission the services necessary for your happiness in the next life.

If you perform honorably from time to time, His Lordship will reward you.' He said nothing about returning alive. When I left my mother alone in Shinobu, I warned her that we would not meet again. 'Someone else dies today; I die tomorrow'—that is a warrior's life. His Lordship is sentimental. Won't some one reason with him?"

"A warrior's words are like an imperial decree. Once spoken, they cannot be withdrawn. Bid him good-bye with a good grace," Benkei advised.

After a short silence, Yoshitsune yielded. "However much I might protest, it would be useless. Do as you wish," he said. Well satisfied, Tadanobu prepared to remain alone in the wild mountains.

Even the proud Tadanobu, who considered himself a warrior equal to Sakanoue Tamuramaro and Fujiwara Toshihito, could not remain unaffected as he thought of saying a last farewell to the lord with whom he had shared so many starlit evenings, misty dawns, freezing winter nights, and sweltering summer mornings, never leaving his side for an instant day or night. His sixteen comrades, taking leave of him one by one, were so deeply moved that they scarcely knew where they were.

Yoshitsune called Tadanobu close. "When you become tired, you will find your present sword too long. A long sword is a handicap to an exhausted man. Fight your last battle with this." He handed him a gold-mounted weapon two and a half feet long, with a narrow groove running the length of its finely wrought blade. "It is short, but the blade is excellent. I have prized it almost as highly as my own life. It was originally a treasure owned by the Kumano Shrine. The abbot obtained permission from the gods to give it to me while I was finding ships to chase the Heike, and since then I have often wondered if my trust in the Kumano deities was responsible for my overthrowing the court's enemies and avenging my father in three years' time. This weapon, which has been as precious as life to me, I give to you now that you are exchanging your life for mine. Think that I am with you."

Tadanobu raised it solemnly to his face. "What a magnificent weapon! Look at it! When my brother Tsuginobu sacrificed his life for Yoshitsune at the battle of Yashima, the mount he received for his journey to hell was Tayūguro, a horse given to His Lordship by Hidehira of Ōshū. Now I, in my turn, have received a priceless sword. But do not think that our lord is partial to me; he would do the same for any of you." They all wept to hear him.

"Is there anything troubling you?" asked Yoshitsune.

"My farewells have been said—there is nothing. Still—if it would not be out of place—I should like to mention one thing which might mar my reputation as a warrior."

"This is the end. Don't stand on ceremony."

Sinking to his knees, Shirobyōe spoke: "I shall be staying here alone while you and the others flee. When the Yoshino monks arrive, they will ask, 'Is Lord Yoshitsune here?' If I admit that I am only Tadanobu, those arrogant clerics may turn back, saying, 'The leader is gone; why should we bother to fight a private battle?' Since that would be a disgrace I could never live down, I should like to make use of the name of Emperor Seiwa,[7] just for today."

"What you ask is quite reasonable, but it would be bad enough for me to share the fate of Sumitomo and Masakado, who perished when they violated the will of heaven,[8] without having people say spitefully, 'Yoshitsune couldn't get the ex-Emperor's approval for an attack on Yoritomo, and all his former friends deserted him. When everyone could see that he was desperate, he allowed someone to impersonate him while he ran away.'"

"We must do what the occasion calls for," said Tadanobu. "If the monks attack, I will shoot arrows as fast as I can until my quiver is empty and then rush in among them to fight with my sword. When I finally draw my dagger to kill myself, I will say, 'Although I wanted you to take me for Yoshitsune, I am Satō Shirobyōe, a retainer who borrowed his master's name to demonstrate his loyalty on the field of battle. Show my head to the Lord of Kamakura.' If I kill myself that way, nobody can criticize the use of your name."

"Of course such a last speech would leave no cause for concern," Yoshitsune agreed. He entrusted the name of his ancestor, Emperor Seiwa, to Tadanobu, who rejoiced to think that he would not only gain fame in the present world but would cut a creditable figure in the nether regions as well.

[7] That is, to impersonate Yoshitsune, who was descended from Emperor Seiwa.

[8] Rebelled against the government. According to Chinese political theory, emperors reigned by virtue of a mandate from heaven. Yoshitsune had been officially declared a rebel.

"What armor is that?" asked Yoshitsune.

"It is the suit Tsuginobu was wearing when he died."

"Armor that failed to stop Lord Noto's arrow is not to be trusted. Some of the monks are first-class archers. Wear these." Yoshitsune gave him his own scarlet armor and silver-studded helmet. When Tadanobu tossed his discarded armor onto the snow, directing that it be given to one of the yeomen, Yoshitsune himself put it on, saying, "I have nothing else to wear." Such a thing had never been done before.

"What about things at home? Do you have any worries?"

"Like any other mortal, I love my family. I left behind a child of three who is old enough now to ask after me; I long to hear the sound of his voice... When we set out from Hiraizumi, I managed to find time to see my old mother, even though His Lordship was in such haste that we passed through Shinobu like a flock of migratory birds. I remember very well how she clung in tears to the sleeves of her two sons and lamented: 'Now that you are going away, I shall be left alone and in misery in my old age. I was very distressed by the loss of Shinobu Shōji, and also by the death of the girl from Date, a neighbor who had the kindness to look after me in numerous ways, but at least I was able to bring up my sons. Although we were not together constantly, I was comforted by the knowledge that you were in the same province. Then for some reason Hidehira saw fit to attach you both to the following of Lord Yoshitsune. Of course I felt resentment at first, but later I was happy in the thought that you had grown up to be such splendid men. Even when you are on the battlefield day and night, never disgrace your dead father by acting in a cowardly fashion. Fight gloriously and come home every year or two as long as you live, even if it means traveling all the way from Shikoku or Kyushu. It would be hard enough if only one of you were leaving. How can I bear to see you both depart for the ends of the earth!'

"We shook off her hands and left with hasty promises, but somehow or other we failed to see her or even to write for the next three or four years. Last spring when I sent word of Tsuginobu's death, she took it very hard, but said, 'Nothing can be done about Tsuginobu now. It is a joy to me that Tadanobu promises to come home in the spring! How I wish this year would end!' When you go to Hiraizumi, she will rush there and say, 'Where is Tadanobu?' You can imagine how she would feel if someone answered bluntly, 'Tsuginobu died at Yashima and Tadanobu at Yoshino.' It would be wicked of me to let such a thing happen. All I ask is that, once you are safe in Ōshū, you show kindness to my mother. Don't worry about masses for me and Tsuginobu." He broke off, pressing his sleeve to his face. Tears flowed from Yoshitsune's eyes as well, and the sixteen warriors sobbed into the sleeves of their armor.

"Do you intend to stay here entirely alone?" asked Yoshitsune.

"Fifty-four retainers came with me from Ōshū. Most of them have either died or been given leave to return home, but the remaining five or six have all sworn to fall here."

"Who among my own men have offered to remain?"

"Bizen and Washinoo volunteered, but I told them to help you instead. Two of your yeomen have declared themselves willing to share my fate."

"They are exceptional men," said Yoshitsune.

TADANOBU'S BATTLE AT YOSHINO

In antiquity, it is said, Deacon Shōkū, a disciple of the Palace Monk[9] Chishō, traded his life for that of his teacher, and the faithful wife of Tung-feng sacrificed herself for her husband's sake. Perhaps someone else in those days may have died for his master—I cannot say with certainty. In our own degenerate times, only the Genji retainers have won fame by laying down their lives to save their lords.

When Tadanobu judged that Yoshitsune was a goodly distance away, he put on the scarlet armor over his speckled corselet, tied the cords of the silver-studded helmet under his chin, and fastened on Yoshitsune's gold-mounted weapon and a three-and-a-half-foot sword called Tsutsurai, a treasure once owned by Tankaikō. High on his hip he slung a twenty-four-arrow quiver, filled with war arrows[10] fledged with black and white eagle feathers. The outer arrows, trimmed with the long wing feathers, were equipped with six-inch humming bulbs to which great pronged arrowheads had been attached. A special war arrow protruded an inch beyond the others—a

---

[9] *Naikō (naiku, naikugu)*. A monk commissioned to perform Buddhist rites in the imperial palace.
[10] *Nakazashi*, an arrow for ordinary combat use, as distinguished from the humming bulb *(kaburaya)*, which was intended to intimidate the enemy by its sound.

Satō family heirloom fledged with crested eagles' feathers. His bow was a serviceable short weapon made of a knotty wood.

Tadanobu and his six men resolved to make their stand at Chūin-no-higashidani. They built a high mound out of snow, cut quantities of *yuzuriha*[11] and *sakaki*[12] branches to make a barricade, and, using five or six great trees as shields, took up positions to await the several hundred monks. The afternoon wore on, but the enemy were still nowhere to be seen. At last, impatient with waiting, the seven set out in pursuit of Yoshitsune; but though they searched in a wide area, swirling winds had drifted the snow across the tracks of the earlier party, and they were obliged to retrace their steps.

Around six o'clock in the evening, there came the cry of three hundred monks in unison from across the valley. Tadanobu's men responded with shouts of their own, which carried faintly to the ears of the enemy from the cedar forest on the mountainside.

"There they are!" exclaimed the monks.

The leader of the monks was a warlike fellow called Kawatsura Hōgen. Though a man of religion, he was dressed like a lay warrior in a light green blouse and knickers, purple armor, and a helmet with three flaps in back. He wore a new sword at his waist and carried arrows fledged with eagles' outer tail feathers[13] in a twenty-four-arrow quiver slung high on his hip. Grasping a rattan-bound bow squarely in the middle, he stepped in front of a four-paneled shield of pasania wood, brought within bowshot by the foremost of five or six imposing warrior monks who formed his escort. (This was a man of about forty, wearing a dark blue blouse and knickers, a black leather corselet, and a black-lacquered sword.)

"We Yoshino monks have come here because people say that Yoshitsune, the younger brother of the Lord of Kamakura, is somewhere in these mountains. We don't bear Yoshitsune any personal grudge. Kindly tell him that he can either run away or stay and be killed, just as he pleases," he announced.

---

[11] *Daphniphyllum macropolium Miq.*, a tall evergreen tree found on Honshu and Kyushu.

[12] *Eurya ochinacea Szysy*, a small evergreen indigenous to Honshu and the western islands. It is frequently planted at shrines, where it is employed in many ways as an adjunct to religious ceremonies. In Chapter Seven (Mitsu-no-kuchi barrier episode), it is apparently to be used to sanctify the barrier house, which would then become inaccessible to the guards.

[13] Arrows fledged with the outer tail feathers of eagles were prized for their strength. They were used only by military commanders.

To these insolent words Tadanobu responded, "For shame! Have you just learned of the presence of Kurō Hōgan Yoshitsune, a descendent of Emperor Seiwa? There was nothing to keep old acquaintances like you from coming to pay your respects earlier. Although lies have come between him and the Lord of Kamakura, Yoritomo won't treat an innocent man this way much longer. What will happen to you then? Do you wonder who I am? I am Shirobyōe-no-jō Fujiwara Tadanobu, the second son of Shinobu Shōji, the grandson of Satō Saemon Noritaka, and a descendent of Tankaikō, the son of the Interior Minister Kamatari.[14] No more arguments! Pay attention to what I say, you Yoshino riffraff!"

Kawatsura Hōgen was so mortified by the insult to his dignity that he charged bellowing across the valley without giving a thought to his strategic disadvantage.

"We can't let them get too close," Tadanobu told his men. "You stay here and argue, while I cross the creek upstream with my bow and two or three arrows, move in behind, and scare them off by shooting one of them in the neck or the back with a humming bulb. Then I'll climb to the top of Chūin Peak with their shields on top of my head. If we're behind the shields, we can force them to use up all their arrows. When our own arrows are gone, we'll draw our swords, rush out, and fight until we drop."

Led by a brave commander, the young retainers were courageous too. "You'll be badly outnumbered. Don't make any mistakes," they said.

"Just keep quiet and watch," Tadanobu advised. He seized a war arrow, a humming bulb, and his bow. Then he ran up the first ravine, crossed the stream near its source, and approached the enemy's rear with his weapon ready, utilizing such shelter as the area afforded until he reached a fallen tree from which branches sprouted in every direction like the disheveled hair on a demon's head. From the trunk of the tree, the monks on Tadanobu's left offered an easy target. He attached the thirteen-fist, three-finger humming bulb to his three-

---

[14] It was customary for one of a chieftain's retainers to act as a spokesman in this way. Tadanobu is, of course, attempting to make the monks believe that Yoshitsune and all the other warriors are with him. The author does not explain why the monks at first accept his identification of himself and later mistake him for Yoshitsune. Perhaps we are to assume that he is concealing his distinctive general's armor in some way, or that the monks are too far distant to see him clearly.

man bow, pulled back the string until the edge of the bulb touched, took careful aim, and released the arrow with tremendous force. It completely severed the raised left forearm of a monk who was holding a standing shield erect and came to rest with its pronged head buried in the shield. The monk slumped to the ground. As the others stared in bewilderment, Tadanobu began to beat on his bow. "Come on, we're winning! You men in front advance; you in back surround them! What has happened to Ise Saburō, Kumai Tarō, Washinoo and Bizen? Are you there, Kataoka Hachirō and Saitō Musashibō? Don't let them get away!" he shouted.

"Those are Yoshitsune's fiercest retainers. We'd better keep out of arrow range," said Kawatsura Hōgen. The monks scattered swiftly in three directions, like autumn leaves in a gale at Tatsuta or Hatsuse.

After the monks had dispersed, Tadanobu rejoined his men with the captured shields. The seven ranged themselves behind this protective wall, hopeful of persuading the enemy to exhaust their arrows, and the monks, now furious, obligingly sent out their best archers. For a full hour the twang of bowstrings reverberated through the forest, and arrows rattled against shields like hailstones on a shingle roof. In all that time, not an arrow was released by the besieged men.

"Why should we try to save our lives? Let us fight," urged the six retainers.

"Wait until their arrows are exhausted," replied Tadanobu. "Those Yoshino monks aren't used to fighting. In a few minutes they will be milling around with their followers, holding useless bows in their hands. That will be our signal to shoot as fast as we can. When our quivers are empty, we'll throw away our scabbards, run in among them, and fight until we drop."

Even as he spoke, the monks began to stand about as if wondering what to do next.

"Here's our chance!" shouted Tadanobu. "Come on!" He moved forward, shielding himself with his left sleeve, and began to release arrows with tremendous speed.

When, after a short time, Tadanobu stepped back he saw that four of his six men had been hit. The two brave survivors stationed themselves in front of him as a protection against enemy missiles, but one died when an arrow shot by Iō-no-zenji found his neckbone, and the other was slain by an arrow in the side from the bow of Jibu Hōgen.

Though all of his retainers had now been struck down, Tadanobu began to search his quiver with an imperturbable countenance. "Those clumsy fellows were only a nuisance," he said. He discovered a pronged arrow and a spearhead. "If I could find an opponent worth fighting, I would shoot one last arrow and then slash open my stomach," he thought.

Kawatsura Hōgen's thirty followers had been standing aimlessly in small knots after their leader's inept handling of the arrow exchange. From behind some of them there now appeared a swarthy six-foot monk, somberly attired in a dark blue blouse and knickers, black leather armor made of double inch-long scales, and a horned helmet with five flaps, which he wore tilted back on his head.[15] He was armed with a three-and-a-half-foot black lacquered sword in a bearskin scabbard, a nine-foot hemp-wound bow which required four men for the stringing, and a high-slung, handsomely furred quiver, loosely filled with black-feathered arrows fourteen fists long, with black lacquered shafts as thick as flute bamboo. Mounting a fallen tree, this man began to speak: "After watching the monks in today's battle, I must say they have made a poor showing! It was a mistake not to take the Genji more seriously, even though they were so few. Yoshitsune is a great general, and every man in his service is worth a thousand ordinary fellows. Now that all the Genji retainers and great numbers of monks have been killed, I call for a match between the Genji chieftain and a captain of the monks! Do you want to know who I am? You have heard, I presume, that the Suzuki League in Kii includes a peerless warrior among its members—a man who is a far cry from Kawatsura Hōgen, the bungler who faced you earlier. Even in my youth people called me a troublemaker. After I was chased out of Kii I entered Tōdaiji Temple in Nara, but they made me leave because I was too much of a fighter. I lived at Yokawa until I wore out my welcome there, and for the last two years I have been at Yoshino as a follower of Kawatsura Hōgen. Because I once stayed at Yokawa, I am called Yokawa-no-zenji Kakuhan. I am going to make a name for myself by shooting a war arrow at you. If you return it, I'll boast of it in the underworld." He fitted a fourteen-fist arrow to his four-man bow, pulled back the string as far as it would go, and released the arrow. The missile grazed Tadanobu's left gauntlet as he

---

[15] To show lack of concern for his personal safety.

stood leaning on his bow, and buried its entire head in a pasania tree behind him.

"That was quite a shot," Tadanobu admitted to himself. "During the Hōgen War, Chinzei Hachirō sent a fifteen-fist arrow from his seven-man bow all the way through a man's armor, but that was a long time ago. I didn't know such an archer existed today. Although the fellow missed the first time, he'll be determined to land his second arrow on the target. I couldn't survive a hit in the middle of my body." He fitted the spearheaded arrow to his bow and tested the string a few times. The distance was somewhat greater than he liked, and a breeze was blowing up from the valley. "The arrow may go astray. Even if it doesn't, a warrior like that always wears a stout corselet under his armor. I would be humiliated if I couldn't penetrate to his flesh. I'll hit his bow instead of risking a shot at him," he decided.

Even Yang Yu of China, who, it is said, once shot a hundred arrows and hit a hundred willow leaves at a distance of a hundred paces, could not equal Tadanobu of Japan, who was able to hit a three-inch target sixty yards away. A bow in an enemy's hand was scarcely a problem for him! "The range is a little long, but there is no reason why I should miss," he thought. He stuck the first arrow upright in the snow, replaced it with the small pronghead, pulled back slightly on the string, and waited while Kakuhan, nettled by the failure of his initial effort, fitted another arrow to his bow and began to pull deliberately on the string. Then Tadanobu pulled back his own string as far as it would go and released the arrow. It cut off the entire top half of Kakuhan's bow.

Kakuhan tossed the bow aside and dropped his quiver. "My fortunes and yours were determined in previous existences. Let's see who is the best man," he roared, lunging toward Tadanobu with his sword flashing above his head like forked lightning. Tadanobu discarded his own bow and quiver, drew the three-foot Tsutsurai, and waited.

Like a trumpeting elephant whetting its tusks, Kakuhan charged. Like a raging lion Tadanobu met him. Their weapons clanged like symbols in a sacred dance. When Kakuhan dodged aside for an instant with his sword held high, Tadanobu darted under his right arm and struck, lowering his head like an untamed hawk entering its coop. Sweat started from the brow of the huge monk as he prepared to die, but Tadanobu had tasted neither food nor wine for three days and could not summon the strength to dispatch him.

"Come on, Kakuhan, you have the advantage! He's on the defensive. Don't blunder now," called the monks in encouragement.

For a time Kakuhan succeeded in carrying the fight to Tadanobu, but he soon found himself in the weaker position again.

"Kakuhan's in trouble. Let's go down and help him," proposed one of the monks.

"All right," agreed others.

As though in a nightmare Tadanobu watched seven mighty monks run shouting to Kakuhan's assistance.[k]

"Behave yourselves, monks! Stand aside and watch when captains fight! Are you trying to destroy my reputation? If you help me, you're my enemies forever," Kakuhan called angrily.

"He wants to fight alone. Let's stand back," said the seven. They abandoned all thought of intervention.

"He's an obnoxious rascal. Still, I'd better retreat a little," Tadanobu thought. He flung his sword whirling over the top of Kakuhan's head, and as the monk flinched he ran forward and stabbed at the inside of his helmet with the tip of his other weapon. The onlookers held their breaths. Tadanobu lowered his head and struck again, but Kakuhan met him with a fearful blow to his neckplate. Even though his flesh was unscathed, Tadanobu retreated thirty or forty yards. He had just hurdled a huge fallen tree when Kakuhan, in close pursuit, struck at him with his sword and caught the blade in the tree trunk. While he struggled to pull it free, Tadanobu fled again.

After Tadanobu had run another thirty-five yards, he reached the awesome four-hundred-foot wall of rock known as Dragon's Return, a precipice so steep that it seemed to offer not the slightest foothold anywhere, and was indeed too dreadful to confront squarely. Meanwhile Kakuhan and the others were coming up from the rear.

"If I am killed here, people will say I was easy game. If I die down there, they'll call it suicide," Tadanobu thought. Holding fast to the skirt of his armor, he faced the cliff, gave a cry, and jumped. After he had fallen about twenty feet, by a fortunate chance his foot caught in a crevice. He looked up, pushing back his helmet, and saw Kakuhan staring down from the edge of the cliff.

"Shame, shame, Your Lordship! Come back and fight! I'm ready to go with you anywhere—to the port of Hakata in the west, North Mountain on Sado in the north, or the barbarian Chishima Isles in the east." He broke off and leaped with a shout.

Perhaps Kakuhan's luck had run out—who can say? The skirt of his armor caught on a branch jutting from a fallen tree, throwing him backward and sending him tumbling slowly down to Tadanobu's waiting sword.

As his adversary staggered to his feet, Tadanobu stepped back and struck. The blow, delivered by a famous blade and a stout arm, split open the front of Kakuhan's helmet and cut his face almost in two. When the sword was withdrawn, he fell in a heap. Although he struggled to rise, he grew weaker and weaker, until at last he died clutching his knees, with only a grunt for a farewell message. He was forty-one years old.

After disposing of Kakuhan, Tadanobu rested for a time. Then he cut off the monk's head, fastened it to the tip of his sword, and climbed back to Chūin Peak.

"Do any of you recognize this head? It belongs to the notorious Kakuhan, and it was cut off by Yoshitsune. If anybody here is a disciple of his, take it and offer masses for him," he shouted, flinging it into the snow.

"If Kakuhan himself failed, how could we possibly hope to succeed? Let us return to the foothills to talk things over again," said a monk. Not one of his comrades protested, "For shame! Let's share Kakuhan's fate!" Instead they chorused, "We agree," and went back toward the temple.

Alone on the mountain, Tadanobu surveyed the scene of the battle, which was strewn with corpses and noisy with the desperate cries of the wounded. When he examined the bodies of his own men, he found that all of them were dead.

The night was by now pitch black, since it was so late in the month that there would be no moon until nearly dawn. Now that Tadanobu had unaccountably escaped death, he was of no mind to throw away his life. He determined to follow the monks back toward the temple. He fastened his helmet to his back armor-cord and tied up his disheveled hair. Then he wiped his bloody sword, slung it over his shoulder, and soon outdistanced his enemies.

"Hello there in the temple!" shouted the monks when they spied Tadanobu nearing the compound. "We defeated Yoshitsune in the mountains, and now he's running away toward the temple. Don't let him escape!" But it had begun to snow, and their voices failed to carry to their comrades in the temple.

Tadanobu entered the main gate, bowed toward the sacred image, and started downhill by way of the south entrance. To his left he observed a large house, the cloister of a monk called Yamashina Hō-gen. It happened that Yamashina was absent, and in a room adjoining the kitchen, two monks and three boys were making merry with a heaping platter of fruits and cakes and a festively bedecked bottle of wine.

"Very nice! I have a feeling that somebody else is going to enjoy your wine," Tadanobu said. He stamped noisily on the veranda planking and burst unceremoniously into the room, his sword still over his shoulder.

It need hardly be said that the boys and monks were terrified. They scurried off in a panic with their rear ends in the air. Tadanobu settled himself heavily, pulled over the fruit and cake, and began to eat.

Presently he heard loud whoops in the distance. "I won't have time to drink the wine if I put it in the warming flask and then transfer it to a saucer," he thought. Being a man of experience in such matters, he seized the neck of the bottle, tilted it until the wine flowed freely, and gulped it down. Then he set his helmet by his side and calmly bent over to warm his face at the fire. The journey through deep snow in heavy armor, the fatigue of battle, the wine, and the warmth of the fire all conspired to lull him into a state of semiconsciousness in which even the shouts of the approaching enemy assumed the quality of a dream.

Soon the monks drew near. "Is Yoshitsune there? Come out!" they demanded.

Awakening with a start, Tadanobu put on his helmet and extinguished the fire.

"Don't hesitate. Come in if you want to," he urged. Anyone with two lives could have entered easily enough, but the monks were content to remain outside, clamoring and jostling one another.

"I won't have that fugitive spending the night in my quarters," said Yamashina Hōgen. "If things go well for us, we'll be rich enough to build a house as good as this every day. Let's set fire to it, force him out into the open, and shoot him down."

"I wouldn't want people to say that the enemy got rid of me by setting a building on fire," thought Tadanobu as he listened. "I'd rather have them say that I died in flames set by my own hand." He forthwith kindled a pair of screens and tossed them up toward the ceiling.

"Look there! He's started a fire himself. Shoot him when he comes out," said the monks. They fitted arrows to their bows, gripped their swords and halberds, and waited.

Soon Tadanobu emerged onto the veranda of the burning building. "Keep still and listen to me, monks," he commanded. "Do you think I'm really Yoshitsune? I don't know when my lord made his escape. I am only one of his retainers, Satō Shirobyōe Fujiwara Tadanobu. Nobody's going to boast of killing me. I'll rip open my own belly! Show my head to the Lord of Kamakura."

Drawing his sword, he pretended to stab his left side. Then he quickly returned the weapon to its scabbard, took a backward leap, and dashed to an inner hall, where he climbed to the ceiling by means of a retractable ladder. The roof near the ornamental tile at the eastern edge of the ridgepole had not yet caught fire. With a vigorous kick, he tore a hole in the wooden ceiling and roof and swiftly mounted to the top of the building, which had been constructed on a terraced hillside and was a mere ten feet from the hill itself.

"If it's my karma to jump short and die, there's nothing I can do about it. Help me, Great Bodhisattva Hachiman," he prayed. He leaped with a shout and flew through the air safely to the hill behind. Then he climbed to a pine grove on the summit, removed his armor, and lay with his head pillowed on his helmet, watching his woefully confused adversaries.

"What a frightful thing to discover that the man we took for Yoshitsune was actually Satō Shirobyōe," the monks were saying. "It is intolerable that we should have been tricked into sacrificing the lives of so many men. If he were a great captain, there would be some reason for showing his head to the Lord of Kamakura. Just let the fellow burn up."

After the flames had subsided, the monks decided to carry Tadanobu's charred head to their abbot, but though they divided into groups and searched, they could find no trace of it—which was scarcely surprising, since Tadanobu had not killed himself.

"A brave man is valiant to the last," said the monks, returning to the temple. "He must have perished in the flames to preserve his corpse from dishonor."

Tadanobu spent the night close to Zaō Gongen. He presented his armor to the shrine, departed from the august peak at dawn on the twenty-first, and re-entered the capital safely at dusk on the twenty-third.

THE YOSHINO MONKS PURSUE YOSHITSUNE

Meanwhile Yoshitsune was at a place called Sakuradani, which he had reached by way of Kōshū-ga-tani on the twenty-third of the twelfth month, after enduring the trials of Kūshō-no-shō, Shii Peak, and Yuzuriha Pass. Exhausted by the tortuous mountain paths, which were buried under snowdrifts and dripping with icicles, the warriors lay with their heads on their swords. Yoshitsune himself was feeling extremely depressed. He called Benkei to his side.

"Have we no friends at the base of this mountain? I should like to get some wine and rest awhile before we go on," he said.

"I don't know of anyone, but the Miroku Hall, a temple in the foothills founded by Emperor Shōmu, is governed from Nara by Kanjubō. Kanjubō's deputy is a layman called Mitake Saemon," Benkei replied.

"There is someone to ask, after all!" said Yoshitsune. He wrote a letter and gave it to Benkei, who went down the mountain to Saemon.

"Why didn't he call on me sooner when he was so close?" lamented Saemon. Summoning five or six trusted men, he sent them off to Sakuradani with two long boxes containing fruit, wine, rice, and other food.

"What could possibly be more welcome!" Yoshitsune exclaimed when the boxes were placed in the midst of the sixteen travelers. Some of his men reached eagerly for the wine and others for the food.

Just as they were about to dine, faint voices floated from a cedar-covered hill to the east. "There are no charcoal burners in the neighborhood, and the trail along the peaks is so far from everything that peasants aren't likely to be cutting firewood there," thought Yoshitsune. He glanced apprehensively behind him. One hundred fifty armed Yoshino monks were approaching, full of anger at their failure to kill Tadanobu at Chūindani two days earlier.

"Enemies!" cried Yoshitsune.

The warriors, unmindful of their reputations, scattered in an instant.

Hitachibō, who had been the first to take to his heels, looked back and saw that Benkei and Yoshitsune had not moved. As he watched curiously, they picked up the empty boxes, threw them over a cliff to the east, and calmly buried the food in the snow. Then they set out.[16]

Although Hitachibō had a good headstart, Benkei soon overtook him. "Following your tracks is like looking into an unclouded mirror. Anyone who prizes life had better wear his shoes backward," he said.

"You always make such odd remarks," replied Yoshitsune. "Why should we do such a thing?"

"You laughed when Kajiwara suggested reverse oars,"[17] Benkei reminded him.

"It is quite true that I knew nothing about reverse oars, and this is certainly the first time I have ever heard of shoes worn backward. But I'm willing to try it if it's not dishonorable."

"In that case, let me tell you a few things," said Benkei. He launched at once into a tale of the reigns and wars of India's sixteen great states, five hundred medium-sized states, and innumerable small states. Though the enemy were approaching to within arrow range, the warriors stood around him in a circle, listening intently.

"Once there were two countries, Shiranai and Vārnaṣt, which were among the sixteen great states of India. On the border between them soared a peak called Incense Mountain, which had at its foot a moor a thousand leagues across. Since the mountain contained all kinds of treasures, people were not permitted to visit it freely.

"On a certain occasion the king of Vārnaṣt decided to take possession of Incense Mountain. He set out toward Shiranai with an army of 510,000 mounted men. The king of Shiranai, who was a clever ruler, had been expecting an attack. A herd of a thousand elephants lived at a place called Thousand Caves on the north side of the moun-

---

[16] This was to keep the enemy from thinking that they had run off in a panic.
[17] See the Introduction, p. *32.*

tain, and the king had captured and tamed one of them. It was such a gigantic beast that it devoured two thousand bushels of food daily.

" 'What is the advantage of keeping that elephant?' the courtiers asked.

" 'Someday he will win a war for us,' was the king's reply.

"Instead of dispatching soldiers to meet the invading force, the king sent the elephant toward the enemy lines, whispering in his ear, 'Don't forget what you owe me.'

"The monster lifted his mighty head with a bellow that was as loud as a thousand giant conch shells blown in unison and seemed to penetrate to the very bones of all who heard it. With a single blow from his left foot he crushed fifty warriors to death. In seven days and nights of fighting, every man of Vārnaṣt's 510,000 riders was struck down. The sole survivors were the king, six high courtiers, and three warriors, who managed to retreat toward the northern edge of Incense Mountain.

"Since the eleventh month was far advanced, scattered maple leaves and patches of snow mantled the ground at the foot of the mountain. The king, in a desperate attempt to save himself, put his shoes on hindside to, with the toes in back and the heels in front.

"When the pursuers saw the king's tracks, they returned to the foothill villages. 'The foreign king must be up to some deviltry. This mountain is full of tigers. If we stay here after sundown we shall all be killed,' they said. So the king survived to return to his own country. Later he mustered a force of 560,000 horsemen and succeeded in defeating the enemy—all because of a pair of reversed shoes.

"That was a story about a wise foreign king. Your Lordship is a great Japanese general, and a tenth-generation descendent of Emperor Seiwa. There is a maxim that says, 'Be humble when the enemy is proud, and proud when he is humble.' I don't know about the rest of you, but as for myself. .." He started to walk straight ahead with his shoes reversed.

"What queer scraps of information you pick up! Where did you learn that?" asked Yoshitsune.

"I ran across it in a Hossō or Sanron text while I was studying under the Bishop of Sakuramoto," replied Benkei.[18]

---

[18] Hossō and Sanron are Buddhist sects.

"You are not only a great warrior, but a scholar as well," said Yoshitsune.

Benkei took this praise complacently. "It would be difficult to find another man as brave and resourceful as I am," he said.

Yoshitsune's party made an orderly retreat, with the monks following closely behind.

"What do you make of this?" Jibu Hōgen, the leader, asked the others. "The tracks have been heading toward the valley all along, but now they're coming away from it toward us."

Iō-no-zenji ran up from the rear ranks to look. "Yoshitsune studied at Kurama and is thoroughly trained in the civil and military arts. His retainers are remarkable men, too. One of his two monks, Hitachibō Kaizon from Onjōji Temple, is a great bookworm, and the other, a disciple of the Bishop of Sakuramoto named Benkei, knows all about every war ever fought in this country or anywhere else. They must be imitating the king of Vārnaṣt who fled with his shoes on backward when he was attacked by an elephant on the north flank of Incense Mountain. Don't let them get away. Follow them!" he urged.

Stealing silently forward until they were within arrow range of the fugitives, the monks shouted a battle cry in unison.

"Don't you intend to reply?" Yoshitsune asked his shaken men. They only pressed on as if they had not heard, jostling one another with their heads down.

Not long after this the party reached a formidable barrier—White Thread Falls in the upper reaches of the Yoshino River, where a fifty-foot cataract tumbled like a tangled skein of threads into a pool fully thirty feet deep, whose boiling waters vividly recalled the bursting flesh of sinners in the Red Lotus Hell.[19] Swollen by melting snows on its long course, the river was pounding against the shoal rocks with a force sufficient to demolish Mount Hōrai itself. On either bank, walls of rock twenty feet high, glistening with snow and ice, rose up like folding screens.

To Benkei, who was the first to reach the shore, it seemed that further progress was impossible. Not wishing to discourage the others, however, he called out with his usual gusto, "What, are you going to

---

[19] A minor Buddhist hell. Its intense cold ruptured the flesh of those consigned to its tortures.

hesitate because of a little mountain stream? Let us hurry and get across."

"How can we?" asked Yoshitsune. "We might as well make up our minds to kill ourselves."

"I don't know about the rest of you, but I'm going over," retorted Benkei. He approached the edge of the bank and, eyes closed, murmured a prayer, "When was our lord forgotten by the Great Bodhisattva Hachiman, protector of the Genji? Hear my prayer; keep us from harm."

When he opened his eyes, he perceived a likely crossing some one hundred fifty or two hundred feet downstream. He ran closer. The river was racing pellmell through a deep, narrow channel between two high banks. On the opposite shore the intertwined, snow-laden tips of three tall bamboos, part of a clump growing in some loose rock, were bent low over the water, trailing icicles like bodhisattva necklaces.[20]

Yoshitsune, too, saw the bamboos. "I'm not sure I can get across, but at least I shall find out how deep the water is. If I fall in, jump in after me," he commanded.

The men promised to do as he asked.

That day Yoshitsune was wearing a red brocade blouse and knickers, a crimson-skirted suit of armor, a silver-studded helmet, and a gold-trimmed sword; a quiver of arrows with black-centered feathers was slung high on his back. He fastened a grappling hook to his bow, held it close against his left side, and walked to the river's edge. Then he gripped his skirts, lowered his head, and with a shout jumped toward the bamboo tips. In an instant he had landed safely on the opposite shore. Shaking the water from his skirts, he called back, "It's much easier than it looks from there. Come along, all of you."

Of the sixteen men in the party, fourteen crossed—Kataoka, Ise, Kumai, Bizen, Washinoo, Hitachibō, the yeoman Suruga Jirō, the servant Kisanda, and others. The two who remained were Nenoo Jūrō and Benkei. As Nenoo was about to cross, Benkei clutched his left sleeve. "The way your knees are trembling, you'll never make it. Take off your armor before you go," he said.

"How can I?" protested Nenoo. "All the others have worn theirs."

[20] *Yōraku,* conventional decorations on bodhisattva images.

"What are you saying, Benkei?" called Yoshitsune.

"I was telling Nenoo to take off his armor before he crosses."

"Force him to do it if necessary."

Unlike Yoshitsune's other retainers, who were vigorous youths in their twenties, Nenoo was a man of fifty-six. "Whether you think it's right or not, you had better stay behind in the city," Yoshitsune had advised him more than once, but he had stubbornly shared his lord's travels. "While you were a prominent man," he said, "my family and I enjoyed your protection. It would be wrong for me to stay in the capital in someone else's service, simply because fortune has deserted you." Now he obediently shed his armor and auxiliary trappings, but since it still appeared that the leap was beyond his powers, the men on the opposite bank unstrung their bows, tied all the strings together, and threw them toward him. "Pull them toward you. Pull hard! Hold fast!" they shouted. In this way they brought him across at a place where the current was slow.

Only Benkei remained. Instead of crossing as Yoshitsune and the others had done, he climbed upstream three hundred fifty feet to a rocky corner and swept off the drifted snow with the handle of his halberd.

"It was disgusting to watch you men holding onto those bamboo stalks and making a big fuss about crossing a mountain stream. Get out of the way while I show you how easy it is to jump across," he yelled.

"He's just jealous; don't pay any attention to him," said Yoshitsune, stooping to retie his shoelaces.

Suddenly there was a desperate cry. Benkei was being carried downstream by the swift current, which pounded him mercilessly against the rocks as he drifted.

"He has fallen in!" exclaimed Yoshitsune. Running to the edge of the water with his grappling hook, he succeeded in snagging Benkei's back armor cord as the stream swept him past.

"Come here, someone!" he shouted.

Ise Saburō ran up. Seizing the handle of the hook, he hoisted the huge monk into the air, armor and all, and deposited him dripping on the shore.

As Benkei, with a rueful laugh, was hauled in, Yoshitsune said sarcastically, "Your legs aren't as clever as your tongue."

"Everyone makes mistakes. Even Confucius had his failures, didn't he?" Benkei retorted gaily.

The party resumed their flight. Benkei paused at the bamboo clump and, standing before the three tall stalks, spoke as persuasively as if they had been human. "Like ourselves, you are living things, but your roots can produce new sprouts in the spring to take your place, whereas we men, once dead, can never return again. I'm going to cut you down. Give your lives for ours!" So saying, he cut the stalks and buried their ends in the snow so that the tips hung over the water. Then he hurried on after Yoshitsune.

Looking back at the seething torrent, Yoshitsune was reminded of stories of antiquity. "The poet Kyōchoku capsized in a boat. The musician Hōcho met the same fate while he was riding on a stalk of bamboo.[21] King Mu of China ascended to heaven from a wall, and Chang Po-wang reached the River of Heaven[22] on a floating log. Now I have crossed a mountain river by means of bamboo leaves."

They ascended the bank to a sheltered hollow. "If the enemy cross the river, we shall shoot at them until our arrows are exhausted and then commit suicide. If they can't cross, we shall laugh in their faces and be on our way," Yoshitsune said.

Almost at once the monks appeared. "Yoshitsune is a wizard; he's managed to get across! Do you think it was here? Could it have been over there?" they clamored.

"Why do you have to say, 'Of course, that's the kind of thing Yoshitsune would do'?" objected Jibu Hōgen. "He's no demon. There must be a crossing." He caught sight of the drooping bamboos on the opposite shore. "He must have used those. Anyone else ought to be able to do the same. Go ahead!" he commanded.

Three black-toothed monks wearing corselets and arm shields pressed their halberds to their sides, joined hands, and leaped with lusty shouts. Though they succeeded in grasping the tips of the bamboos, their tugs only served to draw the severed stalks toward their shoulders. In no time the pounding waves had sent them to the bottom of the river, where they became so much debris.

The discomfited monks silently endured the laughter of the sixteen men on the opposite hill. "This is the work of the clownish oaf they

[21] These legends, apparently current in the Muromachi period, are unknown today.
[22] The Milky Way.

call Benkei," said Hitaka-no-zenji. "We shall look like fools if we stay
here. On the other hand, it would take us days to detour around the
river upstream. We had better return to the temple and talk things
over."

There was not a soul who answered, "For shame! Let us jump in to
die with our comrades." As one, they all turned back, saying, "He is
right. Let's do as he says."

Yoshitsune summoned Kataoka. "Tell the Yoshino monks that I
appreciate their having come so far to see me off, even though they
haven't been able to cross the river. I won't forget their kindness."

Kataoka fitted a large humming bulb to his unlacquered bow and
shot it across the valley. "A message from His Lordship! A message
from His Lordship!" he called out. The monks trudged on as though
deaf.

Still wearing his soaked armor, Benkei climbed onto a great fallen
tree. "If any of you are men of taste, watch the dance that spread
Benkei's fame far and wide in the Western Compound of Mount
Hiei!" When some of the monks showed interest, he said, "Accompany me, Kataoka." Kataoka beat time with a war arrow on the
lower end of his bow, chanting, "*Manzairaku, manzairaku.*"[23] Benkei
began to dance, while the monks looked on, unable to tear themselves
away. Performing with admirable skill, he chanted derisively again
and again, "Since cherry blossoms float on this stream in the spring,
it is called the Yoshino River; since maple leaves float on it in the
autumn, it might also be called the Tatsuta. Now, even though winter
has all but ended, monks are floating down like autumn leaves."

At last one of the monks bellowed, "You stupid ass!"

"If you have anything to say, do speak up," called Benkei.

The party passed the remainder of the day there. At twilight Yoshitsune said to the others, "It is a pity we were chased off before we
could enjoy the food and wine Mitake Saemon was good enough to
send us. If any of you managed to bring along something to eat,
produce it. Let us refresh ourselves before we go on."

"When we saw the monks we tried to get away as fast as we could.
Nobody brought anything," they all replied.

"You're not very foresighted, are you? I saved enough for myself,"
said Yoshitsune. Although it had seemed to the others that all had

[23] A meaningless refrain repeated to keep time.

fled at the same time, Yoshitsune had somehow contrived to make up a paper parcel containing twenty rice cakes wrapped in tangerine leaves, which he now drew from a pocket under his right arm. "Give them one apiece," he said to Benkei.

Benkei placed the cakes on the sleeve of his blouse and transferred four of them to *yuzuriha* twigs broken from a tree. "One for the Buddha of the One Vehicle, one for the Buddha of Enlightenment, one for the patron god of wayfarers, and one for the mountain god," he said. Sixteen cakes remained, exactly enough for the sixteen warriors. After laying one in front of Yoshitsune, he distributed the others to the warriors.

"One is left over.[24] I'll add it to the buddha offerings and consider the five of them payment for my trouble," he said.

The men wept at the sight of Yoshitsune's gifts. "This is a hard life," they lamented. "When our lord was in his rightful place, we considered a fine suit of armor or a stout horse a suitable reward for devotion such as ours, but now we are overjoyed to receive a single rice cake." Though they were warriors who arrogantly challenged demons, gave no thought to wife or child, and held life as lightly as dust, they wept until their sleeves were drenched, unable to express their emotions in words. Yoshitsune himself was deeply affected. Tears started to Benkei's eyes as well, but he pretended to feel nothing. "Why cry when someone gives you a present?" he asked. "It is foolish for you men to say weeping, 'We have taken His Lordship's own things.' Divine assistance is wonderful. I have brought along a little something too. It was extremely thoughtless of the rest of you not to do the same. This is nothing special, but here it is." He pulled out twenty rice cakes. Then he knelt before his delighted master, drew a large black object from a pocket under his left arm, and laid it on the snow. Kataoka, who had come forward for a better look, saw that it was a piece of bamboo filled with wine.

Benkei took two earthenware cups from his blouse, placed one in front of Yoshitsune, and served him three times. He waved the jug in the air. "We have many drinkers and only a little wine. It won't be enough, but at least there is some for every one," he said. After serving his comrades, he drank the last three cupfuls from his own cup.

---

[24] His own.

"Let the rain fall and the wind blow. We have no worries tonight,"
he said.

They rested there throughout the night. The following day was the
twenty-third of the twelfth month. "These mountain paths are too
difficult," said Yoshitsune. "Let's head for the plains." They began
the descent toward the foothills and presently arrived at Kita-no-oka
and Shigemi-ga-tani, where they found a number of huts belonging
to woodcutters from neighboring villages.

"There is no reason to wear armor simply because it's the usual
thing for fugitives. Once we're safe, we can wear it all we like. Just
now nothing is so important as life itself," the sixteen decided. They
tossed their corselets and armor under an old tree at Shigemi-ga-tani
and prepared to flee, each in the direction of his choice.

"I am going to Ōshū late in the first month or early in the second
month of the new year," Yoshitsune told them. "Meet me near Ichijō
Imadegawa." They parted regretfully, some to journey to Kowata,
the Hitsukawa River, Daigo, or Yamashina, some to enter the wilds
of Kurama, and others to seek concealment in the heart of the capital.
Unaccompanied by a single warrior or yeoman, Yoshitsune arrived
at the Nara residence of Kanjubō late on the night of the twenty-
third, wearing a sword and his corselet, Shikitae.

Chapter Six

TADANOBU'S SECRET RETURN TO THE CAPITAL

Since his return to the capital on the twenty-third day of the twelfth month, Satō Shirobyōe Tadanobu had kept himself hidden in outlying districts during the daytime and had entered the city only at night to inquire after Yoshitsune. He had been unable to learn anything definite from the conflicting reports of his informants, some of whom insisted that Yoshitsune had thrown himself into the Yoshino River and others that he had started for Michinoku over the Hokurikudō road; and what with one thing and another, he was still in the capital on the twenty-ninth. Now, to add to his perils, the twenty-ninth being the last day of the old year, there were to be ceremonies in celebration of the new year and the return of spring. No place seemed safe for the night.

It happened that Tadanobu had earlier fallen in love with a girl named Kaya, the daughter of the Koshiba Novice of Shijō Muromachi. He had met and wooed her while Yoshitsune was still in the capital. At the time of Yoshitsune's departure, she had followed him all the way to Kawashiri in Settsu, begging, "I won't object to the roughest sea or frailest craft, if only you will take me with you." Nevertheless, he had bidden her a tender farewell and set out for Shikoku alone, considering it improper to bring a woman on board when he had privately criticized Yoshitsune for doing the same thing.

Tadanobu was still much attached to Kaya, and late on the night of the twenty-ninth he set out to visit her. She greeted him ecstatically, concealed him in her apartments, and did everything possible for his comfort. Then she reported his arrival to her father, the novice, who called him to his room and invited him to see out the old year there.

"We had no notion of your whereabouts after you left the capital. It gives me great pleasure to know that you have trusted this humble novice sufficiently to come here," he said. Tadanobu made a silent vow to go to Michinoku as soon as spring had thawed the mountain snows and brought green leaves to the foothills.

As the proverb goes, "Heaven, which lacks a mouth, must speak through human agents." Though no one deliberately revealed Tadanobu's secret, people soon began to say that he was in the city, and the Rokuhara authorities issued orders for his apprehension. In order to avoid involving others in difficulties, he resolved to leave on the fourth day of the first month, but upon discovering that the date was inauspicious, he delayed his departure. On the fifth, the thought of parting from the lady was so painful that he again temporized, promising himself to leave at dawn on the sixth without fail.

A man can do no worse than trust a woman. Perhaps a demon had gained the ear of that lady, who only yesterday had been exchanging the tenderest of vows with Tadanobu. At any rate, her feelings changed in the course of a single night. After Tadanobu's departure from the capital, she had met a man called Kajiwara Saburō, an eastern warrior living in the city. Since Kajiwara was prospering, while Tadanobu was a fugitive, she now concluded that it would be prudent to transfer her affections to the man of influence. She determined to tell Kajiwara of Tadanobu's presence and urge him to become a hero by killing or capturing Tadanobu for the Lord of Kamakura's inspection.

Kaya sent a messenger to summon Kajiwara, who was living at Gojō Nishi-no-tōin. Having concealed Tadanobu in another room, she provided her guest with refreshment. "I called you because I wanted to tell you that Yoshitsune's retainer Tadanobu escaped alive from the fighting at Yoshino," she whispered. "He has been here since the evening of the twenty-ninth, and he's planning to leave for Ōshū tomorrow. If the authorities were to ask why I didn't inform them I wouldn't know what to do. Even though you may not want to take part in this affair yourself, won't you have some foot soldiers kill him or capture him? You can send him to the Lord of Kamakura and claim a reward."

Kajiwara Saburō was too shocked to reply. Nothing is so loathsome to contemplate, so distressing and irrational, as feminine love, which passes into nothingness more rapidly than a streak of lightning, a May fly, or a snowflake on the water. One can but pity the unsuspecting Tadanobu, doomed to destruction by his trust in a woman.

"I understand what you mean," Kajiwara said at last, "but I have been sent to the capital for three years, of which this is the second, in order to carry out an important family duty.[1] Warriors stationed in the city are forbidden to have two separate assignments at once, so I have not been ordered to take part in the search for Tadanobu. Even if I were selfish enough to seek a reward by attacking him, I wouldn't get anything, because I would be acting on my own. Furthermore, if I blundered I would disgrace my family. I must therefore decline. You had better find someone who is more eager to kill Tadanobu." Abruptly, he departed for home, reflecting as he went on the lady's lack of feeling and principle. He never visited her again.

Angered by Kajiwara's rebuff, Kaya determined to go to Rokuhara herself. She made her way there with a female attendant on the same night of the fifth and asked for Hōjō Yoshitoki. When Yoshitoki had heard her story, he informed Tokimasa, who at once dispatched an arrest party of two hundred riders to Shijō Muromachi.

Meanwhile Tadanobu lay sleeping soundly, stupefied by the wine Kaya had pressed on him that day and evening, using their coming separation as a pretext. The woman in whom he had placed his trust had faithlessly vanished.

"Enemies are approaching!" The servant girl who dressed Tadanobu's hair shook him awake.

TADANOBU'S END

Tadanobu leaped up at the sound of hostile voices, snatched his sword, and knelt to look at the enemy host surrounding the house. There seemed no hope of escape. Standing erect again, he took counsel with himself. "What begins must end; what lives must die. There is no help for it when a man's time comes. I was ready at Yashima, Dan-no-ura, Settsu, and Yoshino, but it wasn't time for me to go. It would be foolish to fly into a panic now that the hour has finally arrived. Still, I won't die like a dog." Quickly he began to prepare for battle, putting on a short-sleeved white undergarment, wide-

---

[1] Guard duty *(ōban)* at the palace and elsewhere. From Yoritomo's time on, this function was entrusted to vassals of the Kamakura regime.

bottomed yellow drawers, knickers, and a blouse, the sleeves of which
he tied over his shoulders. After fastening up his hair, still disordered
from the preceding day, he straightened a cap, pushed it down on the
back of his head, and tied the strings securely around his forehead.
He put on his sword, then crouched low and peered out. Groups of
Hōjō warriors were assembled here and there, the colors of their
armor indistinguishable in the dim light.

Tadanobu thought of trying to slip through the enemy ranks, but
there was little chance of escaping men who enjoyed the advantages
of armor, bows and arrows, and horses. It was likely that they would
wound him a bit so that he could be captured and taken to Rokuhara
to be questioned about Yoshitsune. Professions of ignorance would
merely invite tortures which would paralyze his will and extort the
truth, however much he might seek to conceal it. It would be a sorry
sequel to his resolve to die for Yoshitsune in the wild fastness of
Yoshino.

"I shall have to get away from here if I can," he decided. Entering
the veranda of the middle gate,[2] he saw that it was surmounted by an
ancient room. He climbed up swiftly. Like most old shingled buildings in the capital, this one had a roof so thin as almost to admit the
light of the stars and moon, and there were indeed holes in several
places. With a powerful thrust, Tadanobu broke through the ceiling,
pulled himself out, and fled over the roof like a bird skimming the
treetops.

"Look there! The fellow's making off! Shoot him!" shouted Hōjō
Yoshitoki. He ordered his picked warriors to open fire, but in no time
Tadanobu was beyond arrow range. The pursuers, their movements
impeded by carts of all kinds left in the streets overnight, ended by
losing sight of him.

Although Tadanobu might have escaped completely by continuing
his flight, he reflected that the Kyoto guard would be ordered to
block the exits from the capital while Hōjō warriors ransacked the
city itself. He was sure to be found in the end. Rather than suffer the
indignity of being killed by some low fellow's arrow, he directed his
steps toward Rokujō Horikawa. "Since I can't see His Lordship, I

---

[2] *Chūmon.* In the great mansions of the court nobles there were two gates to the inner
garden, situated in the middle of two corridors leading south into the garden from the east
and west wings. Smaller houses had only one corridor and gate.

shall go to the house where he lived for two years. Let matters take their course there," he decided.

When he reached the building that had been his home until the past year, he found it sadly altered. The gatekeeper was gone, the verandas were thick with dust, the outer shutters and doors were broken, and the blinds had felt the full fury of the wind. Behind their sliding doors, the apartments were hung with spiderwebs. The stouthearted Tadanobu's eyes clouded. "How different from the old days..."

After he had completed a nostalgic round of the places he had longed to see once more, he cut down a number of blinds and raised the shutters in a room which gave on a veranda. Then he wiped his sword with his sleeve and awaited the two hundred Hōjō warriors alone, prepared for the worst.

"Hōjō Tokimasa is a first-rate adversary, better than I have a right to expect," he thought. "In the Kantō he is the respected father-in-law of the Lord of Kamakura, while here in the capital he is the Lord of Rokuhara. I should hate to perish ignominiously before such an enemy. If I had a good suit of armor and a quiver, I could fight one last battle before I killed myself." Suddenly he recalled that a suit of armor had been left in the house.

At the time of his departure for Shikoku on the thirteenth day of the eleventh month of the year just ended, Yoshitsune had left the capital with the greatest reluctance. That night in his lodgings at Toba Port he had summoned Hitachibō.

"What kind of people do you suppose will be living in my house at Rokujō Horikawa?" he asked.

"Who indeed?" replied Hitachibō. "It will probably become a demons' haunt."

"I don't like to think of such a thing. People say that it's possible to ward off evil spirits by leaving a heavy suit of armor and a helmet as house guardians." Having hit upon this notion, he ordered someone to leave behind a suit of cherry blossom armor,[3] a silver helmet, a quiver containing sixteen pheasant-feather arrows, and a rounded bow of untreated wood.

"I wonder if they are still here," thought Tadanobu. He climbed rapidly to the ceiling loft and peered in. There were the helmet studs

---

[3] Armor sewn with thongs printed in a tiny cherry blossom pattern.

glittering in the mid-morning sunlight which came from the eastern hills and was entering through chinks in the roof. He put on the long-skirted armor, slung the arrows on his back, strung the bow, and gave it a few experimental twangs. Then he waited impatiently for the arrival of the two hundred Hōjō warriors.

Soon the enemy appeared, their vanguard pressing into the main courtyard while the rear ranks remained outside the gate. Hōjō Yoshitoki shielded himself behind a shrub in the hedge adjoining the kickball grounds.

"Tadanobu, you coward! You will never escape. Come out into the open. Our commander is Lord Hōjō, and I am Hōjō Yoshitoki. Come out at once!" he shouted.

Swiftly knocking a shutter from the veranda, Tadanobu fitted an arrow to his bow. "I have something to say to Hōjō Yoshitoki. What a pity that you're so ignorant! In the Hōgen and Heiji wars, when the adversaries were exalted personages, men could fight with clear consciences, unawed even by an Emperor or ex-Emperor. This is something entirely different—it's nothing but a private quarrel. Yoshitomo's son Yoritomo is our lord's brother. Even though the two of them have been separated by slanders, Yoritomo will change his mind when he finds out that the stories are lies. Then there will be trouble!" With these words, Tadanobu leaped down from the veranda, took a stance under the eaves, and began to release arrows in rapid succession. Three of Yoshitoki's front retainers fell dead, and two others were wounded; the rest crowded back toward the eastern edge of the pond like leaves scattered by the wind, intent on gaining the outer gate.

"For shame, Yoshitoki!" shouted the men in the rear. "You're not up against five or ten horsemen; the enemy is a lone man. Go back and fight!"

Pressed in from all sides, the retreating warriors swerved their mounts and attacked grimly. Tadanobu soon exhausted his sixteen arrows. He cast aside the quiver, drew his sword, and wheeled and slashed like a madman among the enemy host, killing innumerable men and horses. Then he offered his body as a target for arrows, with his armor pushed up stiffly. The missiles of ordinary soldiers were deflected, but the best archers found their marks, and soon the arrows standing in his armor were so numerous that his senses began to fail.

Since escape was impossible, he determined to kill himself before his increasing weakness permitted the enemy to seize and behead him. Waving his sword, he jumped swiftly to the veranda and turned to the west, palms joined. "Lord Yoshitoki! Although your young retainers from Izu and Suruga are making a disgraceful spectacle of themselves, forget them while you watch the self-destruction of a man of courage! If ever an eastern warrior is driven to suicide by loyalty to his master, calamity, or the prospect of decapitation by an enemy, let this be his example! Inform the Lord of Kamakura of my last words and the manner of my death."

"So be it. Let him cut open his belly in peace, and take his head afterward," said Yoshitoki, loosening his reins and settling back to watch.

Tadanobu, in a calm voice, recited thirty buddha invocations. "Let the benefits of my meritorious conduct be enjoyed by others as well..." he prayed. With his sword he cut cleanly through his armor lacing; resting on one knee, he drew the upper part of his body erect. Then he made a deep incision under his left arm and ripped open his belly from the pit of his stomach almost to the navel, drawing the blade steadily up toward his right side. When he had wiped the sword he inspected his handiwork.

"An excellent blade! Mōfusa was as good as his word when he promised to make me a fine weapon. It cuts a man's belly with no trouble at all. If I leave it behind, I suppose it will be sent to the east with my remains. Rather than allow the youths there to pass on its merits, I shall take it with me to hell." He wiped it again, sheathed it, and placed it under his knees. Grasping the mouth of his wound to force it apart, he plunged his fist into his belly, tossed his bowels onto the veranda, and shoved the hilt of the sword into the pit of his stomach, with the scabbard pointing down below his hipbone. "That's how I treat the sword I take to hell," he said. He began to recite buddha invocations with joined hands, breathing evenly and giving no indication of being about to die. Then, with life still remaining in his body, he reflected aloud on the uncertainty of worldly things.

"The human lot in this world is hard! Young or old, who knows how long he'll last? Why are some men destined to be killed by a single arrow, to the everlasting sorrow of their wives and children, while I cannot die when I cut open my own belly? Mine is an unfortunate karma. Is it because I am too devoted to Yoshitsune that I linger like this? Let me go to hell in peace after I look once more at the sword His Lordship gave me." He picked up the unsheathed weapon, thrust the point into his mouth, and stood erect, gripping his knees. Then he released his hands and fell forward on his face. The sword guard stuck in his mouth and the tip came out through the hair on the side of his head.

What a tragic death! Tadanobu perished by his own hand at the age of twenty-eight, at eight o'clock in the morning on the sixth day of the first month of the second year of Bunji [1186].

HOW TADANOBU'S HEAD WAS TAKEN TO KAMAKURA

One of Lord Hōjō's retainers, an Izu chieftain named Mishima Yatarō, went up to Tadanobu's lifeless body, cut off the head, and carried it back to Rokuhara.

Presently it was rumored that the head would be paraded through the main thoroughfares before it was sent to Kamakura.

"If Tadanobu had been a state enemy, someone whose head was destined for exposure outside the prison gates, it would be appropriate to hold a parade, but wasn't he merely a retainer of Yoritomo's enemy, Yoshitsune? There is no reason for displaying such a conquest," the court nobles said. Admitting the force of these objections, Lord Hōjō refrained from flaunting his prize and contented himself with sending it to Kamakura with an escort made up of Yoshitoki and fifty warriors.

Yoshitoki arrived on the twentieth of the first month. He was received by the Lord of Kamakura on the twenty-first.

"We have taken a rebel head," he reported.

"Who was he, and what was his native province?" asked Yoritomo.

"Satō Tadanobu, one of Yoshitsune's retainers."

"Who attacked him?"

"Lord Hōjō."

Although there had been similar occurrences before, Yoritomo's delight showed that he regarded this as an event of uncommon importance. After listening to a full account of Tadanobu's suicide and last words, he said, "He was a brave man. That is the sort of spirit I should like to see in every warrior. Not one of Yoshitsune's young retainers is a commonplace fellow. Think of the Satō brothers—if they had not been excellent warriors, Hidehira would never have chosen them for Yoshitsune's service from among so many. Why don't we have such men in the eastern provinces? If someone like Tadanobu would leave Yoshitsune for me, I would prefer him to a hundred ordinary men. I would give him any of the Eight Provinces he wanted, great or small."

"What a pity that Tadanobu was foolish enough to kill himself! If only he had stayed alive!" Chiba Tsunetane and Kasai Hyōe Kiyoshige murmured.

At that point Hatakeyama spoke his mind bluntly to Yoritomo. "You admire Tadanobu because his death was so heroic that we can scarcely conceive of it. If he had been brought here as a captive, it would have done him no good to be alive—you would have tortured him to learn where Yoshitsune is hiding. A man who is doomed to death must find it hard to endure the stares of other warriors. Furthermore, even the offer of half of Japan would not have persuaded an honorable man like Tadanobu to desert Yoshitsune for you."

Ōi and Utsunomiya nudged one another. "Well said! That's plain talk, even for Hatakeyama," they whispered.

"Expose the head for the edification of posterity," ordered Yoritomo.

Hori Yatarō obediently withdrew from the hall and hung up Tadanobu's head on the east side of the Hachiman torii at Yui-no-hama. When Yoritomo made inquiry three days later, he was told that it was still there.

"Poor fellow! His home is a long way from here. It's been left because his people don't know about it. If a hero's head is exposed too long, he may become an evil spirit haunting the neighborhood. Take it down," he said. He directed that it be buried behind the Shōjōjuin, the temple which he had erected in memory of the Chief of the Stables of the Left. Feeling perhaps that even this was not enough, he asked the abbot to have one hundred thirty-six sutras copied as an offering on Tadanobu's behalf. "Never has there been such a warrior, either in ancient times or in our own," everyone said.

YOSHITSUNE'S CONCEALMENT IN NARA

Meanwhile, at Nara, Kanjubō had received Yoshitsune warmly and lodged him in a chapel containing images of Fugen and Kokūzō, the monk's special objects of adoration since his childhood, where he attended to his comfort in every conceivable way.

Whenever the opportunity arose, Kanjubō urged Yoshitsune to embrace a life of religion. "You cannot escape punishment for causing all those deaths during your three years of campaigning against the Heike. Will you not sincerely resolve to seek enlightenment? Intone the name of the Buddha as a recluse at Kōya or Kogawa to help yourself in the next life, which must soon follow your present transitory existence," he would beseech him.

"I appreciate your advice," Yoshitsune would respond, "but I want to stay as I am for a year or two to see what happens in the world of men." He showed no inclination to turn his back on society, even though Kanjubō constantly expounded the holy sutras for his benefit, hoping against hope that he would change his mind.

To relieve the tedium of his evenings, Yoshitsune took to playing the flute outside Kanjubō's gate. Just at that time, it chanced that there was a monk at Nara called the Deacon of Tajima. This Tajima approached six of his cronies—Izumi, Mimasaka, Ben-no-kimi, and three others—and said, "People in Nara call us wicked and lawless, but we haven't done much yet to live up to our reputation. Let's wait around at night and steal swords."

"A good idea!" the six replied. From then on they all stole swords nightly.

One day Tajima said, "A small, fair-skinned youth who doesn't ordinarily live in Nara has been loitering outside Kanjubō's gate every night, wearing a handsome corselet and a magnificent gold-mounted sword. Whether the sword is his or his master's, it's much too good for him. Let's take it away from him."

"There's no use thinking about it," Mimasaka replied. "I have heard that Kurō Yoshitsune has been staying with Kanjubō since the Yoshino monks attacked him. We'd better leave him alone."

"You're the worst coward I've ever met. Why shouldn't we take his sword?" said Tajima.

"That's all very well, but what if things go wrong?" said Mimasaka.

"If they do, it will be a case of not having let well enough alone— but after all, we are fellows who are willing to try the impossible.

Foolish or not, let's go." So they agreed to head toward Kanjubō's neighborhood.

"The six of you stand in the shadow of the wall. I'll clap my skirt against his scabbard and cry out, 'This man is assaulting me!' When you hear my voice, run out shouting, 'What sort of rascal behaves in such a rough manner in these holy precincts? Don't kill him! If he's a warrior, cut off his top hair and chase him away from the temple; if he's a commoner, chop off his ears and nose and run him off!' If we can't get the sword then, it will be our own fault," said Tajima. They made their preparations and set out.

Yoshitsune was absorbed as usual in playing his flute. After a time, he became aware of something odd in the behavior of a passer-by. In another instant the stranger had flapped his corselet skirt loudly against Yoshitsune's scabbard cover. "This man is assaulting me!" cried the stranger.

At once six monks ran forward. "Don't let him get away with it!" they shouted.

"What a predicament!" thought Yoshitsune. He stood waiting with his back to the wall, sword in hand. When the first monk approached, brandishing his halberd, he cut the weapon in two. The second man's short-bladed halberd was dispatched in the same way, and soon the flashing sword had claimed five victims. When the wounded Tajima took to his heels, Yoshitsune chased him to a confined area, knocked him down with the back of his sword, and took him prisoner.

"What do they call you in Nara?" Yoshitsune demanded.

"The Deacon of Tajima."

"Do you value your life?"

"Everyone who has received the gift of life values it."

"Coward! You don't live up to your reputation! I'd be happy to cut off your head and throw it away, but you're a monk and I'm not, and it's like harming a buddha for a layman to kill a monk. I'll let you go if you'll stop this sort of business. Tell people in Nara tomorrow that you tackled Gen Kurō and they'll call you a stout fellow. If anyone asks for proof, it would be too bad if you didn't have any—so here!" He pushed the big monk down on his back and stood on his chest. Then he cut off his ears and nose and released him. Tajima would have preferred death, but his laments were futile. He disappeared from Nara that very night.

After this unfortunate encounter, Yoshitsune went back to Kanjubō's cloister. He called the monk to the chapel to bid him farewell. "I had hoped to spend the rest of the year here, but I have had an idea which involves a trip to the capital. It is very hard to say goodbye. Of course I hope you will remember me in your prayers while I am still alive—and if you should hear of my death, please do what you can to help my spirit. Since the bond between a teacher and his disciple lasts for three lives, I am sure we shall meet again in the next world." With these words he prepared to take his leave.

Kanjubō, greatly agitated, held him back. "It is very distressing to hear you talk suddenly of leaving when I had been so certain you would be here for a while at least. You must have taken someone's gossip too seriously. No matter what people may say, I won't pay any attention. Stay until next spring and then go wherever you like, but don't make the mistake of leaving now."

"It is kind of you to regret my departure, but I am afraid I won't be welcome here tomorrow, after you've seen what is in front of your gate," replied Yoshitsune.

"I suppose you've got into a scrape tonight," said Kanjubō. "They tell me that a number of young monks have been abusing the court's indulgence by stealing swords at night lately. Your blade is such a fine one that they've probably got themselves killed by trying to rob you. That's nothing to worry about. I have my resources in case there should be criticism. Of course someone will complain to the military authorities. Hōjō Tokimasa in the capital will ask for instructions from the Kantō, since he won't feel capable of acting alone, but not even Yoritomo himself can send an army into Nara without an order from the Emperor or the ex-Emperor. If it comes to that, you're in as good a position as any to obtain imperial sanction for your acts. You made a good impression on His Majesty while you were living in the capital after the Heike campaigns, and the ex-Emperor also thinks very highly of you. If you were to stay in the city and summon the warriors of Shikoku and Kyushu, they would be certain to come, and so would every fighting man in the Home Provinces and Chūgoku. If the powerful families*l* in Kyushu refused to obey you, you could send Kataoka, Benkei, and some other tough warriors to chasten them a bit. There might be some trouble in other places, but by uniting the western half of Japan, securing Ōsaka Barrier, and blocking the passes through the Arachi Mountains and Ise Suzuka, you could prevent Yoritomo's deputies from penetrating west of the three barriers.[4] Then it would be the easiest thing in the world for me to bring together the Kōfukuji, Tōdaiji, Enryakuji, Miidera, Yoshino, Totsugawa, Kurama, and Kiyomizu temples. What's more, I have done favors for two or three hundred fellows who could build a fortress and shoot from its towers under the command of your retainers. You could leave the battle to them and watch from the sidelines. If by chance we were defeated, I would recite sutras before the buddhas I have worshiped since my childhood, while you repeated the sacred names and killed yourself. Then I would drive a sword into my own body so that I could go with you to the next world. In this world I have recited your prayers; in the next I shall be your spiritual mentor."

Although these loyal words made Yoshitsune long to remain, he left Nara before morning. "Who knows what is in another man's mind?" he thought. "Anyway, it would be a pity to make trouble for Kanjubō. I used to think that no one in Japan had a heart as stout as my own; he is extraordinary!" Kanjubō would not hear of his going alone and ordered six trusted disciples to escort him to the capital, but on the way Yoshitsune said to them, "Wait for me awhile at Rokujō Horikawa," and then disappeared, leaving them no choice but to return to Nara.

From that time on not even Kanjubō knew where to find Yoshitsune. Meanwhile, in Nara, where a number of men had lost their lives, someone (could it have been Tajima?) started a rumor that Yoshitsune had been plotting a rebellion with Kanjubō's connivance, and that the slain monks had been turned over to Yoshitsune by Kanjubō for refusing to take part in the conspiracy.

KANJUBŌ IS SUMMONED TO THE KANTŌ

When the astonished Hōjō at Rokuhara learned of Yoshitsune's presence in Nara, they communicated at once with the Kantō.

"It appears that one of Yoshitsune's Nara friends, the monk Kanjubō, is stirring up all kinds of trouble. A number of monks have

---

[4] Ōsaka, Arachi, and Suzuka.

already been killed there. Do something about him before the warriors in Izumi and Kawachi decide to join Yoshitsune," Yoritomo
told Kajiwara.

"This is serious. It is strange that a monk should do such things,"
said Kajiwara.

At that moment a new courier from the Hōjō entered to report that
Yoshitsune had left Nara and was being hidden elsewhere by Kanjubō. "In that case, it will be necessary to obtain permission from the
Emperor or ex-Emperor to bring Kanjubō here for questioning,"
advised Kajiwara. "After he answers, we can decide whether to
execute him or banish him." Yoritomo at once ordered Hori Tōji
Chikaie to ride to the capital with fifty men.

When Chikaie arrived at Rokuhara with Yoritomo's message, Lord
Hōjō took him to the ex-Emperor's palace to explain matters.

"That is not an easy request," said the ex-Emperor. "Kanjubō
recites prayers for His Majesty himself. Furthermore, he is a pillar of
Buddhism—a miracle worker and a saint. You will have to make a
full statement of your case to His Majesty."

When they went to the palace, the Emperor said, "It is true that
Kanjubō works miracles and serves the cause of Buddhism faithfully,
but we cannot tolerate that kind of behavior. No wonder Yoritomo is
angry. Since Yoshitsune is an enemy of the court, it is only right that
Kanjubō should be arrested."

Armed with this decree, Tokimasa jubilantly led a party of three
hundred mounted warriors to Nara, where he communicated the
Emperor's sentiments to Kanjubō.

"We all know that this is the era of degeneracy,[5] but it is sad to
watch the collapse of imperial authority," said Kanjubō in tears. "In
ancient times, they say, an imperial decree made withered plants
bloom and bear fruit, or struck down birds in flight.[6] If matters have
come to this pass now, what may happen in the future?[7] Imperial
decree or not, I ought to refuse to obey such an order, even if I had
to die fighting here in Nara; but a monk can't resort to violence. As
a matter of fact, I am glad Yoritomo has summoned me. I have been

[5] *Matsudai (mappō)*. See Chapter One, note 6.
[6] A paraphrase of a Buddhist hymn. HM 1.346, n. 12.
[7] He means that if the Emperor is so weak that he must agree to the arrest of an innocent
man, even worse injustices will probably follow.

hoping to have a chance to teach him the doctrines of Buddhism—
people say that he knows very little about them." He began forthwith
to prepare for the journey.

Distressed by the thought of bidding farewell to their teacher, a
number of young noblemen who were Kanjubō's disciples proposed
to travel with him to the east. "That would not do at all. I am being
summoned because I have committed an offense. If you accompanied
me, you would also be accused," he told them reprovingly.

"If word of my death reaches you, mourn for me. If you hear that
I am still alive, join me, even if it is on an isolated moor or deep in the
mountains." With these last words, Kanjubō set out, weeping in
despair. When the sixteen arhats, five hundred disciples, and fifty-
two classes of beings mourned Śākyamuni's entry into Nirvana, the
parting can have been no sadder.

Lord Hōjō took Kanjubō to Kyoto, lodged him in the Rokuhara
chapel, and saw to all his needs. "If you desire anything at all, we
shall be happy to send word to Nara," Yoshitoki told him.

"What can I say?" replied Kanjubō. "I have an old friend near
here who ought to have come to see me by now. Since he has not, I
feel sure that he is afraid. If you have no objection, I should like to
talk to him before I go."

"What is his name?" asked Yoshitoki.

"He used to live at Kurodani, but recently he has been at Higashiyama. His name is Hōnen."

"That is the holy man who lives in this neighborhood," said Yoshitoki. He dispatched a messenger without delay, and Hōnen hastened
to visit Kanjubō.

When the two venerable monks met, they were both deeply moved.
"Though I am delighted to see you, it is all I can do to look anyone in
the face, now that I am about to be carried off to the east with charges
of conspiracy heaped on my shaven head," said Kanjubō. "I have no
expectations of returning safely. Long ago we two made a pact: 'If I
go first, pray for me; if you go first, I will do the same for you.' It
comforts me to know that I can rely on you. Place this at the entrance
to your private chapel, and whenever your eye falls on it remember
me and pray for me in the next world." He gave his nine-piece scarf
to Hōnen, who accepted it in tears. Hōnen in turn presented him with
a *Lotus Sutra* scroll from his blue brocade sutra bag. Then Hōnen

returned to his home, while Kanjubō remained at Rokuhara, weeping disconsolately.

As abbot of the great Tōdaiji Temple, where solemn national religious convocations were held, and as the teacher of His Majesty the Emperor, this compassionate and wise monk had overawed even the mighty Ministers of the Left and Right when he set forth on some such occasion as a visit to the ex-Emperor, riding in a litter or an ox-drawn carriage, with a long train of solemn monks and brilliantly attired pages. Now, with his customary robes of silk replaced by a coarse hempen garment and with soot from the sacred fires darkening his unshaven head, he seemed somehow more saintly than ever.

As if the unfamiliar sight of his warrior escort were not affliction enough, Kanjubō was required to mount a sorry relay beast, from which he slid off time and again in a manner pitiful to behold. After leaving Awataguchi behind, the party climbed Matsusaka Hill, passed the Shinomiya River Beach, which had once been the home of Ōsaka Semimaru, and crossed Ōsaka Barrier. They bowed at Sekidera Temple, where Ono Komachi had lived, passed Ōtsu and Uchi-de Beach with Onjōji Temple on their left, clattered over the Chinese bridge at Seta, and arrived in the vicinity of Noji and Shinohara. Unable to dismiss the capital from his mind, Kanjubō continually looked back as they journeyed until the city had receded far into the distance. Ono-no-suribari, heretofore but a name,[8] mist-veiled Kagami Mountain, and Ibuki Peak drew near in their turn.

Hori Tōji stopped overnight at Kagami post station. On the following day, out of compassion for Kanjubō, he borrowed a litter from the mistress. "I wanted to arrange for you to ride this way from the beginning, but I ordered the horse because I was afraid of what might be said at Kamakura," he explained.

"I am very grateful to be shown this kindness on the way," replied Kanjubō touchingly.

By traveling long hours, they reached Kamakura in fourteen days. Kanjubō was kept in Hori Tōji's house for four or five days, while Yoritomo remained in ignorance of his arrival. At length Hori said, "I have not had the heart to tell Yoritomo that you are here, but since

[8] This phrase, which loses its point in translation, reads literally, "heard but not seen." It introduces a pun on Ono and a homonym meaning "ax." Similarly, "mist-veiled" is intended to suggest "mirror" *(kagami)*.

I cannot keep quiet forever, I am going now to report to him. I dare say he will see you today."

"The uncertainty of waiting is hard to endure. I shall be glad to see His Lordship soon, hear his questions, and explain my position," replied Kanjubō.

When Tōji brought word of Kanjubō's arrival, Yoritomo said to Kajiwara, "I wish to question Kanjubō today. Summon the warriors."^m

"What place would be suitable for the interrogation?" Yoritomo inquired.

"Have him brought to the rear entrance to the middle gate,"⁹ was Kajiwara's advice.

Hatakeyama bowed respectfully. "I suppose that Kajiwara has suggested the middle gate because Kanjubō is accused of conspiring with Yoshitsune. We must remember that this monk belongs to a most illustrious lay family. Furthermore, he is the abbot of Tōdaiji Temple and the teacher of His Majesty the Emperor. His coming to Kamakura merely shows that he is willing to be agreeable. Even though we are country people, we shall be criticized if we are careless in matters like this. It wouldn't surprise me if Kanjubō refused to reply to questions at the middle gate. He ought to be interviewed in the room where His Lordship is sitting."

"I agree," said Yoritomo. Ordering the blinds to be raised high, he settled himself on a purple-bordered mat, dressed in a short-sleeved jacket and high cap, and waited as Hori Tōji ushered Kanjubō in. "Since he is a monk, it will not do to torture him. I shall have to get him to confess by talking to him," he reflected.

When Kanjubō had finished his bow, Yoritomo uttered a short, mirthless laugh and lapsed into grim silence. Kanjubō interpreted this as a sign of hostility. He clasped his hands on his knees and gazed at Yoritomo steadily, while the onlookers swallowed nervously, saying to themselves, "If this is to be the tone of the meeting..."

"This is Kanjubō?" Yoritomo asked Hori Tōji.

"May it please Your Lordship."

Presently Yoritomo spoke. "After a monk begins to study Śākyamuni's precepts in a teacher's cell, he is supposed to live a virtuous Buddhist life—to wear the three garments of black, to support the

⁹ The place where criminals were interrogated.

holy faith, to study the sacred writ diligently, to pray for strangers, and to act as the mentor of those whose karmas are linked with his. What is the meaning of this flagrant conspiracy with a traitor, this attempt to subvert law and order? You had no right to shelter someone like Yoshitsune—a man who wants to start a nationwide war— much less to urge Nara monks to join him, and send them to him to be murdered when they refused. Furthermore, your advice to him was inexcusable. Did you not say the following: 'Unite the warriors of Shikoku and Kyushu, summon men from Chūgoku and the Home Provinces, and send fierce warriors like Kataoka and Benkei to punish anyone who refuses to come. The Tōdaiji and Kōfukuji temples will rise at a word from me. If we fail, we will die in battle here'? You sent men to escort him to the capital, so you must know where he is. Don't attempt to lie. If you fail to tell the truth, I shall be perfectly justified in putting you to the torture."

Upon hearing these savage words, Kanjubō wept for a time with his hands clenched on his knees. Then he said, "I should be obliged if you would all listen to what I have to say. This is unfamiliar language indeed—you are saying to me, 'A miscreant like you does not deserve the name Virtuous Works;[10] there is nothing to respect in a monk like you.'

"People say in the capital that an auspicious karma and a humane nature have made you this country's military lord. We are born with our karmas, but as a man you cannot compare with your brother Yoshitsune. Though it does little good to speak of such things now, let me remind you of the past for a few minutes. Your father, the Shimotsuke Chief of the Stables of the Left, fled to the east in the Heiji era after he and his ally were defeated in the capital. Yoshihira and Tomonaga both lost their lives and your father himself was killed in the first month of the following year. You disgraced the Minamoto name by clinging to life and wandering in the vicinity of Ibuki Peak in Mino until you were captured by people at the foot of the mountains and taken to Kyoto. You would have been executed if it hadn't been for the intercession of Kiyomori's stepmother, who succeeded in having you exiled instead. You were placed in the custody of Yahyo-byōe and sent off (around the eighth month of the first year of Ei-ryaku [1160], as I recall) to Nagoya-no-hirugashima at Hōjō in Izu,

10 *Tokugo*, the ecclesiastical title held by Kanjubō.

where you lived as a rustic for twenty-one years. I am not surprised
that with such a background you have no civilized feelings. You are
utterly heartless! No wonder you hate a merciful, kind, and brave
man like Yoshitsune!

"In the autumn of the fourth year of Jishō [1180], Yoshitsune rode
at breakneck speed from Ōshū to Ukishima Plain in Suruga to accept
a general's commission from you. He pressed a bow to his side,
fastened a sword to his waist, roamed tirelessly over the western
waves, lodged in fields and mountains, and risked his life to conquer
the Heike. But even while he was driving himself pitilessly for your
sake, determined to help you hold your position, it was the old story of
a malicious tongue. All his services were forgotten, and a tragic
mistrust separated him from you.

"We are told that men's ties with their parents endure for one life
and those with their lords for three. As to whether you and Yoshitsune
are now in the first, second, or last, I cannot say, but I have always
heard that the bond between brothers carries over into the next
world. No wonder people call you inhuman for trying to sever it!

"Last year, late at night on the twenty-fourth day of the twelfth
month, Yoshitsune came to me for sanctuary, armed with nothing but
a corselet and sword. His face was hidden under a wicker hat and he
was unaccompanied by a single attendant—he who had once led
thousands and tens of thousands of horsemen. Even if he had been a
complete stranger, how could I have refused to show him mercy?
Please understand my position.

"The stories you have heard are quite untrue. Late last winter, I
urged Yoshitsune again and again to renounce the world, but he said,
'I refuse to let that scoundrel Kajiwara hound me into becoming a
monk.' You may have received some malicious reports about a group
of warrior monks whom Yoshitsune killed when they tried to steal his
sword, but I have never tried to draw people at Nara into a conspiracy. When Yoshitsune was preparing to flee after killing the
monks, I thought that he didn't know what to do, so I gave him this
advice: 'Summon warriors from Shikoku and Kyushu. I shall see to
the Tōdaiji and Kōfukuji temples. You are well liked in the country
and the ex-Emperor favors you. Stay in Kyoto as the ruler of half of
Japan.' But to my dismay he divined my inner feelings and left Nara.

"Although you were not aware of it, I once offered prayers for you.

When Yoshitsune was marching west against the Heike, he asked at Watanabe for a monk who could intercede for the Genji, and someone foolishly suggested me. When we met, he told me to curse the Heike and pray for the Minamoto. I was unwilling to commit such a sin, so I refused repeatedly, until at last he demanded, 'Are you a partisan of the Heike?' He frightened me so much that I did as he wished. At the time I said, 'Although there are not two suns in the heavens or two rulers on earth, let our country fall into the hands of these two brothers.' Yoshitsune has always been unlucky. He failed to establish a position for himself, and the entire nation came under your dominion. Is it not possible that the gods may have answered my prayers?

"However much you may torture me, I shall say no more. There was never anything gained by harassing a man of discernment. Who has been given orders? Let him strike off my head at once to appease the anger of the Lord of Kamakura."

Every warrior with the least shred of human feeling wept at this frank speech, which was followed by a burst of tears. Yoritomo lowered his screen, and for a time all was silent.

"Come forward, some of you," Yoritomo presently commanded.

When Sawara Jūrō, Wada Kotarō, and Hatakeyama Saburō sat before him, he praised Kanjubō in a ringing voice. "I did not expect this! He ought to have been questioned at Rokuhara, but on Kajiwara's advice I brought him here, and now he has given me a fine tongue-lashing. What can I say? That was an answer for you! Kanjubō is a saint. It is entirely proper that he should be the abbot of the greatest temple in Japan and the prayer-monk of the imperial family. Can we not persuade him to stay and teach in Kamakura for the next three years?"

Wada Kotarō and Sawara Jūrō spoke to Kanjubō. "Tōdaiji Temple has already benefited mankind immeasurably during its long history. Kamakura did not exist before the winter of the fourth year of Jishō [1180], and its benighted inhabitants are always violating the sacred commandments. Will you not remain here to help us for at least three years?"

"Your feelings do you credit, but I have no desire to stay in Kamakura, not even for a year or two," replied Kanjubō. When they insisted that it was for the good of Buddhism, however, he agreed: "Very well, I shall stay for three years."

Yoritomo was overjoyed. "Where shall we put him?" he asked.

"I know just the thing," said Sawara Jūrō. "Make him abbot of the Great Hall."

"An excellent idea," said Yoritomo. Sawara Jūrō was put in charge of the construction of the Great Hall, and a cypress-thatched retreat was built for Kanjubō in the rear of the Shōjōjuin.[11] Yoritomo himself worshiped there daily, and there was never a time when saddled horses were not standing outside the gate. In this manner began the propagation of Buddhism in Kamakura.

Whenever the occasion permitted, Kanjubō urged Yoritomo to reconcile his differences with Yoshitsune. Though Yoritomo always agreed readily, he was prevented from following his own desires by Kajiwara Heizō, the Assistant Chief of the Samurai Office supervising the warriors of the Eight Provinces, who made the retainers under his jurisdiction follow his orders or those of his son like so many grasses bending in the wind.

Thus matters stood as long as Hidehira lived. After Hidehira's death, Kanjubō learned that Yoshitsune had been killed by the old lord's heir, Yasuhira, on the twenty-fourth day of the fourth month of the fifth year of Bunji [1189]. He lost no time in returning to Kyoto, telling himself that he had remained in Kamakura only for Yoshitsune's sake and was under no obligation to take formal leave of anyone as heartless as Yoritomo. Owing to the friendship of the ex-Emperor, he was able to return to the Tōdaiji, but he could not bring himself to take charge of the reconstruction, or even to receive callers. He shut himself up behind closed gates, and after copying out in his own hand 226 sutras to help Yoshitsune obtain enlightenment, he refused all food and drink until he entered the Pure Land. He was in his seventh decade.

SHIZUKA'S JOURNEY TO KAMAKURA

As we know, Yoshitsune had been accompanied into the Yoshino

---

[11] This is either a slip on the part of the author or a corruption in the text, since the Shōjōjuin (Great Hall) was built in 1184–85. Possibly the author intended to say that Sawara was ordered to supervise the construction of Kanjubō's cell.

mountains by Shizuka, the dancing girl from Kitashirakawa, who was his favorite among the six noble ladies and five dancers he had selected to join him on the voyage to Shikoku. While Shizuka was living with her mother, Zenji, after having been sent back to the capital, the authorities at Rokuhara learned that she was soon to bear Yoshitsune's child. On Yoshitoki's advice, Lord Hōjō sent a special courier to inform Yoritomo in Kamakura.

Yoritomo summoned Kajiwara. "I have learned that Yoshitsune's favorite concubine, the dancer Shizuka, is with child. What shall we do?" he asked.

"In China, any woman who carries an enemy's child is regarded as a criminal. They think nothing of smashing her head to bits or crushing her bones and extracting the marrow. If the child is a boy, he will be no ordinary youth, whether he resembles Yoshitsune or your own family. There is no danger as long as you are alive, but what of your sons? It would be wise for you to request permission of the Emperor or the ex-Emperor to bring Shizuka to Kamakura where we can watch her until the child is born. If it is a boy you can dispose of him. If it is a girl, she can be turned over to your wife," replied Kajiwara.

As this course recommended itself to Yoritomo, Hori Tōji was dispatched to the capital. With Lord Hōjō's assistance, he laid the matter before the ex-Emperor.

"This is different from Kanjubō's case," said the ex-Emperor. "Have Tokimasa find her and send her to the Kantō."

After a search of the Kitashirakawa area, Shizuka was discovered at Hosshōji Temple, where she had secreted herself in the hope of gaining a brief respite, though she was well aware that she must ultimately be found. She was taken to Rokuhara with her mother, Zenji.

As Hori Tōji prepared to depart for Kamakura with his charge, Iso-no-zenji's emotions were painful beyond description. If she accompanied Shizuka, she would suffer the anguish of witnessing her tragic fate, but if she remained behind she would be sending her off alone to the distant east. "The loss of a child is sorrowful enough to a parent who has five or ten, but Shizuka is my only daughter," the mother thought. "How can I bear to stay in the capital? It might be different if she were a dull clod. Her beauty is famous throughout

Kyoto, and not a dancer in Japan can equal her." Unable to bear the woe of letting Shizuka journey on without her, she ignored the remonstrances of her warrior guards and started out tearfully on foot, accompanied by Saibara and Sonokoma, her attendants since childhood, who refused to be left behind. Hori Tōji treated them kindly on the way, and fourteen days later they reached Kamakura.

As soon as Yoritomo was informed of Shizuka's arrival, he summoned the great chieftains and lesser warriors to witness her interrogation.[n] A huge throng of ordinary folk gathered outside the gate. Lady Masako, who was herself eager for a glimpse of Shizuka, sat with her ladies in waiting behind a curtain.

Presently Shizuka entered, escorted only by Tōji. "What an enchanting creature! If she were not Yoshitsune's concubine..." mused Yoritomo.

Zenji and her two attendants, who had accompanied Shizuka, had stayed weeping outside the gate.

"I hear women wailing at the gate. Who are they?" asked Yoritomo.

"Shizuka's mother and her two maids," replied Tōji.

"Since they are women, there is no reason why they should not come in. Summon them," Yoritomo ordered. When they appeared, he said to Zenji, "Why did you give Shizuka to an enemy of the state instead of marrying her to a nobleman?"

"Shizuka had many suitors before she was fifteen," she replied, "but none of them took her fancy. After Yoshitsune saw her at the pond in the Garden of Divine Waters, where she had gone with the ex-Emperor's party to dance for rain, he called her to his house at Horikawa. I thought it was merely a passing whim, but he fell in love with her. Though he kept a great many other ladies at various places in the city, she was the only one he brought to the Horikawa mansion. I considered it an honor for her to form an alliance with someone who was a descendent of Emperor Seiwa and a brother of the Lord of Kamakura. How could I have dreamed that it would come to this!"

"Well done! 'The sparrows at the Kangakuin chirp the *Meng-ch'iu*,' "[12] said the listeners admiringly.

[12] The Kangakuin was an academy established by the Fujiwara family for the education of its young men; *Meng-ch'iu* is a Chinese text recited by schoolboys. The proverb, which means that one unconsciously learns from environmental influences, is not particularly apt

"She is carrying Yoshitsune's child, is she not? What have you to say to that?"

"Since everyone knows it, there hardly seems anything to discuss. It will be born next month."

Yoritomo summoned Kajiwara. "Shocking! Hear that, Kagetoki! Rip open her belly and kill the child before that scoundrel reproduces his kind."

Shizuka and her mother wailed in anguish with their hands clasped and their faces together. Tears of sympathy rose in Lady Masako's throat, and the other ladies behind the curtain made no effort to control their sobs.

"How heartless he is!" murmured the warriors. "People already call the Kantō a distant land of horrors. We shall be disgraced forever if he kills Shizuka."

Kajiwara overheard them. He arose, approached Yoritomo, and seated himself with formal deliberation, while the warriors watched apprehensively. "This is frightful! What is he going to suggest now?" they wondered.

"I understand your command," said Kajiwara. "We shall no doubt find it necessary to kill the child, but how can you escape retribution for the criminal murder of its mother? It would be different if we had to wait for the entire ten-month period, but since the birth is expected next month, let her go to Genda's house for her confinement. We will inform you of the sex."

The men in the hall nudged one another incredulously. "Era of degeneracy or not, this is extraordinary. Kajiwara has never shown a talent for compassion before," they said.

Shizuka sent a message to Yoritomo by Kudō Saemon. "Ever since we left the capital, the very mention of Kajiwara's name has been almost too much for me to bear. If I die in childbirth at his house, my feeling about him will keep me from attaining buddhahood.[13] Unless there is some objection, I implore you to designate Lord Hori's house instead."

"Her request is quite understandable; there is no reason why it

---

here. The author probably intends to say that remarkable children have remarkable parents.

[13] Only those who have freed themselves from human passions can be reborn as buddhas.

should not be granted," said Yoritomo. He returned Shizuka to the custody of Hori Tōji, who hurried home to his wife, delighted by the honor. "Kajiwara asked to be put in charge of Lady Shizuka, but at her own request she has been returned to me. Do everything possible for her comfort; Yoshitsune himself may hear of it some day," he said. Moving into a subsidiary building, he designated his principal hall as the lying-in place and appointed a dozen or so sensible ladies to attend to Shizuka's needs.

Meanwhile Iso-no-zenji prayed to the gods and buddhas of the capital. "Inari, Gion, Kamo, Kasuga, the Seven Shrines of Hiyoshi Sannō, Great Bodhisattva Hachiman: if the child in Shizuka's womb is a boy, let it be transformed into a girl," she said.

Presently Shizuka's time came. Perhaps because the Earth Goddess[14] pitied her, she suffered no pain. When the birth was imminent, Tōji's wife and Zenji came to her assistance, and the child was delivered with no difficulties whatever. As Zenji began to wrap it in white silk, rejoicing in the sound of its tiny wail, she perceived that in spite of her prayers it was a fine boy.

"What a misfortune!" she cried, bursting into tears.

"Is it a boy or a girl?" Shizuka asked anxiously. She looked at the child in her silent mother's arms, saw that it was a boy, and pulled her cloak over her head with a piteous shriek.

After a time Shizuka said, "Whatever crimes he may have committed in a previous incarnation, it is heart-rending to think that he must return to the nether regions after less than a day in the world of men, without even a proper glimpse of the light of the sun or moon. All things are determined by karma and it is wrong to prize life or regret anyone's death, but all the same I cannot bear to part with him." She pressed her sleeve to her face and wept.

Tōji presented himself courteously. "I must go now to report the child's sex, as Yoritomo ordered," he said.

"There is no hope of keeping it from him, so tell him quickly," Shizuka replied.

After Tōji had reported, Yoritomo summoned Adachi Shinzaburō Kiyotsune. "A boy baby has been born to Shizuka at Tōji's house.

[14] A deity of Indian origin who was believed to protect the earth, promote fertility, and assure her worshipers longevity and freedom from pain.

Ride my bay horse to Yui-no-hama and kill him there," he commanded.

Kiyotsune mounted and rode to Tōji's house. "I come as a messenger from the Lord of Kamakura. He has been informed that the child is a boy. I am to take it to him," he said to Zenji.

"What a foolish thing to say, Kiyotsune!" she cried. "Do you think you can deceive us? Didn't Yoritomo hate this child so much that he was ready to kill its mother too? Of course he has already ordered its death, especially since it's a boy. Give us a few minutes to dress him for his end, I beg you."

Not being made of stone or wood, Kiyotsune agreed to wait; but he soon reminded himself that it would not do to show weakness. "You make too much of the matter. No preparations are needed," he said. He seized the child roughly from Zenji's arms and, holding it close, set out at a gallop for Yui-no-hama.

Zenji cried after him, "I don't ask you to spare his life! Just let me look once more at his tiny face." But Kiyotsune called back heartlessly, "The sight of him would merely make you feel worse," and rode off into the mist.

Zenji ran with Sonokoma toward the beach, not stopping even to put on straw sandals or throw a cloak over her head. Hori Tōji followed her. Shizuka attempted to do the same, but Tōji's wife held her back, remonstrating, "You have just given birth to a child," and she lay weeping at the door through which the others had departed.

When Zenji reached the beach, she could see neither the horse nor the baby. "Though but a fragile bond united us in this life, let me at least see his dead body once more," she lamented. She walked westward along the shore until, on the bank of the Inase River, she encountered a number of children playing in the sand.

"Did a man on horseback abandon a crying baby near here?" she queried.

"He tossed something on top of that pile of wood near the edge of the water," one of them replied. When Tōji's manservant went down to look, he discovered the corpse of the infant who had so recently resembled a budding flower. He took him to Iso-no-zenji, the swaddling clothes apparently undisturbed but the body pitifully lifeless.

Zenji spread the edge of her robe over the warm beach and laid the baby on it to see if he would revive. He showed no sign of life. Rather than torment Shizuka by taking back his body for her to see, she resolved to bury him on the spot. She began to dig in the sand with her hands, but it was painful to think of his grave being trod on by the insensate hooves of passing oxen and horses, and in the end, having found no suitable burial place on the wide beach, she returned to Tōji's house with the baby in her arms. Shizuka pressed its cold body frantically to her breast.

"Your grief is natural, though it is a grave sin for a parent to mourn a child,"[15] said Tōji. He himself attended to the baby's funeral rites, burying him behind the Shōjōjuin, the temple erected in memory of the Chief of the Stables of the Left. Shizuka, unwilling to remain for a single day in a place with such dreadful associations, prepared to return to the capital immediately.

SHIZUKA'S VISIT TO THE LOWER HACHIMAN SHRINE

"How can you go home without visiting Hachiman Shrine?" objected Zenji. "You made a promise to the god: 'I am reconciled to the loss of the child who is to be born, and shall say nothing about that. If I myself survive, I promise to visit the Lower Shrine.' Since a woman cannot enter Hachiman's precincts until fifty-one days after the blood of childbirth defiles her, you will have to wait here until you can purify yourself." Thus they stayed on.

Meanwhile it chanced that Yoritomo had determined to make a pious journey to Mishima and was purifying himself beforehand by daily pilgrimages to shrines in Kamakura. As the attendant warriors were telling stories to dispel the tedium of the rituals, Kawagoe Tarō began to speak of Shizuka. "She will never come back here unless something like this happens again. It is a pity that His Lordship can't see one of her celebrated dances," said some of the others.

"Shizuka puts on airs because Yoshitsune favors her. Besides, I have come between her and her lover and killed the child who was in a sense a keepsake from him. It is hardly likely that she would want to dance for me," said Yoritomo.

"True enough," someone said. "Still, there must be some way of getting a look at her."

"Why are you all so eager to see her perform?" asked Yoritomo.

"She is the best dancer in Japan," replied Kajiwara.

---

[15] Such worldly ties hinder the attainment of enlightenment.

"You flatter her. Where did she earn that title?"

"One year a devastating hundred-day drought parched the Kamo and Katsura rivers and dried up the wells. Someone found an ancient book of precedents which said, 'If one hundred holy, miracle-working monks from Mount Hiei, Miidera, Tōdaiji, and Kōfukuji chant the *Benevolent King Sutra* at the pond in the Garden of Divine Waters, the eight dragon kings[16] will respond.' One hundred august monks were commissioned to recite, but it did no good. Then someone else said, 'I believe the dragon gods would be pleased if a hundred beautiful dancers were summoned to perform before the ex-Emperor at the pond.' The former sovereign journeyed hopefully to the pond and commanded the dancers to perform, one by one. When ninety-nine had done their best, someone remarked, 'Even if Shizuka, the last one, takes her turn, she won't attract the dragon gods' notice. Of course, she has been admitted to the Sacred Mirror Chamber[17] and granted a generous stipend, but still...'

" 'She is one of the hundred. Let her proceed,' the ex-Emperor commanded.

"To the astonishment of all, Shizuka was only halfway through the dance called Shimmujō when black clouds suddenly sailed over the capital from Mikoshi Peak and Atago Mountain. The eight dragon kings thundered, lightning flashed, and the capital was pelted by a drenching rain which continued for three days. The ex-Emperor said that Shizuka had saved the state, and he officially named her the best dancer in Japan."

"It would be amusing to see her perform," Yoritomo agreed. "Who will ask her?"

"Let me do it," offered Kajiwara.

"How do you propose to go about it?"

"Can anyone in Japan refuse to obey a command from the Lord of Kamakura? Furthermore, I was the one who interceded for her after she had been sentenced to death. At any rate, I will try."

"All right, go and make yourself agreeable."

At Shizuka's lodgings Kajiwara called out Iso-no-zenji. "The Lord

[16] Also called eight dragon gods. Rain-bringing divinities described in the *Lotus Sutra*.
[17] *Naishidokoro (Kashikodokoro)*, a palace hall in which the Sacred Mirror, one of the Three Imperial Regalia, was enshrined. Shizuka presumably participated in the Shinto dances which were performed there annually in the twelfth month.

of Kamakura is drinking wine at the moment. He has been listening to Kawagoe Tarō's praise of your daughter and would like to see one of her famous performances. There's nothing to make a fuss about. Tell her that she is to dance," he said.

When Zenji went inside with the message, Shizuka pulled her cloak over her head and fell prostrate, crying, "I cannot bear the thought." After a time she said, "Ours is a cruel profession. If I were not a dancer, I wouldn't be ordered to perform before someone I detest while I'm still overcome with grief. I know it must have pained you to have to tell me this, but even so I can't help envying you. Does Yoritomo really think I shall dance at a word from him?" She refused to send Kajiwara an answer.

The disappointed Kajiwara returned to Yoritomo's mansion, where everyone was eagerly awaiting him. "What did she say?" inquired a messenger from Lady Masako.

"I told her that it was an order from His Lordship, but she refused to give any answer at all," said Kajiwara.

"I expected it," said Yoritomo. "When she returns to the capital, they will ask at the palaces of the Emperor and ex-Emperor, 'Didn't Yoritomo order you to dance for him?' If she answers, 'He sent Kajiwara with a command, but I refused because I didn't feel like it,' I shall look like a weakling. What shall we do? Who can talk to her this time?"

"When Kudō Saemon Suketsune was in the capital, he was a great favorite with Yoshitsune. Besides, he is a city fellow with a glib tongue. Why not call on him?" proposed Kajiwara.

"Summon him," commanded Yoritomo. When Kajiwara had fetched Suketsune from his house at Tō-no-tsuji, Yoritomo said to him, "Will you try to persuade Shizuka to dance for me? I sent Kajiwara to ask her, but she refused to discuss it."

"This is the worst job anybody could possibly be saddled with," thought Kudō. "How am I supposed to persuade her when she has already ignored an outright command from the Lord of Kamakura!" He hurried home in a sad state of nerves. "Yoritomo has given me a terrible task. I am to persuade Shizuka to dance after she has already rejected an order transmitted by Kajiwara. What a prospect!" he complained to his wife.

"It doesn't matter who the messenger is—the important thing is to

treat her sympathetically. Kajiwara is nothing but a country bump-
kin. He probably said, 'Give us a dance!' in his most boorish manner,
and I suppose you would approach her in the same way. I think it
will be quite possible to persuade her if we put her into a good humor
by going to Lord Hori's house with some fruit and cakes, as though
we were simply paying a visit," she said, making it sound like the
easiest thing in the world.

A number of years earlier Suketsune had lost both his ancestral
lands and his beloved wife because of a falling-out with his uncle, Itō
Jirō.[18] At the time of the dispute, Suketsune's future second wife (a
city-bred daughter of Chiba Tsunetane, born while Tsunetane was
on duty in the capital) had been a mature woman in service at the
mansion of Taira Shigemori, where she was called Lady Reizei. To
dissuade Suketsune from going off to Izu to seek revenge against his
uncle, Shigemori had offered him Lady Reizei as a consort. "She is a
bit old," Shigemori had said, "but take her anyway." Suketsune and
Lady Reizei had gradually become deeply devoted to each other.
After the lady had been left without a patron by Shigemori's death,
which occurred in the Jishō era [1177–81], Suketsune had taken her
with him to the east. In spite of her years in the provinces, she had
not forgotten the amenities of city life, and no doubt she thought it
would be an easy matter to cajole Shizuka into dancing. At any rate,
she made a hasty toilet and went with her husband to Tōji's house.

Suketsune, who entered first, addressed Iso-no-zenji politely. "I
have been so busy lately that I have not had an opportunity to call
on you; you must have thought me very negligent. I am to go with
Yoritomo to Mishima Shrine, and because I have had to participate
in the daily purification rituals, I have not been here. Please forgive
me. My wife, who used to live in the capital, has come with me to
Lord Hori's house. Won't you present her compliments to Lady
Shizuka as acceptably as possible?" Pretending to go home, he hid
nearby while Iso-no-zenji went in to Shizuka.

"A visit from Suketsune is always welcome, and his wife's call is
indeed an unexpected privilege," said Shizuka. She set her room to
rights and received the lady, who entered in company with Tōji's
wife. Since the object was to put Shizuka in a good humor, wine was

[18] See Appendix B, Itō Sukechika and Kudō Suketsune.

produced. Before long Suketsune's wife sang an *imayō*,[19] Tōji's wife
responded with a *saibara*,[20] and Iso-no-zenji apologetically sang the
shirabyōshi "Kisen," accompanied by Saibara and Sonokoma, who
rivaled their mistress in skill. Outside, in the quiet spring night, rain
fell softly.

"If there is anyone outside the wall, let him listen too. An evening
devoted to music means a life of a thousand years. I shall sing a song
myself," said Shizuka. She sang the *shirabyōshi* "Parting" in a voice
and style so bewitching that Suketsune and Tōji, listening at the wall,
were quite carried away. "If only that were an ordinary room, nothing could keep us from going in," they said.

When the song was ended, Shizuka produced a lute in a brocade
bag and a cittern in a white-dotted bag. Sonokoma drew out the lute,
tuned it, and placed it in front of Suketsune's wife, while Saibara removed the cittern from its covering, inserted the support beneath the
strings, and gave it to Shizuka.

After the music, Suketsune's wife related elegant anecdotes until
she judged that the time to speak had come. Then she said, "In ancient times the capital was at Naniwa. It was after the establishment
of the new capital in Otagi District that people began to worship the
divine Hachiman at Yui-no-hama, Hizume-no-kobayashi, and the
foot of Tsurugaoka Hill, far away on the Tōkaidō east of the Ashigara
Mountains in the province of Sagami. Since Hachiman is the ancestral deity of the Lord of Kamakura, it goes without saying that he
is Yoshitsune's patron too. By appearing in disguise in our world, a
buddha or bodhisattva takes the first step toward the establishment of
ties with mankind, just as Śākyamuni took the last step for the salvation of living things by appearing in the eight aspects.[21] Can there be
any doubt that Hachiman will answer your prayer?[22]

"Since Tsurugaoka is the holiest shrine in this entire province, it is
as crowded as a market place with petitioners in the afternoon, and

[19] A four-line song form, an outgrowth of the Buddhist hymn, which was popular at
court in the late Heian and Kamakura periods. *Imayō* were often sung by *shirabyōshi*.
[20] A type of court music based on folk songs.
[21] The eight stages in the life of the historical Buddha, beginning with the preliminaries
to his birth and ending with his entry into Nirvana.
[22] Since all Buddhist divinities are sympathetically inclined toward mankind, and
especially since Hachiman is Yoshitsune's guardian deity, Hachiman will grant Shizuka's
petition.

worshipers shoulder one another aside and tread on one another's heels in the morning. You must not think of going during the daytime. Fortunately Lord Hori's wife is quite at home in the Lower Shrine, and so am I. Why don't you fulfill your vow by going early tomorrow while it is still dark? If you dance for the god at the same time, I am sure Yoritomo and Yoshitsune will be reconciled and everything will happen just as you wish. If Yoshitsune were to hear of it in Ōshū, wouldn't he be delighted to know what you were doing to help him? When will you have another opportunity like this? Forgive me if I seem importunate. I have become so concerned for you that I am unable to think of you as a stranger. If you go, I will go with you."

Perhaps Shizuka was convinced by her persuasions. At any rate, she asked Iso-no-zenji for advice. Zenji, who hoped with all her heart that her daughter would visit the shrine, answered, "Hachiman has spoken through this lady's lips. How wonderfully kind she is! Go as soon as you can."

"All right. I will go. And since the daylight hours are not suitable, I shall arrive around four o'clock in the morning, present a formal dance around eight, and then return home," said Shizuka.

Eager to inform her husband as soon as possible, Suketsune's wife sent someone to tell him; but before the messenger had departed, Suketsune himself had left his listening post on the other side of the wall, leaped onto his horse, and galloped posthaste to Yoritomo's mansion.

"What happened? What happened?" asked Yoritomo and the warriors as Suketsune burst into the Samurai Office.

"She will go to worship at four tomorrow morning and dance at eight," Suketsune cried.

Yoritomo set out for the shrine at once.

As word of Shizuka's intention spread, the gate of the Lower Shrine became as congested as a market place. "The rabble are pushing and screaming in front of the sanctuary and in the corridors. They won't listen to reason at all," someone reported.

"Have the attendants put them out," Yoritomo told Genda.

"Disperse in the name of the Lord of Kamakura," Genda shouted.

The crowd paid no attention. Though the attendants showered blows in all directions, knocking off laymen's caps and monks' straw hats and wounding many people, everyone pressed stubbornly forward, determined not to let a few bruises stand in the way of the sight of a lifetime.

Amidst all the commotion Sawara Jūrō commented, "If we had been given advance notice, we could have built a dance platform in the middle of the corridor."

"Who said that?" asked Yoritomo.

"Sawara Jūrō."

"Quite right! Sawara is a man who knows the old customs. Get one ready immediately."

There was no time to spare. Jūrō appropriated some planks which had been intended for shrine repairs, made a stage three feet high, and covered it with Chinese damask and gauze with a woven-in design of crests. Yoritomo announced that he was well pleased.

Ten o'clock came and Shizuka had still not arrived. The spectators at the shrine began grumbling aloud at her tardiness. The sun was high in the heavens before she approached, riding in a litter. She proceeded to the corridor of the sanctuary, accompanied by the wives of Suketsune and Tōji. Zenji, Saibara, and Sonokoma, who were to assist her, seated themselves on the dance platform, and her two escorts entered a viewing stand with a company of some thirty other ladies.

While Shizuka stood in prayer before the sanctuary, Iso-no-zenji told Saibara to beat the drum. "There is nothing remarkable about this, but perhaps it will influence the god favorably," she said. She performed a *shirabyōshi* called "The Amorous Lesser Captain," singing and dancing in such an accomplished manner that the spectators marveled. "Zenji is not particularly famous. If she dances so exquisitely, think how wonderful Shizuka must be," they said.

The curtains and general appearance of the other visitors to the shrine had soon betrayed Yoritomo's presence to Shizuka. "Suketsune's wife has coaxed me into dancing in front of Yoritomo! I must find an excuse for changing my mind," she thought. Calling Suketsune, she said, "I see that the Lord of Kamakura is apparently here today. When I was summoned to the Sacred Mirror Chamber in the capital, I danced to music provided by Nobumitsu, the Chief of the Palace Storehouse Bureau, and when I performed the rain dance at the Garden of Divine Waters, my assistant was Kisuhara of Shijō.

Since I came to Kamakura under a cloud, I did not bring an accompanist. After my mother has dedicated a dance in the correct manner, we shall go to the capital, make arrangements for an accompanist, and return to perform for the god." To the dismay of the assembled chieftains, she appeared to be on the point of departure.

"This is humiliating," said Yoritomo. "We cannot have people saying that she refused to dance in Kamakura for lack of an accompanist. Kajiwara, can none of these warriors beat a measure? Find someone to play for her."

"I have heard that when Suketsune was in Shigemori's service, he was much admired by the nobility for his skill as a drummer at the palace sacred dances," said Kajiwara.

"Very well, beat the drum so that she can dance, Suketsune," commanded Yoritomo.

"I am so out of practice that the tone will not be what I could wish, but since you ask it, I shall do my best. But a drum alone isn't enough; please ask someone to strike a gong."

"Is there anyone here who knows how?"

"Naganuma Gorō."

"Find him and tell him to perform."

"He is absent today because of some trouble with his eyes."

"In that case, I shall try it myself," said Kajiwara.

"How do you rate Kajiwara as a gong player?" Yoritomo asked Suketsune.

"Only Naganuma is better."

"Very well—there's no reason why he should not perform."

"Setting the pitch is very important," said Sawara Jūrō. "Someone should be asked to play a flute."

"Can anyone play the flute?" inquired Yoritomo.

"Hatakeyama's proficiency has been admired by the ex-Emperor himself," replied Wada Kotarō.

"But Hatakeyama is our wisest counselor. We can't ask him to join such a makeshift orchestra."

"Let me speak to him." Going to Hatakeyama's viewing stand, Wada repeated Yoritomo's words.

Hatakeyama promptly agreed to perform. "If the drum is to be beaten by Suketsune, who is one of His Lordship's most trusted retainers, and the gong is to be struck by Kajiwara, who is the assistant chief of the office controlling all the warriors in the Eight Provinces, and the flute is to be blown by myself, there can hardly be anything unrespectable about the orchestra's credentials," he laughed.

The three musicians retired to prepare for the occasion and re-appeared one by one. Suketsune wore a starched skirt of dark blue, an olive-green jacket, and a stiff cap. He carried a sheepskin-covered sandalwood drum with six cords, which he beat with his skirt tucked high as he waited, arousing echoes in the corridor and the pine-covered hill above the shrine. Next Kajiwara entered, also wearing a starched skirt of dark blue, a light green jacket, and a stiff cap. Seating himself to the right of Suketsune, he began to accompany the drum like a chirping insect, using a silver gong embossed with golden chrysanthemums, suspended from a multicolored cord.

After observing the scene through an opening in the curtain, Hata-keyama dressed casually in flaring white drawers, a white blouse and knickers with purple leather cords, and a smartly creased folding cap. He tucked his skirt high, took up Pine Breeze, his long-jointed bamboo flute, swept aside the curtain, and mounted to the dance platform with the measured tread of a hero. Since everyone knows how handsome he was, it is scarcely necessary to say that he was marvelous to behold as he took his place on Suketsune's left. He was just twenty-three years old.

"A splendid orchestra!" praised Yoritomo from behind the blind. They were indeed quite worthy of the occasion. When Shizuka saw them, she thought, "I was right to refuse. It would have been demeaning to go ahead without a second thought. With such accompanists I have no objections whatever to performing." Assisted by Zenji, she began preparing her costume.

Tangled clusters of wisteria blossoms drooped from the pine trees at the edge of the pond, a breeze stirred the mountain mists, and a *hototogisu*[23] tentatively uttered its haunting cry, as if aware of what was about to happen. Shizuka was attired that day in a narrowsleeved white underrobe surmounted by a garment of Chinese damask, a long white skirt, and a jacket embroidered in a diamond pattern. Her flowing hair was tied high, and slender eyebrows accented her slightly painted face, made thin by recent grief. As she opened a crimson fan and faced the sanctuary, she hesitated momentarily,

[23] *Cuculus poliocephalus Latham.* A small melodious bird rather like a cuckoo.

seemingly awed by the presence of the dread Lord of Kamakura.

"Last winter she tossed on the waves of Shikoku and wandered through the snows of Yoshino; this year the long journey over the Tōkaidō has wasted her body. Nevertheless it is hard to believe that our country boasts a woman as beautiful as Shizuka," said Lady Masako.

Soon Shizuka raised her incomparable voice in the strains of "Shimmujō," a *shirabyōshi* which she performed with particular skill. The amazed and delighted spectators of all degrees caught their breath and praised her until the clouds rang. Even those beyond earshot were almost equally moved, simply from hearing her in their imagination. When the song was half finished, Suketsune loosened his sleeve to beat the closing tattoo, as though reluctant to force her to perform longer, and she began to chant, "Long as the imperial reign ..."[24] "Suketsune is an inconsiderate fellow. How delightful it would be to watch her again!" grumbled the crowd.

"After all, this has been a dance in the presence of the enemy. Why shouldn't I express my feelings in a song?" thought Shizuka. She sang:

> Like the *shizu, shizu,*
> *Shizu* bobbin,[25]
> Ever repeating,
> Would that I could somehow
> Make yesterday today.
>
> How I long for him—
> The person who vanished,
> Cleaving a way
> Through the white snows
> On Yoshino's peaks.

[24] *Kimi ga yo no*... It appears to have been customary to end a dance by reciting a suitably auspicious classical verse. Shizuka's choice was probably in the vein of the following poem, which appears in *Shikashū*, a twelfth-century anthology. Okami, p. 296, n. 3.

Kimi ga yo no	The pines of Sumiyoshi
Hisashikarubeki	Planted by the gods—
Tameshi ni ya	Tokens of His Majesty's
Kami no uekemu	Everlasting reign.
Sumiyoshi no matsu.	

[25] The song contains a play on Shizuka's name. *Shizu* was a type of weaving bobbin used in ancient times.

Yoritomo let his blind fall with a clatter. "I am not amused by this *shirabyōshi*," he exclaimed. "That was a brazen exhibition! She thought I was too uncivilized to understand her. 'Like a *shizu* bobbin, ever repeating' means 'If only Yoritomo would lose his power to Yoshitsune!' This is too much! When she sang, 'The person who disappeared, cleaving a way through the white snows on Yoshino's peaks,' she might as well have said outright, 'Yoshitsune is still alive in spite of Yoritomo's efforts to destroy him.' I will not tolerate it!"

"Though we are all fellow pilgrims on the road of life, there has to be a special bond of sympathy between a dancer and her audience," interposed Lady Masako. "How could someone in Shizuka's position be expected to perform before you? No matter what provoking things she says, she is only a weak woman. Forgive her."

Yoritomo elevated one side of his blind slightly. Shizuka, who had noted his displeasure, sang again:

> He has vanished utterly—
> The person who disappeared,
> Cleaving a way
> Through the white snows
> On Yoshino's peaks.

Yoritomo raised the blind all the way—grudging praise indeed!

Shizuka received numerous presents from Lady Masako, all of which she gave to the abbot of the Lower Shrine[26] for prayers on Yoshitsune's behalf. Then she set out toward home with Hori Tōji's wife.

On the following day Shizuka departed for the capital. Back at the Kitashirakawa house, she sank apathetically into memories of the bitter past, finding visitors merely a painful interruption to her ceaseless reveries. Zenji was at her wits' ends to console her. Finally, after closeting herself in her chapel day and night to recite sutras and intone the sacred name of the Buddha, Shizuka determined to linger no more in this world of sorrows. Without a word to her mother, she cut off her hair and shaved her head. Then she built a grass hut near Tenryūji Temple, and there with Zenji she began a life of pious devotion.

[26] The head of the Buddhist temple associated with the shrine.

So the beautiful young Shizuka became a nun at the age of nineteen. Late in the fall of the following year, unable to bear the dreadful weight of her memories any longer, she entered the Pure Land with the name of Amida Buddha on her lips. I have heard that all who learned of her death praised her constant heart.

Chapter Seven

Meanwhile, late in the first month of the second year of Bunji [1186], Yoshitsune was hiding in and about Rokujō Horikawa and the back country of Saga, causing numerous friends in the capital to suffer for his sake. "I am a nuisance and burden to far too many people," he decided. "It is time for me to go to Ōshū." He issued a call to his scattered retainers, and all sixteen responded loyally.

"I propose to go to Ōshū. Which is the best route?" he asked.

"There are too many famous spots on the Tōkaidō and too many narrow passes on the Tōsendō—we could never escape in an emergency. The Hokurikudō would be best. It goes to the port of Tsuruga in Echizen, where we could take passage for Dewa," someone answered.

The matter of the road having been settled in this way, Yoshitsune then put the question, "How shall we disguise ourselves?"

His men offered opinions of all sorts.

"If you want to travel in peace, you'd better take religious vows before you start," Mashio Shichirō advised.

"I may do that some day, but it would be humiliating if people said, 'Kanjubō of Nara urged Yoshitsune over and over to become a monk. He paid no attention then, but now that he has nowhere to go he has renounced the world.' Whatever happens on this trip, I shall travel as my old self."

"Then disguise yourself as a wandering monk," suggested Kataoka.

"How would that do?" Yoshitsune considered. "As soon as we left the capital, we would begin to pass one temple and shrine after another.⁰ Other ascetics might ask us questions which needed a special knowledge of the Peak of the Single Vehicle, the Peak of Enlightenment, Śākyamuni Peak, the Eight Great Vajra Messengers, Mount Fuji, or the etiquette of the fraternity. Could anyone here answer well enough to avoid suspicion?"

"That would be no problem whatsoever," said Benkei. "Since you lived at Kurama, you must have a general notion of how wandering monks behave. Hitachibō, who was at Onjōji Temple, of course knows all about them, and I learned a bit about the Single Vehicle and Enlightenment during my days in the Western Compound. We would certainly be able to give some reply. Pretending to be a wandering monk is the easiest thing in the world for anyone who knows the repentence rites and the *Amida Sutra*. Make up your mind to it."

"In the event that someone inquires, where shall we say we are from?"

"Naoe-no-tsu in Echigo is halfway along the Hokurikudō. While we are on this side of it, we can call ourselves Haguro ascetics returning from a pilgrimage to Kumano; on the other side, we shall be Kumano ascetics going to Haguro."

"Is anyone acquainted with Haguro? What shall we do if someone asks, 'What buildings do you live in at Haguro? What are your names?'"

"When I was at the Western Compound, a Haguro monk staying in a mountain cloister used to say that I looked exactly like Arasanuki in the abbot's quarters at the Daikoku Hall. I shall call myself Arasanuki, and Hitachibō can be Chikuzenbō, the assistant leader," said Benkei.

"Since you two are already monks, there would be no problem even if you didn't take new names. It will sound very odd, won't it, if these laymen call each other Kataoka, Ise Saburō, and Mashio while they're wearing ascetics' caps and robes and carrying panniers on their backs?" said Yoshitsune.

"All right, we'll make clerics of them." Benkei invented a religious name for every man.ᵖ

Since all sorts of people knew Yoshitsune by sight, he disguised himself carefully in a pair of dingy white undergarments, a white hemp robe with an arrow-nock design, wide-bottomed grasscloth drawers, a persimmon-colored cloak with an all-over design of plovers, and a worn black cap pulled down to his eyes. His name was to be Yamatobō.

Each of the others made himself ready in his own way. Benkei, who was to pose as the leader, provided himself with a short-sleeved white robe, dark blue leggings, and straw sandals. He tied his skirt strings high, donned a long cap of the kind affected at the Kumano New Shrine, and hung his sword, Rock Cleaver, at his waist, with a conch shell[1] on his hip. A carved ten-inch ax was fastened to the legs of the pannier carried by the servant Kisanda, his porter, and a four-and-a-half-foot sword lay sideways on its lid. Both in bearing and in costume, Benkei was a convincing leader.

The party of sixteen prepared ten panniers. Into one they put sacred bells, one-limbed vajras,[2] flower dishes,[3] covered censers, water vessels, and images of the vajra messengers; into another, ten unfolded caps and a number of blouses, knickers, and drawers. The remaining eight were filled with suits of armor and corselets.

By the time all this was done, it was the end of the first month. Yoshitsune resolved to set out on the second of the second month, which was an auspicious day for him. He called the warriors together.

"We shall soon be off, but it is hard for many reasons to leave the capital," he said. "I can't help thinking of someone who used to live near the intersection of Ichijō and Imadegawa, and who must still be there. I promised that we would go to Ōshū together, and it would be a great shock if I were to leave without a word. If it won't do any harm, I should like to have that person go too."

"Your traveling companions are all before your eyes. Who is at Imadegawa? You must mean your wife," replied Kataoka and Benkei.

In Yoshitsune's present situation it was impossible to silence them with a sharp word or two, as he had done in the old days. He hesitated miserably.

"Circumstances alter cases," said Benkei. "If we dress in ascetics' caps and robes with panniers on our backs, and then put a woman in our front ranks, we shall never convince people that we are holy men.

[1] *Horagai.* Blown by ascetics during religious rites or as a signal of arrival, departure, or the like.

[2] *Dokko*, a vajra with a single prong at each end. Used for subduing evil spirits.

[3] These were filled with twigs and paper flowers which were scattered during ritual processions.

What if we're pursued by enemies? We can't afford to stay behind a lady who's dawdling along." Nevertheless he could not restrain a feeling of compassion for Yoshitsune's wife, who had lost her father, the Koga Minister of State, at the age of nine and her mother at thirteen, and afterward had had no one upon whom to rely except her guardian, Jūrō Gon-no-kami Kanefusa. Though beautiful and sweet, she had lived very quietly until the age of sixteen, when Yoshitsune had met and fallen in love with her. From that time on she had never been intimate with anyone else. Just as the pine tree supports the frail wisteria, so man is essential to woman, who in the nature of things obeys first a father, then a husband, and lastly a son. "Furthermore," Benkei reflected, "once Yoshitsune arrives in Ōshū, it will be a pity if he has to get along with some coarse eastern woman. What he said just now couldn't have been an idle whim. Why shouldn't we take her?"

"I understand how you feel," Benkei said aloud. "When it comes to human emotions, there is no difference between high and low. As you know, time brings changes. Why don't you visit her, see how she acts, and take her along if you still want her?"

"If you feel that way. . ." said Yoshitsune with every appearance of delight. Wearing his persimmon-colored robe with a thin cloak over his head, he went off at once toward the old Koga mansion near the intersection of Ichijō and Imadegawa. Benkei accompanied him in his white robe and a head-cloak.[4]

Dew-laden grasses glistened in the eaves of the neglected buildings at the mansion, and the fragrance of plum blossoms drifted from a rough-woven fence, recalling the time when the Grand Captain Genji had brushed aside the dew at another ruined dwelling.[5] After concealing Yoshitsune in the corridor adjoining the middle gate, Benkei went up to the door. "Is the lady of the house at home?" he asked.

"Where do you come from?" someone said.

"Horikawa."

When the door was opened, Yoshitsune's wife saw that it was Benkei. Although she had always addressed him through an intermediary,

---

[4] The cloaks were worn to disguise their features and discourage recognition.

[5] See Arthur Waley, *The Tale of Genji* (London: Allen and Unwin, 1957), "The Palace in the Tangled Woods," p. 319.

she was so overjoyed that she went up to the edge of her blind and asked directly, "Where is my husband?"

"At Horikawa. He desires me to tell you that he is leaving tomorrow for Michinoku. I was to say, 'I promised to take you with me no matter what, but the roads are blocked, and I cannot subject you to the trying experiences you would undergo if you went. I shall go ahead alone. If I survive, I swear to send someone for you in the spring. Wait patiently until then.'"

"If he refuses to let me go now, he won't send anyone back just to fetch me! Human life is unpredictable. He will be sorry if I die before he gets to Ōshū. 'People can't escape their destinies. Why did I leave her?' he will lament, but it will be too late. While he still loved me, he took me with him over the waves toward Shikoku and Kyushu, so it is easy to see that he doesn't care about me any more. How can he be so unfeeling? After he sent me back to the capital from Daimotsu-no-ura, or wherever it was, I didn't hear a word, but I foolishly trusted his promises of better times. It is very distressing to receive such a cruel message now!

"Perhaps I ought not say anything, but how do I know that I won't die? It is a sin to carry a secret to the grave... Since last summer I have been feeling wretched, and my people tell me that I must be pregnant. Recently I have been ill even at night. Before long anyone will be able to see what's the matter, and then what will happen if they hear about it at Rokuhara? Yoritomo has no heart at all. He'll have me arrested and sent to Kamakura. Shizuka from Kitashirakawa escaped punishment by singing and dancing, but I am not in the least accomplished. I couldn't bear to have everybody gossiping about me. Of course, if His Lordship won't change his mind, there's nothing for me to do." As she importuned him, sobbing piteously, tears of sympathy rose in Benkei's eyes. In the torchlight he made out a poem which appeared to be in her own hand, written below the handle on a sliding door in her private apartment.

> If he has grown cold,
> My heart, too, should alter—
> Why must I go on loving a man
> Who causes me such anguish?

Deeply moved by this testimony to her constancy, he hurried off to Yoshitsune, who at once made his presence known. "You are very quick tempered," he said. "Here I am, come to fetch you."

His astonished wife wept in relief.

"Even though it is only a disguise, I'm afraid the way I look is enough to destroy your love," Yoshitsune continued.

"Have you renounced the world, as people have been saying?"

"Look." He removed his outer cloak, revealing the persimmon-colored robe, bloused trousers, and black cap.

"All right, what shall I wear?" asked his wife, who, had her affection cooled in the slightest, would certainly have recoiled at the sight.

"Since you will be traveling with a band of ascetics, you had better be a page. It will seem natural for you to wear cosmetics, and your age is right, too. You will look fine, but you'll have to be very careful of your behavior. All kinds of ascetics wander through the Hokuriku-dō provinces. Prepare yourself to talk and act like a boy if one of them should happen to give us a present for you—a spray of blossoms or some such thing. It wouldn't do at all to cling to your old graceful, retiring manners."

"As long as I can go with you, I shan't mind how I act," she replied. "It's already late; let us be quick."

Acting the part of a maidservant, Benkei drew his sword, Rock Cleaver, and remorselessly hacked off her beautiful hair, which trailed on the floor and shimmered like a pellucid stream, until it came only to her waist. Then he trimmed the ends, arranged them high on her head, applied cosmetics sparingly to her face, and painted a pair of delicate brows on her forehead. She dressed herself in five underrobes—the first leaf-green in color, the second deep crimson, the third yellow on one side and red on the other, the fourth of figured Chinese satin, and the fifth of pale yellow Harima cloth with a diamond pattern. Then she put on a pair of flaring drawers tied high on her legs, a blouse and knickers of thin printed silk, figured leggings, straw sandals, and a new bamboo hat. At her waist she hung a vividly colored fan and a sword with a red wooden handle. She carried a Chinese bamboo flute (which she could not possibly have played)[6] and a dark blue brocade bag containing five chapters of the *Lotus Sutra*, draped round her neck by Benkei. As she staggered beneath her

[6] The flute was a man's instrument.

burdens, this lady, who ordinarily found it difficult enough to support her own weight, must have felt very much like Wang Chao-chün being carried off by the Hu barbarians.

After his wife's costume was complete, Yoshitsune ordered Benkei to stand aside while he drew her to her feet and led her back and forth by the hand in the brightly lighted guest room.

"How about it? Do I look like a wandering monk? Does she make a good page?" he asked.

"Since you know the ways of wandering monks from your Kurama days, of course you look authentic. I can't imagine when Her Ladyship learned to impersonate a page, but she's the very image of one. The gods and buddhas must be helping her," said Benkei, concealing tears of pity.

Long before dawn on the second, as the party prepared to set out from the Imadegawa house, Yoshitsune heard a sound at the west door. It was his wife's guardian, Gon-no-kami Kanefusa, wearing indigo-colored trousers over a white blouse and knickers, with his graying hair hanging loose and an ascetic's cap on his head. "Old as I am, I beg you to allow me to go," Kanefusa said.

"Who will look after your wife and children?" asked Yoshitsune's wife.

"A man cannot put his family before his master," he said in tears.

The sixty-three-year-old Kanefusa was a venerable ascetic indeed! At length he succeeded in controlling his sobs and went on: "His Lordship is a Seiwa Genji and Her Ladyship is the daughter of Lord Koga. They ought to be riding in litters and carriages, even if it were only for an outing to look at cherry blossoms or maple leaves, or to visit a shrine or temple. What cruel fate has doomed them to toil on foot over the long road to the far-distant east?" He began to weep again.

"How true," said the spurious ascetics, wringing tears from their jacket sleeves. "Have all the gods and buddhas forsaken the world?"

When Yoshitsune took his wife by the hand to help her walk, the pitifully inexperienced lady stood stock-still. At length he succeeded in distracting her with amusing tales, but though they left Imadegawa while it was still dark, they had barely reached Awataguchi when cockcrows and booming temple gongs foretold the dawn.

"Is there no way to make Her Ladyship walk a bit faster?" Benkei said to Kataoka. "Speak to him about it."

Kataoka went up to Yoshitsune. "We shall never get anywhere if we keep on like this. You travel at your own pace while we go ahead to ask Hidehira to build a house for you. We shall return to meet you," he said.

"It's unspeakably bitter to part from you, but I can't let those men desert me," said Yoshitsune to his wife. To Kanefusa he added, "Take her back to the capital while it's still close." He put her aside and started out.

"No matter how far it is, I won't mind," she said plaintively. "Who will take care of me? Where do you want me to go, now that you're abandoning me?" Until then, she had uttered not a single complaint.

At that Benkei went back for her.

As the party left Awataguchi behind and approached Matsusaka, they heard the faint call of a wild goose, invisible in the hazy spring sky. Yoshitsune recited:

> Enviable indeed—
> The homing goose
> Cleaving the thick white clouds
> On the Hokurikudō.

His wife replied:

> What sorrow evokes his cry?—
> The homing goose,
> Turning away from spring.

Journeying on and on, they came to Semimaru's thatched cottage at Ōsaka, a ruined dwelling behind a hedge overgrown with ferns and day lilies. "Only the moonlight is the same as of old," they mused. Yoshitsune plucked a fern from the eaves for his wife, who found the fragile plant more touching than ever, now that she herself was in hiding.[7] She recited:

> As I leave my home in the capital
> To travel in disguise,

[7] The name of the fern, *shinobugusa*, means "grass in hiding."

How like tears it is—
The clear dew
On the hares' foot fern!

At length they approached Ōtsu Shore. Although they had hoped to travel further in the course of the long spring day, the Sekidera evening bell was signaling the dusk, and with it the necessity of seeking a humble lodging.

ŌTSU JIRŌ

As the saying goes, "Heaven, which lacks a mouth, must speak through human agents." Although there had of course been no announcement, it was rumored that Yoshitsune had left the capital with a dozen men dressed as ascetics, and the lord of Ōtsu, Yamashina Saemon, was preparing to intercept him at a stronghold built with the aid of monks from Onjōji Temple. It happened, however, that there was a large house on the beach at Ōtsu—the home of a merchant captain named Ōtsu Jirōᵠ—and it was there that Benkei went to ask for shelter.

"We are Haguro ascetics on our way home after the year-end retreat at Kumano. Please allow us spend the night with you," he said.

Such requests were common in a post town, and Jirō's people consented willingly. As the night advanced, the party settled down to chant repentence rites and the *Amida Sutra,* the first religious exercises of their journey.

Ōtsu Jirō had been ordered to the stronghold earlier by Saemon. Unseen, his wife watched the arrival of the guests. "What a beautiful page!" she exclaimed to herself. "These people claim to have made a pilgrimage to Kumano from some distant province, but no ordinary boy would be dressed so elegantly. We may get into serious trouble if the people at the stronghold learn that we are sheltering a large band of wandering monks just as Yoshitsune is traveling east in a monk's disguise. I had better call Jirō and tell him about it. If it really is Yoshitsune, we need not say anything to Yamashina Saemon. We can earn a reward by killing or capturing him for Yoritomo." She sent a messenger to the stronghold to call her husband. When he had come, she beckoned him into a tiny room. "Can you imagine! We have taken in Yoshitsune for the night! What shall we do? Why not ask your relatives and my brothers to help us capture him?"

" 'Walls have ears and stones mouths,' " replied her husband. "What difference does it make whether it's Yoshitsune or not? We wouldn't get a reward anyway. If they're ascetics, the vajra messengers might be angry with us, and if they're Yoshitsune and his men, I for one don't intend to interfere with the brother of the Lord of Kamakura. Even if we attacked them, how could we capture them? You talk too much; shut up!"

"You're the kind of man who can't stand up to anybody but a woman," his wife retorted. "Why do you refuse to report something to the authorities simply because it comes from me? Very well—I'll go to the stronghold and tell them myself." She threw a narrow-sleeved robe over her head and ran out.

"See here! This won't do at all!" thought Ōtsu Jirō. He dashed after her and knocked her flat outside the gate. "Listen, you! 'Grass bends before the wind; a wife obeys her husband'—that's nothing new, is it?" he shouted. And he began to curse her roundly, while she lay in the middle of the road screaming and railing, "Ōtsu Jirō is a wicked criminal. He supports Hōgan!"

Although the people in the neighborhood heard the commotion, no one interfered. "Ōtsu Jirō's woman is raving drunk again, yelling because her husband is beating her up," they said. "I've heard lots of monks' names, but Hōgan is a new one. Leave them alone and let him thrash her."

When he had at last tired of hitting his wife, Ōtsu Jirō went away, leaving her lying in the road. He put on a blouse and knickers and entered Yoshitsune's quarters, where his first act was to extinguish the torches. "I can't tell you how much I regret all this," he said. "The woman is out of her mind—listen to her! What must you be thinking? Even so, you will be in trouble tomorrow if you spend the night here. The local lord, a man named Yamashina Saemon, is waiting for Yoshitsune at a stronghold he has built, so you must leave as fast as you can. I have a small boat you're welcome to use if any of you can handle her. Hurry!"

"We have done nothing wrong, but since I don't want to be delayed, we shall say good-bye," Benkei replied, rising to his feet. To Yoshitsune he added privately, "We can leave the boat at Kaizu and cross the Arachi Mountains to Echizen."

Ōtsu Jirō accompanied the party to the wharf and put the boat in readiness; then he hastened back to Yamashina Saemon. "I have just heard that my brother has been injured in an accident at Kaizu. I should like to leave for a while. If he's all right, I shall be back soon," he said.

"I'm very sorry to hear it. Go, by all means," Saemon replied.

Ōtsu Jirō went to his home, fastened a sword to his waist, slung a quiverful of war arrows on his back, and strung a bow. "I'm going with you," he told Yoshitsune. He leaped into the boat and put out from Ōtsu beach.

As they ran under sail before a fresh breeze from the Seta River, Ōtsu Jirō pointed out the sights of interest. "There is the stone pagoda built by King Aśoka; this is the Karasaki Pine; over there is Mount Hiei." While Yoshitsune was looking back toward the Sannō sanctuary, Jirō said, "Ahead lies Chikubu Island." They bowed reverently.

By midnight the wind had sent them to an unknown shore in western Ōmi. When he heard the sound of surf, Yoshitsune asked, "Where are we?" "This is Katada beach in Ōmi," Jirō replied. The lady recited:

> In the swamps where snipes rest
> The water is frozen—
> The waves at Katada break gently.

Passing Shirahige Shrine in the distance, they recalled an ancient verse composed by Jakushō, the Novice of Mikawa:

> Where quail call
> At Mano Inlet,
> The wind on the beach
> Bends the *obana* reeds in waves—
> An autumn eve.[8]

When at last they had rowed past Imazu to Kaizu, the passengers disembarked and Ōtsu Jirō took his leave. Strangely enough, the wind, which had been blowing steadily from the south, had veered suddenly to the north.

"That fellow's social position may be low, but he's a good sort. I

[8] The verse was actually composed by Minamoto Shunrai (1055–1129), one of the leading poets of the late Heian period.

should like to let him know who I am," thought Yoshitsune. He
called Benkei over. "If we tell him the truth before we leave, the
rumors he hears later will have a special meaning for him. Go ahead
and tell him," he said.

Benkei beckoned to Ōtsu Jirō. "Since it's you, I don't mind letting
you know that our lord is Yoshitsune. Take these in case something
happens to us on the way, and have your son and grandson keep them
after you." He took from one of the panniers a pale green corselet and
a sword with gold and silver mountings.

"I wish I could stay with you," said Ōtsu Jirō as he accepted the
gifts, "but it will be best for His Lordship if I leave now. As soon as I
hear that he has found a place to live, I will come to ask for an audience, no matter how far I must travel." With that he set out on the
return journey. "His station in life was low, but he was a good man,"
said the warriors.

When Ōtsu Jirō reached home he found his wife in bed, still seething with two days' anger. "I say, wife!" he shouted. Getting no
answer, he went on, "That was a ridiculous notion you had. You
almost made me lose a lot of money by taking in those monks and then
accusing them of being Yoshitsune and his men. When I asked for my
pay at Kaizu, they said they had been insulted. I was so provoked
that I took these away from them. Have a look!" He slapped down
the sword and corselet with an air of triumph. His wife glared at him
from her mop of sleep-disordered hair, then blinked in astonishment.
Within a flash, her ill humor had vanished, and with a loud guffaw
she remarked smugly, "You owe this good fortune to me, you know."

We expect a woman to restrain masculine impetuosity by gentleness. How could Ōtsu Jirō's wife have conceived a scheme so mon-
strous?

THE ARACHI MOUNTAINS

From Kaizu shore the party approached the Arachi Mountains, on
the border between Ōmi and Echizen. After an arduous walk from
the capital to Ōtsu on one day and the miseries of the rocking boat on
the next, Yoshitsune's wife was scarcely able to move. Blood from her
delicate feet stained the stones with every step as they moved into the
mountains—a lonely and wild place of withered brambles, towering
cliffs, and tortuous paths strewn with sharp rocks and exposed roots.

Although the lady's wounds were perhaps too insignificant to warrant endangering the party's disguise, one or another of the compassionate warriors occasionally risked carrying her on his back, and in that manner they penetrated deep into the interior. As dusk came on, they struck off through the forest, spread their fur rugs under some huge trees about three hundred fifty yards off the path, and laid down their packs to let her rest.

"These are dreadful mountains!" the lady exclaimed. "What are they called?"

"At first they were known as the Arashii Mountains, but nowadays people call them the Arachi Mountains,"[9] answered Yoshitsune.

"How fascinating! Why was the name changed?"

"The new one came into use because the mountains are so rocky that they draw blood from travelers' feet."

"I've never heard such a cock-and-bull story," snorted Benkei. "If a place is going to be called Arachi simply because it makes people's feet bleed, every rocky hill in Japan would have the same name. I know all about this name."

"If you're an expert, why didn't you speak up in the beginning instead of leaving the answer to me? I don't profess to know all about it," Yoshitsune said.

"I started to, but I couldn't very well continue after you interrupted me. This is how these mountains happen to be called Arachi: At a place named Shimoshirayama in the province of Kaga, there was once a shrine in honor of a dragon goddess. The god of Karasaki in the capital of Shiga fell in love with the goddess and begot a child by her. When her confinement approached, she set out for Kaga, telling him, 'If you have no objection, I wish the baby to be born in my own province.' Just as she reached the highest point in these mountains, she felt a sudden pain in her belly. 'The baby is about to arrive,' said the god of Karasaki. He held her loins and the baby was born. Because of the blood spilled at the time of that birth, the mountains are called Arachi. You should understand now how the name Arashii became Arachi."

"I knew it all along," laughed Yoshitsune.

[9] Arachi means either "blood shed from a wound" or "blood shed during childbirth."

HOW YOSHITSUNE PASSED THE MITSUNOKUCHI BARRIER

Early the next morning they began to descend into Echizen. On the northern edge of the mountains at a place called Mitsunokuchi, where roads branched off to Wakasa and Nomiyama, two local chieftains, Tsuruga Hyōe of Echizen and Inoue Saemon of Kaga, had built a barrier house protected by formidable stakes. Day and night three hundred guards were alert to detain and question all travelers who had white skin and crooked front teeth.

"Those wandering monks won't be able to escape a grilling," predicted wayfarers who observed Yoshitsune.

As the party journeyed on, full of gloomy forebodings, they encountered a man in a pale yellow blouse and knickers, hastening with a letter from the direction of Echizen.

"I am sure his errand has some significance for us," Yoshitsune said. He continued to move on, hiding his face beneath the brim of his bamboo hat, but the man made his way through the entire group and dropped to his knees in front of him.

"I am astonished to see Your Lordship! Where are you going?" he asked.

"What do you mean, 'Your Lordship'?" said Kataoka. "There is no one here who could be your lord."

"Do you mean Kyō-no-kimi or Senji-no-kimi?" said Benkei.[10]

"What makes you talk that way? I say Your Lordship because I see His Lordship. I once served Ueda Saemon, one of the most powerful warriors in Echizen. I fought in the campaigns against the Taira, so of course I recognize His Lordship. Am I mistaken in thinking that I also see Benkei, who kept the roster of men from Echizen, Noto, and Kaga at the battle of Dan-no-ura?"

At this even the glib Benkei lowered his eyes in silence.

"It's an extremely awkward situation," continued the stranger. "Enemies are waiting for His Lordship farther along the road. You had better turn back here and head east from the pass along the Nomiyama road...[11] Then you will cross a pine-covered hill and see Hidehira's mansion just before you. Be sure to go that way."

[10] *Kimi* can mean "lord." Kyō-no-kimi and Senji-no-kimi were the names bestowed by Benkei on two of the warriors. See Appendix C, note *p*.

[11] The man goes on to describe his suggested route in great detail. I have omitted twenty-three lines here (pp. 321–22, *kan* 7).

"This is extraordinary! Hachiman must have sent him. Let us follow his advice," said Yoshitsune.

"You mean to take his route? Go ahead then, if you don't mind asking for trouble. Anyone can tell that the fellow is lying his head off. Whether he urges you to go on or to turn back, he's up to no good," said Benkei.

"Do as you think best," Yoshitsune shrugged.

Approaching the stranger with a question concerning the road, Benkei suddenly seized him by the nape of the neck with his left arm, flipped him over onto his back, and stepped on his chest. "Let's have the truth," he demanded, touching his sword to the pit of the man's stomach.

Trembling violently, the stranger replied: "I was once one of Ueda Saemon's retainers. Then I grew dissatisfied and went into service with Inoue Saemon of Kaga. When I told Inoue that I knew Yoshitsune by sight, he said, 'Look for him and try to draw him into a trap.' Just the same, I'd never fail to do my duty by His Lordship."

"Those were your last words," said Benkei. He stabbed the man twice in the belly, cut off his head, buried it in the snow, and stamped on the spot. Then the party went on as though nothing had happened. The stranger was one of Inoue's servants, Heizaburō by name. His fate was a good illustration of the saying, "A servant with a big mouth is apt to devour himself."

Yoshitsune and his men walked boldly toward the barrier house. When they were about a thousand yards away, they separated into two groups which advanced five hundred yards apart. Benkei, Kataoka, Ise Saburō, Hitachibō, and three others accompanied Yoshitsune, and Kanefusa, Nenoo, Kumai, Kamei, Suruga, and Kisanda escorted his wife. As the first party approached the gate of the stockade, the barrier guards raised a great shout. A hundred of them swiftly surrounded the false monks, clamoring, "We've got Yoshitsune at last!"

"There's the man who inflicts such terrible suffering on innocent people! That's him, all right!" yelled other travelers who had been detained in ropes at the station.

"What have we done to arouse all this excitement? We're only Haguro ascetics," said Yoshitsune, stepping forward.

"Haguro ascetics indeed! You're Yoshitsune and his men," a guard answered.

"Who are the officers in charge here?"

"Tsuruga Hyōe, a chieftain in this province, and Inoue Saemon of Kaga. Hyōe left this morning for Kamakura, and Inoue is at Kanazu."

"I advise you not to make trouble for your absent masters by laying hands on Haguro ascetics. If you annoy us we'll put up sacred ropes,[12] wave *sakaki*[13] branches, and proclaim your barrier house as the holy sanctuary of our image of Kannon, the bodhisattva whose god-manifestation is worshiped at Haguro."

"If you weren't Yoshitsune, you'd say so. Why are you threatening our lords?" asked a guard belligerently.

"This group has a leader, as is proper. You don't have to argue with a subordinate. Get back over there, Yamatobō," interrupted Benkei. Yoshitsune sat down meekly on the veranda.

"I am Sanukibō, a wandering monk from Haguro, on his way home from the year-end retreat at Kumano," Benkei explained. "As for Yoshitsune, I've heard that he was captured in Mino, Owari, or somewhere of the sort. People say he's being taken to the capital—or was it to Kamakura? Anyway, there's no reason why you should accuse Haguro monks like us of being him and his men." The guards, unmoved, continued to menace them with fixed arrows and naked swords and halberds.

Meanwhile the second party had also been surrounded by a mob of excited guards, who were shouting exultantly, "Let's shoot them down!" Yoshitsune's wife was almost unconscious.

"Quiet down for a minute," said a sensible-looking guard. "It will be a serious business if we kill some ascetics who aren't Yoshitsune and his men after all. Why not try asking them for the passage fee? Yoshitsune wouldn't know that Haguro ascetics have never paid ferry or barrier charges, and he'd be in a great hurry to pay and get through. If they're really wandering monks they won't want to pay. That's how we can tell."

He walked over to Benkei. "Ascetics or not, you'll have to pay the

---

[12] *Yae no shime (shimenawa)*. A straw rope used to indicate the presence of a deity or to mark off a sacred area.
[13] See Chapter Five, note 12.

toll. If there were only four or five of you it might be different, but we can't let sixteen or seventeen pass scot free. Pay the charge and go on through. By order of the Lord of Kamakura we're required to pay for our own food by collecting fees from all travelers without exception. Please hand over your money," he said.

"This is unheard of!" Benkei cried. "Since when have Haguro ascetics had to pay barrier fees? Nobody else has ever done it, and we won't either."

"It's not Yoshitsune," said some of the guards. But others objected, "Don't be so sure. A great man has unusual retainers. That's just what Benkei would say."

"In that case," the spokesman said to Benkei, "we'll send someone to the Kantō for instructions. You'll have to stay here in the meantime."

"This must be the work of the vajra messengers," replied Benkei. "While your man is going back and forth between here and Kamakura, we can eat the barrier's rice instead of our usual miserable diet, recite our prayers, and rest awhile in comfort." So saying, he led the party, laden with their panniers, into the building, where they stood about nonchalantly.

Seeing that the guards were still casting suspicious glances in their direction, Benkei struck up a conversation with some of them. "Our page is the son of Sakata Jirō of Dewa. At Haguro we call him Kunnō. We had planned to make the year-end retreat at Kumano, stay in the capital until the snow disappeared from the Hokurikudō, and then head for home, going from one mountain dwelling to another to ask for millet, and eating whatever other monks' fare we happened to find, but the child got so homesick that we decided to start out along the road, even though the snow hadn't melted completely. We've been having a pretty hard time, and we're more than happy to spend a few days here." He and the others took off their straw sandals and washed their feet; some stretched out to rest, others sauntered about, all with such complete lack of concern that at last the guards opened the barrier gate. "You don't seem to be Yoshitsune's party; be off with you," they urged.

Showing no undue eagerness, the warriors drifted through the gate casually by ones and twos. Hitachibō, who was the first to pass, looked back and saw Yoshitsune and Benkei still sitting on the veranda.

"It was very good of you to absolve us of suspicion and excuse us from paying the fee," Benkei was saying. "Our only regret is that we haven't been able to give our page a bite of food for the last two or three days. Won't you let us have a little rice for him before we go? You can think of it both as charity and as payment for prayers on your behalf."

"You ascetics had better learn a few manners. When we asked if you were Yoshitsune and his men, you were high and mighty enough, but now you beg for food," said the guards.

"Still, it would be nice to have them pray for us; let's give them some rice," proposed one who was more kindhearted than the rest. Filling the lid of a chest with white rice, he carried it over to Benkei.

"Take it, Yamatobō," Benkei said as he accepted it. Yoshitsune rose obediently from his position beside him. Then Benkei crouched on the threshold, blew a mighty blast on his conch shell, and began to chant impressively, rubbing the beads of the rosary suspended around his neck.

Ye Gods of the Three Kumano Shrines, the greatest miracle workers
    in Japan,
Ye Eight Great Vajra Messengers of Ōmine,
Ye Hundred Thousand Law Guardians of Katsuragi,
Ye Great Seven-Hall Monasteries of Nara and Eleven-Headed Kannon
    of Hase,
Ye Gods of Inari, Gion, Sumiyoshi, Kamo, Kasuga, and of the Seven
    Shrines of Hiei Sannō:
May Yoshitsune travel over this road,
May the barrier guards of Arachi win eternal fame by capturing him,
And may the munificence of their rewards reveal to them the powers
    of Sanukibō of Haguro!

The guards listened in reverent attention, blissfully unaware of the moving petition Benkei was silently uttering: "Hear me, Great Bodhisattva Hachiman! Manifest thyself as the innumerable escorting and welcoming Protectors of the Law and deliver Yoshitsune safely to Ōshū."

Thus, as if in a dream, Yoshitsune and his men succeeded in passing Arachi Barrier. They reached Tsuruga Harbor on the same day and prayed throughout the night at Kehi Shrine. Then they made inquiries concerning vessels bound for Dewa, but could learn of none that was prepared to risk the fierce gales of the early second month. After another night at the harbor, they set out again by way of Kinome Pass, choosing a road which brought them to the capital of the province of Echizen. There they remained for three days.

YOSHITSUNE'S VISIT TO HEISENJI TEMPLE

"Even though it isn't quite on our way, I should like to see Heisenji Temple. It is one of the most famous places in this province," said Yoshitsune. His warriors did not welcome the excursion, but they set off obediently, journeying monotonously through a dismal world of rain and wind until they reached the temple's Kannon Hall.

When the Heisenji monks became aware of the visitors' presence, they informed the abbot, who at once assembled his officials and arranged for a meeting of the entire religious community.

"The Kantō has forbidden ascetics to travel, has it not? There is something odd about these men. One must not forget that Yoshitsune is supposed to have passed Ōtsu, Sakamoto, and the Arachi Mountains. Let's take a closer look. I'm sure it's he," said one of the monks.

"You are indeed right!" His comrades began to prepare for battle.

At Heisenji Temple, which was a subsidiary of the Enryakuji, monastic discipline was quite as rigid as on top of the mountain.[14] Late that night the two hundred ordinary monks and one hundred officials all advanced in full armor toward the Kannon Hall, where the warriors were occupying the east corridor and Yoshitsune and his wife the west.

Benkei rushed over to the west corridor. "Now we're in real trouble! This isn't like the other places. What are you going to do? I'll try my best to talk our way out, but if it's no use I'll draw my sword and jump down among them, yelling, 'You scum,' or something of the sort. When you hear me, you'd better commit suicide." Off he dashed, leaving an agitated Yoshitsune straining his ears for the fateful words.

"Where did you come from?" the monks demanded of Benkei. "This is not an inn."

---

[14] "Top of the mountain" probably means either Enryakuji Temple, which was frequently called "the mountain," or Hakusan Shrine, situated on the summit of Mount Hakusan. See Appendix B, Heisenji Temple.

"We are ascetics from Haguro in Dewa," Benkei replied. "I am the chief monk of the Daikoku Hall, the Deacon of Sanuki."

"Who is the boy?"

"The famous page Konnō, a son of Sakata Jirō."

"These men cannot be Yoshitsune and his party. If they were, how could they possibly know so much about Haguro? It's true that the Haguro monks have a page called Konnō," said the monks to one another. They went back to report to the abbot.

Seating himself ceremoniously in his reception room, the abbot summoned Benkei.

"I should like a few words with you," he said.

Benkei sat opposite him with his legs crossed in formal fashion.

"I have heard your page praised in most glowing terms. How does he rank as a scholar?" the abbot inquired.

"He has no equal at Haguro. Perhaps I shouldn't say so, but I doubt that any boy at Mount Hiei or Miidera is as handsome, either. Furthermore, he is the best flute player in Japan."

One of the abbot's men, a crafty rascal called Izumi Mimasaka, murmured to his master, "One naturally assumes that a woman will play the lute. It seems rather odd that this fellow makes a point of mentioning the page's skill as a flautist, just when he's suspected of being a woman. Let's see if the boy can actually play."

"Quite right," agreed the abbot. "Splendid!" he said to Benkei. "Do permit me to listen to this celebrated performer! It will be something to talk about for the rest of my life."

"With pleasure," Benkei replied in a faint voice. "I shall call him."

"A frightful thing has happened," Benkei told Yoshitsune and his wife back at the west corridor. "Thanks to my lies, they have asked to hear our page play the flute. What shall we do?"

"You had better make an appearance, even if you don't play," Yoshitsune advised.

"How terribly distressing!" His wife prostrated herself with her cloak over her head.

Meanwhile the monks were setting up a great clamor. "Why is the page taking so long?" they asked impatiently.

"Just a minute, just a minute," Benkei replied over and over.

"After all, Haguro is one of the holiest shrines in Japan," said the monk Izumi. "Heisenji Temple will be disgraced if people say we dragged out this famous page to make him amuse us. We ought to invite him to be our guest; then at the proper time we can request him to play the flute."

"A very good idea," said the others.

The abbot himself had two famous pages, Nen'ichi and Midaō, who were now borne in, charmingly attired, on the shoulders of young monks. The abbot was seated in the central position, with his officials on the east, the ascetics on the west, and the sacred image in the rear. Places had been prepared for the pages at the edge of the altar, facing south.[15] When the two Heisenji pages had settled themselves, Benkei went to the west corridor. "Come now," he said.

With hesitant steps Yoshitsune's wife moved forward, ravishingly beautiful in her pale green underrobe and intricately patterned blouse and knickers of silk gauze, still damp from the previous day's rain. Her hair was modishly coiled, and a bright fan and a red-handled sword hung at her waist. She advanced flute in hand, accompanied by Kanefusa, Kataoka, and Ise Saburō, with Yoshitsune himself hovering near by. As she reached the center of the hall, the monks raised the torches high. She arranged her fan, adjusted her garments, and seated herself.

So far everything had gone so smoothly that Benkei's spirits rose. Nevertheless he continued to sit knee to knee with the abbot, ready to stab him if the deception failed.

"This page is the best flute player in Japan," Benkei repeated. "There is something I must tell you, however. At Haguro he thought of nothing but music morning and night, sadly to the detriment of his studies. When we left in the eighth month last year, his teacher asked him to promise not to play at all during the trip, and he swore a solemn oath in front of the sacred image, so I hope you will excuse him from performing. Our colleague, Yamatobō, is an excellent flautist; in fact, he frequently instructs the page. Won't you accept him as a substitute?"

"That's the way a parent ought to handle his child, or a teacher his pupil," said the abbot, nodding approval. "We wouldn't dream of distressing him by asking him to break such a solemn vow. Let us hear the substitute, by all means."

Beside himself with relief, Benkei put his hands on his hips, raised

[15] The position of honor.

his eyes, and drew a long breath. "Come up at once, Yamatobō, and perform in the boy's place," he ordered.

Yoshitsune advanced from the shadow of the altar to a seat behind his wife.

"If he is going to play, bring on the other instruments," said the monks. Someone fetched a *kusaki-no-kō*[16] cittern and a lute in a brocade bag from the abbot's quarters. "Let us give the cittern to the guest," they said, placing it before Yoshitsune's wife. The page Nen'-ichi was given the lute, Midaō received a set of pipes, and the flute was offered to Yoshitsune. The concert proceeded in the most pleasant fashion imaginable, to the astonishment of the travelers, who could only suppose that divine intervention had saved them from fighting a battle.

"What an exquisite page! What an incomparable flautist! We've always been tremendously proud of our own pages, Nen'ichi and Midaō, but it's impossible to mention them in the same breath with that boy," whispered the young monks to one another.

After a time the abbot retired inside the temple. As the night advanced, he sent messengers from his own quarters to the Kannon Hall with trays of fruit and bottles of wine.

"Let's have a drink!" proposed the tired warriors.

"What a worthless bunch you are!" said Benkei in exasperation. "Men expose their real selves in liquor. At first you'll say, 'Give some to the page,' 'Our leader,' and 'Kyō-no-kimi,' but as soon as you've had enough to drink you'll begin to talk like laymen—'Give some to Her Ladyship,' 'Come on, Kumai and Kataoka, let's toast each other,' 'Hey, Ise Saburō, bring some over here,' 'Come on, Benkei, let's have another!' You'll be exactly like a pheasant in a burning field with its head hidden and its tail sticking out." He sent all the wine back to the abbot. "We are forbidden to drink during our pilgrimage," he told the messenger.

"These are remarkable wandering monks," marveled the abbot. He ordered suitable food prepared and sent to the hall.

Toward dawn, after they had recited the night's repentence rites and sent Ise Saburō to take leave of the abbot, Yoshitsune's party set out across lingering patches of snow, escorted for the first two or three hundred yards by a number of sociable monks. Free at last, they

[16] Meaning uncertain. Okami, p. 333, n. 15.

hastened away from the scene of their ordeal like men escaping from the jaws of a crocodile.

Presently they arrived at Kanazu-no-uwano by way of Sugō Shrine. They were just in time to meet a long procession made up of fifty imposing warriors, with innumerable box-laden porters and horses on leads.

"Who is your lord?" Yoshitsune's men asked.

"Inoue Saemon of Kaga. He's traveling to Arachi Barrier."

"It is useless to try to escape. We have reached the end of the road," said Yoshitsune. He put his hand on his sword, drew his wife close, and tried to pass with his face hidden under his tilted hat. Just as Inoue glanced in his direction, a strong gust of wind lifted the brim of the hat. Their eyes met, and Inoue leaped from his horse to kneel in the road.

"What a surprise! I am so sorry that I happen to be on a journey. It is a great honor to be able to greet a party of ascetics; I only wish that my fief at Inoue weren't so far away, so that I could invite you to visit me there. Please pass on at once," he said. He led his beast aside, remaining on foot until long after the party had passed. Only when Yoshitsune and his men had receded far into the distance did he and his warriors remount.

The astonished Yoshitsune was quite unable to continue without looking back repeatedly. "May his descendents to the seventh generation enjoy divine protection on the field of battle," he and all his men prayed.

That day Inoue stopped at a place called Hosorogi. He called his kinsmen and retainers together. "Who do you think those ascetics were?" he asked. "That was Yoritomo's brother Yoshitsune and his men. What a shame! In the old days the whole province would have known he was passing, and the procession would have been a rare spectacle! It is pitiful to see him now. I won't live forever myself. I couldn't bear to kill him, so I let him go." At these words his men's trust in him deepened. "He is a truly compassionate man," they thought.

Yoshitsune and the warriors lodged for the night at Shinohara. The next morning they viewed Ai Pond, where Saitō Sanemori was killed by Tezuka Tarō Mitsumori, and journeyed by way of Adaka Crossing to the Neagari Pine. Since they thus found themselves in a

neighborhood where sutras were traditionally recited in honor of the
goddess of Shirayama, they determined to go to the goddess's shrine.
They spent a night worshiping Eleven-Headed Kannon at Iwamoto,
and the next day they continued to Shirayama to do honor to the
goddess. All that night they presented sacred dances at Tsurugi
Shrine.

The following day they passed behind the rear entrance to Hayashi
Rokurō Mitsuakira's house and approached Togashi in Kaga. Togashi-no-suke, one of the great chieftains of Kaga Province, was understood to be quietly on the lookout for Yoshitsune, even though no
orders had come to him from Yoritomo.

"It is best that you go on alone from here to Miya-no-koshi,"
Benkei said to Yoshitsune. "I will join you after I look around at
Togashi's place."

"There's nothing to keep us from traveling along this road without
being seen. Why call on him?" asked Yoshitsune.

"No, I think I ought to go. It wouldn't do to have him chase after
us with a band of warriors. I'll go alone." He slung his pannier on his
back and set out.

It so happened that it was the third day of the third month, and
the people at Togashi's house were playing kickball, shooting sparrows with tiny bows, watching cockfights, listening to music, drinking, and otherwise enjoying themselves.[17] Some of them were already
drunk. Benkei entered the premises without incident, passed the
guardhouse veranda, and looked toward the interior where a concert
was in progress.

"An ascetic here," he bawled, disrupting the harmony of the instruments.

"The master is indisposed," someone answered.

Benkei took a step forward. "In that case, let me talk to someone
who can act for him," he persisted, loftily ignoring two or three servants who were bearing down on him with irate shouts.

"That fellow's creating a disturbance. Throw him out," said the
servants, seizing his arms and pushing and pulling vainly. More men
came up. "Don't let him stay here. Give him a drubbing and chase
him off," they said.

[17] The third day of the third month was the occasion of a festival of Chinese origin
(*sangatsu no sekku*) celebrated by entertainments such as these. (It is now observed as a doll
festival for girls.)

Benkei doubled up his fists and began to strike out furiously, knocking off the caps of some of his adversaries, and sending others into empty rooms with their hands clasped to their heads.

"Here's a monk running wild!" everyone began to shout.

Presently Togashi himself appeared at the guard quarters, wearing wide-bottomed trousers and a soft cap and carrying a lance.

"Look at the scene your retainers are creating," said Benkei, promptly climbing up to the veranda.

"Where are you from, ascetic?" asked Togashi.

"I am collecting for the Tōdaiji building fund."[18]

"How do you happen to be alone?"

"There are some others with me, but they went ahead toward Miya-no-koshi while I came here to ask for a contribution. My uncle, the Deacon of Mimasaka, is going to Shinano by way of the Tōsendō Road, and I'm on my way to Echigo over the Hokurikudō. I'm called the Deacon of Sanuki. Now how about your contribution?"

"Please make yourself at home," said Togashi. He gave Benkei a hundred yards of fine Kaga silk, and his wife added a pair of white trousers and an octagonal looking glass as tokens of repentence for past sins. The Togashi kinsmen, the retainers, the ladies-in-waiting, and even the maidservants made contributions of their own, until 150 names had been added to the register.

"I ought to accept your contributions gratefully now, but I'll take them when I go back toward Nara around the middle of next month," said Benkei. He left the things in their care and departed astride a horse lent to him by Togashi, who also provided him with an escort as far as Miya-no-koshi.

After searching in vain for Yoshitsune and the others at Miya-no-koshi, Benkei found them at Ōno-no-minato.

"Where have you been all this time? What happened?" asked Yoshitsune.

"They entertained me in various ways, and then I recited some sutras. They sent me here on a horse," he replied. The warriors stared at him openmouthed.

That night the party lodged at Take-no-hashi, and the next day they crossed Kurikara Pass. At Hasekomi Valley, where so many of

---

[18] Tōdaiji Temple had been burned by Taira soldiers a few years earlier as a reprisal for the temple's support of Prince Mochihito. See the Introduction.

the Heike had perished, they all recited the *Amida Sutra,* intoned the
sacred name of the Buddha, and prayed for the spirits of the dead.
Then they continued their journey, as the afternoon sun sank in the
west and twilight fell. They stayed that night at Hachiman Shrine
in Matsunaga.

HOW BENKEI FLOGGED YOSHITSUNE AT NYOI CROSSING

The next morning Yoshitsune and his men prepared to cross the
river near Nyoi-no-jō.

"There's a little matter I must mention," said the ferryman, Hei
Gon-no-kami. "The warden of Etchū lives near here. It's all right for
me to pass three or four ascetics without any questions, but I'm supposed to report to him before I take over any party of ten or more.
Since there are seventeen or eighteen of you, I shall have to be careful. I'll let you cross after I tell the warden."

"Come now, is there anyone on the Hokurikudō who doesn't recognize Sanuki from Haguro?" asked Benkei in an annoyed tone.

A man who was seated in the middle of the boat looked at him
closely. "Yes, yes, I'm sure I've seen him before. That's the monk
who purified me with sacred strips of paper the year before last, and
the year before that, not only when I went up the mountain, but also
when I came down," he said.

"Your memory is excellent," said Benkei jubilantly.

"Pretty sure of yourself, aren't you?" said Gon-no-kami to the
passenger. "Since you recognize him, I suppose you won't mind taking the responsibility for letting him cross."

"If you think anybody in this boat is Yoshitsune, point him out,"
invited Benkei.

"The fellow in the bow looks suspicious—the one wearing the robe
with the design of a plover flock," replied Gon-no-kami.

"That's a monk we took in tow at Shirayama in Kaga. We can't
afford to be objects of suspicion everywhere just because of him,"
grumbled Benkei.

While Yoshitsune hung his head in silence, Benkei leaped angrily
onto the gunwale of the boat, seized his master's arm, hoisted him
over his shoulder, and jumped to the beach. Then he dumped him
roughly onto the sand and with a fan which he pulled from his waist
began to beat him so mercilessly that the onlookers averted their

eyes. Though Yoshitsune's wife forced herself to appear unconcerned, she was hardly able to refrain from shrieking aloud.

"Nobody is more cruel than a Haguro ascetic," said Gon-no-kami. "If you had simply said, 'That's not Yoshitsune,' it would have been enough. It's painful to watch you beat him so harshly; I feel as though I'd been hitting him myself. What a pitiful sight! Get back in." He pulled the boat over and took them aboard. "All right, hurry up and pay your fare," he said.

"Since when have Haguro ascetics been paying to ride ferries?"

"As a rule we don't ask, but you're much too rough. You can go across after you pay and not before. Hurry up now!" He still had not pushed off.

"You're bound to visit Dewa some time during the next year or two. You'll get your just deserts if you treat us this way," Benkei threatened. "Our page's father, Sakata Jirō, is the lord of Sakata Harbor."

"I don't care what you say. If you won't pay, I won't take you across," repeated the ferryman, still not lifting a hand.

"There's absolutely no precedent for this. I suppose it's divine retribution because I did something wrong," said Benkei. "Let me have that, won't you." He obliged Yoshitsune's wife to take off a handsome underrobe, which he handed to the ferryman.

"I accept this because the regulations compel me to, but I want to give it to that poor monk over there," said the ferryman, transferring it to Yoshitsune.

Benkei grasped Kataoka by the sleeve. "That's a good one, eh? What's his is hers," he whispered.

With the Rokudōji crossing successfully behind them, they walked on toward Nago Woods, while Benkei tried vainly to forget his recent actions. At length he ran up to Yoshitsune, caught hold of his sleeve, and burst out crying. "What kind of business was that—protecting my master by beating him? I shall be punished by everybody—gods, bodhisattvas, and men. Forgive me, Great Bodhisattva Hachiman! Oh, what a wretched world this is!" The other warriors wept loudly at the sight of the indomitable Benkei groveling miserably on the ground.

"It wasn't your fault," said Yoshitsune. "I can't hold back the tears when I think of what will become of you men who have stood by an unlucky master for so long." He pressed his sleeve to his eyes, and the tears of the others fell all the faster.

Wearily they plodded onward in the gathering dusk. "People say that travelers who cross the River of Three Ways[19] are stripped of their garments," remarked Yoshitsune's wife. "That's exactly what happened to me."

They spent the night at Iwase Woods. The next morning, after a brief rest at Kurobe post station, they traveled' to a place called Iwato Cape, where they found shelter in some thatched fishermen's huts.

While they were chatting that evening, Yoshitsune's wife saw the neighboring folk diving for seaweed. She recited:

> Many a province's wave-swept strand
> Have I approached
> As night has followed night,
> Yet only now have I encountered them—
> The maidens diving for seaweed.

This vexed Benkei, who countered:

> Following the wave-swept strand
> Night after night,
> We've reached this spot.
> What a relief![20]

From Iwato Cape they went on to the Hanazono Kannon Hall at Naoe-no-tsu, the capital of Echigo Province. Throughout the night, Yoshitsune remained in prayer inside the building, which for many generations had been associated with the house of Minamoto. It had been founded during the campaign against Abe Sadatō, when Yoshiie gave thirty suits of armor to a rich man named Naoe Jirō, requesting him to have prayers for a court victory recited in Echigo.

[19] In Buddhist tradition, a river in the intermediate existence where souls await rebirth. It is crossed in the course of their wanderings by those who have been neither exceptionally virtuous nor exceptionally wicked on earth. There are three crossings of various degrees of difficulty, to one of which each traveler is assigned by his karma. An old man and an old woman wait on the far shore to strip off the garments of the wayfarers.

[20] The point of the lady's poem is in the play on *ukime*, which can mean either "distress," "floating seaweed," or "diving girls." The last line of Benkei's reply, a parody on the lady's last line, carries the alternative meaning, "For the first time, I have seen some pretty girls."

THE BAGGAGE SEARCH AT NAOE-NO-TSU

The warden of the Echigo capital was absent at Kamakura, but his deputy at the beach, Ura Gon-no-kami, soon heard that a party of wandering monks had appeared. He assembled the local folk, armed them with clubs made of oars, and surrounded the Kannon Hall with an unruly mob of some two hundred fishermen and others. All the warriors had gone off in search of food, leaving Yoshitsune alone.

"Something is happening at the Kannon Hall," Benkei heard someone say. He rushed back in a great state of alarm to find Yoshitsune addressing the mob. Since they could no longer call themselves Haguro ascetics now that Haguro itself was so close, Yoshitsune was saying, "We are on our way from Kumano to Haguro and are hoping to find a boat here. Our leader is out visiting the homes of the pious while I look after things at the hall. What do you want?"

Benkei spoke up. "There are thirty-three images of Kannon in those panniers. We have brought them from the capital to enshrine in the sanctuary on the fourth of next month. Don't crowd in and sully the sacred images with your unclean bodies. If you have anything to say, say it outside. If you defile them, we shall be obliged to purify everything, panniers and all."

Ignoring his bluster, the mob shouted insults. "Any fool can tell that Yoshitsune is talking his way past all sorts of people," said Gon-no-kami. "Our warden is away at the moment. As his deputy, I am required to report to the authorities. I must ask you to relieve my doubts by showing me one of your panniers."

"Something terrible is bound to happen if impure hands search a pannier with a sacred image in it," Benkei warned. "You seem to be a suspicious chap who enjoys bad luck. Go ahead—it's your own lookout if you're punished. Here, inspect it." He tossed out a pannier.

The piece of baggage which Benkei had carelessly selected was Yoshitsune's own. Benkei caught his breath as Gon-no-kami drew forth thirty-three combs.[21]

"What about these?" asked the deputy.

Benkei gave a scornful laugh. "Don't you know anything at all? Did you ever hear of a page who didn't comb his hair?"

---

[21] This perplexingly large number may have had a significance which is no longer understood. Note that Benkei pretends to be carrying thirty-three images of Kannon in the panniers.

This appeared reasonable to Gon-no-kami. He laid the combs aside and extracted a Chinese mirror. "How about this?"

"We have a page with us on this trip; why shouldn't we be carrying toilet articles?"

"That's true enough."

Next Gon-no-kami found an eight-foot sash, a wig five feet long, a crimson skirt, and a woman's robe. "What about these? Does a page need these too?"

"My aunt, who is the chief shamaness at Haguro, has been pestering me to buy her a wig, a skirt, and a pretty sash in the capital, so I decided to make her happy by bringing them with me this time."

"I suppose that's possible. Hand over another pannier; I want to have a look inside."

"Pick out whichever one you please." Benkei threw him a second one.

This time the pannier, which was Kataoka's, contained a helmet, arm shields, leggings, ax-heads, and such things. Gon-no-kami tried to open it but it was tied fast, and, in the darkness, the knots defied his efforts to unravel them.

Benkei joined his palms in a silent prayer to Hachiman. "That one has sacred images in it," he said aloud. "I beg of you—don't risk the wrath of the gods by laying impure hands on its contents. You can tell whether the images are there or not without opening it." Picking up the pannier by the shoulder strap, he whirled it around so that the arm shields, leggings, and axes clanked together noisily.

Gon-no-kami's heart missed a beat. "This is more than I bargained for. They must be images after all," he thought. "Here, have it back," he offered.

"I told you so," said Benkei. "Don't accept it until it's cleansed, any of you." All the members of the party shrank back. "Didn't I warn you? If it isn't cleansed, we shall start to pray. We need all kinds of things for a purification."

"Overlook it and take it back," pleaded Gon-no-kami.

"Unless it is purified, we shall leave the images beside you, go to Haguro to call up the monks, and come back after it." At this threat the mob scattered in every direction, leaving Gon-no-kami to deal with matters as best he could.

"How many things do you need to purify it?" Gon-no-kami asked.

"Since Kannon is a compassionate bodhisattva, always ready to help humanity, the ordinary ritual will be sufficient. If you will bring us a hundred quires of thick white paper for sacred strips, sixteen bushels of white rice, sixteen bushels of unpolished rice, a thousand yards of white cloth, a thousand yards of dark blue cloth, a hundred sets of eagle feathers, a thousand grains of gold, seven horses with identical coats, and a hundred straw mats, we will cleanse it for you, although that is actually the fee for just an ordinary ritual."

"Willing as I am to give you those things, I am a very poor man. I cannot possibly provide all of them." He brought fifteen bushels of rice, thirty yards of white cloth, seven sets of eagle feathers, two hundred grains of gold, and three sacred horses with identical coats. "This is all I have. If it is enough, please recite the prayers," he said apologetically.

"In that case, I'll attempt to placate the deity," said Benkei. Facing the pannier containing the arm shields, leggings, and axes, he muttered under his breath, "*Mutsumutsu kankan ranran sowaka sowaka . . . onkoro onkoro Prajna Heart Sutra. . .*" Then he said, "I've explained matters to the deity, and the pannier has now been purified in the customary manner. We should appreciate your arranging for delivery of the goods to Haguro."

In the small hours of the morning, Kataoka went down to Naoe Harbor to look about. Before long he spied a boat from Sado with its awning rolled up, its master nowhere to be seen, and its oars and rudder moving slackly with the waves. "Splendid!" he said to himself. "We'll take it." He went to the Kannon Hall to tell Benkei.

"Good—let us get started while the morning breeze is still blowing," said Benkei.

The party hurried down to the harbor, launched the vessel, and hoisted a sail to catch the wind from Myōkannon Peak. As they passed Mount Yonayama and came within sight of Mount Kakuta, they said to one another, "Look there, the wind is as fresh as ever. We won't have to row unless it dies down."

Presently, however, they observed white clouds billowing high in the heavens from the mountainous region north of Ao Island. "I don't know anything about the local weather traditions, but those look like storm clouds to me. What shall we do?" asked Kataoka. Even as he spoke a north wind raised sand on the beaches and began whipping up the sea. Around them, fishing craft were bobbing crazily up and down. "The same thing will probably happen to us," Yoshitsune thought gloomily.

Within a short time they had been driven far out to sea.

"We'll simply have to go where the wind takes us," they said.

They lowered the sail and turned the boat toward Sado Island, hoping to land at Kamo Lagoon; but towering waves barred the way, and soon the wind sent them in the direction of Matsukage, where a new gale whistled down fiercely from Shirayama Peak and drove them away from Sado toward Cape Suzu in Noto.

Meanwhile the approach of night increased their alarm. They prepared sacred paper strips, inserted them behind the legs of their panniers, and prayed to the dragon gods. "We have no objection to your worshiping heaven; all we ask is that you abate this wind long enough for us to reach land. Then do as you please." Yoshitsune took a silver-mounted dagger from one of the panniers and cast it into the sea. "I offer this to the eight great dragon kings," he said. His wife threw in a crimson skirt and a Chinese mirror. "For the dragon kings," she repeated, but the wind blew on. Dusk had now settled in, and everyone was in a miserable state.

At last a west wind from Yusurugi Peak in Noto sent the boat off toward the east. "A fair wind!" they rejoiced. They ran before it until midnight, when to their great relief both wind and waves subsided. Toward dawn the lingering breeze deposited them on an unknown shore. They landed and approached a thatched hut.

"What is the name of this place?" they asked.

"Teradomari in Echigo."

"The very place we wanted to go!" they exclaimed.

The party succeeded in reaching Kugami before daybreak. They secured lodgings at Mikura-machi and continued their journey the following morning, traveling past one renowned place after another until they reached the heavily fortified barrier of Nenju. There seemed, at last, no possibility of going further.

"What shall we do?" asked Yoshitsune.

"You've got out of lots of other tight places. This is nothing to worry about. But we shall have to be careful." Benkei made up Yoshitsune to resemble a porter monk, loaded two panniers on his back, and started forward, beating him smartly with a big switch and shouting, "Get along, monk!"

"What has he done to make you treat him so harshly?" the barrier guards asked.

"We are Kumano ascetics," replied Benkei. "This fellow and his ancestors before him have all been servants. He gave me the slip the other day, but I found him again. I'm only too happy to punish him in any way I can think of. Do you blame me?" He came closer, beating Yoshitsune cruelly, and the guards opened the gate to let them through.

So they entered the province of Dewa. They reached a place called Harakai on the same day and the next morning proceeded by way of Mount Kasatori to the Yakushi Hall at Sanse in Tagawa District, where they were delayed for two or three days by the rain-swollen river.

It happened that the lord of Tagawa District, a man by the name of Tagawa Tarō Sanefusa, had fathered a fine large family of boys, only to see them die one by one. He was now threatened with the loss of his last son, a lad of thirteen, who had contracted a fever that baffled the ministrations of the most celebrated Haguro ascetics. When Sanefusa heard of the arrival of Yoshitsune's party, he said to his household, "As a shrine, Haguro is just as important as Kumano, but the Kumano gods are a little more sacred, so their monks ought to be holier too. I think I shall ask those ascetics to come here and pray for us."

"Send a messenger at once," begged his wife, who had been driven to the point of distraction by her son's sufferings.

Sanefusa dispatched his deputy, Ōuchi Saburō, to the Sanse Yakushi Hall.

"It's all very well for him to ask," said Yoshitsune to the others. "What good would it do for impure men like us to recite prayers? There's no use going unless we can help them."

"You may be unclean, but the rest of us have been scrupulously abstinent ever since we left the capital. We aren't miracle workers, of course, but the mere forms of our rites ought to frighten away sinister influences and phantoms. As long as we've been asked, I'm in favor of going," said Benkei. The others gathered around them, laughing and joking.

"We're already in Hidehira's domains," said someone to Yoshitsune. "This Sanefusa must be one of his retainers. There's nothing to
prevent you from telling him who you are."

"What's that?" interrupted Benkei. " 'Even a son doesn't know
his father's heart.' Nobody can say what another man is thinking. If
we get into trouble, it will be a case of 'regret doesn't precede the
deed.' After His Lordship reaches Hiraizumi, Sanefusa will go there
to pay his respects. Let's not spoil the joke by telling him ... Now, who
will recite the prayers? His Lordship can be the protector,[22] and I shall
be the best person, I think, to tell the beads."

Yoshitsune went to Tagawa's house with Benkei, Hitachibō, Kataoka, and Kanefusa. They were ushered to a chapel, where Tagawa
presently joined them, followed by his son and a nurse.

When Yoshitsune was ready to commence, he summoned a boy of
twelve or thirteen to receive the possession. He began to pray, while
Benkei rubbed his beads and the others chanted. One might almost
suppose that an evil spirit was indeed frightened by their rituals. The
young proxy raved incoherently, and after the sacred paper strips
were stilled the invalid appeared to have been entirely liberated from
malignant influences. Yoshitsune and the others, considerably awed
by their own effectiveness, remained overnight at Tagawa's insistence.
The fever, which had recurred daily in the past, had disappeared
without a trace. Tagawa's faith in the gods of Kumano grew stronger
than ever, and his happiness was quite beyond description. For their
part, Yoshitsune and his men trembled before the august power of
the gods, which had manifested itself even through such makeshift
vehicles as themselves.

As a token of his gratitude, Tagawa gave Yoshitsune a bay horse
with a black saddle. He also presented him with two thousand grains
of gold dust, and—saying that it was the local custom—with a
hundred sets of eagle feathers. To each of the other four monks he
gave two underrobes. Then he sent them off to the Sanse Yakushi
Hall with an escort.

When Tagawa's men were about to return home, Yoshitsune returned all the gifts to them. "Although we appreciate your offerings,

---

[22] Meaning uncertain. In this instance, possibly the monk who would recite protective
spells on behalf of the sufferer. Okami, p. 351, n. 23.

we are going to Haguro for a retreat in the usual manner. Please keep them for us until we stop on our return journey," he said.

From Tagawa the party went on past Ōizumi Domain and Dai-bonji. Yoshitsune would have liked to go to Haguro, whose peaks loomed in the distance, but the month of his wife's confinement had arrived, and out of concern for her welfare he deputed Benkei to go alone, while he and the others continued by way of Nitsuke-no-takaura to the Kiyogawa River. Benkei rejoined them beyond Age-namiyama.

They spent that night in prayer at Gosho-no-ōji Shrine. The Kiyogawa River, in which Haguro-bound pilgrims perform their ablutions, flows northward from the top of Mount Gassan and is as famous for its purity as the Iwata River in Kumano. After Yoshitsune and his men had cleansed their bodies, they offered sacred dances before each of the five deities, hoping to rid themselves even of sins committed in previous existences. In addition, each performed individually for the divine pleasure. In this way the night passed.

The following day they set out on the river with a boatman called Iya Gon-no-kami. The snow waters from the upper reaches were so strong that he was barely able to force his stout craft upstream. For the first time they understood the emotions of the Chigusa Lesser Captain, who after his exile to Shō-no-sarashima had recited:

> The Tanakai's upper reaches, visited by moonlight alone;
> The Mogami's rapids, tormenting the sheaf-laden boats—
> Strains of a lute somewhere
> Heard through rifts in the fog.

As the boat pressed on, they saw a waterfall cascading down the side of a mountain. "What is its name?" inquired Yoshitsune's wife. "White Threads," the boatman answered. She composed two verses.[23]

> Mogami River—
> Stop the rock-tossed waves in your rapids,
> Lest we pass without approaching
> White Thread Falls.

---

[23] In both, the word *yoru* ("approach," "night") is intended to suggest a homonym meaning twist, as in twisted threads.

The moon shines on the rock-tossed waves
Of the Mogami River—
How pleasant the evening
At White Thread Falls.

Beyond the shrines of the armor and helmet gods,[24] they reached a difficult passage known as Takayari Rapids. While the boat attempted to make its way through, they heard monkeys chattering on the fringe of the mountains ahead. Yoshitsune's wife recited:

My moving fan
Is not a bow,
Yet someone's arrow, it seems,
Has struck a monkey.

They continued upstream past Mirutakara, the Height-Measuring Cedar, and Yamuke Shrine. At Aizu Port Yoshitsune said to his wife, "We can get to Hiraizumi in another two days. By way of Minato it would be a three-day journey past Miyagino Plain, Tsutsuji Hill, and Chiga Beach. If we cross the Kamewari Mountains and go from Nomura-no-sato to the Aneha Pine, we shall be traveling almost in a straight line. Which places do you want to see?"

"I should enjoy looking at all those famous spots, but let us take the shorter road, even if we only save one day. I should rather go by way of the Kamewari Mountains," she pleaded. So the party headed for the mountains.

THE BIRTH IN THE KAMEWARI MOUNTAINS

To the great concern of Kanefusa, Yoshitsune's wife began to feel the pangs of approaching childbirth as they were crossing the Kamewari Mountains. She seemed closer to unconsciousness with each step further into the wilderness, and Kanefusa was obliged to help her along as best he could. Since there was no possibility of obtaining shelter without descending to the villages far below, they left the trail at the pass, spread a fur rug under an ancient tree some two hundred fifty yards away, and placed the lady there to await the birth.

Soon her agony became so great that she could no longer think of modesty. "It distresses me to have everyone standing around; please

[24] On the middle course of the Mogami.

go away," she implored, taking a deep breath. All the warriors except Kanefusa and Yoshitsune moved off.

"Even Kanefusa's presence is embarrassing, but the pain is so dreadful that I can do nothing about it," she said, fainting again.

To Yoshitsune she appeared on the point of death. No longer the hard warrior, he began to lament grievously, tears streaming down his face. "Even though I knew that this might happen, it is indescribably bitter to feel that I have taken you away from the capital and brought you here to die by the side of the road. During all this wearisome journey, which has compelled you to suffer hardships in strange hamlets and submit to unspeakable privations for my sake, I haven't known an instant's ease. That you should die now is more than I can bear. I won't be separated from you.... I'll go too."

"He never acted like that on the field of battle," said the warriors, pressing their sleeves to their eyes.

Presently the lady gasped, "Water."

Benkei took a jug and struck off blindly down hill through the dark, rainy night, trusting to his feet to guide him to a valley. He strained his ears for the sound of running water, but a protracted spell of fine weather had dried up the small rivulets in the ravines.

"No matter how bad His Lordship's luck may be, it's too much not even to be able to find a common thing like water," Benkei thought with a sinking heart. He continued the descent in tears.

At last he heard the murmur of a brook. He filled the jug and started to climb back up, but the hillside was shrouded in dense fog. After hesitating for a time lest a mountain settlement be concealed near by, he blew his conch shell, saying to himself, "I must not take too long." An answering blast came from above.

When Benkei finally brought the water to the lady's side, Yoshitsune spoke to him in a tear-choked voice. "Your errand was futile; she has stopped breathing. Who is going to drink it after all your trouble?" He wept aloud, while the grief-stricken Kanefusa threw himself down beside his ward. Struggling to restrain his own tears, Benkei touched the lady's hair. "I begged His Lordship to leave you in the capital, but he couldn't bring himself to do it. What a cruel fate you have met! Even though it may be your karma from a previous life, before you die please drink a little of the water I worked so hard to get for you." He gave her a sip of water, and as though revived she caught at Yoshitsune's hand. Then she fainted again.

Seeing that Yoshitsune was also on the point of losing consciousness, Benkei said, "Buck up! Circumstances alter cases. Get out of the way, Kanefusa!" He pulled the lady to a sitting position, braced her hips, and prayed, "Hail, Great Bodhisattva Hachiman! Let this lady be delivered successfully. Have you deserted our lord?" Hitachibō also joined his palms and prayed, while Kanefusa sobbed loudly. Yoshitsune lay as though dazed beside his wife.

"Ah, how it hurts!" the lady exclaimed, holding fast to Yoshitsune as she regained her senses. Benkei at once pressed her hips from behind, and the child was born with no further trouble.

Benkei wrapped the wailing infant in his ascetic's cloak, clumsily cut the umbilical cord, and bathed the baby in water from the jug. "Let us name him at once. We're in the Kamewari Mountains. Since *kame* means tortoise, and since the tortoise is long-lived, let's pair it with the *tsuru* crane, which lives for a thousand years, and call him Kametsuru," he proposed.

"Poor little beggar! Will he ever grow up?" said Yoshitsune. "If my own future were brighter, he would be all right. It would better to abandon him in these mountains while he's still too young to mind."

His wife forgot her recent suffering. "What a shocking thing to say!" she shrieked. "Now that he's been fortunate enough to enter the world of men, how can you talk about killing him before he's even caught a glimpse of the sun and moon! Kanefusa, take the baby if His Lordship is displeased. He shan't die, even if you and I have to go back to the capital with him."

"Up to now we have only had His Lordship to rely on. If anything had happened to him, we would have been masterless. I am very happy indeed to have this young lord as well. Could anyone kill such a beautiful baby?" asked Benkei. To the child he said, "May your karma resemble that of your uncle, the Lord of Kamakura. Even though I am not an influential man, may you have abilities to equal mine, and may you live to be a thousand—no, ten thousand years old." He added, "It's still a long way from here to Hiraizumi. Don't cry and fuss at me when we meet people on the road." He put the child in his pannier, still wrapped in the cloak. Oddly enough, it did not utter a single cry during the remaining three days of the journey.

After allowing Yoshitsune's wife to rest for a day or two at a place called Sehi-no-uchi, they procured a horse for her, and that day reached Kurihara Temple. From there they sent Kamei Rokurō and Ise Saburō as messengers to Hiraizumi.

The moment Hidehira learned that messengers from Yoshitsune had arrived, he made haste to grant them an audience. "I knew in a general way that His Lordship was traveling along the Hokurikudō in this direction, but since I hadn't received any definite news I didn't go to meet him. Though he may have enemies in Echigo and Etchū, Dewa is my territory. Why didn't you make yourselves known so that the local people could escort you here? I'll send men to welcome him at once." He dispatched his eldest son, Yasuhira, with one hundred fifty horsemen and a litter for the lady.

"This is what I have come to," said Yoshitsune when the escort arrived.[25]

So at last Yoshitsune reached Iwai District. Instead of quartering him unceremoniously in his own house, Hidehira presented him with the Moon Viewing Hall, a building reserved for special use, and entertained him daily in the most hospitable manner imaginable. To Yoshitsune's wife he gave twelve beautiful and cultivated ladies in waiting, in addition to maids and other servants; to Yoshitsune himself, in accordance with an old promise, a hundred fine horses, fifty suits of armor, fifty quivers of war arrows, fifty bows, and five of the best districts in his provinces,[i] containing over nine thousand acres of rice fields apiece. Each of the warriors received a share of three excellent domains, Isawa, Ezashi, and Hamashi. Hidehira also considerately offered Yoshitsune ten stout mounts, as well as shoes and leather breeches, to be used for pleasure excursions to whatever places suited his fancy. Tadahira, his son, was instructed to select three hundred sixty warriors from the Two Provinces to provide daily entertainment. "There's nothing to worry about now—it's up to us to see that His Lordship enjoys himself," the old lord said.

Soon Hidehira built a new residence for Yoshitsune at Koromogawa, west of his own home. In this Koromogawa stronghold, protected by the Koromo River in front, Hidehira's house on the east,

---

[25] He is comparing his present misery with his former high position as Yoritomo's deputy.

and the Tōku Cavern mountains on the west, Yoshitsune was as proud as an eagle. Yesterday's sham ascetic had suddenly become today's man of consequence, with a glorious future stretching before him. From time to time, he recalled events of the Hokurikudō journey, or spoke of his wife's behavior, while his retainers joined in his laughter. Thus the year ended and the third year of Bunji [1187] began.

Chapter Eight

THE MEMORIAL SERVICES FOR TSUGINOBU AND TADANOBU

To the great satisfaction of his men, Yoshitsune had frequently sent messages of cheer to Satō Shōji's widow since moving to Taka-dachi. On a certain occasion, he told Benkei that he wished to cele-brate memorial services for Tsuginobu and Tadanobu. "Get the names of all the men who died fighting in Shikoku and Kyushu, heroes and cowards alike, so that we can hold services for them too," he said.

Benkei could not restrain his tears. "This is very good of you. Not even the emperors of Engi and Tenryaku[1] were so considerate of their subordinates. Please don't put it off," he said.

Yoshitsune instructed a number of high monks to make the neces-sary arrangements; Benkei informed the Novice Hidehira, who was deeply touched by Yoshitsune's thoughtfulness as well as by the memory of the Satō brothers' sad fates. The lady nun, the mother of the two brothers, attended the services with her grandchildren and the widows and watched as Yoshitsune reverently made an offering of a copy of the *Lotus Sutra* written in his own hand. "Has such a thing ever been done before?" everyone marveled.

"I am most appreciative of your kindness in arranging these ser-vices for my sons," said the nun. "Nothing could be a greater post-humous honor. I cannot help weeping when I think of how grateful they would be if they were alive; but I have reconciled myself to

---

[1] The eras known as Engi (901–23) and Tenryaku (947–57) were regarded as high points in the history of the imperial house, not so much for their intrinsic brilliance as because they were followed by a permanent eclipse of the authority of the throne.

their loss. I should like to present their young sons to you in their stead, even though they are still using children's names."

"By rights Hidehira ought to give them names, but I should like to do it myself in memory of their fathers. I shall speak to Hidehira about it," said Yoshitsune.

When a messenger was dispatched, Hidehira agreed readily. "I have often wished to suggest the same thing. This is a great honor," he said.

"In that case, have Hidehira make the arrangements," ordered Yoshitsune.

Hidehira dressed the two boys' hair, placed caps on their heads, and presented them to Yoshitsune, who, after gazing upon them, named Tsuginobu's son Satō Saburō Yoshinobu, and Tadanobu's, Satō Shirō Yoshitada.

"Now then, Izumi Saburō," said the delighted nun, "give His Lordship the things I have ready." Saburō presented Yoshitsune with a sword which had been handed down for generations in the Satō family. Yoshitsune's wife received a robe of Chinese damask and a roll of fine silk, and each of the warriors was suitably remembered.

"How I wish Tsuginobu and Tadanobu could have come back to see my grandsons capped in their master's presence," said the nun in tears. The two young wives began to wail pitifully at the thought of their dead husbands, even as they had done at the time of parting. Yoshitsune, too, shed tears of sympathy, and Hidehira and the other spectators pressed their sleeves to their faces.

Presently Yoshitsune handed a wine cup to Yoshinobu, who performed the courtesies of the occasion with perfect poise.

"You are very much like Tsuginobu," Yoshitsune told him. "At the battle of Yashima your father gave his life for mine in front of all the Minamoto and Taira warriors. People said that they had never seen anything like it, and everyone called him the greatest hero in three nations. 'Of course there have been plenty of other loyal retainers in Japan, China, and India, but none of them ever did such a thing,' they said. From today on, think of me as your father." He beckoned the boy close to stroke his hair, weeping in spite of himself. Kamei, Kataoka, Washinoo, Mashio Jūrō, Kanefusa, Benkei, and all the rest sobbed audibly.

After Yoshitsune had regained his composure, he handed a cup to

Yoshitada. "When the monks were pursuing us at Yoshino, your father offered to stay behind on a mountain to protect me. I begged him over and over to come along, but he said, 'A warrior's word is like an imperial decree. It cannot be retracted any more than a man can recover his own sweat.' I had to leave him there ready to take his own life. He held off five or six hundred enemies with a handful of men, killed the ferocious Kakuhan of Yokawa, and fought his way out of an attack by Hōjō Yoshitoki in the capital. An ordinary fellow would have come back here after that, but Tadanobu's only thought was to find me. Since he didn't know where I was, he went to my old house at Rokujō Horikawa and killed himself there. What he did will never be forgotten! People say that Yoritomo himself praised his bravery and held services in his memory. I feel quite certain that you will be a man to equal Tadanobu," he told the boy, weeping again.

Next Yoshitsune directed Ise Saburō to present each of the two youths with a suit of armor, one of them dyed in a tiny cherry blossom pattern and the other in contrasting shades of white and dark blue.

"How very kindly His Lordship has spoken to you!" exclaimed the weeping nun. "A warrior is expected to be more courageous than other men, but though I say it of my own sons, if they had not been exceptionally valiant His Lordship would not have talked like that. When you have grown to manhood, you too must be of service to your lord so that your names will not be forgotten. If you behave dishonorably, your comrades will sneer, 'They aren't the men their fathers were.' Never disgrace the house of Satō by allowing other people to speak lightly of you. Listen to these words of mine, uttered in the presence of your lord, and remember them always." All who heard nodded in approval: "It is not surprising that her sons were heroes! That was an admirable speech!"

HIDEHIRA'S DEATH

Hidehira became very ill on the tenth day of the twelfth month of the fourth year of Bunji [1188]. Day by day his condition worsened. When it was apparent that not even the arts of a Jīva or Pien Ch'üeh could save him, he tearfully addressed his assembled sons, daughters, and retainers.

"I have always been impatient with mortally ill men who clung to life, but now that it is my own turn I understand their feelings. Yoshitsune came here with his wife and child because he relied on me, and I have not been able to give him even ten years of peace. If I die today or tomorrow, I greatly fear that he may be compelled to wander over fields and mountains like a man bereft of his torch on a dark night. This is the only worry standing in the way of my journey to the next world; but alas, I can do nothing about it now. I should like to visit His Lordship to say good-bye, but I am in too much pain; and since I won't presume to ask him to come here, I want you to repeat my words to him. Do you mean to respect my dying wishes? If you do, listen carefully to what I have to say."

"Is it conceivable that we should disobey?" they all protested.

"After my death," he continued haltingly, "Yoritomo will tell you that the court has ordered Yoshitsune's death. He will probably offer you Hitachi Province as a bribe. Pay no attention. Dewa and Ōshū alone have been more than enough for me, and since my sons are no better than I am, they have no need for anything more. Whenever a messenger comes from Kamakura, cut off his head. Yoritomo will not send any more after you have executed two or three. If by any chance he does, you will have to recognize that the matter is serious and prepare accordingly. Have Nishikido guard the Nenju and Shirakawa barriers, and don't be remiss in your duty to His Lordship. Don't seek to exceed your station. As long as you obey my last words, you needn't fear the future, however degenerate the times may be. Even though we shall be in different worlds..." Those were Hidehira's last words before he died at dawn on the twenty-first day of the twelfth month, leaving his wife, children, and household to lament his passing.

When Yoshitsune was informed, he rode frantically to Hidehira's house. "I would never have come all the way here if I had not depended on Hidehira. My father died when I was two years old. My mother and I were estranged after she sided with the Heike, my brothers were so widely scattered that I never saw them as a child, and now Yoritomo and I are enemies. No parting between parent and child could be harder to bear than this," he said, gazing sorrowfully at the lifeless body. He grieved inconsolably, as though his old courage had quite forsaken him.

On the day of the funeral, even the child born in the Kamewari

Mountains joined the mourners on the moor, touchingly arrayed like his father in garments of white. Yoshitsune himself would gladly have lain beside Hidehira in the grave. He said his last farewells on the barren moor and turned away, a sad and lonely figure.

HOW HIDEHIRA'S SONS CONSPIRED AGAINST YOSHITSUNE

After Hidehira's death, everything went on as before until the end of the year, with each of the sons serving Yoshitsune in turn. Around the second month of the new year, however, one of Yasuhira's retainers, having, it appears, heard some sort of rumor, called upon his master secretly in the dead of night.

"Yoshitsune and Tadahira are going to attack us. It is poor strategy to let an enemy seize the initiative; we had better get ready as fast as we can," he urged.

Yasuhira nervously agreed. He abandoned preparations for a service in Hidehira's memory which he had been planning to hold on the twenty-first day of the second month, and, in a night attack, vilely struck down his brother Tadahira. Immediately his older brother Kunihira, his kinsman Suehira, and his younger brother Takahira struck off on their own, each fearful for his own safety. This is the sort of thing people mean by the old saying, "When kinsmen fall out, divine protection fails."

"They are certain to attack me next," Yoshitsune decided. He ordered Benkei to compose a circular letter, which he entrusted to a servant, one Suruga Jirō. "Tell the warrior families" in Kyushu to report to me here immediately," he ordered. Suruga traveled day and night to the capital, but news of his mission somehow reached the Rokuhara authorities just as he was about to set out for Tsukushi. They arrested him and sent him to the Kantō with a guard of twenty-four soldiers.

Yoritomo took one look at the letter and flew into a rage. "Yoshitsune's behavior is intolerable! Why does he persist in attempting to usurp his own brother's position! Fortunately, with Hidehira dead and his family declining, it shouldn't be hard to conquer Ōshū," he said.

"I don't agree," objected Kajiwara. "People say that once when the Emperor ordered Hidehira to come to court, he answered, 'Long ago Masakado commanded 80,000 horsemen, but I have 108,000 at my disposal. If the court will pay half the expenses of my journey, I will go.' Since His Majesty was in no position to accept, the subject was dropped, and Hidehira never visited the capital. If Hidehira had fortified the Nenju and Shirakawa barriers under Yoshitsune's command, we couldn't possibly have beaten him, even by attacking with all the warriors in Japan for a century or two—we would only have caused suffering everywhere. It is useless to strike at Yasuhira unless we can persuade him to kill Yoshitsune first."

"He is right," thought Yoritomo. Reflecting that a command from him would be unlikely to move Yasuhira, he prevailed upon the ex-Emperor to decree Yoshitsune's execution and promise Hitachi to Yasuhira and his descendents in perpetuity. Then he sent word of the edict, reinforced by an order of his own, to the Fujiwara chieftain, who had already begun to disregard his father's deathbed injunctions. Yasuhira declared himself ready to act when he had the imperial command in his hands.

"Very well, he shall have it," said Yoritomo. He sent off Adachi Shirō Kiyotada to Ōshū. "Yoshitsune has probably grown a beard in the last two or three years. Make sure of his identity," he said.

One day, as Yoshitsune joined a hunt which Yasuhira had suddenly arranged, he was positively identified by Kiyotada, who had mingled unobtrusively with the other participants. This formality having been satisfied, the conspirators resolved to attack him at ten o'clock in the morning on the twenty-ninth day of the fourth month of the fifth year of Bunji [1189]. Yoshitsune himself had, meanwhile, not the faintest intimation of their plans.

It chanced that a man known as Motonari, the Provisional Assistant Vice-Minister of Popular Affairs, was living in Hiraizumi at the time. He had been exiled to the east because of his brother Nobuyori, the martial Commander of the Gate Guards who perished in the Heiji War. Hidehira had treated him with great consideration, and had taken his daughter to wife and begot numerous children by her. As the grandfather of Yasuhira, Hidehira's second son and legal heir, and of Izumi Saburō Tadahira, the lord's third son, Motonari was a highly respected personage, to whom people referred as the Honorable Assistant Vice-Minister.

(Hidehira's son Nishikido Tarō Yorihira, who had been born before either Yasuhira or Tadahira, was a man of heroic stature, superior intelligence, and varied accomplishments—a fine archer and all-around warrior, who would have made an excellent heir for his father. However, Hidehira's legitimate wife had borne a son before Yorihira was fifteen, and Hidehira had named the baby his heir, thinking that it would be inappropriate to allow an illegitimate child to succeed him. It must be said that this was a disappointing act on Hidehira's part.)

Motonari, who was extremely fond of Yoshitsune, was much disturbed by the rumors which reached his ears. Though he wished to restrain his grandson, he was in the humiliating position of not having ceded him any lands whatever[2]—and indeed of being a man under imperial censure, dependent upon Yasuhira's generosity for his own livelihood. In any case, it was futile to seek to thwart an imperial decree. He could only send an anxious letter to Yoshitsune, weeping as the messenger departed. "The ex-Emperor has ordered Yoritomo to kill you," he wrote. "Did you think that the hunt the other day was merely an agreeable excursion? Nothing is as precious as life—you must do everything you can to escape from here. When we recall that your father was put to death for conspiring with my brother, it is evident that a strong karma tie has banished me to the east and brought you to the very same place. It would be infinitely distressing to have to mourn your death. I would go with you if I were not so old and feeble, but I can offer masses for you here just as well as anywhere."

Yoshitsune returned his answer with a Chinese box. "It was a great pleasure to receive your message. I should like to escape as you suggest, but no one can evade an imperial decree, even by flying through the air or burrowing under the ground. It is best therefore for me to prepare to kill myself here without releasing a single rusty-headed arrow. Though I cannot repay your kindness in this life, I look forward to seeing you in Amida's paradise. This letter is written in the strictest confidence; please do not allow it to leave your person." He ignored all subsequent communications from Motonari with the explanation that he was fully occupied with preparations for his suicide.

After learning of Yasuhira's intentions, Yoshitsune summoned his

[2] A man was expected to make over his property to his heirs when he reached a certain age. Motonari, as an exile, had had no land to relinquish.

wife, who only seven days earlier had given birth to a child. "Yoritomo has sent Yasuhira an imperial edict demanding my execution. It has never been the custom to kill women who have committed offenses, so I want you to go elsewhere while I prepare to take my life," he told her.

His anguished wife pressed her sleeve to her face. "When I left everything behind, even my beloved nurse, to follow you here, was it only to say good-bye? Though I know that a woman ought to be ashamed to confess to an unrequited passion, I beg you not to turn me over to someone else," she said. Since she refused to leave his side, he made ready an apartment in the eastern corner of his chapel and installed her there with many tears.

HOW SUZUKI SABURŌ SHIGEIE CAME TO TAKADACHI

[Meanwhile one of Yoshitsune's old retainers, Suzuki Shigeie of Kumano, had journeyed alone to Hiraizumi to join him.][3]

"I am sorry indeed to involve you in this affair, now that you have been good enough to relinquish Yoritomo's benefactions for the sake of a ruined master," Yoshitsune told him.

"It is true that I received a piece of land in Kai Province from Yoritomo, but my thoughts dwelled on Your Lordship so constantly that I could not keep away any longer. I have sent my family to my wife's people in Kumano, and there are no worries left to bind me to this world. My only regret is that I didn't come sooner. I arrived two days ago, but I was loath to let you see me until I had recovered from a trifling leg injury inflicted by my horse. Now I am once again in fine shape. This will be the battle I have always been ready for. Had I not arrived in time, I would simply have died far away instead of close by—there would have been no reason for me to live after you died. If we had died apart, we would have traveled separately along the road to hell; this way, I shall be able to go with you." He spoke so cheerfully that Yoshitsune bowed before him, choked with tears.

"I came here wearing nothing but a corselet," Shigeie continued. "The quality of one's armor is of no concern to a dead man, but it would be embarrassing, I must admit, for people to gossip about it later."

"We have armor of all descriptions waiting to be used," Yoshitsune

---

[3] Part of the original text appears to have been lost here.

said. He presented him with a horse and a stout metal-reinforced suit of red armor. The corselet was handed on to Shigeie's brother.

THE BATTLE OF KOROMOGAWA

Not long thereafter Takadachi was assaulted by a combined force of 20,000 warriors under the command of Nagasaki Tayū-no-suke.

"Who is leading today's attack?" Yoshitsune inquired of his men.

"One of Hidehira's retainers, Nagasaki Tarō Tayū."

"If it were Yasuhira or Nishikido, I would fight a last battle, but I shall kill myself rather than trade arrows with an eastern retainer."

While Kanefusa and Kisanda released arrows with lightning speed from the roof, using shutters as shields, eight men met the attack in front—Benkei, Kataoka, the Suzuki brothers, Washinoo, Mashio, Ise Saburō, and Bizen Heishirō. Hitachibō and the other ten retainers, who had gone to pray at a neighboring mountain temple that morning, had never returned. Such conduct is better passed over in silence.

Benkei was dressed that day in a suit of black armor with several butterflies of yellow metal on the skirt. He leaped onto a plank, grasping his great halberd in the middle. "Keep time, men," he shouted. "I'll give the eastern rabble something to look at. When I was a youth at Mount Hiei, they called me a warrior and an artist in a thousand. Here's a dance for you, eastern dogs!" He danced to the Suzuki brothers' accompaniment, chanting:

> How delightful are the waters of the cataract—
> How pleasant the sound of the cataract's waters,
> Never ceasing in the driest of weather!
> Sing on, sing on!
> Ah, the armor and helmets of the eastern rabble—
> Heads and all, they are cut off,
> Tossed into the Koromo River
> And carried away!

"Yoshitsune's men have admirable nerve," commented the attackers. "There are 30,000 of us and only ten of them inside their stronghold. What kind of fight do they intend to make, dancing like that?"

"You can talk all you want to—there are 30,000 of us," they shouted to Benkei. "Leave off your dancing!"

"Numbers don't mean a thing. Quality is what counts. Ten or not, we are not an ordinary ten. If you want to know why I'm laughing, it's because you look so foolish in your battle array—like a mob at the fifth-month horse races at Hiyoshi or Kasuga! Now then, Suzuki, show these eastern dogs what you can do!" said Benkei. Heads lowered, he and the Suzuki brothers charged with terrifying whoops, holding their swords poised at helmet level. The enemy retreated like leaves blown by an autumn wind.

"What has come of all your big talk? Quality, not numbers—that's what counts! Come back, you cowards!" Benkei and the others roared after them.

Suzuki Saburō sought to engage Terui Tarō. "What are you called?" he shouted.

"Terui Tarō Takaharu, a retainer of Lord Yasuhira."

"Then your master is one of Yoritomo's retainers. I have certainly heard it said that your master's ancestor, Kiyohira, became a Minamoto retainer at the time of the Later Three Years' War. Kiyohira was the father of Takehira, who was the father of Hidehira, who was the father of Yasuhira, so your family have only been vassals of our lord's house for five generations.[4] I can't even count the number of my ancestors who have served the Genji, and I certainly have no business bothering with you, but a man ought to be ready to fight any enemy he meets on the field. All right! They tell me that you at least are one of Yasuhira's men who knows the meaning of shame. Will you show your back to another honorable man? Stop, coward!"

Shamed by these words, Terui returned to the fight, only to suffer a wound on his right shoulder and retreat again. Then Suzuki cut down five warriors, two on his left and three on his right, and wounded seven or eight more. In the fighting he himself was severely injured.

"Don't sell your life cheaply, Kamei Rokurō. I am finished." Those were Suzuki's last words before he ripped open his belly and fell dead.

"On the day I left Suzuki in Kii, I vowed to give my life for His

---

[4] A variant text, *Yoshitsune monogatari*, inserts Iehira between Kiyohira and Takehira, but this is an historical inaccuracy. Hidehira was Kiyohira's grandson.

Lordship. Nothing could make me happier than to die in the same place as my brother. Be sure to wait for me at Shide Mountain,"[5] said Kamei. He jerked off his armor skirts.[6] "You'll be hearing about me; see me as well! I am Kamei Rokurō, twenty-three years old and younger brother to Suzuki Saburō. Everybody knows what kind of warrior I am, but perhaps you eastern yokels have not yet heard of me. Gaze on me now for the first time!" Before the words had left his mouth, he began cleaving a path through the center of the enemy host, slashing left and right so savagely that no one ventured to face him. When he had killed three men, wounded six, and sustained innumerable wounds himself, he loosened his armor-belt, cut open his belly, and died on the battlefield along with his brother.

After engaging first one enemy and then another, Benkei had by now suffered a jagged wound in the glottis which bled as though it would never stop. The loss of so much blood would have made an ordinary man's senses reel, but Benkei seemed all the livelier for it and was fighting as though the enemy were hardly worth his attention, while the blood poured down his chest and flowed steadily onto the ground from his moving armor.

"That monk is crazy," said one enemy warrior. "He's got his *horo*[7] on backward."

"Stay away from him; there's no telling what he'll do," warned another.

They all pulled back on their reins and kept their distance from the wily veteran, who was managing somehow still to spring erect whenever he appeared on the verge of collapse. Not a soul was willing to confront him as he dashed up and down the river bank.

Mashio Jūrō, meanwhile, had perished, and Bizen Heishirō had taken his own life after killing many enemies and suffering grievous wounds. Kataoka and Washinoo fought as a team until Washinoo died with five enemies to his credit. Since Kataoka was then in an exposed position, Benkei and Ise Saburō hastened to his assistance. Ise Saburō fought gloriously, killing six warriors and wounding three more, before his own injuries forced him to turn his sword on himself. "I will wait for you at Shide Mountain," he promised the others.

[5] According to Buddhist tradition, a steep mountain in hell.

[6] For greater freedom of action.

[7] A baggy piece of cloth which was sometimes suspended from the shoulders of a warrior's armor in order to deflect arrows coming from the rear.

Then Benkei forced a path through the enemy and made his way to Yoshitsune. "Here I am," he said.

Yoshitsune had been reciting the eighth book of the *Lotus Sutra*. "What have you to report?" he asked.

"The battle is over. Washinoo, Mashio, the Suzuki brothers, and Ise Saburō have all fallen after magnificent fights. Kataoka and I are the only ones left. I desired to see you once more in this life. If you die before me, wait for me at Shide Mountain. If I am the first to go, I shall wait at the River of Three Ways."

"It is very hard to say good-bye like this. Long ago, we swore to die together, but if I go out with you I will not find a decent opponent. If I keep you here now that all the others have been killed, boors will humiliate me by intruding on my suicide. It cannot be helped. If I go first, I will wait at Shide Mountain. If you are first, promise to wait for me at the River of Three Ways. I have but a few lines more of this sutra to recite. Protect me with your life until I finish."

"I will do so." Benkei raised the blind and looked fixedly on his master's face, while tears constricted his throat. At the sound of enemy voices he took his leave and started off, but in a moment he returned to recite a verse.

> Though one of us may die before the other,
> Wait for me, my lord,
> Where the road to hell branches off.

Since Benkei had alluded to the future in such a desperate hour, Yoshitsune responded:

> Join me in the next world
> And the next,
> Until we mount to paradise
> On a purple cloud.

At that Benkei wept aloud.

With their backs to each other Benkei and Kataoka charged, splitting the two-acre courtyard into two sectors while the besiegers retreated as one man. Kataoka attacked a group of seven warriors. When his shoulders and arms were limp with exhaustion and his body was covered with wounds, he ripped open his belly and died, as if in the knowledge that he could do no more. Benkei thereupon broke off a twelve-inch length from his halberd and threw it aside.

"This is more like it! Those worthless helpers got in my way!" he shouted, taking a bold stance. He advanced with his sword flashing, ripping open the bellies and knees of horses and dispensing with their unseated riders by slashing off their heads with the tip of his halberd or striking them down with the flat of his sword. Singlehanded he checked the entire enemy host, not a man of whom dared meet him face to face. One could not even guess at the number of arrows lodged in his armor. He bent them and let them hang, for all the world like a straw raincoat wrongside up, with their black, white, and colored feathers fluttering in the breeze even as *obana* reeds in an autumn gale on Musashi Moor.

With Benkei charging this way and that like a man possessed, the attackers were reduced to showering curses on his head. "How can it be that with enemies and friends dying on all sides, Benkei is the only one to survive, no matter how reckless he is? Not even his old exploits have prepared us for this. Since we can't defeat him, may our guardian gods strike him dead!" they begged.

The victorious Benkei, hearing this, planted his halberd upside down on the ground, rocking with laughter. He stood there like one of the two Guardian Kings.[8]

"See how that monk keeps looking over here! He's getting ready to attack. There's something uncanny about his laugh. Don't get near him unless you want to be killed," the besiegers warned one another.

After an interval during which none of the enemy ventured to approach, someone spoke up. "I have heard it said that heroes sometimes die on their feet. Let someone go up and take a look." None of his comrades volunteered, but just then a mounted warrior came galloping past and the swish of wind caught Benkei, who had indeed been dead for some time. As he fell, he seemed to lunge forward, gripping his halberd. "Look out, here he comes again!" the warriors cried, retreating hastily. Only after he had remained motionless on the ground for some minutes was there an unseemly rush to his side.

In time, people realized that Benkei had stood like a statue to protect his lord from intrusion while he was committing suicide.

---

[8] *Niō*. Two fierce deities whose statues are frequently placed at temple gates.

YOSHITSUNE'S SUICIDE

As Kanefusa and Kisanda were descending hurriedly from the roof, Kisanda was killed by an arrow in the neck. Kanefusa, who had been protecting his rear with a shield, took hold of a crossbeam and leaped into the narrow inner corridor of the chapel. There he encountered Shasō, a servant whom Hidehira had once praised warmly to Yoshitsune.

"That fellow will be useful in an emergency. Take him and put him to work," Hidehira had said. Yoshitsune, who ordinarily refused to grant warriors' privileges to men of Shasō's status, had permitted him to ride a horse. Now he had remained faithful after many warriors had taken to their heels.

"Tell His Lordship I shall stay here to hold them off with my arrows. I am but a servant, but I shall go with him to Shide Mountain as Lord Hidehira commanded," Shasō said to Kanefusa. As he spoke, he continued to lay about him so furiously that no enemy dared meet him face to face. It was touching that this mere servant should have stayed with Yoshitsune to the end, just as Hidehira had predicted.

"The moment has come for me to kill myself," said Yoshitsune to Kanefusa. "How shall I do it?"

"People are still praising Satō Tadanobu's suicide in the capital," Kanefusa replied.

"There is no reason why I should not choose the same method. A wide wound would be best."

Shortly after Yoshitsune's arrival at Kurama as a page, the abbot had given him a six-inch dagger. It was a weapon forged by Sanjō Kokaji and presented to the temple in fulfillment of a vow; the abbot himself had later removed it from the sanctuary, christened it Ima-no-tsurugi, and stored it carefully away. Yoshitsune had kept it on his person always, secreting it under his armor throughout the western campaigns. With that very dagger he stabbed himself below the left nipple, plunging the blade so deep that it almost emerged through his back. Then he stretched the incision in three directions, pulled out his intestines, and wiped the dagger on the sleeve of his cloak. He draped the cloak over his body and leaned heavily on an arm rest; then he summoned his wife.

"I want you to go to Hidehira's widow or to his father-in-law. They are both city people who will treat you kindly and arrange for your return to the capital. Even in the life to come, I shall be worried by the thought that you are grieving with no one to protect you. Remember that everything comes from our deeds in previous existences, and do not mourn unreasonably."

"Always since our departure from the capital, I have been ready to die without warning," she said, clinging to him. "I was certain that I would be killed if anything happened on our journey here, so I am not in the least frightened now. Make haste and kill me."

"I wanted to urge you to die while I still lived, but the words refused to come. You must ask Kanefusa now. Come close, Kanefusa."

Kanefusa fell at Yoshitsune's feet, horrified at the thought of plunging a dagger into the lady's body.

"Had my father not been such a deplorable judge of character, he would never have selected such a coward to be my guardian," the lady said. "You ought to kill me without waiting to be ordered. Is it a kindness to humiliate me by forcing me to remain alive? Here, give me the dagger."

"It is not surprising that I should be a coward in this one matter. Three days after your birth, when your father committed you to my care, I went to the lying-in chamber and held you in my arms for the first time. From that day to this, you have never left my thoughts for a moment, even when we were parted. I had hoped to make you a junior imperial consort, and perhaps in time an empress, but all that was out of the question after your mother and father died. Never for an instant did I dream that my prayers to the gods and buddhas would be in vain! Never did I think I should see you in such a plight as this!" He pressed his armor sleeve to his face, weeping bitterly.

"Cease at once! Grief is useless now. Enemies are approaching," she insisted.

Though Kanefusa's eyes clouded and his senses reeled, he agreed that it must be so. Drawing the dagger from his waist, he seized the lady's shoulder and swiftly made an incision from her right side to her left. She died instantly, gasping the name of Amida Buddha.

Kanefusa drew a cloak over her body, laid her beside Yoshitsune, and rushed to the place where a nurse was holding Yoshitsune's five-year-old son. "His Lordship and Her Ladyship are crossing Shide Mountain on their way to the remote boundary of hell. They instructed me to send their son after them at once." The child put his arms around the neck of his executioner, saying, "Let us hurry to that mountain, whatever it is called. Take me there now, Kanefusa."

Kanefusa, all but fainting, and weeping uncontrollably, said, "He must have committed a crime in his last life. What a tragedy that he should meet such a fate after being born the son of Minamoto Yoshitsune! I can still hear His Lordship saying, 'Abandon him' in the Kamewari Mountains." His tears flowed bitterly again, but the enemy were drawing very near. "It must be done now," he thought. He stabbed twice and the child died with but a single cry. Kanefusa laid his body under Yoshitsune's cloak. Then he killed Yoshitsune's seven-day-old daughter, laid her under her mother's cloak, and staggered to his feet, intoning over and over, "Hail, Amida Buddha! Hail, Amida Buddha!" Yoshitsune was still breathing. He opened his eyes to ask, "My wife?" "She lies dead by your side." Yoshitsune's hand groped for her. "Who is this, the boy?" He reached over the child's body and touched his wife. Kanefusa's grief became unendurable. "Quickly, quickly, set fire to the house." With these last words Yoshitsune died.

THE DEATH OF KANEFUSA

"Nothing remains for me to worry about," said Kanefusa in anguish. He darted about setting the fire, for which arrangements had long ago been made, and with the aid of a west wind the house was soon enveloped in leaping flames.

After wrenching shutters from their fastenings and piling them onto the bodies to hide them, Kanefusa hesitated briefly in the suffocating smoke. No doubt he was deciding to finish the last battle for his lord's protection. At any rate, he threw off his armor, tied the cord of his corselet securely, and burst out through a door. The enemy general, Nagasaki Tarō, and his brother Jirō were calmly sitting their horses in the middle courtyard, feeling themselves quite safe now that their adversaries had committed suicide.

"I know nothing about the customs of China and India, but in Japan we don't sit a horse in front of an important man's private apartments," Kanefusa said to them. "Do you care to know who I am? I am Jūrō Gon-no-kami Kanefusa, a retainer of Kurō Yoshitsune, the younger brother of the Lord of Kamakura, who was a descendent in the fourth generation of Hachiman Tarō, who was a descendent in the tenth generation of Emperor Seiwa. Once in the service of the Koga Minister of State, and now a retainer of the house of Minamoto, I am a warrior better than Fan K'uai himself! Shall I show you what I can do, you shameless curs?" With a single blow he cut through Nagasaki Tarō's right armor skirt, his kneecap, his stirrup ring, and five of his horse's ribs. Rider and beast crashed to the ground instantly.

As Kanefusa pounced on Tarō to take his head, Jirō charged to save his brother's life. Kanefusa dodged aside, pulled Jirō from his horse, and ran into the flames, holding him against his left side. "I had intended to cross Shide Mountain alone, but I don't mind letting you go with me," he said. When one stops to consider, it was a frightful thing to do—the act of a very demon. Kanefusa, to be sure, had been determined from the outset to die in the fire, but poor Nagasaki Jirō was indeed to be pitied! Instead of receiving rewards and lands from a grateful court, he was snatched up willynilly and roasted alive.

HOW HIDEHIRA'S SONS WERE HUNTED DOWN

It was in this manner that Yasuhira obtained Yoshitsune's head to be sent to Kamakura.[9]

"Those men are despicable," said Yoritomo. "They killed Yoshitsune after he had gone to them for protection. Worse than that, they had the effrontery to use the ex-Emperor's command as an excuse to lay hands on my brother." He cut off and exposed the heads of Yasuhira's entire delegation—the two senior retainers who were its leaders, and all the others as well, down to the lowliest servants.

Soon afterward it was agreed at a council of war to send a punitive force against Yasuhira at once. So many warriors[v] clamored for permission to march in the vanguard that Yoritomo declared himself unable to choose among them. He went to pray at the Hachiman Lower Shrine and returned with word that the god had designated Hatakeyama. It was thus that Hatakeyama received the position of honor in the combined army of more than 70,000 warriors which presently set out toward Ōshū.

Whereas in ancient times twelve years had been required to subdue

---

[9] We are to understand that Yasuhira's men recovered Yoshitsune's body and beheaded it.

Ōshū, on this occasion it fell within ninety days. Hatakeyama took the heads of three hundred chieftains, including Nishikido, Hizume, and Yasuhira, and the heads of all their men as well, down to the very servants. It is impossible to estimate the total number who perished. If only they had obeyed Hidehira's dying injunction—if only Nishikido and Hizume had guarded the two barriers and Yasuhira had fought under Yoshitsune's direction—they would never have been defeated with such tragic ease! By wickedly betraying their lord in defiance of their father's last wish, they forfeited their lives, destroyed their family, and allowed their hereditary lands to become the treasured possessions of other men. Nothing is so important in a warrior as loyalty and filial piety. One can but pity them.

Appendixes

Appendix A

Yoshitsune in Hiding

(Summarized from Kuroita Katsumi,
Yoshitsune-den [Sōgensha, 1939], pp. 240–76.)

When Yoshitsune parted from Yukiie after the shipwreck, there were two potential sources of aid available to him: (1) his old friend, Go-Shirakawa, and (2) more or less sympathetic Ki'nai temples and shrines, such as Kurama, Mount Hiei, Kōfukuji, Tōnomine, and Yoshino, which were not yet firmly enough under *bakufu* control to permit Yoritomo's warriors to enter their precincts at will. From Tennōji Temple, he went first to Yoshino, where he remained for several days in an effort to enlist the monks' support. When this failed, he separated from Shizuka, Satō Tadanobu, and the others (twenty-second day, eleventh month), agreeing to meet them again in the capital, and made his way over snowy mountain paths to the quarters of a monk called Jūjibō at Tōnomine in Yamato. After remaining there for a time, he retreated to the more remote Totsu-gawa area in Kumano, escorted by a band of warrior monks. Soon he set off again, this time toward the capital, hoping that the assistance denied him at Yoshino and Tōnomine might be forthcoming from Go-Shirakawa, Mount Hiei, and Kōfukuji Temple. He seems to have entered the city less than three weeks after Yukiie's death, which occurred in the fifth month of 1186.

Around the middle of 1186, the *bakufu* was informed that Yoshi-tsune was conspiring with monks at Enryakuji Temple. A communication from Kamakura requested the court to intensify its search, threatening to invade Mount Hiei with eastern warriors if necessary. The court's answer, which contained assurances of unremitting efforts, requested that Kamakura refrain from antagonizing the

Enryakuji until proof of the temple's guilt was obtained (sixth day, fifth month). There is reason to believe that either Go-Shirakawa himself or men close to him were hiding Yoshitsune at the time.

After Yoshitsune's first flight, Yoritomo had seized some of the ex-Emperor's lands, ousted some of his favorites from office, and otherwise stiffened his attitude to such an extent that, it is said, the outraged Go-Shirakawa had shut himself up in his chapel, refusing to shave his head, cut his nails, or eat his meals. The regent, Motomichi, and others who had lost their posts appear to have protected Yoshitsune because they regarded him as the sole instrument by means of which they might oppose Yoritomo successfully. Yoshitsune probably found shelter either with Motomichi or within the ex-Emperor's palace.

On the twenty-ninth day of the fifth month, a Kurama monk reported to one of his superiors that Yoshitsune had appeared at Kurama Temple. The superior informed Ichijō Yoshiyasu, Yoritomo's deputy in Kyoto, who told Go-Shirakawa on the second day of the sixth month. Professing to fear that warriors could not be trusted to respect the sanctity of the temple, Go-Shirakawa promised to order his own men to arrest the fugitive. After a day or two of waiting, Yoshiyasu returned to the ex-Emperor's palace. His visit produced an announcement to the temple that soldiers were to comb the premises, to which the abbot replied with a denial of Yoshitsune's presence. The abbot suggested that they search elsewhere, and also said that there was a monk at the temple friendly to Yoshitsune, who ought to be questioned. Needless to say, Yoshitsune was not found.

In a dispatch to Kamakura on the twenty-sixth of the sixth month, Yoshiyasu reported a rumor that Yoshitsune was at Ninnaji Temple; he had sent men to investigate, and it had proved false. He said that Yoshitsune seemed to be on Mount Hiei at the time. Since it was impossible for warriors to invade Enryakuji Temple, which was the strongest of all the religious military establishments, the Kantō was obliged to be content with urging Go-Shirakawa to exert pressure upon the abbot.

During the sixth and seventh months of 1186, two of Yoshitsune's chief lieutenants, Izu Saemon-no-jō Aritsuna and Ise Saburō Yoshimori, were killed.

Around the intercalary seventh month, one of Yoshitsune's servants, who had fallen into Yoshiyasu's hands, confessed that his master had been at Mount Hiei as late as the twentieth of the sixth month, and named monks who were acting as his accomplices. Yoshiyasu promptly informed both the ex-Emperor and the monastery. The monks replied that Yoshitsune had already fled. On the eleventh day of the intercalary seventh month, upon receiving further reports of Yoshitsune's presence on the mountain, Yoshiyasu renewed his representations to Go-Shirakawa, with the result that a council of nobles was convened, attended by the regent, Kanezane, and others. When questioned by the council, high monks from the temple insisted that Yoshitsune was nowhere to be found. The courtiers communicated this answer to Yoshiyasu, in turn asking for information concerning a rumor that warriors were about to attack Mount Hiei. Yoshiyasu replied that only firm action by the imperial police could prevent an armed search.

Because of military pressure and the anxiety of the court, the Enryakuji finally handed over three warrior monks, who were fruitlessly questioned by the authorities.

On the twentieth of the ninth month, the *bakufu* captured another of Yoshitsune's retainers, Hori Yatarō Kagemitsu, who confessed under severe examination that his lord was hiding at Kōfukuji Temple in the quarters of Kanjubō Tokugyō. A force sent to Nara threw a cordon of hundreds of men around Kanjubō's residence, but a search failed to disclose either Yoshitsune or his host.

Meanwhile, Yoritomo's men seem to have discovered an anti-*bakufu* plot in Kyoto, in which Go-Shirakawa was a leader. From the scanty information preserved in *Gyokuyō*, it appears that the principal figure in the background was the ex-Emperor's redoubtable favorite, Lady Tango, who made even Kanezane quail. The former regent, Motomichi, probably also was involved. Other names are mentioned, including Kanezane's own steward, Fujiwara Norisue. When Norisue was interrogated by Kantō representatives, he denied everything, and the matter does not appear to have been pressed, possibly to avoid embarrassment to Kanezane. Following this incident the efforts of the *bakufu* increased, while the court, with no immediate prospect of using Yoshitsune for its own ends, grew less and less willing to protect him.

Around this time, Yoshitsune's chief sympathizer was the abbot of the Ninnaji, a son of Go-Shirakawa, whose diary, *Saki*, seems to imply that Yoshitsune stayed at the temple briefly.

Late in 1186, Yoritomo presented Go-Shirakawa with an ultimatum. Admitting that Yoshitsune's many supporters at Kyoto, Nara, the Enryakuji, the Kōfukuji, Yoshino, Tōnomine, and elsewhere had made it impossible to apprehend him by measures theretofore employed, he told the ex-Emperor that he must either produce Yoshitsune or be prepared to see an army of twenty or thirty thousand warriors search for him, mountain by mountain and temple by temple. The threat resulted in a conference at the ex-Emperor's palace on the eighteenth of the eleventh month, at which various methods of capturing Yoshitsune were discussed in dead earnest. It was decided to commission prayers, ransack the city, and send arrest warrants to the Ki'nai and Hokurikudō. At the same time, the court changed Yoshitsune's name to Yoshiaki, as a token of its hope that his whereabouts would soon become known.[1]

Around the end of the fourth month of 1187, it was rumored in the capital that Yoshitsune had killed himself at a remote mountain temple in Mimasaka Province. The report, an apparent answer to the court's prayers, produced great rejoicing until it was discovered to be false. It is not impossible that it was deliberately circulated as a blind to facilitate the hazardous journey to Ōshū, which took place at approximately the same time.

Yoshitsune could no longer count on Go-Shirakawa's help, nor on that of the Kōfukuji, since Kanjubō, his sole trustworthy friend in Nara, had been captured and sent to Kamakura soon after his flight. Even at Mount Hiei, the only safe hiding place remaining, *bakufu* pressure was intense. His old protector, Hidehira, was his last hope. The long journey to Ōshū, through hostile territory in which every province and temple held a warrant for his arrest, was a desperate undertaking which could not have succeeded without the help of sympathizers along the way.

Azuma kagami, in its entry for the tenth day of the second month of 1187, reported that Yoshitsune had traveled to Ōshū with his family by way of Ise and Mino, disguised as a wandering monk. If he had

---

[1] Somewhat earlier, his name had been changed to Yoshiyuki to avoid confusion with Kanezane's son, Yoshitsune. The character used for "-yuki," which means "go," was now considered inauspicious; "-aki" means "come to light."

actually chosen the Ise-Mino route, he would have been obliged to follow the Tōsendō through territories held by leading *bakufu* retainers. It appears that this was merely gossip, particularly in view of a considerably later entry in the same source, which says: "Yoshitsune's whereabouts being completely unknown, prayers were ordered at Tsurugaoka..." (fourth month, fourth day).

On the other hand, the mention of the *yamabushi* disguise, which is supported by *Gikeiki* and *Gempei seisuiki*, is quite credible. In later times, the safest way to penetrate enemy lines was in monk's garb, and genuine ascetics were frequently used as spies.

Hōryaku kanki, a late but generally reliable work, agrees with *Gikeiki* concerning the route. There is evidence to suggest that Yoshitsune was escorted to Ōshū by a Hiei monk named Shunshō (the prototype of Benkei?). In any case, it would have been natural for the journey to begin at Mount Hiei and continue north into Echizen via Lake Biwa. Powerful religious establishments in the north, such as Heisenji and Mount Hakusan, were closely associated with Mount Hiei, and there were also large numbers of *yamabushi* on the Hokurikudō, going back and forth from Mount Haguro and Mount Gassan in Dewa.

The date of Yoshitsune's departure for Ōshū is unknown. *Azuma kagami*'s entry of the second month was premature, and *Gikeiki*'s account is based on nothing more than the author's imagination. *Hōryaku kanki*'s choice, the end of the third month, has no discernible justification. One can say only that he set out at some time during the second, third, or fourth month, after waiting for the northern snows to melt.

APPENDIX B

Persons and Places Mentioned in the Text

This appendix contains notes on identifiable persons (including Buddhist and Shinto divinities) and places mentioned in the text. Omission of a name indicates that nothing is known of the individual or locality from sources other than *Gikeiki*. As a general rule, entries for persons consist only of surnames and formal personal names. Thus, Minamoto Yoshiie, not Hachiman Tarō; Hatakeyama Shigetada, not Hatakeyama Jirō Shigetada. Final elements of place names, such as *yama* (mountain), *hara* (plain), *tera/ji* (temple), *no* (moor), and *kawa* (river), have been translated if the first part of the name occurs elsewhere by itself as a geographical entity. Thus, Ashigara Mountains, not Ashigarayama Mountains; Hayakawa River, not Haya River. Hyphenated words will be found after nonhyphenated. Thus, Miura Yoshitsura precedes Miura-no-suke. Reference to Okami mean either that the note is based entirely on data supplied in the *Nihon koten bungaku taikei* edition of *Gikeiki* (ed. Okami Masao, Iwanami Shoten, 1959), or that supplementary information is available there.

Abe Gon-no-kami, *see* Abe Yoritoki

Abe Ietō. Seventh son of Yoritoki. He surrendered to Minamoto Yoriyoshi at the end of the Former Nine Years' War.

Abe Moritō. Probably a mistake for Noritō, Yoritoki's eighth son, who surrendered at the end of the Former Nine Years' War.

Abe Munetō. Known as Torinomi Saburō. Third son of Yoritoki. He was banished to Iyo after being captured at the end of the Former Nine Years' War.

Abe Sadatō (1019–1062). Known as Kuriyagawa Jirō. Second son of Yoritoki. Killed in action during the Former Nine Years' War.

Abe Shigetō. Sixth son of Yoritoki.

Abe Yoritoki (d. 1057). First called Yoriyoshi; known as Gon-no-kami. Head of a powerful family of Ezo descent which controlled six districts in Mutsu. He was killed while fighting Minamoto Yoriyoshi in the Former Nine Years' War.

Abukuma. The Abukuma River, mentioned in many old poems. It flows northward to Sendai Bay between the Abukuma and Ōu Mountains.

Abura-no-kōji. A minor north-south street between Horikawa and Nishi-no-tōin in the capital.

Adachi. **1.** A district in Mutsu (Fukushima Prefecture). **2.** A district in Musashi, corresponding to Adachi Ward, Tokyo and part of Kitaadachi District, Saitama.

Adachi Barrier. A barrier in Date District, Mutsu (Fukushima Prefecture). Also called Date Barrier.

Adachi Kiyotada. Called Shirō. Possibly a yeoman like Adachi Kiyotsune. Okami, p. 370, n. 7.

Adachi Kiyotsune. Called Shinzaburō. According to the war tales, a yeoman *(zōshiki)* from Ōmi.

Adachi Morinaga (d. 1200). Known as Tō Kurō. One of Yoritomo's chief retainers.

Adachi Shinzaburō, *see* Adachi Kiyotsune

Adachi Shirō Kiyotada, *see* Adachi Kiyotada

Adaka Crossing. Said to have been located on the left bank of the Kakehashi River at Adaka-machi in Komatsu City, Nomi District, Ishikawa Prefecture (Kaga). Okami, p. 336, n. 6.

Agatsuma. A Genji family in Agatsuma District, Kōzuke (Gumma Prefecture).

Aika. A mistake for Ahiru, an old district name in Kazusa (Chiba Prefecture), where there was presumably an Ahiru family. Okami, p. 131, n. 20.

Aizu. A mistake for Aikawa, in southwest Shinjō City, Yamagata Prefecture (Uzen).

Akagashira Shirō. Akagashira is said to have been the name of a rebel lieutenant of Akuroō, subdued with his master in Ōshū by Sakanoue Tamuramaro. *Gikeiki*'s author mistakenly connects him with Toshihito.

Akashi Shore. The area facing Akashi Strait in Akashi District, Hyōgo Prefecture (Harima Province).

Akugenda, *see* Minamoto Yoshihira

Akuji Takamaro. The chronicles represent Tamuramaro as conquering two rebel chieftains, Akuroō (or Aguru) and Takamaro, who seem gradually to have coalesced into one man. (The *ro* of Akuroō can also be read *ji*.)

Akushichibyō Kagekiyo, *see* Taira Kagekiyo

Akuzenji, *see* Zenjō

Amanō. Southeast of the location of the present Great Buddha in Kamakura.

Amatsukoyane. Divine ancestor of the Fujiwara family.

Amida. The buddha most revered in Japan, particularly by adherents of the Pure Land faith. Ruler of the Western Paradise (Pure Land), into which those who believe in him and recite his name are reborn.

Aneha. In Kannari Township, Kurihara District, Miyagi Prefecture (Ōshū). The famous Pine of Aneha is frequently mentioned in classical literature.

Annai-no-taifu. Probably a mistake for Anzai-no-taifu. An Awa family named Anzai appears in *Azuma kagami* and other records.

Ano, Monk of, *see* Zenjō

Ao Island. Probably Awa Island, in the Japan Sea off Iwafune District, Niigata Prefecture (Echigo).

Aohaka. An old post station on the Tōsendō. Now a part of Akasaka Township, Fuwa District, Gifu Prefecture (Mino).

Arachi Mountains. Mountains between Ōmi and Echizen, crossed by travelers going from Kyoto to Tsuruga and the Hokurikudō.

Arachi Pass. A pass through the Arachi Mountains between Ōmi and Echizen, connecting the present Makino Township (Takashima District, Shiga Prefecture) with Tsuruga City.

Arakai. Possibly an old place name in the vicinity of Arakawa Township, Kitakambara District, Niigata Prefecture (Echigo). Okami, p. 349, n. 23.

Ariwara Narihira (825–880).

Known as the Zaigo [Fifth Ariwara Son] Middle Captain. A poet of the early Heian period, remembered both for his distinguished verse and for his romantic adventures. He is said to be the anonymous hero of *Ise monogatari*, a tenth-century collection of anecdotes built around his poetry, in which many places in eastern Japan figure.

Asaka Marsh. Said to have been located in the vicinity of Hiwada, Asaka District, Fukushima Prefecture (Mutsu). It was famous for its iris.

Asaka Mountain. A round hill in the present Hiwada, Yamanoi Village, Asaka District, Fukushima Prefecture (Mutsu).

Ashigara. **1.** A post station at the present Hakone Township, Ashigara District, Kanagawa Prefecture (Sagami). **2.** In Chapter Two, apparently a corruption in the text. There is no Ashigara in or near Kōzuke. *Yoshitsune monogatari* has, "He is from such-and-such a place in Kōzuke." Okami, p. 78, n. 6.

Ashigara Mountains. A range of low mountains on the border between Sagami and Suruga.

Ashikura. A temple at the foot of the Tateyama Mountains in Tateyama Township, Nakaniikawa District, Toyama Prefecture (Etchū); old starting point for pilgrims to the mountains, which were the center of a vigorous mountain-god cult. There are said to have been seven shrines and temples in the area at the foot of the mountains, of which Ashikura, the most important, and Iwakura still survive.

Ashiya. The present Ashiya City, Muko District, Hyōgo Prefecture (Settsu).

Aśoka, King (fl. *ca.* 3d c. B.C.). The most important early Indian royal patron of Buddhism. He was responsible for the erection of thousands of stone pagodas, one of which was said to have been brought to Ishidō in the present Gamō Township, Gamō District, Shiga Prefecture. *Gikeiki*'s author seems to have had the legend in mind in Chapter Seven, although Ishidō is not visible from Lake Biwa. Okami, p. 315, n. 12.

Atago Mountain. In Katono District, Yamashiro, southwest of Kyoto. It seems to have been regarded as the abode of a dragon god. Okami, p. 284, n. 5.

Atari. A mistake for Adachi.

Atari Pine. Unidentified. It appears as Ataka Pine in other *Gikeiki* texts.

Atsukashi. A strategic height, located in the present Ōkido Village, Date District, Fukushima Prefecture (Mutsu).

Atsuta. Atsuta Shrine, in the present Nagoya City, Aichi Prefecture. Said to have been founded by the semilegendary Prince Yamatotakeru around the beginning of the Christian era. The Sacred Sword, one of the Three Imperial Regalia, is enshrined there.

Awa. **1.** A Tōkaidō province, corresponding to part of Chiba Prefecture. **2.** A Shikoku province, corresponding to Tokushima Prefecture.

Awaji. A Nankaidō province, corresponding to part of Hyōgo Prefecture. Awaji Island.

Awaji, Strait of. In Chapter Four, Akashi Strait, between Honshū and Awaji Island, is meant.

Awataguchi. The Tōkaidō exit from Kyoto, leading to Ōtsu. The term applied to the area east of the Sanjō Shirakawa bridge, extending to the mountains.

Awazu. A harbor located in the present Ōtsu City, Shiga Prefecture (Ōmi).

Azukashie. Probably to be identified with Atsukashi.

Bamba. A post station in Sakata District, Ōmi, northeast of Surihari Pass (Surihari Mountain) and southwest of Samegai.

Bandō. Synonymous with Kantō. "Bandō and Banzai" in Chapter Three should probably read "Andō and Anzai." Andō is east of Tateyama City in Chiba, and there is evidence to suggest that Anzai was once current as the name of an area to the west.

Banzai, *see* Bandō

Benkei. Semimythical retainer of Yoshitsune. *See* the Introduction.

Bishamon. Skt. Vaiśravana. Also

called Tamon. One of the Four Heavenly Kings (*Shitennō*) who guard the world. Often worshiped as a god of wealth. He was the principal deity at Kurama.

Bizen. **1.** A San'yōdō province, corresponding to part of Okayama Prefecture. **2.** *See* Bizen Heishirō

Bizen, Governor of, *see* Minamoto Yukiie

Bizen Heishirō. One of Yoshitsune's retainers. Possibly to be identified with Bizen Shirō, a warrior mentioned in *Gempei seisuiki*. Okami, p. 165, n. 7.

Bodai, *see* Enlightenment, Peak of

Bungo, A province in Kyushu, corresponding to part of Ōita Prefecture.

Chang Ch'ien (d. 114 B.C.). Called Po-wang. Famous Chinese traveler of the Han period.

Chang Liang (d. 168 B.C.). One of the architects of the Han dynasty. According to legend, he was given the military treatise *San-lüeh* by a mysterious old man, the Ancient of Huang-shih, while in hiding after an unsuccessful attempt on the life of Ch'in Shih Huang-ti. He later became one of Han Kao Tsu's chief assistants.

Chang Po-wang, *see* Chang Ch'ien

Chiba Hirotsune. A Kazusa warrior, called Kazusa-no-gonnosuke in *Azuma kagami*. Also called Suke Hachirō. Okami, p. 131, n. 22.

Chiba Tsunetane (1118–1201). Called Chiba-no-suke. A *bakufu*

mainstay from 1180 on. His home was at Chiba domain (*shō*) in Shimōsa.

Chiba-no-suke, *see* Chiba Tsunetane

Chichibu Jūrō Shigekuni, *see* Chichibu Shigekuni

Chichibu Shigekuni. Jūrō; also called Taketsuna. A Minamoto retainer; ancestor of the Hatakeyama.

Chichibu-no-shōji, *see* Hatakeyama Shigeyoshi

Chiga Beach. Chiga-no-shiogama. Now a part of Shiogama City, Miyagi District, Miyagi Prefecture (Ōshū). Shiogama Shrine (Rokusho Shrine), the principal shrine of Ōshū, is situated there.

Chikubu Island. An island with a circumference of about two kilometers, located in the northern part of Lake Biwa. Site of a Shinto shrine and a Buddhist temple.

Chikuzen. A province corresponding to part of Fukuoka Prefecture in Kyushu.

Chinzei. An old name for Kyushu.

Chinzei Hachirō, *see* Minamoto Tametomo

Chishō. Mistake for Chikō. *See* Shōkū, Deacon.

Chōhoku. Apparently a family in Nagara District (the present Chōsei District), Chiba Prefecture (Kazusa). Okami, p. 131, n. 20.

Chōnan. Presumably a family who lived in the vicinity of Chōnan Township, Isumi District, Chiba Prefecture (Kazusa).

Chūgoku. A general term for the San'yōdō and San'indō provinces in western Honshu (Harima, Bizen, Mimasaka, Bitchū, Bingo, Aki, Suō, Nagato [San'yōdō], Tamba, Tango, Tajima, Inaba, Hōki, Izumo, Iwami, and Oki [San'indō].

Chūindani. In the Yoshino Mountains, not far from Zaō Gongen.

Daibonji. Also Daihōji. Old name of Tsuruoka City in Nishitagawa District, Yamagata Prefecture (Uzen). Probably at one time a Buddhist temple attached to Haguro Shrine. Okami, p. 352, n. 4.

Daigo. In Fushimi Ward, Kyoto.

Daimotsu. Also called Daimotsu-no-hama and Daimotsu-no-ura. A harbor at Ōkawajiri, near the mouth of the Kanzaki River, a tributary of the Yodo, in Kawanobe District, Settsu. (Now a part of Amagasaki City, Hyōgo Prefecture.) During the Heian period, it was one of the principal ports of embarkation for western Japan.

Daimotsu-no-ura, *see* Daimotsu

Dan-no-ura. In Shimonoseki Straits. *See* the Introduction.

Date. A district in Ōshū (Fukushima Prefecture).

Dazaifu Anrakuji Temple. A Buddhist temple on the site of the grave of an exiled minister of state, Sugawara Michizane (845–903). Now Dazaifu Tenjin Shrine. In Tsukushi District, Chikuzen, Kyushu.

Dewa. An old province in northeast Honshu, corresponding to the modern prefectures of Yamagata and Akita. After the Meiji Restoration, it was divided into the two provinces of Uzen and Ugo.

Dohi. A general term for the area embracing Yoshihama and the villages south of it in Ashigarashimo District, Sagami (now a part of Yugawara Township, Kanagawa Prefecture). Yoritomo hid there after his defeat at Ishibashiyama.

Dohi Jirō Sanehira, *see* Dohi Sanehira

Dohi Sanehira (d. 1191). Called Jirō. A retainer of Yoritomo from the time of his revolt on.

Earth Goddess. Kenro Jijin, a Buddhist deity who makes the ground strong and firm.

Echigo. A Hokurikudō province, corresponding to part of Niigata Prefecture.

Echizen. A Hokurikudō province, corresponding to Fukui Prefecture.

Echizen Capital. The present Takefu City, Nanjō District, Fukui Prefecture (Echizen).

Eda Genzō, *see* Eda Hiromoto

Eda Hiromoto. Called Genzō. A warrior mentioned in *Gempei seisuiki*. Okami, p. 152, n. 18.

Edo, *see* Edo Shigenaga

Edo Shigenaga. Called Tarō. Owner of Edo domain (*shō*), Toyoshima District, Musashi (Tokyo Prefecture). Okami, p. 133, n. 8.

Edo Tarō, *see* Edo Shigenaga

Eight Great Vajra Messengers. Hachidai Kongō Dōji. Minor Buddhist deities of fierce aspect, usually said to be attendants or messengers of Fudō, but apparently regarded as messengers of Zaō by the ascetic fraternity. They seem to have been worshiped at the Kumano Ōji shrines, Mount Kimpu, and the Ōmine Mountains. Okami, pp. 202, n. 1 ; 431, suppl. n. 4; 301, n. 23.

Eight Provinces. The Kantō provinces.

Ema Koshirō, *see* Hōjō Yoshitoki

En no Gyōja (fl. Nara period). En no Ozune, an early Buddhist ascetic who was the first well-known monk to practice austerities in many of the remote mountain regions in Yamato Province. He is said to have founded Kimpusan Temple (the Zaōdō) on Mount Kimpu.

Enlightenment, Peak of. Bodai-no-mine. A name for Mount Kimpu used by wandering ascetics.

Enryakuji Temple. Called Sammon (Mountain Gate). The great headquarters of the Tendai sect on Mount Hiei near Kyoto, founded by Dengyō Daishi in 788. It was the leading religious institution of the Heian period in terms of wealth, political influence, and military strength.

Eshima. On the eastern outskirts of Iwaya Township, Tsuna District, Awaji. Often mentioned in classical verse.

Etchū. A Hokurikudō province, corresponding to Toyama Prefecture.

Ezashi. A district in Iwate Prefecture (Rikuchū).

Fan K'uai (d. 189 B.C.). A renowned Chinese general, with whose assistance Han Kao Tsu founded the Han dynasty.

Four Heavenly Kings. *Shitennō.* Buddhist guardians of the four directions and protectors of the state against evil spirits. Their warlike figures are frequently encountered in Japanese temples.

Fudō. Skt. Acala. The most important of the Five Great Bright Kings; a fierce manifestation of Vairochana Buddha, whose mission is to crush evil. In Chapter Five, the author appears to be confusing him with Zaō, another angry deity, and the Buddhist novice, or lay monk, with En no Gyōja, who is traditionally said to have founded the Zaōdō, though not as a result of an incident such as the one described.

Fugen. Skt. Samantabhadra. A bodhisattva, usually depicted as riding a white elephant, who is worshiped in esoteric rites intended to avert calamity and assure longevity.

Fuji, Mount. In Suruga. A favorite resort of wandering monks.

Fujiwara. Part of Minakami Township, Tone District, Gumma Prefecture (Kōzuke).

Fujiwara Fubito (659–720). Son of Kamatari. Nara statesman; ancestor of the great Northern House of the Fujiwara. His posthumous name was Tankaikō.

Fujiwara Hidehira (d. 1187). Lord of Ōshū and protector of Yoshitsune. *See* the Introduction.

Fujiwara Hidesato. Called Tawara Tōda Hidesato. Early Heian military chieftain in Shimotsuke, who with Taira Sadamori put down Taira Masakado's revolt.

Fujiwara Hōshō (958–1036). Yasumasa. Mid-Heian warrior, poet, and provincial official.

Fujiwara Kamatari (614–669). Statesman-founder of the Fujiwara family; the leading political figure of his day.

Fujiwara Kiyohira (fl. *ca.* late 11th c.). Ancestor of the Ōshū Fujiwara; also known as the Mitsū Lesser Captain, or Watari Kiyohira. *See* the Introduction.

Fujiwara Kunihira. Called Tarō Nishikido. Oldest son of Hidehira. Sometimes called Yorihira in *Gikeiki*. Okami, p. 367, n. 15.

Fujiwara Michinori (d. 1159). Also called Shinzei. Opponent of Yoshitomo and Fujiwara Nobuyori in the Heiji War. *See* the Introduction.

Fujiwara Michitaka (953–995). Eldest son of the regent Kaneie, elder brother of the celebrated Michinaga, and regent and father-in-law of Emperor Ichijō (r. 986–1011). His name is also read Tōryū.

Fujiwara Motohira, *see* Fujiwara Tadahira

Fujiwara Motonari. Half-brother of Nobuyori and father-in-law of Hidehira. Okami, pp. 371, n. 11; 445, suppl. n. 1.

Fujiwara Nobuyori (1133–1159). Minamoto Yoshitomo's principal ally in the Heiji War. *See* the Introduction.

Fujiwara Noriakira. Known as Gotōnai Noriakira. A retainer of Yoriyoshi from Shimotsuke; son of Yoshiie's wet nurse. He was one of the survivors of the Former Nine Years' War.

Fujiwara Sanekata (d. 998). Mid-Heian courtier and poet; a member of the great Northern House of the Fujiwara. He is said to have been sent off to serve as governor of Mutsu in 995, as a punishment for having become involved in a quarrel at the palace. He died in Mutsu in 998. His poetry was particularly admired in the Kamakura period.

Fujiwara Suehira. Called Hizume Gorō. A kinsman of the Ōshū Fujiwara who lived at Shiba District, Iwate Prefecture (Rikuchū). Okami, p. 369, n. 14.

Fujiwara Sumitomo (d. 941). An ex-official who stayed in Iyo Province as a local chieftain after the expiration of his term of office in 936. As the leader of the powerful local families ("pirates") in the area, he virtually controlled the Inland Sea for a period of about five years. After becoming an open rebel in 939, he was

finally suppressed by a punitive
force in 941.

Fujiwara Tadahira (d. 1189). Third
son of Hidehira. Known as Izumi
Kanja or Izumi Saburō. (Incorrectly identified as Motohira in
Gikeiki, Chapter Two.) The only
one of Hidehira's sons who remained loyal to Yoshitsune, he
died in the battle of Koromogawa.

Fujiwara Takahira. Called Motoyoshi Kanja. Fourth son of
Hidehira.

Fujiwara Toshihito. Famous early
tenth-century court general.

Fujiwara Yasuhira (1155–1189).
Second son and heir of Hidehira.
See the Introduction. *Gikeiki* errs
in calling him Motoyoshi Kanja.
Okami, p. 79, n. 18.

Futami. Futami Township, Wata-
rai District, Mie Prefecture (Ise).

Futami Coast. A famous scenic area
on the beach at Futami.

Futoi River. The lower reaches of
the present Edo River, east of the
Sumida, along the Chiba-Tokyo
border.

Ganda, *see* Minamoto Yoshiie

Garden of Divine Waters. Shinzen'-
en. An imperial garden and
pleasure ground in Kyoto. Prayers for rain were offered there
during seasons of drought.

Gassan, Mount. A volcanic peak in
central Yamagata Prefecture.
One of the Three Mountains of
Dewa (elevation 1,979 meters).
Since ancient times, it has been a
holy region, frequented by reli-

gious ascetics.

Gate Guards, Chief of the, *see*
Fujiwara Nobuyori

Gen Kurō. Yoshitsune.

Genda, *see* Kajiwara Kagesue

Gien (d. 1181). Childhood name
Otowaka. Second of Yoshitomo's
three sons by Tokiwa Gozen; full
brother of Yoshitsune. *See* the
Introduction, note 7, and Chapter One, note 2.

Gion. Gion Shrine in Higashiyama,
Kyoto.

Gion Highway. A street running
east and west in front of Gion
Shrine in Kyoto.

Gojō. An east-west avenue which
traversed the center of Kyoto,
corresponding approximately to
the present street of Matsubara;
also, a strip section of the city
which lay between Gojō and
Shijō avenues and extended to the
city's eastern and western limits.

Gojō Higashi-no-tōin. The area
near the intersection of Gojō and
Higashi-no-tōin in the capital.

Gojō Nishi-no-tōin. The area in the
vicinity of the intersection of Gojō
Avenue and Nishi-no-tōin, a
north-south avenue in the capital
east of the imperial palace, a
little west of the present Nishi-no-
tōin Street.

Gojō Tenjin Shrine. A popular
shrine dedicated to Amaterasu
and other deities at Tenjimmae-
chō in Shimokyō Ward, Kyoto.
It was traditionally believed to
protect its devotees against disease and calamity.

Gosho-no-ōji. A shrine at Kiyogawa Village. The name indicates that five deities are worshiped there, but their identities are uncertain. Okami, p. 353, n. 10.

Gotōnai Noriakira, *see* Fujiwara Noriakira

Grand Shrine, *see* Ise, Grand Shrine of

Hachijō. A major east-west avenue in the southern part of Kyoto; also, a strip section of the city, lying between Hachijō and Shichijō avenues.

Hachijūhachiri Beach. An area corresponding to the present Shimami Beach in Kitakambara District, Niigata Prefecture (Echigo).

Hachiman. Ancestral god of the Minamoto. A state-protecting Shinto deity, usually identified with Emperor Ōjin (r. 270–310 A.D.?). His most important early shrine was at Usa in Kyushu. He was given the title Great Bodhisattva when he was brought to Nara to protect the great new Tōdaiji Temple in the eighth century. He was later adopted by the Seiwa Genji as their special guardian, and gradually came to be worshiped by the entire military class.

Hachiman Lower Shrine, *see* Hachiman Shrine, **3**

Hachiman Shrine. **1.** (Iwashimizu). A shrine near Kyoto, founded by a Buddhist monk in 859 on Mount Otokoyama in Tsuzuki District, Yamashiro. Deeply revered by the court from the beginning, it ranked in importance with the great Shinto sanctuaries at Kamo and Kasuga. Minamoto Yoriyoshi and his son Yoshiie, who were among the first Genji to make a special cult of the worship of Hachiman, were faithful Iwashimizu patrons, as was Yoritomo. **2.** (Matsunaga). Possibly the Hachiman Shrine at Haniyū, Isurugi Township, western Nishitonami District, Toyama Prefecture (Etchū), although Matsunaga (Matsunaga *shō*) seems to have been a little farther north. Okami, p. 340, n. 14. **3.** (Tsurugaoka). The great shrine dedicated to Emperor Ōjin (i.e., the war god, Hachiman), Emperor Chūai, and Empress Jingū at Yukinoshita in Kamakura. In effect, the official shrine of the Kamakura government. There were two main shrines in the compound, an Upper Shrine on Daijin Mountain and a Lower Shrine, called Wakamiya, at the foot of the mountain. *See also* Yui-no-hama.

Hachiman Tarō, *see* Minamoto Yoshiie

Haguro, Mount. One of the Three Mountains of Dewa, located at Tamuke Township, Higashitagawa District, Yamagata Province (Dewa). Haguro Gongen (also Hagurosan Gongen; now Ideha Jinja), the shrine on its summit, is still visited by wandering ascetics. During the medieval period, the god worshiped there was regarded as a manifestation of Kannon. Okami, p. 442, suppl. n. 21.

Hakata. In the present Fukuoka City, Kyushu. One of the chief ports of the medieval era.

Hakusan, Mount, *see* Heisenji Temple

Hakusan, Seven Shrines of Mount. The Shirayamahime Shrine and its subsidiaries. The main Hakusan shrine was on top of Mount Hakusan, but because of its inaccessibility Shirayamahime tended to usurp its place.

Hamana Bridge. A bridge at the sea outlet of Hamana Lake, Hamana District, Shizuoka Prefecture (Tōtōmi).

Han Wu Ti (156–87 B.C.). Great Chinese emperor of the Han dynasty (r. 141–87 B.C.).

Harada. A warrior family in Harada, Tsukushi Village, Tsukushi District, Higo Province, Kyushu.

Harakai. Possibly Harami in Nishitagawa District, Yamagata Prefecture (Dewa). Okami, p. 350, n. 5.

Harima. A San'yōdō province, corresponding to part of Hyōgo Prefecture.

Hase. Hatsuse. A township on the upper reaches of the Hase River in Shiki District, Nara Prefecture (Yamato). (Also a mountain north of the town.) Site of ancient imperial residences, and of the celebrated Hase Temple, dedi-

cated to Eleven-Headed Kannon.

Hasekomi Valley. Also Kurikara Valley. The valley below Kurikara Pass, into which a Taira army was driven with great loss of life by Kiso Yoshinaka in 1183.

Hata. Hata Village (now a part of Kōchi City), Tosa District, Kōchi Prefecture (Tosa); site of Shinsenji Temple.

Hatakeyama, Hatakeyama Jirō, *see* Hatakeyama Shigetada

Hatakeyama Saburō. Presumably a mistake for Hatakeyama Jirō.

Hatakeyama Shigetada (1164–1205). Called Jirō. Member of a Musashi family. Although unable to join Yoritomo at first because his father was in Taira hands in Kyoto, he soon became one of the *bakufu*'s most valued retainers.

Hatakeyama Shigeyoshi. Father of Shigetada. Called Chichibu-no-shōji or Hatakeyama-no-shōji.

Hatsuse, *see* Hase

Hayakawa River. Called Kobayagawa River in Chapter Three. A stream which rises at the north end of Lake Ashinoko, flows down through the Hakone Mountains, and empties into Sagami Bay southwest of Odawara. There is no record of a battle there. *Gikeiki*'s author is probably thinking of the defeat suffered by Yoritomo at Ishibashiyama, a mountain at Ishibashi, Kataura Township, Ashigarashimo District, Kanagawa Prefecture (Sagami).

Hayashi Mitsuakira. Called Rokurō. A relative of the Togashi, who lived at Hayashi Township, Ishikawa District, Ishikawa Prefecture (Kaga). He fought under Yoshinaka against the Heike. Okami, p. 337, n. 12.

Hayashi Rokurō, *see* Hayashi Mitsuakira

Hayashiro. Possibly a mistake for Miyashiro, Shinobu District, Fukushima Prefecture (Ōshū).

Heisenji Temple. An ancient Tendai temple in Heisenji Village, Ōno District, Fukui Prefecture (Echizen), which was a subsidiary of the Enryakuji, and itself supported a large contingent of warrior-monks. It was patronized especially by the military. Its tutelary deity was Hakusan Gongen, the Shinto god worshiped at the top of Hakusan, the highest mountain of the Hakusan volcanic chain, situated on the border between Ōno District in Echizen and Nomi District in Kaga.

Hetsugi. Apparently a warrior alliance at Hetsugi Domain (*shō*), Ōita District, Bungo, Kyushu.

Hidehira, *see* Fujiwara Hidehira

Hie Sannō, *see* Hie Shrine

Hie Shrine. Also Hiyoshi Shrine, Hiyoshi Sannō, Hie Sannō, Hiei Sannō. Its many buildings still occupy a broad area on the flank of Mount Hiei, within the administrative confines of Ōtsu City. Founded by imperial order in 668, and recognized by Dengyō Daishi as the guardian of the Enryakuji. Because of its close connection with the Hiei warrior-monks, who frequently blackmailed the court by taking its sacred car into the city, it was an important political force in the Heian, Kamakura, and Muromachi periods.

Hiedori Pass. Hiyodori. A passage through the mountains between Fukuhara in the present Kobe City and Mino District in Harima.

Hiei, Mount. A mountain northeast of Kyoto, on the boundary between the provinces of Yamashiro and Ōmi; also, a synonym for the Enryakuji Temple, whose buildings it supported.

Hiei Sannō, *see* Hie Shrine

Higashi-no-tōin. A north-south avenue in the eastern part of the old capital, corresponding in position to the present street of the same name in Kyoto.

Higashiyama. A mountainous area on the eastern side of the old capital.

Higuchi Karasumaru. Higuchi corresponded to the present Manjuji Street in Kyoto; Karasumaru was a north-south street in the eastern section of the city. The Buddhist hall mentioned in Chapter Three was perhaps the Rokujō Midō (Manjuji), a well-known temple not far from Karasumaru. Okami, p. 119, n. 19.

Hiraizumi. Old seat of the Ōshū Fujiwara (*see* the Introduction). Now a village on the right bank of the Kitakami River in northern

Nishiiwai District, Iwate Prefecture.

Hirazuka. Hiratsuka City, Naka District, Kanagawa Prefecture (Sagami).

Hitachi. A Tōkaidō province, corresponding to part of Ibaragi Prefecture.

Hitsukawa River. Now called the Yamashina. It rises in North Yamashina, flows east of Higashiyama, joins the Otowa, and empties into the Uji in Fushimi Ward, Kyoto.

Hiyoshi Sannō, Hiyoshi Shrine, *see* Hie Shrine

Hizume, Hizume Gorō, *see* Fujiwara Suehira

Hizume-no-kobayashi. Probably Kobayashi, one of the Seven Districts of Kamakura. The Hachiman Lower Shrine is situated there.

Hōgan. Yoshitsune.

Hōjō. **1.** An area in Takata District, Shizuoka Prefecture (Izu). **2.** ——, Lord. Hōjō Tokimasa.

Hōjō Masako, *see* Taira Masako

Hōjō Shirō, *see* Hōjō Tokimasa

Hōjō Tokimasa (1137–1215). Called Shirō. Originally one of Yoritomo's two Heike guardians, and later, as his father-in-law, a mainstay of the Kamakura government. Founder of the Hōjō line of regents. Yoritomo's deputy in Kyoto after Yoshitsune's defection.

Hōjō Yoshitoki (1163–1224). Called Ema Koshirō, after the locality in which he lived (Ema, Takata District, Izu). Son of Tokimasa; second of the Hōjō regents in Kamakura (1205–1224).

Hōjūji Temple. Formerly the residence of Fujiwara Tamemitsu (942–992), converted into a temple by its owner. It is said to have been situated in the vicinity of the present Sanjūsangendō in Higashiyama Ward, Kyoto. It was not rebuilt after its destruction by Minamoto Yoshinaka's troops in 1183.

Hokurikudō. Hokurokudō. The provinces northeast of Kyoto, fronting on the Japan Sea (Wakasa, Echizen, Kaga, Noto, Etchū, Echigo, and Sado); also, the road leading from Kyoto through those provinces.

Home Provinces, *see* Ki'nai

Homma. Homma Yoshitada. Okami, p. 132, n. 50.

Hōnen (1133–1212). Founder of the Japanese Pure Land sect of Buddhism.

Hōrai, Mount. In Chinese legend, a fairy mountain in the eastern seas, whose inhabitants are immortal.

Hori Chikaie. Called Tōji. A Kamakura vassal.

Hori Tōji, *see* Hori Chikaie

Hori Yatarō. Possibly to be identified with Hori Yatarō Kagemitsu (*Azuma kagami*) or Hori Yatarō Chikatsune (*Heike monogatari*). *Gyokuyō* says that Hori Yatarō Kagemitsu, a retainer of Yoshitsune, was captured at the time of

Satō Tadanobu's death. Okami, pp. 254, n. 18; 138, n. 6.

Horikane Well. Horikane-no-i. In Horikane Village, Iruma District, Saitama Prefecture (Musashi). Frequently mentioned in classical literature.

Horikawa. A broad north-south avenue in the eastern sector of the old capital.

Horikawa Mansion. Yoshitsune's house in the capital. *Gikeiki* locates the house at Horikawa Rokujō (i.e., in the vicinity of the intersection of Horikawa and Rokujō), *Azuma kagami* at Rokujō Muromachi, and *Gyokuyō* at a place "near the ex-emperor's palace." Okami, p. 153, n. 20.

Hoshika. A district in Rikuzen; the area of Hoshika Peninsula in Miyagi Prefecture.

Hōshō, *see* Fujiwara Hōshō

Hosorogi. A village north of Kanazu in Sakai District, Fukui Prefecture (Echizen).

Hosshōji Temple. A temple founded by Emperor Shirakawa at Okasaki in the present Sakyō Ward, Kyoto. It appears to have survived until the Muromachi period.

Hsüan Tsung (685–762). Chinese emperor of the T'ang dynasty (r. 712–756).

Huang-shih. The old man who gave Chang Liang the *San-lüeh* (*see* Chang Liang). In Chapter Three, *Gikeiki*'s author has apparently confused him with the semilegendary philosopher Lao-tzu (fl. be-tween 5th and 3d centuries B.C. ?), who is said to have remained in the womb for eighty-one years. There is no known precedent for the association with Hachiman's name.

Hyōe-no-suke. Minamoto Yoritomo.

Hyōgo-no-shima. The Fukuhara region in the present Kobe City.

Ibuki Peak. On the border between Sakata District in Ōmi and Ibi District in Mino.

Ichi-no-tani. On the coast near Kobe. *See* the Introduction.

Ichifuri. A village (now a part of Aomi Township) situated in Nishikubiki District, Niigata Prefecture (Echigo).

Ichijō, *see* Katsuragi, Mount

Ichijō. The northernmost of the nine great east-west avenues in the capital; also, the section of the city lying between Tsuchimikado and Nakamikado avenues.

Ichijō Horikawa. The vicinity of the intersection of Ichijō and Horikawa avenues in the old capital. This was an area traditionally associated with yin-yang practitioners. Okami, p. 83, n. 16.

Ichijō Imadegawa. The capital area in the vicinity of the intersection of Ichijō and Imadegawa.

Ichikawa. In the vicinity of the present Matsudo City, Chiba Prefecture.

Ietō, *see* Abe Ietō

Iga. A Tōkaidō province, corresponding to part of Mie Prefecture.

Ihō. A family who lived at Ihō, in the vicinity of Ōtaki Township, Isumi District, Kazusa (Chiba Prefecture).

Ihō Gorō, *see* Ihō Morinao

Ihō Morinao. Called Gorō. Probably a member of the Ihō family in Kazusa.

Ikaishiri. Other *Gikeiki* texts read Kawajiri, a name for the mouth of the Kobitsu River at Kisarazu City, Chiba.

Ikuta Woods. Ikuta-no-mori. An area in the vicinity of Ikuta Shrine, in the present Kobe City.

Imadegawa. Originally a small stream, whose name was preserved in an east-west street in the northern section of the capital, near the imperial palace. Oni-ichi's house was in the area. Okami, p. 95, n. 4.

Imai. In Edogawa Ward, Tokyo.

Imawaka, *see* Zenjō

Imazu. In the present Makino Township, Takashima District, Shiga Prefecture (Ōmi).

Inaba. One of the eight San'indō provinces, corresponding to part of Tottori Prefecture.

Inaba, Governor of. Ōe Hiromoto.

Inage, Inage Saburō, *see* Inage Shigenari

Inage Shigenari (d. 1205). Called Saburō. A Musashi warrior, related to Hatakeyama Shigetada. He died with Shigetada when the Hōjō attacked him.

Inamu Barrier. Usually called Uya-

muya; also Muyamuya, Moyamoya. Said to have been located at the present Sasaya Pass, on the border between Yamagata City and Natori District in Miyagi Prefecture.

Inan. A family mentioned in *Azuma kagami* as being related to the Ihō. Okami, p. 131, n. 20.

Inari. Fushimi Inari Shrine in Kyoto.

Inase River. A small stream in southwest Kamakura, which rises in the hills behind Fukazawa and empties into Sagami Bay at Yui-ga-hama.

Incense Mountain. A mountain in India, which was said to be the dwelling place of a bodhisattva. Okami, pp. 204, n. 5; 229, n. 12.

Inner Princess' Household, Chief of, *see* Minamoto Tomonaga

Inomata. A family in the present Kodama District, Saitama Prefecture (Musashi).

Inoue Saemon. Possibly a warrior from Inoue Domain (*shō*) in Kahoku District, Kaga, an area believed to lie within the modern Tsubata Township. Okami, p. 441, suppl. n. 19.

Isawa. A district in Iwate Prefecture (Rikuchū).

Ise. A Tōkaidō province, corresponding to part of Mie Prefecture.

Ise, Grand Shrine of. The foremost shrine in Japan, dedicated to the Sun Goddess Amaterasu, progenitor of the imperial family.

Ise Katōji, *see* Katō Kagekado

Ise Saburō, *see* Ise Yoshimori

Ise Suzuka, *see* Suzuka

Ise Yoshimori (d. 1185). Called Saburō. Unlike Benkei, Ise Saburō is clearly a historical person. He lived as a brigand in Kōzuke, to which province he had been exiled for murder, until he met Yoshitsune and became his retainer. Chronicles of the period mention his presence at Yashima and Dan-no-ura. When Yoshitsune fled from the capital, Yoshimori returned to Ise, where he was eventually forced to commit suicide by the local Kamakura warden (*shugo*).

Ishihama. In the present Asakusa district, Taitō Ward, Tokyo.

Ishikawa Hōgan Yoshimichi, *see* Minamoto Yoshimichi

Ishiyama Temple. A seventh-century temple in the present city of Ōtsu. During its heyday in the Heian period, it was patronized by the imperial family and high nobility, and by such literary figures as Murasaki Shikibu.

Iso, Cape. Probably Isone Cape, on the east coast of Sanuki Township, Kimitsu District, Chiba Prefecture (Kazusa).

Iso-no-zenji. Mother of Shizuka; according to one tradition, the first *shirabyōshi* dancer.

Itabashi. In Itabashi Ward, Tokyo.

Itahana. West of Takasaki City, in the present Annaka Township, Usui District, Gumma Prefecture (Kōzuke).

Itō Jirō, *see* Itō Sukechika

Itō Sukechika (d. 1182). Called Jirō. He was the cousin of Kudō Suketsune, not the uncle (see Kudō Suketsune). As one of two Heike-appointed guardians of Yoritomo, he remained consistently hostile to his ward after the latter's revolt. Though pardoned through the intercession of his son-in-law, Miura Yoshizumi, he finally committed suicide.

Iwafune. A township (now part of Murakami City) in Iwafune District, Niigata Prefecture (Echigo).

Iwai. A district in Mutsu Province (corresponding to modern Higashiiwai District and Nishiiwai District, Iwate Prefecture), in which Hidehira's Hiraizumi residence was located.

Iwaki, *see* Mutsu

Iwakura, *see* Ashikura

Iwamoto. One of the Seven Shrines of Mount Hakusan. It was close to Shimoshirayama, in Iwamoto Village, Nomi District, Ishikawa Prefecture (Kaga). The god was regarded as a manifestation of Eleven-Headed Kannon, or, according to another view, of the bodhisattva Jizō.

Iwase. Higashiiwase Township (now a part of Toyama City), Kaminiikawa District, Toyama Prefecture (Etchū).

Iwashimizu, *see* Hachiman Shrine 1 (Iwashimizu)

Iwashiro, *see* Mutsu

Iwata River. Also called the Tomita or Kurusu. It rises at Mount Ando in Nishimuro District,

Wakayama Prefecture (Kii), and flows through Iwata Village, east of Tanabe City. In medieval times, its waters were apparently used for purification rituals by pilgrims to Kumano. Okami, p. 353, n. 15.

Iwate. A district in northwestern Iwate Prefecture (Mutsu).

Iwato Cape. East of Naoe-no-tsu (Naoetsu) on the coast at Kota, Nakakubiki District, Niigata Prefecture (Echigo).

Iyo. A province in Shikoku, corresponding to Ehime Prefecture.

Izu. A Tōkaidō province, corresponding to part of Shizuoka Prefecture.

Izu Provincial Capital. The present Mishima City, Shizuoka.

Izumi. A Ki'nai province, corresponding to part of Osaka Prefecture.

Izumi Hangan Kanetaka, *see* Taira Kanetaka

Izumi Kanja Motohira, Izumi Saburō, *see* Fujiwara Tadahira

Jakushō (d. 1034). A member of the Ōe scholar family in Kyoto. He became a monk after the death of his wife, which occurred while he was serving as governor of Mikawa, and in 1003 went to China, where he died thirty-one years later.

Jīva. Son of Bimbisāra. A legendary Indian physician.

Jōdo. Near Ichifuri in Nishikubiki District, Niigata Prefecture (Echigo).

Jūzenji Shrine. A shrine at Awataguchi in the capital, dedicated to Ninigi-no-mikoto Gongen, one of the gods of Hie.

Kaba. 1. Eastern Hamana District, Shizuoka Prefecture (north of Hamamatsu City). 2. Minamoto Noriyori.

Kaba Kanja, *see* Minamoto Noriyori

Kaba Onzōshi. Noriyori, who grew up in Kaba, was called Kaba Kanja or Kaba Onzōshi. He is said to have been the son of a local harlot. The son of the daughter of the Atsuta chief priest was actually Yoritomo. For *onzōshi*, *see* the Introduction, note 18.

Kaga. A Hokurikudō province, corresponding to part of Ishikawa Prefecture.

Kagami. Until the Tokugawa period, a post station north of Kagami Mountain in Gamō District, Ōmi.

Kagami Mountain, *see* Kagami Kagetoki, *see* Kajiwara Kagetoki

Kai. A Tōkaidō province, corresponding to Yamanashi Prefecture.

Kaihatsu Beach. Now a part of Kisarazu City, Chiba.

Kaizu. A post station at Lake Biwa (in the present Makino Township, Takashima District, Shiga Prefecture), on the main road to the Hokurikudō provinces.

Kajiwara, Kajiwara Heizō, *see* Kajiwara Kagetoki

Kajiwara Kagesue (1162–1200).

Called Genda. Eldest son of Kagetoki, and himself a warrior of note.

Kajiwara Kagetoki (d. 1200). Called Heizō. One of Yoritomo's senior retainers. *See* the Introduction.

Kakuta, Mount. Situated in Nishikambara District, Niigata Prefecture (Echigo).

Kamada Jirō, Kamada Jirobyōe Masakiyo, *see* Kamada Masakiyo

Kamada Masakiyo (1123–1160). Jirō, Jirobyōe. Also called Masaie. A Sagami warrior who fought for Yoshitomo in Hōgen and Heiji. After the Heiji defeat, he and Yoshitomo sought refuge in the home of Masakiyo's father-in-law, Taira Tadamasa, in Noma, Chita District, Owari (Aichi Prefecture). Tadamasa murdered Yoshitomo in the bathroom, and his son killed Masakiyo.

Kamakura, Lord of. Minamoto Yoritomo.

Kamakura Akugenda Yoshihira, *see* Minamoto Yoshihira

Kamakura Gongorō, *see* Kamakura Kagemasa

Kamakura Kagemasa. Called Gongorō. A warrior of Taira descent. He fought not in the Former Nine Years' War but in the Later Three Years' War, during which, at the age of sixteen or thereabouts, he is said to have killed an enemy while an arrow dangled from his own eye.

Kamatari, *see* Fujiwara Kamatari

Kambara. Now a part of Aomi Township, Nishikubiki District, Niigata Prefecture (Echigo).

Kambara-no-tachi. Probably a mistake for "Kambara and Nuttari." Kambara was a port in the vicinity of the present Niigata City, and Nuttari an area corresponding to Nuttari-machi in Niigata City. Okami, p. 349, n. 21.

Kamei Rokurō. A retainer of Yoshitsune, whose historicity is attested by *Azuma kagami*. *Gempei seisuiki* gives his name as Shigekiyo. According to *Gikeiki* and the *kōwakamai Takadachi*, he was the younger brother of Suzuki Saburō Shigeie from Kumano. Okami, p. 165, n. 6.

Kamenashi. In Katsushika Ward, Tokyo.

Kamewari Mountains. A low range of hills along the course of the Funakata River, on the border between Mogami District and Shinjō City in Yamagata Prefecture (Uzen).

Kamo. A general term for the great Upper and Lower Kamo Shrines, northeast of the old capital on the bank of the Kamo River. (Now a part of Sakyō Ward, Kyoto.)

Kamo Lagoon. At Ryōtsu City, Sado Island.

Kamo River. A stream which rises in northern Yamashiro and runs through the eastern part of Kyoto.

Kanatsu, *see* Kanazu

Kanazawa Fortress. Abe Sadatō's home; also called Kuriyagawa.

Situated in Kanazawa, Semboku District, Dewa (Akita Prefecture), near a small stream, the Kuriyagawa River (not to be confused with the Kuriyagawa in Iwate District, Iwate Prefecture).

Kanazu. Kanatsu. A domain (*shō*) in central Nakakambara District, Echigo (Niigata Prefecture). Later a village.

Kanazu-no-uwano. Possibly Kanazu Township in Sakai District, Fukui Prefecture (Echizen). However, a party traveling north by way of the Heisenji and Sugō would have had to double back in order to reach Kanazu.

Kanjubō, *see* Shōgu

Kannon. Skt. Avalokiteśvara. Kanzeon. Most widely revered of the bodhisattvas; a compassionate divinity who helps mankind. Although popularly known today as the Goddess of Mercy, this bodhisattva's early images show him as a male. He is depicted in various guises (Thousand-Armed Kannon, Horse-Head Kannon, Eleven-Head Kannon, etc.).

Kannonji Temple. Possibly Imakumano Temple in Higashiyama Ward, Kyoto. Okami, p. 39, n. 13.

Kantō. Also Bandō. The eight provinces east of Hakone Pass (Sagami, Musashi, Kōzuke, Shimotsuke, Awa, Kazusa, Shimōsa, and Hitachi).

Karasaki. On the western shore of Lake Biwa (now a part of Ōtsu City). The ancient pine which once stood there was among the Eight Sights of Ōmi.

Kasai. A family in what was formerly Kasai District, Shimōsa (now a part of Tokyo).

Kasai Hyōe, *see* Kasai Kiyoshige

Kasai Kiyoshige. Called Hyōe. The Kasai and the Edo were related to one another. Okami, p. 132, n. 7.

Kashima. A district in Ibaragi Prefecture (Hitachi).

Kasuga. Kasuga Shrine, located on Mount Mikasa in the present Kasugano, Nara. It enjoyed enormous prestige as the Fujiwara family shrine.

Katada. A township in Shiga District, Shiga Prefecture (Ōmi), on the shore of Lake Biwa. Frequently mentioned in classical poetry.

Kataoka. A retainer of Yoshitsune. Although little is known of him, he seems to have been a historical figure, since the name Kataoka Hachirō Hirotsune appears in an *Azuma kagami* list of Yoshitsune's men. The names Kataoka Tarō Tsuneharu, Kataoka Hachirō Tameharu, and Kataoka Jirō Tsuneharu also occur in *Azuma kagami*, *Heike monogatari*, and/or *Gempei seisuiki*, but it is impossible to say whether these represent one man or two or more. Kataoka occurs as a place name in Kashima District, Hitachi, which is identified as Kataoka's home in Chapter Four. *Azuma kagami* states that Kataoka Hachirō Tsuneharu was a *shōen* officer at Misaki Domain, Unakami District, Shimōsa, which is in the same general area as Kashima. Okami, p. 177, n. 25; Shimazu, p. 163.

Katō Kagekado (d. 1221). Called Ise Katōji. A retainer of Yoritomo, who participated in his rebellion from the beginning. He served the Kamakura government until his death in 1221.

Katōji, *see* Katō Kagekado

Katsura River. A stream on the outskirts of Kyoto. It empties into the Yodo.

Katsuragi, Mount. Also called Mount Kongō. The highest peak in the Katsuragi Range, situated on the border between Minamikawachi District in Osaka Prefecture and Minamikatsuragi District in Nara Prefecture. Called Peak of the Single Vehicle (Ichijō) by wandering ascetics.

Katte. Katte Shrine, near the Zaōdō on Mount Kimpu. Six gods, of whom Ame-no-oshiomi is usually said to be the most important, are worshiped there.

Kawachi. A Ki'nai province, corresponding to part of Osaka Prefecture.

Kawagoe. The Kawagoe, a branch of the Chichibu League, lived at Kawagoe Domain (*shō*) in Iruma District, Musashi (Saitama Prefecture).

Kawagoe Kojirō, *see* Kawagoe Shigetoki

Kawagoe Kotarō, *see* Kawagoe Shigefusa

Kawagoe Shigefusa. Called Kotarō. A member of the Musashi Kawa-

goe; son of Shigeyori.

Kawagoe Shigetoki. Called Kojirō. Second son of Shigeyori.

Kawagoe Shigeyori (d. 1185). Called Tarō. A Musashi warrior, related to the Hatakeyama. His daughter's marriage to Yoshitsune, though arranged by Yoritomo himself, resulted in his execution after Yoshitsune's flight to Ōshū.

Kawagoe Tarō, *see* Kawagoe Shigeyori

Kawashiri. Same as Ōkawajiri. *See* Daimotsu.

Kazusa. A Tōkaidō province, corresponding to part of Chiba Prefecture.

Kazusa-no-suke Hachirō, *see* Chiba Hirotsune

Kehi. A famous Hokurikudō shrine, located in Tsuruga City.

Kembutsu. A Buddhist monk who lived at Matsushima for many years. His piety is said to have attracted the admiration of Emperor Toba (r. 1107–1123).

Kemmotsu Tarō, *see* Kemmotsu Yorikata

Kemmotsu Yorikata (d. 1184). Called Tarō. A Taira warrior. He gave his life for Tomomori at the battle of Ichi-no-tani.

Kibune, *see* Kibune Shrine

Kibune Shrine. Located in the present Kurama Township, Sakyō Ward, Kyoto, in a ravine formed by the Kibune River (upper course of the Kamo). Said to have been founded in 678; one of the major shrines listed in the

Engishiki. It was much patronized by the court, particularly during the Heian period, when its god, Takaokami-no-kami, was regarded as a bringer of rain.

Kichijō Komagata. A horse-headed deity, believed to be a manifestation of Horse-Head Kannon, who was worshiped at some of the Kumano Ōji shrines. Okami, p. 67, n. 17.

Kii. A Nankaidō province, corresponding to Wakayama Prefecture and part of Mie Prefecture.

Kikuchi. A powerful warrior family in Kikuchi District, Higo Province, Kyushu.

Kikuchi Jirō, *see* Kikuchi Takanao

Kikuchi Takanao. Called Jirō. A warrior from Kikuchi District in Higo; member of one of the Nine Leagues of Chinzei. Okami, p. 171, n. 2.

Kikuta Barrier. Also called Nakoso Barrier. One of the Three Barriers of Ōshū, located in the present Nakoso City, Iwashiro District, Fukushima.

Kimmei (509–571). Twenty-ninth emperor of Japan (r. 540–571). There is no historical evidence connecting him with the Zaōdō.

Kimpu, Mount. The highest peak in the Yoshino Mountains. Site of the Zaōdō. Called the Sacred Peak of Yoshino.

Ki'nai. Home Provinces. The five provinces surrounding the ancient capital at Naniwa: Yamashiro, Yamato, Kawachi, Izumi, and Settsu. Also called Goki'nai (Five Home Provinces).

Kinome Pass. In the mountains of Echizen (Fukui Prefecture), on the border between Tsuruga and Nanjō districts.

Kinora. A mistake for Kinome Pass.

Kinugawa River. A subsidiary of the Tone. It rises in the Nikkō mountains, flows south on the plain beyond Utsunomiya, and joins the Tone at the southwest corner of Ibaragi Prefecture.

Kiribe-no-ōji. Also Kirime-no-ōji. One of the chief of the Kumano Ōji shrines, situated in Hitaka District, Wakayama Prefecture (Kii).

Kishi-no-oka. Possibly a part of Ryūmon Village (now Yoshino Township), on the north bank of the Yoshino River in Yoshino District, Nara Prefecture (Yamato). According to *Heiji monogatari*, Tokiwa fled to Ryūmon in Uda District. (Ryūmon is actually not in Uda, but in the adjoining Yoshino District.)

Kiso, Lord, Kiso Kanja, Kiso Yoshinaka, *see* Minamoto Yoshinaka

Kisōto Beach. Possibly to be identified with the present Kisarazu City in Chiba.

Kitashirakawa. The northern part of Shirakawa in Kyoto; i.e., the southern part of the present Sakyō Ward.

Kiyogawa River. A tributary of the Mogami which rises at Tachiyasawa in Higashitagawa District,

Yamagata Prefecture (the valley north of Mount Gassan). Now called the Tachiyasawa River.

Kiyomizu, Kiyomizu Kannon, *see* Kiyomizu Temple

Kiyomizu Temple. A well-known temple dedicated to Kannon at the foot of Otowa (or Kiyomizu) Mountain, in the hills east of the old capital (Kiyomizu Itchōme, Higashiyama Ward, Kyoto).

Kiyomori, *see* Taira Kiyomori

Kizukawa. Possibly Kitsuregawa Township in Shionoya District, Tochigi Prefecture (Shimotsuke).

Kobayagawa River, *see* Hayakawa River

Kōfukuji Temple. In Nara City. Family temple of the Fujiwara; one of the great religious institutions of premodern Japan, and still an important repository of art treasures. Like the Tōdaiji, it supported a large number of soldier-monks.

Koga Minister of State. Probably Minamoto Michichika (1145–1202), a prominent political figure and poet of the late Heian and early Kamakura periods. There is no historical evidence that Yoshitsune was married to his daughter. Okami, p. 304, n. 4.

Kogawa. A temple in Kogawa Township, Naga District, Wakayama Prefecture.

Kokawaguchi. Possibly Kawaguchi City, Kitaadachi District, Saitama Prefecture (Musashi).

Kokūzō. Skt. Ākāśagharbha. A bodhisattva revered especially in esoteric Buddhism. His central attributes are wisdom and intellectual power, which he imparts to his devotees.

Kominato. Possibly refers to the mouth of the Heguri River (Minato River) at Tateyama City, Chiba.

Kōmyō, Mount. A peak in the mountainous region east of Kawada, Tanakura Village (now Yamashiro Township), Sagara District, Kyoto Prefecture (Yamashiro). The Kōmyō Temple, a subsidiary of the Tōdaiji, was situated on the mountain.

Kongō, Mount, *see* Katsuragi, Mount

Koromogawa. **1.** A place in northern Hiraizumi Township (Nishiiwai District, Iwate Prefecture), northeast of the Chūsonji Temple, which is said to have been the site of Yoshitsune's Takadachi residence. The exact location of the house is in doubt. Okami, p. 360, n. 13. **2.** An Abe stronghold, probably situated in the general area of the Koromogawa River in the present Koromogawa Village, Isawa District, Iwate Prefecture. Koromogawa Fortress. **3.** A stream which flows mainly through Isawa District in Iwate Prefecture, and joins the Kitakami River in the vicinity of Hiraizumi. According to one tradition, Yoshitsune's house faced it.

Koromogawa Fortress, *see* Koromogawa, **2**

Koromogawa River, *see* Koromogawa, **3**

Koshigoe. Now in eastern Kamakura City, Kanagawa Prefecture.
It appears to have been a post
station at one time.

Kowata. A part of Uji City, Kyoto
Prefecture.

Kōya. Kongōbuji Temple. A Shingon temple founded by Kōbō
Daishi on Mount Kōya in Wakayama Prefecture.

Koyasu Woods. Koyasu-no-mori.
Another name for Koyasu Shrine
in Akasaka Township, Fuwa
District, Mino.

Kōzuke. A Kantō province, corresponding to Gumma Prefecture.

Kubiki. An old district in Echigo,
comprising the present Higashi-
kubiki, Nishikubiki, and Nakakubiki districts in Niigata Prefecture.

Kudō Saemon, *see* Kudō Suketsune

Kudō Suketsune (d. 1193). Called
Saemon or Saemon-no-jō. A
vassal of Taira Shigemori, who
held the Itō area in Izu. After
being despoiled of his lands by
his cousin, Itō Sukechika, he
retaliated by wounding Sukechika and killing Sukechika's son,
Sukeyasu. He was subsequently
active as a Kamakura retainer.
In 1193 he became the victim of
the famous revenge slaying of the
Soga brothers, sons of Sukeyasu.

Kugami. A village in Nishikambara

District, Niigata Prefecture
(Echigo). Site of Kugami Temple.

Kujō. A major east-west avenue in
the old capital; also, a strip section of the city, lying between
Hachijō and Kujō avenues.

Kujō-no-in, *see* Teishi, ex-Empress

Kujūkuri Beach. Possibly a mistake
for Igarashi Beach in Nishikambara District.

Kumano. The three shrines of
Kumano in Higashimuro District, Wakayama Prefecture (Kii
Province): Hongū (Main Shrine),
or Kumano-nimasu, in Hongō
Township; Shingū (New Shrine),
or Kumano-hayatama, in Shingū
City; and Nachi, or Kumano-
nachi, in Nachi-katsuura Township. Though widely separated,
they were organized as a single
entity, unified by the "Kumano
faith," a peculiar form of Buddhism devoted especially to the
prolongation of life and rebirth
into paradise. Kumano was one
of the great religious institutions
of the Heian and Kamakura
periods, frequently visited by
ex-emperors and other notables,
as well as by wandering ascetics
and ordinary pilgrims.

Kumano New Shrine, *see* Kumano

Kumano Ōji Shrines. A large
number of shrines subsidiary to
Kumano Shrine, located at various places on the route from
Kyoto to Kumano.

Kurama. A township in Sakyō
Ward, Kyoto, about an hour by

train northeast of the present city proper. Kurama Temple on Kurama Mountain, founded in honor of Bishamon by imperial command in 796, was believed by the court to be a guardian of the city, and by the townspeople to be a source of good fortune.

Kurama Temple, *see* Kurama

Kurihama. In Miura District, Sagami (now a part of Yokosuka City), just across from the Bōsō Peninsula at the mouth of Tokyo Bay.

Kurihara. A district in Miyagi Prefecture.

Kurihara Temple. A temple which was formerly situated in the present Kurihara Township, Kurihara District, Miyagi Prefecture (Rikuzen).

Kurikara Pass. A 277-meter pass on the Hokurikudō, in the Tonami Mountains on the Echizen-Etchū border. Scene of a major battle between Kiso Yoshinaka and the Taira in 1183.

Kurikawa. Location uncertain; perhaps in the vicinity of Imai.

Kuriyagawa. **1.** A fortress, said to have been situated on a bluff facing the Kitakami River in Kuriyagawa Village (now Morioka City), Iwate District, Iwate Prefecture (Mutsu). Scene of the Abe's last stand in the Former Nine Years' War. **2.** Probably the stream which flowed beside Kanazawa Fortress.

Kuriyagawa Fortress, *see* Kuriyagawa, **1**

Kuriyagawa Jirō Sadatō, *see* Abe Sadatō

Kuriyagawa River, *see* Kuriyagawa, **2**

Kurō Hōgan. Yoshitsune.

Kurobe, Forty-Eight Currents of. Traditional name for the numerous swift-flowing channels of the Kurobe River in central Shimoniikawa District, Toyama Prefecture (Etchū).

Kurobe Station. Apparently an invention. There is a Kurobe River which flows through central Shimoniikawa District, Toyama Prefecture (Etchū).

Kurodani. A valley in the Western Compound of Mount Hiei.

Kuwanokami. This family's name appears in one *Gikeiki* text as Kawakami, which is probably correct, although no such place is now known. Okami, p. 131, n. 20.

Kuze River. The Kuize River. It rises around Ikeno in Ibi District, Gifu Prefecture (Mino), and flows generally southward past Akasaka on the west and Ōgaki on the east, until it empties into the Makita River in Yōrō District, a total length of about twenty-five kilometers. The chief crossing was at Akasaka post station, in the present township of Akasaka, Fuwa District, Gifu Prefecture (Mino).

Kyō-no-kimi, Kyō-no-kimi Enshin, *see* Gien

Kyōgoku. A broad north-south avenue on the eastern edge of the old capital, corresponding to the present Teramachi Street in Kyoto.

Li, Lady. Concubine of Han Wu Ti, routinely invoked as a standard of feminine beauty in Muromachi literature.

Lower Hachiman Shrine, *see* Hachiman Shrine **3** (Tsurugaoka)

Lü Shang (fl. *ca.* 1100 B.C.). Minister of Wen Wang and Wu Wang of Chou, who is reputed to have been a military and political genius. Known as T'ai-kung Wang.

Magaki Island. Off Chiga Beach.

Main Shrine, *see* Kumano

Manazuru, Cape. In Manazuru Township, Ashigarashimo District, Kanagawa Prefecture (Sagami).

Mano Inlet. Mano-no-irie. Mano, now a place name in Katada Township, probably referred originally to the area around the mouth of the Mano River, north of the old Katada. Okami, p. 316, n. 3.

Manonotachi. Possibly to be identified with Mano, east of Andō in Chiba. Okami, p. 129, n. 20.

Maro Tarō. A warrior from Maro in Awa District, Awa (Chiba Prefecture).

Masakado, *see* Taira Masakado

Masako, Lady, *see* Taira Masako

Matano, Matano Gorō, *see* Matano Kagehisa

Matano Kagehisa. Called Gorō. A

nephew of Ōba Kagechika.

Matsudo. A private domain (*shō*) in the vicinity of the present Matsudo City, Higashikatsushika District, Chiba Prefecture (Shimōsa).

Matsukage. Possibly Matsu-ga-saki, in the former Hamochi District, Sado. Okami, p. 348, n. 7.

Matsumoto. A harbor at Ōtsu City, Shiga Prefecture (Ōmi).

Matsunaga, *see* Hachiman Shrine **2** (Matsunaga)

Matsura. **1.** A district in Hizen Province, Kyushu. **2.** The Matsura League, a famous military alliance in Kyushu, made up primarily of warriors from the four Matsura (Matsuura) districts in Hizen Province.

Matsura Sayohime. A legendary beauty. She is supposed to have waved to her departing husband's ship until she turned to stone.

Matsusaka. A name applied to the hill road leading out from Awataguchi to Yamashina.

Matsushima. A general name for more than 260 islands in and around Matsushima Bay in Miyagi Prefecture, and for the surrounding scenic area. One of the Three Scenic Wonders of Japan.

Michinoku. Another name for Mutsu.

Miidera, *see* Onjōji Temple

Mikasa. In the present Tsukushi District, Fukuoka Prefecture, Kyushu.

Mikawa. **1.** One of the fifteen provinces of the Tōkaidō, corresponding to part of Aichi Prefecture. **2.** ——, Lord. Minamoto Noriyori.

Mikura-machi. Variant texts read Sakura-machi, which may be a mistake for Sakurai, in Yahiko Village, Nishikambara District, Niigata Prefecture (Echigo). Okami, p. 349, n. 18.

Minamoto Noriyori (d. 1193). Called Kaba, Kaba Kanja, and Kaba Onzōshi (*q.v.*). Younger brother of Yoritomo, and one of his generals in the campaigns against the Taira. *See* the Introduction.

Minamoto Raikō (d. 1021). Yorimitsu. Late Heian general; son of Mitsunaka. Hero of numerous legendary exploits.

Minamoto Tametomo (1139–1170). Eighth son of Tameyoshi and brother of Yoshitomo. Known as Chinzei Hachirō (Hachirō of Chinzei). Famous for his physical strength and prowess with the bow. After a turbulent early career in Kyushu (Chinzei), he joined his father on ex-Emperor Sutoku's side in the Hōgen War. At the end of the war, he was banished to Ōshima in Izu, where his seditious activities finally led to his death.

Minamoto Tameyoshi (1096–1156). Father of Yoshitomo. *See* the Introduction.

Minamoto Tomonaga. Called Chief of the Inner Princess' Household. Second son of Yoshitomo. While fleeing with his father after the Heiji War, he was

so severely wounded by hostile monks from Mount Hiei that Yoshitomo was forced to kill him at Aohaka.

Minamoto Yorimasa (1104–1180). Real leader of Prince Mochihito's revolt against the Taira in 1180. *See* the Introduction.

Minamoto Yoriyoshi (999–1075). Prominent warrior of the midtenth century; ancestor of Yoshitsune. *See* the Introduction.

Minamoto Yoshihira (1141–1160). Called Kamakura Akugenda. Oldest son of Yoshitomo. After fighting gallantly in the Heiji battles, he accompanied his father as far as Aohaka in Mino, and from there went to Hida Province to muster support. Later, when Yoshitomo's death made it impossible to find adherents, he returned to the capital area, where he was eventually captured and beheaded.

Minamoto Yoshiie (1041–ca. 1108). Called Genda (Ganda), Hachiman Tarō. The greatest warrior of his day; ancestor of Yoshitsune. *See* the Introduction.

Minamoto Yoshimichi. Probably a member of a Genji family living in Ishikawa District (modern Minamikawachi District), Kawachi. The name Yoshimichi appears to be a mistake. Okami, p. 43, n. 16.

Minamoto Yoshimitsu (d. 1127). Called Shiragi Saburō or Secretary of the Punishments Ministry. Younger brother of Yoshiie, known primarily for his role in the Later Three Years' War.

Minamoto Yoshinaka (1154–1184). Called Kiso, Kiso Kanja. Cousin of Yoritomo and Yoshitsune, whose home was in Shinano. *See* the Introduction.

Minamoto Yoshinobu. A son of Tameyoshi living in Hitachi. Known as Shida Saburō Senjō. His personal name appears as Yoshinori in *Heike monogatari* and as Yoshihiro in *Azuma kagami*. Okami, p. 43, n. 22.

Minamoto Yoshitomo (1123–1160). Called the Chief of the Stables of the Left. Father of Yoshitsune. *See* the Introduction.

Minamoto Yukiie (d. 1186). Brother of Yoshitomo and uncle of Yoritomo and Yoshitsune. His name was Yoshimori until the time of Prince Mochihito's revolt, when he changed it to Yukiie. He was known as Shingū Jūrō because he had hidden at Kumano Shingū after the Hōgen War. He was appointed Governor of Bizen in 1183. *See* the Introduction.

Minamoto Yukitsuna. Called Tada Kurōdo. Member of a family of descendents of Mitsunaka, who lived at Tada Domain (*shō*) in Settsu. He attacked and defeated Yoshitsune when the latter was fleeing through Settsu in 1185.

Mino. A Tōsendō province, corresponding to part of Gifu Prefecture.

Misasagi Hyōe. *Heiji monogatari* (*kan* 3), which briefly mentions a meeting between Yoshitsune and "a Genji from Shimōsa, Misasagi-no-suke Yorishige," is probably the source from which this name was taken. Okami, p. 67, n. 27.

Mishima. In Chapter Six, probably either the well-known Mishima Shrine in Takata District, Shizuoka Prefecture (Izu), or the Seto Mishima Shrine in Yokohama (near the Kanazawa Bunko), which, according to tradition, was founded by Yoritomo in honor of the gods of Izu Mishima. Okami, p. 282, n. 4.

Mito, Great God of. Mito Daimyōjin. Tamakushiirihikoizu-no-kotoshirunushi, the god of the principal shrine of Izu Province, Mito (Mishima) Shrine, in the Izu provincial capital (Mishima Township, Takata District, Shizuoka Prefecture).

Mitsu-no-kuchi. Also Michi-no-kuchi. Later called Nakagō. The starting point of the Hokurikudō, which ran through Tsuruga. Now in southern Tsuruga City, Tsuruga District, Fukui Prefecture (Echizen). The presence of roads branching off to Wakasa Province and the neighboring Tochigi Pass (Nomiyama) seems to have led to the dual reading Michi-no-kuchi (beginning of the road) and Mitsu-no-kuchi (three beginnings).

Miura. **1.** Miura District in Kanagawa Prefecture (Sagami); the Miura Peninsula. **2.** A powerful family who lived at Kinugasa (now a part of Yokosuka City) in Miura District, Kanagawa Prefecture (Sagami).

Miura Heidayū, *see* Miura Tametsugi

Miura Tametsugi. Also Tametsugu. Called Heidayū. A Genji retainer who fought in both the Former Nine Years' War and the Later Three Years' War.

Miura Yoshitsura, *see* Sawara Yoshitsura

Miura-no-suke. Probably Miura Yoshizumi (1127–1200), brother of Yoshitsura, and a leading *bakufu* retainer, who is known to have participated in the Ōshū campaign. He was called Miura-no-suke.

Miya-no-koshi. Old name for the coast at the mouth of the Saikawa River in northwest Ishikawa District, Kaga (in the present Kanazawa City, Ishikawa Prefecture). Site of Ōno-no-minato Shrine (also called Sanatake or Saratake Shrine).

Miyagino Plain. Renowned for its bush clover (*hagi*). The plain in the vicinity of Tsutsuji Hill, in the present Sendai City, Miyagi District, Miyagi Prefecture.

Mochihito, Prince (1151–1180). Second son of Go-Shirakawa. Nominal leader of a revolt against the Taira in 1180. *See* the Introduction.

Mōfusa. An Ōshū swordsmith. Okami, p. 251, n. 26.

Mogami. **1.** A district in Dewa (Yamagata Prefecture). **2.** A swift river, about 216 kilometers long, which rises in the mountains of southern Yamagata Prefecture and flows by way of the Yonezawa, Yamagata, and Shinjō basins and the Shōnai Plain to the Japan Sea near Sakata.

Monō. Monō District in Rikuzen. South of Toyoma District, near Ishinomaki City in Miyagi Prefecture.

Moritō, *see* Abe Moritō

Motohira, *see* Fujiwara Tadahira

Motonari, *see* Fujiwara Motonari

Motoyoshi Kanja, *see* Fujiwara Takahira

Motoyoshi Kanja Yasuhira, *see* Fujiwara Yasuhira

Mountain Gate, *see* Enryakuji Temple

Mu, King (traditionally said to have reigned 1002–947 B.C.). Fifth king of the Chou dynasty in China, who is supposed to have traveled to celestial realms in a chariot drawn by eight magnificent horses. *Gikeiki*'s statement that he ascended to heaven from an eight-foot wall (Chapter Three) seems to represent a garbled form of this legend. Okami, pp. 82, n. 1; 122, n. 6; 235, n. 12.

Muko, Mount. A 932–meter mountain on the northern border of Muko District, Hyōgo Prefecture (Settsu). Now called Rokkōzan.

Munemori, *see* Taira Munemori

Munō Castle. Conceivably a mistake for Monō Fortress in Monō District, Mutsu (Miyagi Prefecture), which, however, is nowhere near the Kuriyagawa River. It may have been a place-name in the vicinity of Kanazawa Fortress. Okami, p. 141, n. 16 and n. 22.

Murasaki Shrine. Also called Matsushima Shrine. In the present Matsushima Township, Miyagi District, Miyagi. The local god of Matsushima is worshiped there.

Muro-no-yashima. A place frequently mentioned in early literature, said to have been located in what is now Tochigi City, in central Shimotsuga District, Tochigi Prefecture (Shimotsuke).

Muromachi. A minor north-south street in the capital, between Nishi-no-tōin and Higashi-no-tōin.

Musashi. A Kantō province, corresponding to the Tokyo metropolitan district, Saitama Prefecture, and part of Kanagawa Prefecture.

Musashi, Seven Leagues of, *see* Appendix C, note 1

Musashi Moor. The part of the Kantō plain extending south from Kawagoe City in Saitama to Fuchū in Tokyo. More broadly, Musashi Province.

Musashibō. Benkei.

Mutsu. An old province in northeast Honshu, corresponding to the modern prefectures of Fukushima, Miyagi, Iwate, and Aomori. After the Meiji Restoration, it was divided into the five provinces of Iwaki, Iwashiro,

Rikuzen, Rikuchū, and Mutsu.

Myōkannon Peak. Possibly Mount Myōkō in Nakakubiki District, Niigata Prefecture (Echigo).

Nagamori. Probably Tsumori Nagamori (d. 1220). The Tsumori were hereditary priests at Sumiyoshi Shrine.

Naganuma Gorō, *see* Naganuma Munemasa

Naganuma Munemasa (1412–1490). Called Gorō. Son of Oyama Masamitsu and brother of Oyama Tomomasa. He lived at Naganuma Domain (*shō*) in Tsuga District, Tochigi Prefecture (Shimotsuke).

Nagasaki Tarō, *see* Nagasaki Tayū-no-suke

Nagasaki Tayū-no-suke. Called Tarō in *Gikeiki* and Shirō in the *kōwakamai Takadachi*. He is said to have lived at Ichihazama Township in Kurihara District, Miyagi Prefecture (Rikuzen). Okami, p. 375, n. 11.

Nago. The coastal area at Bōjōtsu, west of Shimminato City, Imizu District, Toyama Prefecture (Etchū). Famous for its wisteria.

Nagoya-no-hirugashima. In Nirayama Village, Takata District, Shizuoka Prefecture (Izu).

Nako Kannon. The Nakoji, a Shingon temple, in Nako Township, Tateyama City, Chiba.

Namba. A Taira retainer; exact identity uncertain.

Namekata. **1.** A district in Hitachi. **2.** A Chiba branch family in

Namekata District, Ibaragi Prefecture (Hitachi).

Naniwa. The present Osaka and its environs. The court was situated there briefly during the fourth (?) century, and again in the seventh.

Naniwa Bay. Osaka Bay.

Naoe, *see* Naoe-no-tsu

Naoe-no-tsu. Naoe, Naoetsu. A harbor in Nakakubiki District, Niigata Prefecture (Echigo). During the medieval period it was a busy port, serving the Echigo provincial capital.

Narihira, *see* Ariwara Narihira

Narishima. Unidentified. It appears as Nagashima in other *Gikeiki* texts.

Narumi Beach. An inlet in Ise Bay at the mouth of the Tempaku River (north of the present Narumi Township, Aichi District, Aichi Prefecture [Owari]), famous for its strong tides. Frequently mentioned in literature.

Neagari. East of Adaka in Nomi District, Ishikawa Prefecture (Kaga). Its ancient pine was a well-known landmark.

Nenju. One of the Three Barriers of Ōshū, on the Echigo-Dewa border at Atsumi Township, Nishitagawa District, Yamagata Prefecture (Dewa).

New Shrine, *see* Kumano

Niidono, *see* Taira Masako

Nikaidō. An area in Kamakura, which took its name from Nikaidō Temple (Eifukuji).

Nishikido, *see* Fujiwara Kunihira

Nishisakamoto. The area at the foot of Mount Shosha; a name used in imitation of the better known Nishisakamoto at the base of Mount Hiei on the Kyoto side.

Nobuyori, *see* Fujiwara Nobuyori

Noji. In Kurita District (the present Kusatsu City), Shiga Prefecture (Ōmi). Famous in classical poetry.

Nomiyama, *see* Mitsu-no-kuchi

Noriyori, *see* Minamoto Noriyori

North Mountain. Probably Kimbokuzan, the highest mountain on Sado Island (1,173 meters).

Noto. **1.** A Hokurikudō province, corresponding to part of Ishikawa Prefecture. **2.** ——, Lord. Taira Noritsune.

Nyoi-no-jō. Possibly a mistake for Goi-no-shō (Goi Domain), in the general area of the present Goiyama Village, near the Konade River in Tonami District, Toyama Prefecture (Etchū). Okami, p. 340, n. 15.

Ōba, *see* Ōba Kagechika

Ōba Kagechika. Called Saburō. A Sagami partisan of the Taira, who defeated Yoritomo at Ishibashiyama but was later forced to surrender to him.

Ōba Saburō, *see* Ōba Kagechika

Ōe Hiromoto (1148–1225). Governor of Inaba. A senior civilian official in Yoritomo's Kamakura government. *See* the Introduction, note 23.

Ogata Koreyoshi. Called Saburō. A warrior from Ogata Domain

(*shō*) in Ono District, Bungo, Kyushu.

Ogata Saburō, *see* Ogata Koreyoshi

Ōgo Takayoshi. Called Tarō. Member of an Ashikaga branch family from Ōgo Village, at the southern base of Mount Akagi in Seta District, Gumma Prefecture (Kōzuke). Okami, p. 132, n. 44.

Ōgo Tarō, *see* Ōgo Takayoshi

Ohara-no-bessho. At the foot of Mount Hiei, in the present Sakyō Ward, Kyoto.

Ōi. Possibly Ōi Hyōe Jirō Saneharu, a warrior mentioned occasionally in *Azuma kagami*. Okami, p. 254, n. 15.

Ōizumi. An old domain (*shō*) in Dewa, located in the general area of the present Tsuruoka City, Nishitagawa District, Yamagata Prefecture.

Ōji. Now a part of Kita Ward, Tokyo.

Oka Tayū. Presumably Abe Tadayoshi, the father of Yoritoki.

Okachi Pass. Probably refers to the pass between the modern towns of Okachi (in Okachi District, Yamagata) and Shinjō (in Mogami District, Yamagata).

Okuyama. A domain (*shō*) in Kitakambara District, Niigata Prefecture (Echigo).

Ōmi. A Tōsendō province, corresponding to Shiga Prefecture.

Ōmine. The Ōmine Mountains. *See* Eight Great Vajra Messengers, Śākyamuni Peak

Ōmine Mountains, *see* Śākyamuni Peak

Onjōji Temple. Also called Miidera. A Tendai temple in Ōtsu City, Shiga Prefecture. The neighbor and ancient rival of the Enryaku-ji.

Ono Komachi. Celebrated poetess and beauty of the early Heian period. She is said to have lived at Sekidera, near Ōsaka Barrier, as a lonely old woman.

Ōno-no-minato. This presumably refers to Ōno-no-minato Shrine, on the beach at Miya-no-koshi. Ōno-no-minato was another name for Miya-no-koshi; not, as the text implies, a separate place.

Ono-no-suribari, *see* Surihari Mountain

Onodera Michitsuna. Called Zenji Tarō. Member of a leading family in Onodera Village, Tsuga District, Tochigi Prefecture (Shimotsuke).

Onodera Zenji Tarō, *see* Onodera Michitsuna

Onzōshi. Yoshitsune.

Osada Bailiff. Taira Tadamasa (or Tadamune). *See* Kamada Masakiyo.

Ōsaka, *see* Ōsaka Semimaru

Ōsaka Barrier. Probably the most celebrated of all ancient barriers, invariably mentioned in travelers' poems. It was situated on a mountain between Kyoto and Ōtsu.

Ōsaka Semimaru. A legendary blind poet and musician, said to have lived on Ōsaka Mountain (between Ōtsu and Kyoto) early in the Heian period. According to one account, he was a son of Emperor Daigo (r. 897–930).

Ōshū. Another name for Mutsu.

Otagi. An old district in Yamashiro. It corresponded roughly to the present Kyoto City.

Otowaka, *see* Gien

Ōtsu. The present Ōtsu City, situated on Lake Biwa in Shiga Prefecture.

Ōu. Mutsu and Dewa; the modern Tōhoku region.

Owari. A Tōkaidō province, corresponding to part of Aichi Prefecture.

Ōyake, *see* Takahashi Mitsutō

Oyama Shirō, *see* Oyama Tomomasa

Oyama Tomomasa (1158–1238). Called Shirō. Member of an influential warrior family at Oyama Domain (*shō*), Tsuga District, Tochigi Prefecture (Shimotsuke). He is mistakenly called Yamada Shirō Tomomasa in Chapter Four.

Oyamada Arishige. Called Oyamada-no-bettō. An uncle of Hatakeyama Shigeyoshi. He sided with the Taira.

Oyamada-no-bettō, *see* Oyamada Arishige

Pien Ch'üeh. Ch'in Yüeh-jen, a Chinese physician of the fourth century B.C.

Pond, Nun of the. Ike no ama, Ike no zenni. Wife of Taira Tadamori and stepmother of Kiyomori. After her husband's death, she lived in retirement as a Buddhist nun at the Ikedono (Hall of the Pond), Rokuhara. She is said to have been attracted to the youthful Yoritomo because of his resemblance to her dead son.

Punishments Ministry, Secretary of, *see* Minamoto Yoshimitsu

Pure Land, *see* Amida

Raikō, *see* Minamoto Raikō

Rikuzen, Rikuchū, *see* Mutsu

Rokudōji Crossing. Probably at Fushiki Township (now a part of Takaoka City), on the left bank of the Shōkawa River (Imizu River) in Himi District, Toyama Prefecture (Etchū), across from Shimminato City in Imizu District. It is uncertain whether this was regarded by *Gikeiki's* author as synonymous with Nyoi Crossing, or whether the two were thought to be different places. Okami, p. 340, notes 15 and 16.

Rokuhara. The region in the vicinity of Rokuhara Mitsuji Temple, east of the Kamo River in Kyoto. It contained the residences and administrative offices of the Taira family, and later became the Kamakura government's Kyoto headquarters.

Rokujo. Now a part of Fuchū City, Kitatama District, Tokyo Prefecture (Musashi).

Rokujō. An east-west avenue running across the northern side of the present Nishihonganji and Higashihonganji temples in Kyoto; also, a strip section of the city, lying between Gojō and Rokujō avenues.

Rokujō Horikawa, *see* Horikawa Mansion

Rokujō River Beach. The beach of the Kamo River in Kyoto, near the intersection of Rokujō and Kyōgoku (between the modern Gojō and Shichijō bridges). Rokuhara was near by.

Rokujō-no-bōmon. The present Gojō, an east-west street in the capital.

Ryōshima. A settlement in Awa District, Chiba Prefecture (Awa Province), north of Kachiyama Township.

Ryōzō. A Buddhist monk who seems to have been Abe Sadatō's uncle, not his brother. Known as Sakai Kanja and Sakai Kōshi. His name appears in other texts as Ryōshō or Kanshō. He was taken to Kyoto as a prisoner after the Former Nine Years' War. Okami, p. 396, n. 23.

Sabashi. A domain (*shō*) located in Kariwa District, Niigata Prefecture (Echigo).

Sado. A large island in the Japan Sea off the coast of Niigata. Place of exile for numerous important personages.

Saga. West of Udano in the present Ukyō Ward, Kyoto.

Sagami. A Tōkaidō province corresponding to part of Kanagawa Prefecture.

Sagehashi. Now a part of Kawachi Village, Kawachi District, To-

chigi Prefecture (Shimotsuke).

Saitō, *see* Western Compound

Saitō Musashibō, *see* Benkei

Saitō Sanemori (1111–1182). Called Bettō. A warrior from Musashi who fought with distinction in the Hōgen and Heiji wars as a retainer of Yoshitomo. After Yoshitomo's death he entered the service of the Taira. He joined in the Hokurikudō campaign against Yoshinaka at his own request at the age of seventy-one, and perished in the battle of Shinohara.

Sakai Kanja Ryōzō, *see* Ryōzō

Sakamoto. **1.** The area at the eastern base of Mount Hiei, in southern Shiga District, Shiga Prefecture (Ōmi). Site of Hie Shrine. **2.** The area at the western base of Mount Hiei (also called Nishisakamoto, or West Sakamoto), in Yamashiro. Now a part of Kyoto.

Sakanoue Tamuramaro (758–811). Early Heian general, renowned for his exploits against the alien tribes (Ezo) in northeastern Japan.

Sakata. **1.** The present Sakata City, Akumi District, Yamagata Prefecture (Dewa). It appears to have been a flourishing port in the medieval period. Okami, p. 341, n. 5. **2.** Probably a family at Sakata, Akumi District, Yamagata Prefecture (Dewa). Okami, pp. 326, n. 7; 341, n. 5.

Sakawa. An old post station in Ashigarashimo District, Sagami.

Now a part of Odawara City, Kanagawa Prefecture.

Sakuramoto. Presumably a place on Mount Hiei. Benkei's teacher there seems to have been connected in some way with Yoshino. Okami, pp. 105, n. 27; 202, n. 9.

Śākyamuni Peak. A 1,799-meter peak in the Ōmine Mountains east of Totsugawa, frequented by ascetics.

Samegai. A post station in Sakata District, Ōmi.

Sammon, *see* Enryakuji Temple

Samukawa Shrine. North of Ichinomiya. On Mount Miyayama, Samukawa Village, Kōza District, Kanagawa Prefecture (Sagami).

Sanekata, *see* Fujiwara Sanekata

Sanjō. A major east-west street in the northern part of the old capital; also, a strip section of the city, lying between Nijō and Sanjō avenues.

Sanjō Kokaji, *see* Sanjō Munechika

Sanjō Kyōgoku. The area near the intersection of Sanjō and Kyōgoku streets in the capital.

Sanjō Munechika (d. 1033). Called Kokaji. A metalsmith who lived at Sanjō in Kyoto.

Sannō. Hie Shrine.

Sanse. There is a place of this name in Nishitagawa District, Yamagata Prefecture (Dewa), but evidence from other *Gikeiki* texts suggests that the Yakushi Hall in Chapter Seven was at Atsumi Peak in the same district. Okami, p. 350, notes 7 and 8.

Sanuki. A province in Shikoku, corresponding to Kagawa Prefecture.

Sanuki-no-edahama. Probably in the vicinity of Sanuki Township, Kimitsu District, Chiba Prefecture (Kazusa).

Sasaki Genzō, *see* Sasaki Hideyoshi

Sasaki Hideyoshi. (d. 1184). Called Genzō. A Genji who lived at Sasaki Domain (*shō*) in Gamō District, Shiga Prefecture (Ōmi); a partisan of Yoshitomo in Hōgen and Heiji. He died in battle against Satake Hideyoshi the Taira in Ōmi in 1184. (1151–1225). Called Satake-no bettō. The Satake were a family living at Satake Village in Kuji District, Ibaragi Prefecture (Hitachi). Hideyoshi, fought for the *bakufu* in the Ōshū campaign and the Shōkyū War of 1221.

Satake Masayoshi. Known as Satake-no-bettō and Satake Kanja. Founder of the Satake family; grandson of Minamoto Yoshimitsu. A powerful Hitachi warrior with court connections.

Satake-no-bettō, *see* Satake Hideyoshi and Satake Masayoshi

Satō Shirō, *see* Satō Tadanobu

Satō Shōji, *see* Satō Tadatsugu

Satō Tadanobu (1161–1186). Called Shirō or Shirobyōe. Retainer of Yoshitsune. *See* the Introduction.

Satō Tadatsugu (d. 1189). Shinobu Shōji, Shinobu Satō Shōji, Motoharu. Father of Tsuginobu and Tadanobu. According to *Azuma kagami*, he died in battle against Yoritomo's Ōshū expeditionary force in 1189. Okami, p. 362, n. 3.

Satō Tsuginobu (1158–1185). Called Saburō Hyōe-no-jō. A retainer of Yoshitsune. *See* the Introduction.

Sawara Jūrō, *see* Sawara Yoshitsura

Sawara Yoshitsura. Called Jūrō. The Sawara family were a branch of the Miura. Yoshitsura, a son of Miura Yoshiaki and an uncle of Wada Yoshimori, played an active role in the campaign against the Heike.

Second Rank, Lady of, *see* Taira Masako

Sehi-no-uchi. Possibly a corruption of Semi Hot Springs, just south of the Kamewari Mountains in Mogami Township, Mogami District, Yamagata Prefecture (Dewa). Okami, p. 359, n. 7.

Seiwa (850–880). Fifty-sixth emperor of Japan (r. 858–876). Ancestor of the Seiwa Genji and thus of Yoshitsune. *See* the Introduction.

Sekidera Temple. Near Ōsaka Barrier.

Sembon-no-matsubara. A stretch of seacoast in Suntō District, Shizuoka Prefecture (Suruga).

Sembuku. Also Semboku. A general term for Okachi, Hiraga, and Yamamoto districts in Ugo Province (Akita Prefecture).

Semimaru, *see* Ōsaka Semimaru

Senami. A township (in the present Murakami City) in Iwafune District, Niigata Prefecture (Echigo).

Senjuin. One of a school of metalsmiths which began around 1260, after Yoritomo's death.

Senoo. A Taira retainer; exact identity uncertain. The family came from Senoo in Bitchū Province (Okayama Prefecture). Okami, p. 37, n. 18.

Seta. A settlement on the east bank of the Seta River just south of where the river emerges from Lake Biwa (Seta Township, Kurita District, Shiga Prefecture). The old bridge over the river, which was apparently of Chinese design, is famous in Japanese history and literature.

Seta River. The outlet of Lake Biwa (known as the Uji River after it reaches the flat land around Uji).

Settsu. A Ki'nai province, corresponding to parts of Osaka and Hyōgo prefectures.

Seven Leagues of Musashi, *see* Appendix C, note 1

Seven Shrines of Mount Hakusan, *see* Hakusan, Seven Shrines of Mount

Shibochi Michitsuna. This name appears to be the result of an omission from the original text, which in the Tanaka MS. reads, "Shionoya Torimasa, Naganuma no Gorō Munemasa, Onodera no Senji Michitsuna..." Okami, p. 132, n. 43.

Shibuya. Shibuya Shigekuni. Okami, p. 132, n. 51.

Shichijō Shushaka (Suzaku). Near the present intersection of Sembondōri and Shichijō in Kyoto. Kiyomori had a house near by. Okami, p. 38, n. 10.

Shida. **1.** A district in Rikuzen (Miyagi Prefecture). East of Kurokawa District, Miyagi Prefecture. **2.** Probably a family who lived in the vicinity of Edosaki Township, Inashiki District (formerly Shida District), Hitachi (Ibaragi Prefecture).

Shida Saburō Senjō, *see* Minamoto Yoshinobu

Shido. Shido Temple in Shido Township, northwest Ōkawa District, Tokushima Prefecture (Sanuki). It appears to have been a mecca for Shingon ascetics. Okami, p. 109, n. 18.

Shiga Capital. Also called Ōtsu Palace. The capital was located at Ōtsu in Shiga District, Ōmi (Shiga Prefecture), during the reign of Emperor Tenchi (r. 668–671).

Shigemori, *see* Taira Shigemori

Shigetō, *see* Abe Shigetō

Shijō. A major east-west street in the central part of the old capital; also, a strip section of the city, lying between Sanjō and Shijō avenues.

Shijō Muromachi. The area near the intersection of Shijō Avenue and Muromachi Street.

Shikarazaru. Probably to be identified with Shihōzaka, a strategic location in Katta District, Miyagi Prefecture. Okami, p. 51, n. 8.

Shimokōbe Domain. In the Kamakura and Muromachi periods, an extensive private tract (*shō*), which seems to have stretched from its center, in Higashikatsushika District, Chiba Prefecture (Shimōsa), to Sashima District in Ibaragi Prefecture (Shimōsa) and Kitakatsushika District in Saitama Prefecture (Musashi). See Okami, p. 403, suppl. n. 13.

Shimōsa. One of the fifteen provinces of the Tōkaidō, corresponding to parts of Chiba and Ibaragi prefectures.

Shimoshirayama. Shirayamahime Shrine (also called Hakusan or Shirayama), at Tsurugi Township, Ishikawa District, Ishikawa Prefecture (Kaga). The principal shrine of Kaga Province. The main object of worship is the goddess Kukurihime.

Shimotsuke. A Tōsendō province corresponding to Tochigi Prefecture.

Shinano. One of the thirteen Tōsendō provinces, corresponding to Nagano Prefecture.

Shingū Jūrō Yoshimori, *see* Minamoto Yukiie

Shinobe. South of Futtsu Township on Tokyo Bay in Kamitsu District, Chiba Prefecture (Kazusa).

Shinobu. **1.** A village in northern Nishishirakawa District, Fukushima. **2.** A district in Fukushima. The text in Chapter Two should probably read Shinobu District rather than Shinobu Village. The district was famous for *shinobuzuri*, a special kind of white cloth with a design made by pressing the plant called *shinobu-gusa* (hare'sfoot fern [*Davallia bullata*]), treated with paint, against the fabric. In the Chapter Two passage, there is a reference to the cloth which becomes meaningless in translation.

Shinobu Satō Shōji, Shinobu Shōji, *see* Satō Tadatsugu

Shinohara. **1.** In Yasu District, Shiga Prefecture (Ōmi). In Chapter Six, one text has "the bamboo plain at Noji" (*Noji no shinohara*), instead of "Noji and Shinohara." **2.** Shinohara Village (now a part of Kaga City), Enuma District, Ishikawa Prefecture (Kaga).

Shinomiya River Beach. A place at Yamashina on the road to Ōtsu (now within Higashiyama Ward, Kyoto). It is associated with the name of Prince Hitoyasu, a blind son of Emperor Nimmyō (r. 833–850), who seems to have become confused with Semimaru because both were patron gods of the blind.

Shinzei, *see* Fujiwara Michinori

Shiozu. A trading port on Lake Biwa at Shiozu Village (the present Nishiasai Village), Ika District, Shiga Prefecture (Ōmi).

Shirahige Shrine. In Shiga Township, Shiga District, Shiga Prefecture (Ōmi).

Shirakawa. **1.** An old name for a region east of the capital in the present Sakyō Ward of Kyoto, bounded on the west by the Kamo River and on the east by the Higashiyama hills. **2.** Seventy-second emperor of Japan (r. 1072–1086; cloister government 1086–1129).

Shirakawa Barrier. An ancient barrier located in the present Nishishirakawa District, Fukushima Prefecture (Mutsu). One of the Three Barriers of Ōshū.

Shirato. Possibly a family in Shira-to Township, Nishiibaragi District, Ibaragi Prefecture (Hitachi).

Shirayama, *see* Shimoshirayama

Shirayama Peak. Possibly Mount Hitotsutsumuri, a prominent elevation north of Matsu-ga-saki in Sado; or perhaps another name for Mount Kimboku, the highest mountain on the island. Okami, p. 348, n. 8.

Shirayamahime Shrine, *see* Shimoshirayama

Shirobyōe, Shirobyōe Fujiwara Tadanobu, *see* Satō Tadanobu

Shirokiyama. Another name for Kurosawa Pass, between Hiraga District in Dewa (Akita Prefecture) and Waga District in Rikuchū (Iwate Prefecture).

Shishichi. Unidentified. Evidence in a variant text suggests that this may be a mistake for Shirakawa Barrier. Okami, p. 134, n. 6.

Shitennō, *see* Four Heavenly Kings

Shō Saburō, *see* Shō Takaie

Shō Takaie. Called Saburō. A warrior belonging to the Kodama League. His family lived at Honjō in Kodama District in southwest

Saitama Prefecture (Musashi). Okami, p. 143, n. 12.

Sho-no-sarashima. In Tosawa Village, Mogami District, Yamagata Prefecture (Uzen), on the right bank of the Mogami River.

Shōgu. Called Kanjubō, after the name of his residence. Identified in *Azuma kagami* and *Gyokuyō* only as a Nara monk who sheltered Yoshitsune. There is no apparent justification for *Gikeiki*'s statement that he was abbot of the Tōdaiji. Okami, p. 255, n. 24.

Shōgū (d. 1007). An ascetic who founded Enkyōji Temple at Mount Shosha in Hyōgo Prefecture (Harima).

Shōjōjuin. A temple at Yukinoshita in Kamakura, built by Yoritomo in memory of Yoshitomo. Also called the Great Hall (Ōmidō).

Shōkū, Deacon. According to an old legend, an Onjōji monk called Chikō (d. 970) was dying of a possession when one of his disciples, Shōkū, volunteered to transfer the malignancy to himself by letting his name be used in the attendant yin-yang master's prayers. The ruse succeeded, and Shōkū's resultant illness was magically cured by Fudō. Okami, p. 432, suppl. n. 9.

Shōmu (701–756). Forty-fifth emperor of Japan (r. 724–749); a notably pious Buddhist.

Shosha, Mount. Site of the Enkyōji, a famous Tendai temple within the boundaries of the present Himeji City in Hyōgo Prefecture.

Single Vehicle, Peak of the, *see* Katsuragi, Mount

Sōma Kojirō Masakado, *see* Taira Masakado

Sōtō Gongen. Also Izu Gongen. The buddha-manifestation (buddha in Shinto god form) of Izuzan Shrine in Atami City, Shizuoka, renowned in the medieval period as one of the Two Gongen. (The other was Hakone Gongen, the god of Hakone Shrine in Motohakone Village, Ashigara District, Kanagawa Prefecture.)

Stables of the Left, Chief of the, *see* Minamoto Yoshitomo

Suekawa River. Possibly the present Koito River in central Kimitsu District, Chiba Prefecture.

Sugiyama. This name appears to designate the wooded hills in the Dohi area (*see* Dohi). Yoritomo hid there for a time after the battle of Ishibashiyama, until he was forced by Ōba to flee further into the back country.

Sugō. **1.** Now a part of Kuma Township, Iyo District, Ehime Prefecture (Iyo). Site of the Taihōji, a celebrated temple dedicated to Kannon. **2.** A shrine (Sugō Isobe Jinsha) in Kaga City, Enuma District, Ishikawa Prefecture (Kaga).

Suketsune, *see* Kudō Suketsune

Sumida Crossing. In the vicinity of Sumida Village, Musashi (in the present Honjō Ward, Tokyo).

Sumida River. A river which flows through east Tokyo to Tokyo Bay; the lower reaches of the

Arakawa. The reference in Chapter Two is probably to the present Tone River, the largest river in the Kantō, which carries waters from the five prefectures of Gumma, Tochigi, Saitama, Ibaragi, and Chiba into the Pacific Ocean at Chōshi City, Chiba. *See also* Tone River. Okami, p. 404, suppl. n. 14.

Sumitomo, *see* Fujiwara Sumitomo

Sumiyoshi. Sumiyoshi Shrine in Sumiyoshi District, Settsu (now a part of Osaka City). Its gods were believed to protect seafarers. The god who appears to Kataoka in Chapter Four is probably to be associated with Ubara Sumiyoshi (Suminoe) Shrine, located in the vicinity of Ashiya (now a part of Kobe City).

Sung-kao, Mount. In Honan Province, China.

Sunomata River. A name applied to the Nagara River in the vicinity of the present township of Sunomata in Ampachi District, Gifu, where there was a strategic crossing.

Sunosaki, Cape. At the tip of the Bōsō Peninsula in Tateyama City, Awa District, Chiba Prefecture (Awa).

Surihari Mountain. Within the confines of Hikone City in Sakata District, Shiga Prefecture (Ōmi). Also called Ono-no-surihari or Ono-no-suribari.

Suruga. A Tōkaidō province corresponding to a portion of Shizuoka Prefecture.

Suruga Jirō. A low-ranking soldier in Yoshitsune's service. His name was Kiyoshige. Okami, p. 170, n. 5.

Surukami River. A tributary of the Abukuma River, forming the boundary between Date and Shinobu districts in Fukushima Prefecture.

Sutoku (1119–1164). Seventy-fifth emperor of Japan (r. 1123–1141).

Suzu, Cape. Northeast of Suzu City, Ishikawa Prefecture (Noto).

Suzuka. Mountains in western Suzuka District, Mie Prefecture (Ise Province); site of the ancient Suzuka Barrier.

Suzuki League. A warrior aggregation in Kumano.

Suzuki Saburō, *see* Suzuki Shigeie

Suzuki Shigeie. Called Saburō. A member of the Suzuki League, one of the Three Leagues of Kumano. Retainer of Yoshitsune. Okami, p. 373, n. 14.

Suzumeshima Shrine. Possibly on Suzumeshima, an island west of Nako near Cape Daibō, Chiba. Okami, p. 130, n. 3.

Tada Kurōdo Yukitsuna, *see* Minamoto Yukitsuna

Tadahira, *see* Fujiwara Tadahira

Tadamori, *see* Taira Tadamori

Tadanobu, *see* Satō Tadanobu

Tagawa. A district in Uzen (Yamagata Prefecture).

Taira Great Counselor. Taira Tokitada (1127–1187). *See* the Introduction, note 22.

Taira Kagekiyo. Son of Tadakiyo;

a leading Taira warrior. He survived the destruction of the family but died soon afterward. Also called Fujiwara Kagekiyo.

Taira Kanetaka (d. 1180). A Taira warrior who lived near Yoritomo in Izu. Called Yamaki Hangan after the locality in which he lived (Yamaki, Nirayama Township, Takata District, Shizuoka Prefecture); also known as Izumi Hangan. He was attacked and killed by Yoritomo's deputy, Hōjō Tokimasa, in 1180.

Taira Kiyomori (1118–1181). The de facto ruler of Japan after the Heiji War. *See* the Introduction.

Taira Masakado (d. 940). Known as Soma Kojirō. Member of an influential Kantō family. After serving the Fujiwara regent, Tadahira, as a youth, he returned to Shimotsuke with frustrated ambitions, and soon began a series of bloody quarrels with relatives and neighbors. By 939 he was in open revolt against the court, styling himself the New Emperor and controlling the chief Kantō provinces. In 940, as he was moving against Izu and Suruga, he was killed by forces under his cousin, Taira Sadamori, and Fujiwara Hidesato, a government police officer in Shimotsuke.

Taira Masako (1157–1225). Daughter of Hōjō Tokimasa and wife of Yoritomo. Known as the Lady of Second Rank (*niidono*).

Taira Masamori (d. *ca.* 1150).

Grandfather of Kiyomori. *See* the Introduction.

Taira Munekiyo. Called Yahyobyōe or Yahyō Saemon. The Taira retainer who captured Yoritomo after the Heiji War, and in whose Kyoto house Yoritomo was detained. It was at his request that Kiyomori's stepmother intervened to save Yoritomo's life.

Taira Munemori (1147–1185). Son and heir of Kiyomori, executed after the Taira defeat. *See* the Introduction.

Taira Noritsune (1160–1185). Son of Norimori. One of the best of the Taira warriors; famous as an archer. He held the office of Governor of Noto.

Taira Shigehira (1156–1184). Fifth son of Kiyomori; a Taira general.

Taira Shigemori (1138–1179). Oldest son and heir of Kiyomori, whom he predeceased.

Taira Tadamori (1096–1153). Father of Kiyomori. *See* the Introduction.

Taitōji. Possibly to be identified with Taitō, a place in Ōuda Township, Uda District, Nara Prefecture (Yamato). Okami, p. 38, n. 30.

Takadachi. Yoshitsune's residence at Koromogawa.

Takahashi Mitsutō. A Suruga chieftain who fought under Yoriyoshi in the Former Nine Years' War. His family, who lived at Takahashi in Ihara District, Shizuoka Prefecture (Suruga), were called both Ōyake and Takahashi. Mitsutō himself was known as Daizō Tayū. (Ōkura-no-tayū is a mistaken reading, resulting apparently from ignorance of the characters with which Daizō was written.) Okami, p. 397, suppl. n. 24.

Takahashi Ōkura-no-tayū, *see* Takahashi Mitsutō

Takano. *Gikeiki* is incorrect in locating this place in Shimotsuke. It was a part of the vast Shimokōbe Domain (*shō*) in Shimōsa, situated on the course of the Sumida River. Okami, p. 67, n. 22.

Takayari Rapids. Possibly a mistake for Takaya, on the upper reaches of the Mogami near the Kiyogawa.

Take-no-hashi. In Kurikara Village, Kahoku District, Ishikawa Prefecture (Kaga).

Takechi-no-hei Musha Tarō. Possibly a warrior from Takechi in Kuji District, Ibaragi Prefecture (Hitachi).

Takehira. A mistake for Motohira, Hidehira's father (*see* the Introduction, note 12), who should not be confused with Hidehira's son Tadahira, incorrectly called Motohira in *Gikeiki*.

Takekuma. An old name for Iwanuma Township, southern Natori District, Miyagi Prefecture, on the north bank of the Abukuma River. Its two pine trees were often mentioned in poetry.

Takinoguchi Shrine. Probably a mistake for Sunosaki Shrine in Tateyama City on the tip of the Bōsō Peninsula, an ancient shrine dedicated to Amehiritome, the deity of the cape, at which Yoritomo is said by other chronicles to have worshiped upon his arrival in Awa. Takinoguchi is a place east of the cape. *Gikeiki* appears to be perpetuating an error in *Gempei seisuiki*, which identifies the god of the shrine as Hachiman. Okami, p. 129, n. 15.

Tako. A private domain (*shō*) in northwestern Tano District, Kōzuke (Gumma Prefecture), once owned by the father of Minamoto Yoshinaka.

Tamatsukuri. A district in Rikuzen (Miyagi Prefecture). West of Kurihara District.

Tameyoshi, *see* Minamoto Tameyoshi

Tamon, *see* Bishamon

Tamura, *see* Sakanoue Tamuramaro

Tan. The Tan League was concentrated in Chichibu and Kodama, with a few families in Kōzuke and Shinano.

Tankaikō, *see* Fujiwara Fubito

Tateyama Mountains, *see* Ashikura

Tatsuta. A township in southern Ikoma District, Nara Prefecture; also a river and mountain in the same locality. Tatsuta's scarlet autumn foliage was frequently mentioned in classical literature.

Tawara Tōda Hidesato, *see* Fujiwara Hidesato

Tayū of Matsura. Probably a leader

of the Matsura League, an alliance of warriors in Matsura District, Hizen Province, whose chief members appear to have belonged to the Watanabe Genji. Okami, p. 119, n. 15.

Teishi, ex-Empress. Known as Kujō-no-in. Fujiwara Teishi, adopted daughter of the regent Tadamichi and consort (*chūgū*) of Emperor Konoe (r. 1141–1155).

Tenjin. Gojō Tenjin Shrine.

Tenryūji Temple. A Zen temple in Kyoto founded in 1340 by Ashikaga Takauji for the repose of Emperor Go-Daigo's soul. The mention of it in Chapter Six shows that *Gikeiki* could not have existed in its present form before 1340.

Teradomari. A port opposite Sado Island in Santō District, Niigata Prefecture (Echigo).

Terui Takaharu. Called Tarō. A retainer of Yasuhira; ancestor of the Terui family, who lived in Terui, Iwai District (near Hiraizumi).

Terui Tarō, *see* Terui Takaharu

Tezuka Mitsumori. Called Tarō. A Shinano retainer of Kiso Yoshinaka. Okami, p. 336, n. 4.

Tezuka Tarō, *see* Tezuka Mitsumori

Third Rank, Lord of. Probably Takashina Yasutsune (d. 1192), a senior courtier who was deprived of his office in 1185 on suspicion of complicity with Yoshitsune.

Three Shrines. The Kumano shrines.

Tō Kurō Morinaga, *see* Adachi Morinaga

Tō-no-tsuji. In Kamakura.

Toba Port. This refers to a place called Kusatsu, or Shimotoba, on the east bank of the Katsura River in Kii District, Yamashiro (Kyoto Prefecture). Passengers for the west set out from there on their journey down the Yodo River (into which the Katsura flows) to Osaka Bay.

Tōdaiji Temple. A temple in Nara City founded in 749. During the Nara period, the headquarters of Buddhism in Japan; in the Heian and Kamakura periods, a rich, politically influential institution, whose many soldier-monks militantly protected its interests.

Togashi. Togashi Domain (*shō*) in Ishikawa District, Ishikawa Prefecture (Kaga). Seat of the Togashi family, who acted as local officials in the district.

Togashi-no-suke. This name was borne by successive generations of the Togashi family, who appear to have wielded considerable power as wardens (*shugo*) of Kaga in the early Muromachi period. Its use in *Gikeiki* is probably an anachronism. Okami, p. 337, n. 15.

Tōji, *see* Hori Chikaie

Tōjō. Probably a family at Tōjō near Shida.

Tōkaidō. The road between Kyoto and the east; also, the provinces of the Tōkaidō Circuit (Iga, Ise,

Shima, Owari, Mikawa, Tōtōmi, Suruga, Kai, Izu, Sagami, Musashi, Awa, Kazusa, Shimōsa, and Hitachi.)

Tokimasa, *see* Hōjō Tokimasa

Tokiwa. Mother of Yoshitsune. *See* the Introduction.

Tōkōbō, Deacon of. Tōkōbō-no-ajari. According to *Heiji monogatari*, his name was Rennin. There was apparently a monks' residence hall (*bō*) called Tōkōbō at Kurama. Okami, p. 40, n. 2.

Tōku Cavern. Tatsukoku Cavern, about six kilometers southwest of Hiraizumi.

Tomonaga, *see* Minamoto Tomonaga

Tomotoshi Kanja. Probably a corruption of Motoyoshi Kanja.

Tone. A Genji family in Tone District, Kōzuke (Gumma Prefecture).

Tone River. In the Kamakura-Muromachi period, the Tone appears to have flowed toward Shimotsuke from Takasaki, and to have been called the Sumida in its lower reaches. It apparently emptied into Tokyo Bay after forming the Shimōsa-Musashi border. *See also* Sumida River. Okami, p. 404, suppl. n. 14.

Torikai Middle Counselor. Probably Fujiwara Korezane. No daughter of his is known to have been married to Yoshitsune.

Torinomi Saburō Munetō, *see* Abe Munetō

Tōryū, *see* Fujiwara Michitaka

Tosa. A province in Shikoku corresponding to Kōchi Prefecture.

Tōsandō, *see* Tōsendō

Tōsendō. Also Tōsandō. One of the Eight Circuits, lying east of the Ki'nai, and, for the most part, between the Tōkaidō and the Hokurikudō. It included the provinces of Ōmi, Mino, Hida, Shinano, Kōzuke, Shimotsuke, Mutsu, and Dewa.

Toshihito, *see* Fujiwara Toshihito

Tōta. A district in Rikuzen (Miyagi Prefecture), east of Shida District.

Tōtōmi. A Tōkaidō province corresponding to part of Shizuoka Prefecture.

Totsugawa. The wild, mountainous region along the upper reaches of the Kumano River (Totsugawa River) in southern Yoshino District, Nara Prefecture (Yamato).

Toyota. Probably a family at Toyota Domain (*shō*) in Yuiki District, Shimōsa (Ibaragi Prefecture).

Toyota Tarō. Mentioned in *Azuma kagami*. Possibly a Chiba collateral in Toyota Domain, Shimōsa. Okami, p. 266, n. 8.

Tsuginobu, *see* Satō Tsuginobu

Tsukushi. An old name for Kyushu.

Tsukushiumi. Possibly a mistake for Tsukuromi, the old name of Takegaoka in Kimitsu District, Chiba Prefecture (Kazusa).

Tsuru Peak. Probably Mount Tsurugi, a towering peak in southern Mima District, Tokushima Prefecture, on the border between Awa and Tosa, which, like Shōsanji, seems to have been a favorite resort of wandering monks. Okami, p. 109, n. 17.

Tsuruga. A trading port in Tsuruga District, Fukui Prefecture (Echizen), which carried a heavy volume of capital-bound traffic in the medieval period.

Tsurugaoka Hachiman Shrine, *see* Hachiman Shrine 3 (Tsurugaoka)

Tsurugi Shrine. East of Shimoshirayama. One of the Seven Shrines of Mount Hakusan.

Tsutsuji Hill. Famous for its cherry blossoms. On the eastern outskirts of Sendai, where it is now part of a municipal park.

Tung-feng. A Ch'ang-an man whose wife is said to have saved his life by tricking an enemy into killing her in his place. Okami, p. 212, n. 3.

Two Provinces. Mutsu and Dewa.

Uchide Beach. An old place name in the vicinity of Matsumoto, Ōtsu City, Shiga Prefecture (Ōmi).

Uda. A mountainous district (*kōri*) in the Yoshino area of Yamato.

Ugo, *see* Dewa

Ukawa. A private domain (*shō*) in the vicinity of Kashiwazaki City, Kariwa District, Niigata Prefecture (Echigo).

Ukishima Island. An island in Kasumi-ga-ura, Chiba Prefecture.

Ukishima Plain. The coastal plain in the vicinity of the Fuji Marsh in Suruga, between the Fuji and Kano Rivers. Now a part of Suntō District and Yoshiwara City in Shizuoka Prefecture.

Unakami Jirō. Possibly a kinsman of the Chiba. Called Shigetane in *Yoshitsune monogatari*.

Usa. Probably to be identified with the Musa family who lived in the old Musa District in Kazusa (now northern Yamamu District, Chiba Prefecture). Okami, p. 131, n. 20.

Ushima. Other *Gikeiki* texts have Ushishima, an old name for a place in Sumida Ward, Tokyo.

Ushiwaka. Childhood name of Yoshitsune.

Usui Pass. A steep pass on the route from the Kantō to Shinano Province. On the boundary between Usui District, Gumma, and Kitasakuma District, Nagano, near the present resort town of Karuizawa.

Usuki. Warriors living in Usuki Domain (*shō*), Amabe District, Bungo Province, Kyushu.

Uta-no-waki. Near Ichifuri.

Utsu Mountain. A 279-meter hill on the border between the present Shida District and Shizuoka City in Suruga. Famous in poetry.

Utsunomiya. 1. Utsunomiya City, Tochigi Prefecture. 2. *See* Utsunomiya Tomotsuna.

Utsunomiya, God of. *Utsunomiya no Daimyōjin*. A deity identified as a son of Emperor Sujin (traditionally said to have reigned 97–30 B.C.), worshiped at Futarasan (Futarayama) Shrine in Utsunomiya. He was particularly revered by Yoshiie, Yoritomo, and others of the Minamoto.

Utsunomiya Tomotsuna. Called Yasaburō or Saemon-no-jō. Originally a member of ex-Emperor Shirakawa's guards, he joined Yoritomo when the latter rebelled, and served with distinction in the Ōshū campaign. A few years later he was banished on charges of misconduct.

Utsunomiya Yasaburō, *see* Utsunomiya Tomotsuna

Uzen, *see* Dewa

Vajra Messengers, *see* Eight Great Vajra Messengers

Wada, *see* Wada Yoshimori

Wada Cape. A cape southeast of Kobe at the entrance to Kobe Harbor.

Wada Kotarō, *see* Wada Yoshimori

Wada Yoshimori (1147–1213). Known as Saemon-no-jō Kotarō; a grandson of Miura Yoshiaki. He lived at Wada in Miura District, Sagami. Yoshimori joined Yoritomo in 1180, and in the same year was made head of the Samuraidokoro (Warrior Office). He continued to play a leading role in *bakufu* affairs until 1213, when he came into conflict with the Hōjō and was killed.

Wakamiya Hachiman, *see* Hachiman Shrine **3** (Tsurugaoka)

Wakasa. A Hokurikudō province adjacent to Echizen, corresponding to part of Fukui Prefecture.

Wang Chao-chün. A Han beauty in the imperial harem. The emperor gave her to a barbarian chieftain in 33 B.C.

Washinoo. One of Yoshitsune's warriors. Perhaps to be identified with the Washinoo Saburō Yoshihisa mentioned in *Heike monogatari*, although he appears later in *Gikeiki* as Shichirō. Okami, p. 159, n. 19.

Watanabe. Near Temman in Osaka.

Watari. A district in Miyagi Prefecture (Rikuzen).

Watari Kiyohira, *see* Fujiwara Kiyohira

Western Compound. Saitō. One of four main valleys at the Enryakuji on Mount Hiei. The Eastern Compound was the central area of the temple, the Western Compound lay to the northwest, the Mudōji to the south, and Yokawa to the north.

Western Shrine. Nishinomiya Shrine at Nishinomiya City, Muko District, Hyōgo Prefecture (Settsu).

Yabase. A harbor in the present Kusatsu City, Kurita District, Shiga Prefecture (Ōmi).

Yahiko Shrine. Iyahiko Shrine, the principal shrine of Echigo Province, located at the foot of Mount Iyahiko in Iyahiko Village, Nishikambara District, Niigata Prefecture.

Yahyobyōe, *see* Taira Munekiyo

Yakata. Appears in other *Gikeiki* texts as Yawata. Possibly the vicinity of Yawata Township (now Ichihara Township) in Ichihara District, Chiba Prefecture (Kazusa).

Yakeyama. Probably refers to the Shōzanji, a Shingon temple in Nasai District, Tokushima Prefecture. (Shōzan can be pronounced Yakeyama.)

Yamada. A port at Yamada Village (now Kusatsu City), Kurita District, Shiga Prefecture (Ōmi).

Yamada Shirō Tomomasa, *see* Oyama Tomomasa

Yamakami Nobutaka. Member of an Ashikaga branch family in Yamakami, at the southeast edge of Mount Akagi in Seta District, Gumma Prefecture (Kōzuke). Okami, p. 132, n. 44.

Yamamomo-machi. Probably in the vicinity of Yamamomo-nozushi on Yamamomo Street, between Gojō and Rokujō in Shimokyō Ward, Kyoto. Okami, p. 38, n. 31.

Yamanobe. Probably a family in the old Yamanobe District in Kazusa (now southern Yamamu District, Chiba Prefecture).

Yamanouchi. A Sagami family.

Yamashina. Now within the bounds of Higashiyama Ward, Kyoto. Site of the tombs of Emperor Tenchi (r. 668–671) and Sakanoue Tamuramaro.

Yamashiro. A Ki'nai province, corresponding to part of Kyoto Prefecture.

Yamato. A Ki'nai province corresponding to Nara Prefecture.

Yamuke Shrine. At Mount Yamuke in Shinjō City, Mogami District, Yamagata Prefecture (Uzen).

Yang Kuei-fei (719–756). Favorite concubine of the Chinese Emperor Hsüan Tsung.

Yang Yu[-chi]. An archer in the Chinese state of Ch'u (740–330 B.C.). His exploits are described in the *Shih-chi*.

Yashima. Near Takamatsu City in Shikoku. *See* the Introduction.

Yasuhira, *see* Fujiwara Yasuhira

Yatsuhashi Bridge. Famous in literature since the early Heian period. It was located in Chiryū Township, Aomi District, Aichi Prefecture (Mikawa).

Yokawa, *see* Western Compound

Yokota Plain. South of the present Utsunomiya City in central Tochigi Prefecture (Shimotsuke).

Yokoyama. The Yokoyama League's main seat was at Yokoyama in Minamitama District, Tokyo Prefecture (Musashi).

Yonayama, Mount. On the border between Kariwa and Nakakubiki districts in Niigata Prefecture (Echigo). There is a temple dedicated to Yakushi on its summit.

Yorihira, *see* Fujiwara Kunihira

Yorimasa, *see* Minamoto Yorimasa

Yoriyoshi, *see* Minamoto Yoriyoshi

Yoshihira, *see* Minamoto Yoshihira

Yoshiie, *see* Minamoto Yoshiie

Yoshimori, *see* Ise Yoshimori

Yoshino, Sacred Peak of, *see* Kimpu, Mount

Yoshino Mountains. A ridge of

high, wild mountains in Yoshino
District, Nara Prefecture.

Yoshino River. A stream which
rises in the mountains of Yoshino
District, Nara Prefecture, flows
northwest and then west, and
becomes the Kinogawa River in
Wakayama Prefecture.

Yoshitoki, *see* Hōjō Yoshitoki

Yoshitomo, *see* Minamoto Yoshitomo

Yū-wang, Mount. Mount A-yü-
wang, site of A-yü-wang Temple
in Ning-po-fu, Chekiang Province, China.

Yui-no-hama. Yui-ga-hama. A
beach in the present Kamakura
City. The torii mentioned in
Chapter Six was probably connected with the old Hachiman
Shrine in the area (founded by
Minamoto Yoriyoshi in 1063 as
a branch of Iwashimizu Hachiman Shrine), which had been
moved to the center of Kamakura
by Yoritomo in 1180.

Yukigata Plain. In Nishishirakawa
District, Fukushima Prefecture.

Yusurugi Peak. A 565-meter hill in
Kashima Township, Kashima
District, Ishikawa Prefecture
(Noto).

Zaigo Middle Captain, *see* Ariwara
Narihira

Zaō, Zaō Gongen, *see* Zaōdō

Zaō Hall, *see* Zaōdō

Zaōdō. A temple on Mount Kimpu,
also called Kimpusenji. Dedicated to Kongō Zaō Gongen, a
deity of fierce aspect who is said
to be a manifestation of Śākyamuni.

Zenji. 1. *See* Iso-no-zenji. 2. *See*
Zenjō.

Zenjō (d. 1203). Childhood name
Imawaka. Oldest of Minamoto
Yoshitomo's three sons by Toki-
wa Gozen; full brother of Yoshi-
tsune. Called the Monk of Ano
(Ano no Zenji), Akuzenji, etc.
See the Introduction, note 7.

APPENDIX C

Omissions

a. There were Shingū Jūrō Yoshimori in Kii, Ishikawa Hōgan Yoshimichi in Kawachi, Tada Kurōdo Yukitsuna in Settsu, Lord Yorimasa of Third Rank and Kyō-no-kimi Enshin in the capital, Sasaki Genzō Hideyoshi in Ōmi, Kaba Kanja in Owari, the Monk of Ano in Suruga, Hyōe-no-suke Yoritomo in Izu, Shida Saburō Senjō Yoshinobu and Satake-no-bettō Masayoshi in Hitachi, and Tone and Agatsuma in Kōzuke.

b. He went to Naniwa Bay by way of Kawashiri in Settsu, journeyed past Hyōgo-no-shima to Akashi Shore, and embarked for Awa Province, where he worshiped at Yakeyama and Tsuru Peak. Next he visited the holy ground at Shido in Sanuki, and from there proceeded to Sugō in Iyo and Hata in Tosa. He returned to Awa late in the first month.

c. He journeyed past Bandō and Banzai, crossed to Kominato from Manonotachi, paid his respects to the Nako Kannon, and presented formal sacred dances at Suzumeshima Shrine.

d. Wada Kotarō Yoshimori and Sawara Jūrō Yoshitsura.

e. Maro Tarō and Annai-no-taifu.

f. The Kazusa chieftains Ihō, Inan, Chōhoku, Chōnan, Usa, Yamanobe, Aika, and Kuwanokami and their followers.

g. Shirato, Namekata, Shida, Tōjō, Satake-no-bettō Hideyoshi, Takechi-no-hei Musha Tarō, and Shibochi Michitsuna came from Hitachi, Ōgo Tarō and Yamakami Nobutaka from Kōzuke, Kawagoe Tarō Shigeyori, Kawagoe Kotarō Shigefusa, and Kawagoe Saburō Shigeyoshi from Musashi, and Tan, Yokoyama, and Inomata from the leagues.[1] Hatakeyama and Inage had not yet appeared, and

---

[1] The league *(tō)* was an alliance of warrior families claiming descent from a common

Chichibu-no-shōji and Oyamada-no-bettō were away at the capital. Homma and Shibuya came from Sagami, but Ōba, Matano, and Yamanouchi remained aloof.

h. Imai, Kurikawa, Kamenashi, and Ushima.

i. They passed Kizukawa, rested the horses at Sagehashi post station, crossed the Kinugawa River, bowed before the god of Utsunomiya, and glimpsed Muro-no-yashima in the distance.

j. . . . such as the Eight Great Vajra Messengers associated with Kichijō Komagata, the gods of Katte, Himeguri, Shikiōji, Sōke, and Kosōke.

k. Iō-no-zenji, Hitachi-no-zenji, Tonomo-no-suke, Yakui-no-kami, Kaerisaka Kohijiri, Jibu Hōgen, and Yamashina Hōgen.

l. Kikuchi, Harada, Matsura, Usuki, and Hetsugi.

m. The men whom Kajiwara called together were Wada Kotarō Yoshimori, Sawara Jūrō, Chiba Tsunetane, Kasai Hyōe, Toyota Tarō, Utsunomiya Yasaburō, Unakami Jirō, Oyama Shirō, Naganuma Gorō, Onodera Zenji Tarō, Kawagoe Kotarō, Kawagoe Kojirō, Hatakeyama Jirō, Inage Saburō, Kajiwara Heizō, and Heizō's son Kagesue.

n. Wada, Hatakeyama, Utsunomiya, Chiba, Kasai, Edo, Kawagoe, and all the others assembled.

o. Hie Sannō, Kehi and Heisenji in Echizen, Shimoshirayama in Kaga, Ashikura and Iwakura in Etchū, Kugami in Echigo, and Mount Haguro in Dewa.

p. . . . christening Kataoka Kyō-no-kimi, Ise Saburō Senji-no-kimi, Kumai Tarō Jibu-no-kimi, and others Kōzukebō, Kazusabō, Shimotsukebō, and so on.

q. . . . who was well known in Shiozu, Kaizu, Yamada, Yabase, Awazu, and Matsumoto.

r. . . . by way of the Forty-Eight Currents of Kurobe, Ichifuri, Jōdo, Uta-no-waki, Kambara, and Nakahashi. . .

s. . . . after a visit to Yahiko Shrine, traveling by way of Kujūkuri Beach, Kambara-no-tachi, Hachijūhachiri Beach, the pine grove of Arakai, Iwafune, Senami, Hidariyanagui, Migiutsubo, Sengakakehashi, and other places of renown. . .

---

ancestor. The reference here is to the famous Seven Leagues of Musashi, made up of the Tajimi, Kodama, Inomata, Yokoyama, Kisaichi, Murayama, and Nishino.

t. Monō, Hoshika, Shida, Tamatsukuri, and Tōta.

u. Kikuchi, Harada, Usuki, and Ogata.

v. Chiba-no-suke, Miura-no-suke, Sama-no-suke, Daigaku-no-kami, Ōi-no-suke, Kajiwara, and the other warriors.

Index

Abbot: of Kumano, 110–12; of Kurama, 71–72, 75–76, 82, 85

Abe family, 8, 13n, 264

Achievement register, 162

Adachi Kiyotsune, 223–24, 303

Amida Buddha, 106n, 107, 167, 235–36, 262, 291f, 304. *See also* Buddhism

Amida Sutra, 238, 245, 262

Arachi Mountains, 248f, 304

Archery: feats of, 156, 184; in battle, 161–63, 181–83, 204, 289. *See also* Arrow; Bow

Architecture, 187f, 219; houses, 90, 98, 203f; *izumidono*, 150

Ariwara Narihira, 88, 129, 304

Armor, 83, 91, 104, 146, 151; Yoshitsune's, 75, 147, 193, 198; Benkei's, 143, 148, 164, 285, 287; of warrior monks, 174, 180, 183; Tadanobu's, 178, 179–80, 203–4; cherry blossom, 203, 279; gift of, 248, 279, 284–85. *See also* Costume

Arrow: humming bulbs, 92, 162, 179n, 181, 196; described, 146f, 156, 161–62, 163, 179–80, 183–84; war, 179, 196; of commanders, 180n; pheasant-feather, 203; "like a straw raincoat," 289

Asahi, Lady, 51f

Ascetics, 115–19 *passim*, 250–72, 301; Yoshitsune disguised as, 28, 238–39, 300f. *See also* Monk

Aśoka, King, 247, 305

Ataka, 5, 39f, 54, 57, 58–61

Atsumori, 64–65

Auspicious days, 80, 137, 140–41, 200, 239

Azuma kagami: historical source, 6n, 14n, 46, 55f, 61, 300f, 315, 319f, quoted, 16n, 22–23, 25; Benkei in, 32; mentioned, 34, 306, 314, 316, 319f, 344

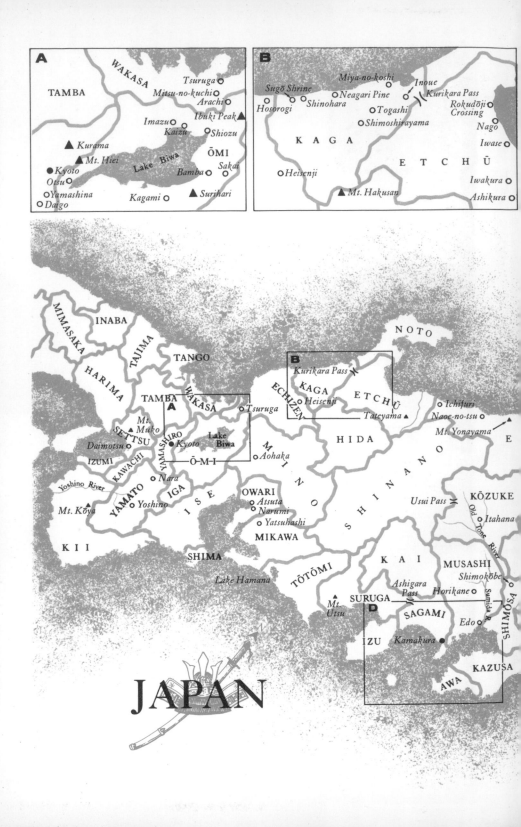

A

WAKASA

TAMBA

Tsuruga ○
Mitsu-no-kuchi ○
Arachi ○
Imazu ○
Kaizu ○
Ibuki Peak ▲
Shiozu ○
▲ Kurama
▲ Mt. Hiei
Lake Biwa
ŌMI
● Kyoto
Otsu ○
Yamashina ○
Daigo ○
Bamba ○
Sakai ○
Kagami ○
▲ Surihari

B

Sugō Shrine ○
Hosorogi ○
Miya-no-koshi ○
Neagari Pine ○
Shinohara ○
Inoue ○
Kurikara Pass
Rokudōji Crossing
Togashi ○
Nago ○
Shimoshirayama ○
Iwase ○
KAGA
Heisenji ○
ETCHŪ
Iwakura ○
▲ Mt. Hakusan
Ashikura ○

MIMASAKA
INABA
TAJIMA
TANGO
NOTO
HARIMA
TAMBA
WAKASA
Tsuruga ○
B
Kurikara Pass
KAGA
ECHIZEN
ETCHŪ
Ichifuri ○
Naoe-no-tsu ○
Mt. Yonayama ▲
E
Mt. Muko ▲
SETTSU
A
YAMASHIRO
Kyoto ●
Lake Biwa
HIDA
Tateyama ▲
Daimotsu ○
IZUMI
Ō-MI
Aohaka ○
MINO
SHINANO
KAWACHI
Nara ○
IGA
ISE
OWARI
Usui Pass
KŌZUKE
Yoshino River
YAMATO
Yoshino ○
Atsuta ○
Narumi ○
Yatsuhashi ○
Itahana ○
Old Tone River
Mt. Kōya ▲
MIKAWA
KAI
MUSASHI
KII
Shimokōbe ○
SHIMA
TŌTŌMI
Ashigara Pass
Horikane ○
Edo ○
Sumida R.
Lake Hamana
Mt. Utsu ▲
SURUGA
D
SAGAMI
SHIMOSA
IZU
Kamakura ●
KAZUSA
AWA

JAPAN